The Shepherd of Princes

The Shepherd of Princes

Mike Bonikowsky

A thought-provoking journey that weaves narrow strands of brotherly love and hope through the mire of selfishness, doubt, fear, and desperation. Bonikowsky creates a world that immediately consumes you with the weight of moral responsibility, and allows the reader to contemplate what it means to care for others above yourself when self-sacrifice is directly challenged by self-preservation. A unique dystopian tale worth reading.

— **Veronica McDonald**, Editor of *Heart of Flesh Literary Journal*

A haunting tale of a caregiver's heart amidst the fall and rise of civilizations. Mike Bonikowsky expertly captures the nuances of a community where people with and without developmental disabilities work, worship, and live alongside one another. This harrowing, but thrilling, quest challenges the protagonist and reader alike to examine their values and worldview.

— **Jasmine Duckworth**, Disability Advocate and Accessibility Trainer

The world that Bonikowsky has built inside and outside the Fold is itself a character, both singing of undeniably permanent beauty and crying for the revealing of long-suppressed justice. Every step of Micah's cross-country pilgrimage towards death or salvation is at once breathtaking and heart-wrenching in the midst of poignantly developed characters caught up in the deep, pulsing question: Who truly are "the least of these" and what does it mean to leave everything behind—even oneself—for the sake of leading them? Every now and then, we're touched by a story that both takes us out of ourselves and also plunges us painfully deeper into our own conflictingly selfish hearts. From both places—above and within—*The Shepherd of Princes* refuses to let us remain indifferent to the injustices that characterize the lives of those "at the bottom" of a problematic social pecking order, instead asking us to consider the limits of human kindness and where we will go when its rations are gone. Woven through a masterfully rendered story and fiercely real characters made of heart, whimsy, grit, and pig sausage, Bonikowsky's tale of internal wrestling, self-sacrifice, and the bounds of love is one that will stick with you long past the logbook's final entry.

— **Shannon Baker**, Author of *When the Mountains Called*

Michael writes with the strange joy that can only come from the exhausted chaos of a soul set on laying down its life for another.

— **Conor Sweetman**, Editor of *Ekstasis Magazine* by *Christianity Today*

Cover art, illustrations, and interior design by Sarah Christolini
Page 185 image credit to Ronelle Bonikowsky,
'Michael and Ronelle in the woods,' 2009

Library of Congress Cataloging-in-Publication Data
Name: Bonikowsky, Mike, author.
Title: The shepherd of princes / Mike Bonikowsky
Description: Scottsdale, AZ: Solum Literary Press, 2024.
Identifiers: LCCN 2023949709
ISBN: 979-8-9879514-7-7 (print)
ISBN: 979-8-9898558-2-7 (ePub)
Subjects: BISAC: YOUNG ADULT FICTION / Dystopian / Social Themes—Religion & Faith / Neurodiversity
LC record available at https://lccn.loc.gov/2023949709

Solum Literary Press
15850 N Thompson Peak Pkwy, 2176
Scottsdale, AZ 85260
(480) 371-9053

For Tzegai Habte, who taught me about Princes,
and
David J. Busuttil, the Shepherd of this book.

Acknowledgements

This book would not exist without the love and support of a great many people. First and foremost, I would like to thank my wife Nelle for loving me so well and encouraging and enabling me to be my truest, strangest, and most embarrassing self (and for leading by example), and my kids, Wimmy and Micah Bonikowsky for being Wimmy and Micah Bonikowsky, no matter what. I would like to thank my parents, Gary and Sharon, for showing me what the love of God, the love of other people, and the love of beautiful things looks like in such a world as this.

I would also like to thank the friends who would not let me give up on this book even when I expressly requested it. Thank you Peter, and Rob, and Jeff, and to Dave. Dave, you were the most annoying, and so this book is dedicated to you.

I will always be deeply grateful to Riley Bounds and the team at Solum Literary Press, for taking a chance on some guy from Canada and making his dreams come true, and to Sarah Christolini, whose art is honestly my favorite part of the books I've written.

Finally, neither I nor this book would be what we are if I had not met Sarah Godfrey, Christopher Dawe, Jason Armstrong, Tzegai Habte, and John Garballa. The times I have spent with you have been the most important and transformative minutes, hours, months and years of my life. Thank you for teaching me what it means to be fully human. I am so much better for having known you.

Contents

Prologue: Continuity of Operations

An Excerpt From the Daily Shift Logs of the Tecumseth Regional Center, Residential Unit

Date: March 21st
Shift: 7:30 AM–10:30 PM
Staff On Shift: Beanka Peterson, Rex Olenko, Susan Raikkonen. Recording Staff: Martin Safarian.

First day of staff reductions. New union rubrics (seniority + level of education) mean Martin Safarian is now shift supervisor of the residential unit. New directives from management concerning staggered outing and exercise schedule for clients have been initiated.

RL, MB, TZ, and RG very agitated by routine change. Attempted elopement from residential area into program area. Redirection resulted in >5 aggressions. MB, TZ and RG restrained/escorted back to Res (see incident reports / PRNs administration paperwork attached).

Daytime routine proceeded otherwise without further incident. All clients vocal in their disappointment re: new restrictions. BL refused dinner, RT resumed intentional soiling / self-injurious behaviors (see incident reports). SA requested to telephone her mother, who was extremely concerned about changes to the program/ cancellation of scheduled activities, and is threatening legal action. SA's mother directed to bring concerns to the Executive Director as per protocol.

SA's mother called back after attempting to do so, but was unable to reach ED's office for several days. Email regarding concerns sent to ED on her behalf. Automated out-of-office reply received.

Medications delivered on schedule. However, double check revealed that several medications were missing, all of them psychotropics (see attached list). Pharmacist contacted: listed medications are no longer available in this province and will not be for the foreseeable future. Homeopathic remedies suggested as alternatives (see notes). Changes have been made to MAR sheets accordingly. All protocols we have attempted to follow are per Continuity of Operations binder (emergencies: house, local, national), but protocols proving inadequate for current situation.

Rex, Susan and Martin would like to officially register concerns regarding the new protocols (as previously stated at the March 16th staff meeting). Rex would also like to state for the record that any further budget cuts will result in his resignation, as in his opinion they would render quality support impossible. Statements forwarded to the Executive Director's office. Automated response received.

Date: March 28th
Shift: 7:00 AM–11:30 PM
Staff On Shift: Beanka Peterson, Susan Raikkonen. Recorder: Martin Safarian.

Outbreak of infectious illness discovered in Residential this morning. Osa Adebayo reported coughing and sounds of vomiting during the night but was forbidden by protocols to enter locked ward alone. SB, TZ, GH and RB have contracted what appears to be a stomach virus. Dr. Montoya contacted, but is unable to come in until next week due to increased demand / reduced subsidized hours. Prescription for antibiotics has been sent to the pharmacist on our behalf and will arrive with the next delivery.

Assistance with cleanup requested from Sanitation Dept. Unavailable until tomorrow afternoon due to backlog. Most of the morning spent attempting to sanitize Residential Unit. All clients moved from Residential to the Program area. Clients extremely agitated by change in routine. DL and ON became aggressive, but due to staffing ratios, proper restraint protocols were not possible. Susan injured and required medical assistance (see report), leaving only two staff on shift. ON also injured in incident (see report). Clients were therefore returned to Residential Unit before cleanup completed. Locked containment was required for the remainder of the shift (see report and statement of intent).

At 4:45 PM, Ministry representative called to inform the Unit that eight more clients have been approved for transfer and are arriving Friday morning. Objections raised by all staff. Objections dismissed on the grounds that the additions are to be temporary.

The recording staff would like to state for the record that in his opinion the situation at TRC Residential has become unsafe for both clients and staff, and is not sustainable. A letter to this effect has been drafted and sent to the Executive Director's office and to the Ministry, signed by Martin, Osa, and Beanka.

RN's mother and sister visited today. Both were very upset over declining conditions and quality-of-life and became verbally abusive towards staff. Explanations given re: new Ministry protocols. Directed to proper channels for lodging a complaint.

RN's family returned at 7:45 PM, requesting RN be discharged. Discharge completed under new simplified guidelines (see Discharge report), authorized by senior ranking staff on shift (the recording staff). As of 9:30 PM, Roberta Nuñez is no longer a resident of TRC.

RB and SE very agitated by footage aired on the news during TV time tonight. News channels no longer recommended during viewing hours due to increases in anxiety. Cartoons, gameshows, and reality television (as per preference) deemed better options for time being. Reminder: BT's old movie collection is still in the storage room.

Date: April 7th
Shift: 7:30AM–
Staff On Shift: Beanka Peterson. Recorder: Martin Safarian

Osa Adebayo has resigned and will not be working his next shift (tomorrow's overnight). He apologized but in light of current circumstances he is no longer willing to leave his family alone at night. Keys, ID badge, walkie-talkie, and PPE returned.

Shift proceeded as per ongoing lockdown protocols (see hourly observation notes). No new signs of illness among clients. Tecumseth County Coroner arrived at 8:45 AM to remove the bodies of Robert Ballantyne and Gwen Harvey (see attached ADPF 7.3, [Death of A Person Supported]).

I (Martin) have made the decision to call the emergency contacts of all remaining clients to inform them of the situation and to give them the opportunity to discharge their loved ones if they see fit. I was only able to make contact with three. BR's sister will be coming to complete his discharge on Tuesday morning. All remaining clients: no valid emergency contacts / Crown Wards. Beanka and I have begun to prepare the facility for inevitable closure, though no statement has been received to this effect.

On-duty manager (Miranda Paulson) contacted. Was informed she resigned this morning. Advised to "proceed according to your best judgment" until further notice.

Multiple aggressive and self-injurious behaviors observed among the clients (see reports). Interventions not possible under recent Ministry guidelines (improper ratios and unacceptable risk). First-aid administered to JL, RB, and BZ at first opportunity.

I would like to take this opportunity to commend Beanka Peterson for repeatedly going above and beyond the call of duty in her services to the people supported by the Residential Unit.

In light of Osa's resignation, I will be covering the night shift, to be relieved by Beanka tomorrow morning. Tomorrow afternoon we will petition the Ministry to implement a full facility closure, as lack of staff, supplies, and the ongoing medical crisis have made operations untenable.

Date: April 8th
Shift: Ongoing
Staff On Shift: Martin Safarian. Recording Staff: Martin Safarian

Beanka didn't come in this morning and isn't answering her phone. Working single-staffed today, in violation of Ministry protocols. On-call manager, executive director, ministry office contacted. No one is picking up, and all voicemail inboxes are full.

We are on our own.

April 12th — I have moved into the residence full time, in violation of Ministry protocols. I sleep in SA's old room, and share the living space with the clients. At night I have been instituting lockdown procedures for safety. However, two nights ago JA badly hurt himself while locked in his room, and since then I only lock my own door.

I listen to them wandering the facility. They call out to me, and I answer their questions if I can. They talk to themselves, but never to each other. Some of them wander the halls all night, because they can, I guess. After so long.

April 15th — Attempted to disinfect Residential as Sanitation Dept. unreachable. Administered first aid to JA, again. No aggressions or attempted aggressions. Will be disregarding lockdown protocols in the future except in the cases of RB and BZ.

Received and implemented rationing protocols from the Ministry via email. No mention of the fact that I appear to be their sole remaining employee. Everyone extremely distressed concerning alterations to the menu. Also received protocols outlining new drills and precautions to be taken in event of "extraordinary events." Most impossible due to staffing ratios. Emergency kits renewed and expanded as per Ministry recommendations. Stockpile of nonperishable goods, medical supplies, and a diesel generator was delivered this evening by government courier.

The courier indicated that this would probably be the last delivery of psychotropic meds "for a while."

Discovered among other supplies: a voucher for a sporting goods store. Called the store for clarification. The voucher entitles the government employee to which it is issued to one 9mm handgun and corresponding ammunition, "against extreme eventualities." It will be delivered tomorrow, if I am there to sign for it.

After sunset a group of looters forced entry into the Program area and stole or destroyed most of the electronics and exercise equipment there. Attempted to enter Residential but unable to get past mag-locked fire doors. Emergency Services called. Due to high demand, the situation was deemed low priority. Looters dispersed after fire alarms triggered.

April 16th — The gun arrived this morning. Private courier this time. He asked if I was going to be OK, which was kind. He said he's leaving the City with his family.

I had never held one before today. It sits, as I write this, on the office desk next to the Program calendar that informs me that today we are supposed to be doing beading and karaoke.

I hate the shape and the weight and the smell of it. But I'm glad it's here, relieved, and I hate that more than anything.

I believe we are still safe here. I have chained and bolted the fire doors. We have a stockpile of non-perishable food, and a generator. This place was built to keep the outside world safe from the people inside it. It will serve the opposite purpose just as well.

April 20th — What is going to happen to this facility? What are my instructions? I have consulted every guideline I could, but they all depend upon communication from further up the Ministry's command structure. But that structure appears to be gone.

We are so far down on the list of priorities that we no longer functionally exist. There is only this dead building, and those left inside of it. Me, and my "clients," sick and lonely and hungry and off their meds.

We called them clients because they (or their families, or the government) paid us to provide them with a service. That service is no longer being provided, and no one is getting paid, so I'll give them back their names: Richard, Janine, Barry, Vikram, Erica, Bill, Paul, Glen, Lee, Philip.

This office is useless. I cannot sit in here anymore, staring at these buzzing monitors hour after hour. I can't take the silence. I am lonely. When I'm with them I am not. They seem calmer when I'm there too. The separations are disappearing.

We watch a lot of TV together, like scared kids around a campfire: first night in the woods. There's not much on anymore but the news, and the news is never good. The news tells part of the story, and the view out of the wire-reinforced window tells the rest. Black smoke on the southern horizon. It keeps on billowing and doesn't dissipate A lot more cars, then suddenly almost none. Military helicopters making the north-south run from the base up by Angus, all day, every day.

We have enough food left for two and a half weeks, at current rations. I have to come up with a plan in case the power goes out. So far that doesn't seem to be a problem. Someone is still paying a bill somewhere.

April 22nd — The phones are out, dead plastic as useful as the people on the other end. The last real call: Mom asking me to come home.

I told her what I tell myself: If I leave, who is left here? She didn't like that answer. Told me I was stupid, that I was throwing my life away, and for what? For a bunch of retards, a word I've never heard her use before. Then she started crying, and apologizing, and then begging me to come home, not to try to be a hero. She said she was scared too; didn't she need taking care of too? I didn't know what to say to that, so I didn't say anything. And now I can't call her back. After she hung up, I just sat, for a long time, until Vikram asked me what was wrong. Nothing, I said. But that's not true.

April 28th — I used the gun today. A man named Colin Dancey had broken into the facility with a bolt cutter and a handgun of his own. He was filling a backpack with cans of beans and Lorazepam PRNs when Glen found him and tried to stop him. He shot Glen in the stomach.

I was showering Barry when I heard the shot. By the time I got to the storeroom the floor was covered in blood to the walls and Glen was unconscious. I heard the girls screaming in Program. He had his gun in Erica's face, yelling that if she didn't tell him where to find more he'd kill her. I shot him in the back. He died there in the craft room.

His wallet was in his back pocket. He was a civil engineer with the City, and then he was a looter and murderer, and now he is just his parts without a person attached. Glen died before I returned. I put the bodies in the walk-in freezer. What else could I do? I haven't said anything to the rest of them, and nobody has asked. I was wrong, Glen. As long as there are other people around, we are not safe. I was wrong, and I'm sorry.

May 3rd — Brownouts are becoming more frequent. I don't know what's going on out there, but if there isn't an intervention soon the power will go out for good and with it the lights and fridges and the mag locks on the doors. If that happens, we are going to have to leave TRC. Maybe even before it happens. We are running out of food.

May 10th — This logbook is never to leave the Unit. But as I write this, it sits on a fake granite tabletop at an abandoned rest stop beside the northbound highway, five kilometers outside of town. The men and women who sit at the tables around me were also never meant to leave the unit. But here we are, together.

Grandma and Grandpa's farm was all I could think of. If we stayed in that town we were going to die. Once the lights go out, there will be nothing in the towns but metal and glass and cold concrete and desperate starving people. And the lights will go out soon.

Grandma and Grandpa barely had lights to go out. They had the land, and the old farmhouse and the tools in their hands. The land and the house are still there, and so are the tools. There's life there. There's less here every day, and soon there'll be none at all.

I talked to everyone about it before we left, and the ones that understood seemed to like the idea. They talked about tractors and red barns and roosters going cock-a-doodle-doo. I let them talk. I didn't interrupt to explain the thirty kilometers of broken road through what amounts to enemy territory. I didn't tell them that in the original plan we were driving the van, the stolen van, not walking.

We aren't all here. Barry absolutely refused to leave. Even when I pushed and pulled him outside and dragged him along by one arm, the first chance he got he broke my grip and ran back into the facility and locked the door behind him. I told him if he stayed he was going to die, but he just shook his head at me over and over through the wired glass until finally we had to go.

Erica died on the road that first evening. I think it was a heart attack, but I don't know. We were making our way up the shoulder of the highway, where it starts to climb the escarpment outside of town. She told me her arm was hurting, but everybody's hurting. Everybody's scared, everybody's sick. I checked it but couldn't see anything. Then her face was very red and she looked like she was having some trouble breathing, but there wasn't time to stop. We had to find somewhere with walls and a roof and a locking door by nightfall, and it had taken us so long to leave, so long to get all the food and all the clothing and all the tools packed, so long to get everyone moving.

She gave a little cry, and just dropped. By the time I got back to her she had no pulse. We took her child's backpack and shared what she was carrying around. Richard started to cry and stroke her hair. It took a long time to get him moving again.

We left her there on the shoulder of that empty highway, her old blue coat flapping in the wind. I made them leave her, though they didn't want to. I made them climb the hill, though they shouted and cried and tried to hit me. I told them that if they didn't keep moving they would die like Erica. It was a monstrous thing to say, but it was the truth and it worked. We made the rest stop before darkness fell. It is insulated and the windows are intact. It'll be warm enough tonight. There is no sign that anyone has been here for at least a week.

We spread our sleeping bags on the floors around the big battery-powered lantern. We eat our cold meals; beans, pudding cups, bottled water. Janine and Paul wouldn't eat the beans, but they will.

While they sleep, I write these words and I look out, over the parking lot and down the hill, to where the town is and the City beyond it. There are some lights on down there, the streetlight grids still marking out the skeleton of the town. But there is firelight, too. And even as I sit here, even as I write this, the electric lights do battle with the flame across the night sky, a war waged against a backdrop of cloud and smoke.

The lights flicker out, then come back on, once, twice, three times. Then they go out a fourth time, and I wait and I wait, but they do not come on again.

Now there are only fires.

May 16th — It is a Tuesday morning, according to the logbook. The old farmhouse is silent except for the same old creaks I remember from when I was a little kid. I've never known them to all sleep at the same time, but there's not a sound coming from any of the bedrooms but snoring.

I didn't think we would make it. There were so many reasons why we wouldn't, and not all of us did. Up the empty highway, the endless line of abandoned cars. Off the highway as soon as we could manage it, up the backroads in the shadow of the escarpment, paved and then dirt, the "scenic route" that Dad used to take. I knew it all by heart, locked away in memories of childhood summers.

It stopped being frightening after the second day and just became toil, just trying to put one foot in front of the other, to keep each of them putting one foot in front of the other, bribing, lying, threatening, dragging in the end.

On the third day we found an abandoned gas station in Adjala that hadn't been looted, and we ate and ate and ate until some of us threw up. The rest we packed into our bags and kept going.

7

We got here as the sun went down on the fifth day. The light of the sunset was still in the valley under the cliff. I almost cried when I saw the house, the barn, the stable, the silo, all still there, all still safe, somehow. I led them down into the valley, barely letting myself breathe until I found the key, still on the windowsill where it always was, and opened the door and smelled the old familiar smell.

I got them all into bed and onto couches and then I fell into Grandpa's old chair in the living room and was asleep before I knew I was sitting down.

And now it is morning, and everything is starting over, and nothing is the same.

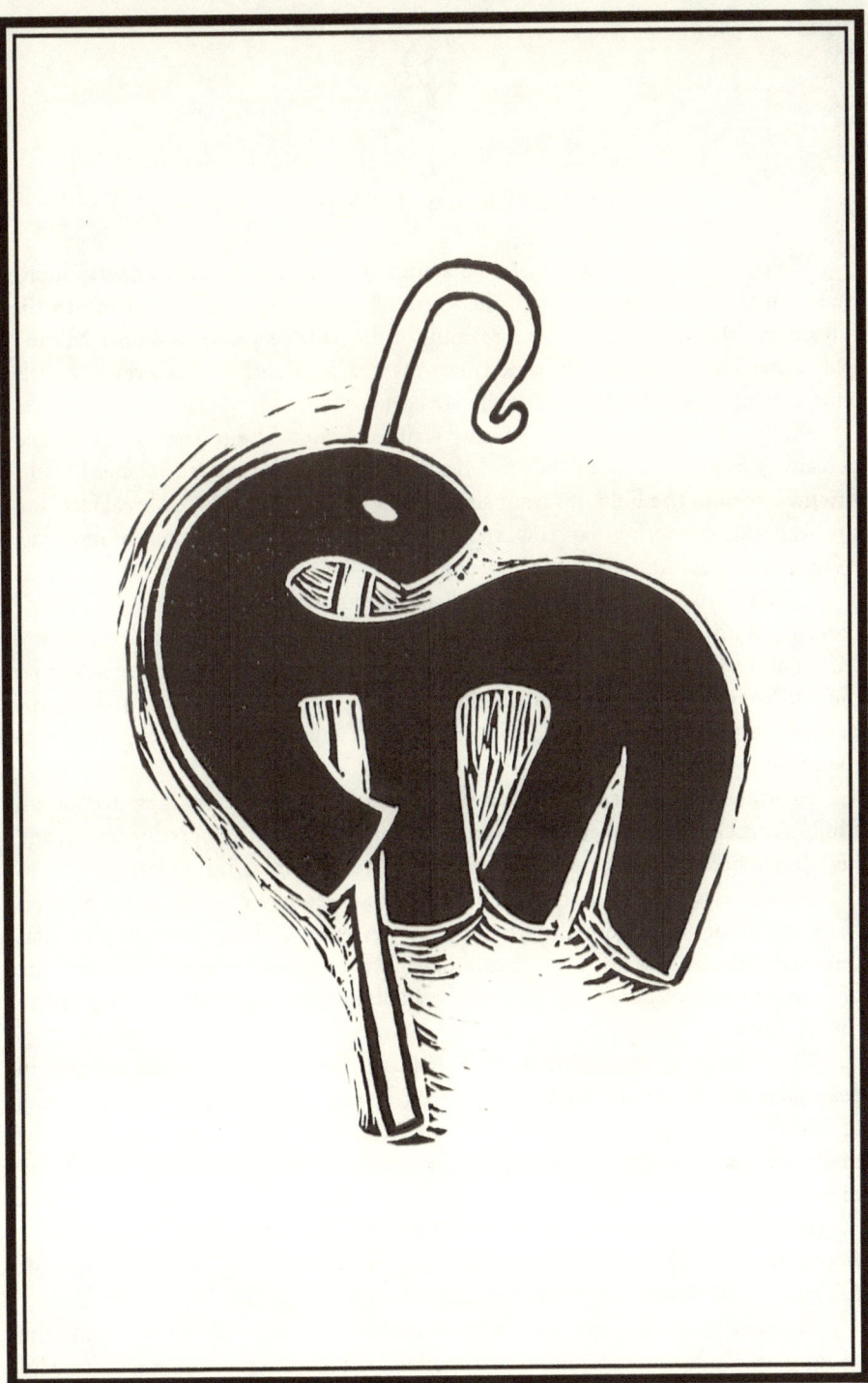

1

The Familiar Sound of Screaming

Micah Gault awoke to the familiar sound of screaming, and the understanding that something was very wrong. The sense of wrongness was not related to the screaming. That was only Philip screaming, as he had every morning since Micah's ordination, lying on his freshly soiled mattress with his sightless eyes screwed tightly shut, signing "Eat," over and over and over again.

Philip could maintain this keening wail for hours. The unfamiliar ear would perceive it as a cry of agony, but to Micah, in his seventh year as Shepherd to the Friendly Men of the Fold, it meant simply that Philip was ready for breakfast, and the beginning of another day. It was something else that troubled him this morning, a vague and unsettling sense of disharmony.

Micah's brother Thomas did not share his powers of adaptation, and Philip's morning routine alarmed him anew each day. He leapt from his place between Micah and the attic wall and began to buffet him with the frightened smacks that meant, "Something is amiss. You are the fixer. Fix!" When this failed to produce the desired reaction, Thomas hauled Micah to his feet and dragged him roughly over to the corner where Philip lay.

Reflexively, Micah took Thomas by his shoulders and steered him away from Philip's corner. Thomas needed calming. His lungs were bad and getting worse, and his labored breathing became a high-pitched wheeze as his agitation increased.

Micah helped Thomas through his breathing exercises while they put on their coats and boots. The door, frozen shut, opened with a sharp kick, and Thomas followed Micah outside, into the bone-chilling predawn darkness, down the fire escape that ran down the back of the Hall, and through the door that led to the kitchens.

Karen and Adi were already at their posts, firing the ovens and engaged in passionate debate at full volume. They waved Thomas in without a pause, gesturing to Micah that they would take it from here. Thomas loved the warm moist air that eased his struggling lungs, and he loved the smell of the kitchens, and he loved these women.

Micah turned and ran back upstairs. Philip was still keening, but now the others were also beginning to stir. The smell of baking bread filtered up through the ancient oak floorboard, which creaked as they began to warm from the ovens beneath.

Flint and tinder in practiced hands lit the stump of the tallow candle, and the rising glow slowly revealed the attic room around it. After all these hundreds of identical mornings, Micah still held his breath as he waited for that first glimpse. With the Friendly Men, as Donny had christened the group under Micah's care seven years ago, you never really knew what morning would bring. It was only eight months ago that he had discovered the corpse of Jonas Fisher, his face blue and contorted from the seizure that had taken him silently in the night.

The flickering candlelight crept into the corners beneath the eaves to reveal the sleeping forms of Sam and Jonathan, and of Donny, awake yet calm, as if Philip were not howling out his hunger five feet away.

Each new morning found two scents fighting for possession of the air: the morning's fresh bread, and the last night's accidents. It was Micah's job to ensure the triumph of the former. He sighed and got to work, putting his hands gently over Philip's. Philip did not speak and his understanding seemed to wax and wane, but he knew Micah and he knew that hands on hands meant the long night of hungry soiled waiting was over. Philip could smell the torturous ecstasy of breakfast below.

Philip was nothing if not stubborn, and it had taken many years and many painful falls for him to learn that sometimes it was better to wait for assistance. Micah helped him to his feet and led him past the snoring Sam, who slept until shaken awake no matter what was for breakfast, through the door and down the back stairs into the dark ice-bound yard. There stood the shed where Micah wiped him clean and broke the ice in the bucket to wash off what he could. Micah threw the armful of dirty straw into the huge mouse-heaven pile in the forest, then gathered a clean bundle from the adjacent barn. Donny and Jonathan were stumbling down the stairs when they returned. As soon as Donny saw Micah, he sucked in a deep breath and began the daily monologue that would last until sleep claimed him once again at close of day:

"What's for breakfast Micah and I hope it's porridge and pig sausage what I would is porridge and pig sausage oh yes and it had better not be eggs again it was eggs yesterday and if it's eggs again the chickens won't have any left and we won't have eggs for Saturday and we have to have eggs every Saturday fried eggs not boiled eggs and not poached eggs Micah do you know if we are having porridge and pig sausage this morning? Can you go down and talk to Karen and Adi please because if it's eggs again I am afraid I am going to be upset at them and I don't want to have to yell . . ." Donny continued on, despite Micah's assertion that they would in fact be having porridge and toast this morning, that pig sausage was only for Sunday, as he very well knew.

The monologue continued as Micah woke Sam and helped him down the stairs and through the kitchen. Thomas was waiting in his favorite corner by the ovens, his arms locked around his knees and his eyes closed, lost in the warmth. At the sound of Micah's voice, he leaped to his feet and took his accustomed place on Micah's left arm.

In the kitchen, fresh bread was being buttered while vats of oatmeal porridge bubbled on the long cast-iron wood stove. At the service window, four gentlemen were beseeching, in their outdoor voices, the implacable kitchen staff. They demanded sustenance in harmony, lest they should die. He heard Joey's distinctively high-pitched repetition of "MRS. PATTERSON I WOULD LIKE A LARGE BREAKFAST WITH TOAST AND EGGS AND WAFFLES AND TEA MRS. ANDREWS I WOULD LIKE A BIG BREAKFAST WITH TOAST AND EGGS AND WAFFLES AND TEA," his every-morning song.

It was still before sunrise, but nearly every Brother, Sister and Shepherd in the Fold was there. The Friendly Men were early risers as a rule, and the rest of their Brothers and Sisters (as they were officially known) were generally of the same mind. Micah held up a hand in greeting to Rosie with her Cool Guys and Bethlehem with her Pretty Girls, who responded with identical gestures. No one had time for anything like conversation, not until the morning routine was finished.

That routine was strict and taxing, and Micah was feeling it, body and soul. The previous night had not been a good one. Jonathan was sick, and twenty years experience had taught him that there was no reason to leave the warmth of the attic to throw up if someone was willing to clean your vomit up for you in the morning. He tried to keep it in the bucket, but his eyesight was poor, and Micah had been up with him almost every hour. Micah's clothes smelled like Jonathan's illness, and his turn to do his laundry was still three days away. Not that he was alone in this. Everyone shared the single pump while the pond was frozen, making winter an unkempt and odorous time in the Fold.

As Micah struggled to settle the Friendly Men down to their meal (Jonathan had stolen one of Philip's slices of toast and Donny had launched into a high-pitched renunciation of Jonathan's obvious moral failings), a large, bald, and heavily bearded man in his late thirties came sliding down the scarred and pitted bench, an impish grin on his face. "Hey Micah," he queried with mock concern, "why do you always smell like other people's throw up?"

"Hey Rufus," Micah returned. "Why are your eyes so red?" The handyman roared with laughter and folded his massive arms behind his head. "You know why, skinny boy. It's because I'm the only one around here who knows how to relax." His laughter was impossible not to share. Soon Micah was laughing, joined by several Brothers. While they may not have been in on the joke, enjoyed laughter on principle.

"Jonathan! Was it you that threw up on the good Shepherd here?" Rufus barked, with his effortless benevolent volume. Jonathan nodded vigorously, a look of awe on his face. Jonathan loved Rufus because he sometimes let him ride around on his back, despite the protests of the Shepherds.

"Then here is the agreed-upon fee!" he said, tossing Jonathan his piece of toast. Jonathan giggled delightedly, the toast already in his mouth.

The old community hall groaned and bounced with the weight of humanity. It echoed with shouted conversations between men and women mostly deaf, with steady rhythmic banging of tin plate on wooden table by men and women who could not see or hear at all and who craved the news vibration brought them, with the wail of Victoria Mackenzie, who once, many years ago, received a second and a third helping in exchange for her cessation of that sound.

But sooner than would have seemed possible, everyone in the Hall had received their breakfast, and soon the room was filled with the quieter sounds of men and women eating as quickly as possible. It was the closest to silence the group would experience all day. As that brief window in which everyone was eating and everyone was satisfied opened, Micah relaxed his watchfulness and allowed himself to make his way to the kitchen window for his own meal.

Porridge bowl filled to the brim by Adi, who thought him too thin, Micah made his way over to one of the windows that lined the Hall and sat on the wide sill. He kept his eyes on the Friendly Men. He didn't expect to be needed, but when things happened to the Friendly Men, they happened quickly. Convinced that no one was in imminent danger of choking, he allowed his gaze to wander out the window and onto the morning prospect of the tilled and snowbound fields that lapped at the feet of the cliffs.

The Brothers, the Sisters, and their Shepherds lived hidden in a deep fold of the land, huddled against the high wall of the escarpment. The escarpment was a long bulwark of limestone sixty feet high that ran for two hundred miles, through deep woods and dead cities, under farms and pastures, until it dove down to find its rest in the cold waters of the great lake to the north. In the mornings the sun washed its white limestone face rose. In the winter the cliff acted as a snow fence, and the village beneath was often buried. The children climbed it like a jungle gym and hung from the ancient cedars that overhung its edge, and the adults set their watch from its crest. The village that lived beneath it had always been a small place and mostly a hidden one, until autumn came and people would drive from miles around to see the turning of the leaves, for which its woods were famous.

But nobody came up the winding road to the village these days, though the last few autumns had been some of the most beautiful in living memory. The yellow line that divided it had faded and its pavement was broken and potholed. Most of the bridges had been claimed by spring runoff, and the signs that marked the exit from the highway had been carefully removed. The forest, once carefully preserved against the encroaches of men and ribboned with groomed trails and interpretive signage, had been given back to the wild, and had finally taken its long revenge on the farmers who had cleared it three centuries before. Many a pasture and many a parking lot were now the nursery of saplings. As the forest grew, the towns disappeared. Only the escarpment remained unchanged, a silent white wall from which the cedars watched the fall of empire.

Renamed and repurposed, the Fold, once the village of Monora, remained. The old red-brick church still stood to hold the wine and host on its altar. The brick and fieldstone houses, the oldest now nearly three hundred years old, were home to families still. The fields to the south were still neat brown corduroy squares, tilled and planted in the spring and harvested in the fall, though their crops were a fraction of what they were. The orchards still bore fruit in their season, but were now eaten and preserved by their farmers, no longer making the journey south. Smoke rose from the chimneys in the winter and lights burned in the windows at night. The community hall that had seen so many decades of craft fairs and wedding receptions beneath the same faded picture of the long-dead queen still stood. It was from its windows that Micah looked out into that first morning in March.

It was usually a sight to quiet the heart. But on this morning, the peace of the prospect before him served only to set into sharp relief the unease and unrest to which Micah had awoken. It wasn't stress, or anxiety, or boredom (the psychological maladies so common to Shepherds). It was some other, deeper thing.

The sudden sound of a bench grating on the floor tore through Micah's reverie. He turned instinctively towards the sound, too late, and found himself on the floor, lights flashing across half his field of vision, his cheekbone throbbing with the force of an open-handed blow.

Philip had discovered the theft of his toast, and a familiar expression of blank fury marred his face as he wound up for another swing. With a long-practiced motion, Micah blocked the second blow with one open palm, while using the other to block the approaching left hand, then held on with both as he scrambled off the sill and onto his feet. He held Philip's thin wrists in his hands and waited for him to stop struggling to hit him. The fury passed away, and Philip stared expressionless as Micah spoke in a voice of well-rehearsed calm.

"Safe hands, Philip. It's OK. I know. I know."

Micah expected no answer nor apology from Philip. It was just a thing he did sometimes, and more often at this time of year, when the winter stores were getting low. He was hungry, and Jon should not have stolen his toast, but there could be no consolation for Philip, not in March, only restraint and words like "later" and "wait." Micah held his wrists, trying to predict when the headbutt would come, but there was none this time. Philip gave a shy smile, and, once released, went groping back to his spot on the bench, leaving Micah with a bruise blossoming across his cheek.

The paperwork would be worse than the injury, as it generally was. Everything would have to be written down. It was one of Martin's policies, a rule held over from the old days. Micah leaned heavily against the chicken wire protecting the glass of the windows for a moment, then pushed himself off and into the hooting crowd to gather the Friendly Men.

It was a Thursday, which meant Nature Walk for Philip Ramirez and The Friendly Men, as their official title read. Donny, the author, had insisted on prefacing it with Philip's name because it sounded "better" that way, and took great offense at any attempt at abridgment.

14

Nature Walk began directly after Morning Bathroom, rain or shine or sleet or snow or apocalypse. Philip Ramirez and the Friendly Men followed a very strict schedule, policed by Donny and enforced by Sam. Sam did not speak, but knew exactly where everyone was meant to be at any one time, knowledge gleaned from his careful study of the giant calendar beside the food service window in the Hall. Anyone found out of place anywhere in the village quickly found themselves escorted back to their proper task by the very large Sam and his very acute obsessive-compulsive disorder. This was often an alarming experience.

Today, however, Sam's careful check revealed everyone to be happily on schedule. When at last every boot had found its way onto the correct foot, every coat had been buckled all the way up and every thumb had its place in each mitten, Micah pulled on his own patched green parka. He ensured his whistle and his knife were in their places, and opened the door of the Hall.

The Friendly Men poured out of the door with their usual intensity of purpose. Thomas clung to Micah's arm, eyes screwed tightly shut against the light despite his near-blindness, a heavy scarf triple-wound around his mouth and throat. He hated Nature Walk, especially in winter, but he could bear a separation from his brother even less. Jonathan was not fond of the outdoors either, but he had long since learned that Sam would not allow division among the Friendly Men, and grudgingly acquiesced.

As the path curved away from the village and up into the forest, the last lingering sounds of the mill and the forge and the whooping of the Cool Guys at work in the woodshop below them failed utterly. Silence fell like a heavy blanket onto Micah, Philip Ramirez, and the Friendly Men. The silence of the woods was like medicine to Micah after the madness of the morning routine. He took his usual position near the end of the line, from which he could monitor the entire group. Philip hung off of his left arm, which Thomas had reluctantly relinquished to take his traveling position close behind Micah, holding on to a cord that hung from Micah's backpack for that purpose.

Donny took the lead, as always. Jonathan and Sam could always be trusted to follow Donny. They formed a deadly serious procession, scanning the still-green cedars for any sign of movement. There was a master-list tacked to the wall of their home above the kitchens, written up by Lorne the librarian by special request, which tallied each of the mammals, birds, reptiles and fish they had seen, and how many of each. It was a very serious matter for the Friendly Men to be able to return home from Nature Walk to put a checkmark beside Red Squirrel or Blue Jay or even (hearts beat faster) Beaver or Muskrat. At the end of every month the list was taken to Lorne, who carefully collated the data into his master chart. Any sightings that seemed suspicious or unlikely drew ruthless cross-examination from Lorne, who had proclaimed the matter to be of the utmost scientific importance.

Micah grinned wearily to himself as Donny roared out "Chickadee!" This incited much unconcealed jealousy, but the grumbles were soon replaced by panting as the path began to climb the rocky switchback up through the cedars to the birch woods on top of the escarpment.

Here the old woods petered out as they skirted the borders of what had been a provincial park, in the days when wild places had needed to be preserved from the predation of man. The path ran along what had been the dividing line between the wild wood and the cleared pastureland. The old property line was still visible, marked by vast and shattered oaks now three hundred years old, a long watchful line looking out onto a pasture now wild with their children.

The sun had broken through as they neared the traditional turn-around point for Nature Walk. This was the Watch Tree, a massive living oak a century old. Micah called a good morning to Emmanuel, who sat on the high cold platform, the Fold's one precious pair of binoculars in hand, watching the north-south roads. Jonathan, who loved him, insisted on climbing the steps nailed to the tree's hide to shake Emmanuel's hand and smell his hair. Sam nodded impassively, satisfied that the schedule was being adhered to.

Micah leaned his back against the tree, tasting the purity of his exhaustion, and looked out over the valley below. It was a startlingly beautiful view, even to one born there, when the pale gold of the late winter sunrise came lancing in over the snowy roofs of the village. It was lovely, and charming, and perfect, and Micah was weary of it down to the marrow of his bones.

Having reached the Watch Tree and the culmination of Nature Walk, Philip Ramirez and the Friendly Men returned to the village and were led by Donny to the Workshop, a repurposed bank barn on the eastern edge of the village. Workshop was a very popular destination in the winter months due to the eternal heat of Wayne's forge, which was housed there.

The rest of the morning was spent at what Donny referred to as "Nails," one of the tasks given to the Friendly Men as a means of helping their community. Nails consisted of using claw hammers to pull the nails out of old barnwood the foragers (a position usually held by the Cool Guys) had found. The wood was left in one pile if it was usable and another if it was not, to be used as firewood. The collected nails were then taken to Wayne the blacksmith who straightened them for reuse, or melted them down to make other needful things. All metal was precious in the Fold. As Wayne put it, often, "Ain't nobody around here doing any mining or smelting anytime soon," a statement the Friendly Men always agreed with, loudly and with great seriousness. They prided themselves on their proficiency at Nails, and kept careful track of the number pulled each session. The quest for a new record was a matter of great importance.

While the Friendly Men were busy at their work, Micah sat at the old scarred workbench in the back and pulled out the heavy notebook all Shepherds carried. It was black, with a hard smooth cover and an elastic strap that kept it closed. There were crates of these journals in the storage barns, and boxes upon boxes of pens to be used with them. Martin was very particular about certain things.

Flipping open the worn cover of the notebook, Micah found his current page and began to write the morning's log. It was an old practice, more of a tradition than a practicality now that there was rarely a shift change to necessitate the transfer of information, but Martin and the older Shepherds insisted it be done. It was a daily record of the Brothers' movements and moods and activities, of medical concerns and aggressions and victories and struggles. He carefully recorded the progression of Jonathan's illness and the time and nature and likely cause of Philip's morning aggression. He wrote about the morning's walk, marking down Donny's chickadee. He marked down the total of the nails pulled for that day. There were fifty-two, well short of the record.

As they worked, Robert Sanderson came ambling down to speak to Wayne. "Would you come up to the farm sometime next week? Plough needs sharpening and I just can't manage it myself anymore. There's a side of ham in it for you." Wayne acquiesced with a gruff nod, without missing a hammer-blow. "And you, young Micah? How goes the battle?"

"It, um, goes pretty good. Pretty good I guess." Micah had known Robert his entire life but had never learned to relax around him. One of the several farm-family patriarchs that formed the secular arm of the Fold, Robert never missed a chance to let it be known whose land, whose crop, whose animals kept Martin's "little project" watered and victualled. His low opinion of the men (but not the women) who had taken on the role of Shepherd was well-documented, and he had been vocally disappointed when Micah had declined to apprentice with him as a farmer.

When all the day's nails had been pulled and the salvaged wood had been piled, the Friendly Men used the remaining time before lunch to work on their own small projects. Donny was building a birdhouse with walls, at his own insistence, four feet long, a home for a bird one would hope never to meet. Sam simply enjoyed cutting wood into progressively smaller and smaller pieces, while Philip and Thomas huddled as close to Wayne's forge as he would allow them to get. They loved the heat, the spit and crackle of the sparks and the steady rhythm of Wayne's hammer as he slowly transfigured the hood of an ancient pickup truck into a plough blade. They loved Wayne and were terrified of him, that grim old god of hammer and flame, but a god who sometimes gave them treats out of his lunch. It was a warm, merry place, the din a welcome thing after the relentless silence of the wilderness that always sought a way into the village.

Micah was doodling in the margins of his shift log, drawing that tree he always drew. This sort of thing was not discouraged, as it would have been in the old days of the institutions. Your notes were personal until the journal was full. Then it was added to the dozens of others in the library and became public domain, a rarely-read history of the Fold and those who dwelt there. Micah looked out the window and saw that it had begun to snow. He was so very tired of the snow. But surely this must be nearly the last of it. Spring was coming soon. He had smelt the first of its warmth and its moisture in the wind, two days ago. He had written it down in his shift log.

Micah's mind began to wander back to the Watch Tree, and what he had felt as he looked down into the valley that held his entire life. His hand began to move, his exhausted mind still up there on the cliff, and when he looked down he saw that he had written in his log a single word:

"Goodbye."

The lunch bell began to toll.

. . .

People came streaming in from all over the village and the woods and fields that surrounded it. The rumble of rusted and repaired wheelchairs on wooden boardwalks echoed through the town. The ratty end of winter was a hungry time, and no one had had as much breakfast as they would have liked. He waved to Bethlehem and the Pretty Girls, coming in from the Crafts house where he knew they had been mending clothes. Rosie and her Cool Guys were coming down the road from the high pastures, all bundled up from their shepherding, already starting to use their crooks on one another.

All of them converged at the blue steel fire doors, and after the usual bumps and chaos everyone got inside and seated. Martin said a mostly unheard prayer over the lentil stew and the bread and the well water, and those who had not already began to eat. Micah ate with the Friendly Men as he always did, slowing Thomas with a word and a hand when he forgot to chew, directing Sam to take his dishes to the ladies in the kitchen when he had finished, helping Philip find the remaining bits of food in his bowl. When everyone had finished and when he himself was finally able to get some food down, Micah called out "Barn duty!" to Sam and Jonathan and Donny, already milling impatiently by the door. Philip and Thomas attached themselves each to an arm and when everyone had dressed they pushed outside.

The sun, already westering, had broken through again and set the red barn that was their destination to glow like a beacon against the snowy pasture. Jim, father of Amanda of the Pretty Girls and one of the founders of the community, was waiting by the door for them, sitting in the rotten armchair he loved so well, his feet on a milking bucket.

"Hello the Friendly Men! And a good afternoon to ya. We'll be doing some mucking out, if that's all right by everyone," he boomed, while handing out shovels and pitchforks to those who would accept them. Thomas gave a shut-faced scowl that indicated that it was very much not all right, but joined in when Micah took his pitchfork and began to work to the backdrop of Donny's shrill litany on the duty and the many virtues of service to one's community. Philip curled up in a warm corner and refused to participate, as was his custom.

18

Micah hated mucking out, because this was work that actually had to get done. It wasn't a time-filler for the men or a way to burn energy and keep warm like some of the scheduled activities. The dung had to be wheelbarrowed to the pile, and new straw had to be put down, or the animals would get sick and the entire community would suffer. The job had to be finished, and Micah always ended up doing most of it, with Thomas hanging off of his arm. It took five hours with breaks, and he was still finishing, the rest of the guys having long since given up, when the dinner bell began to ring out through the swiftly falling darkness.

It was lentil stew again, the leftovers from lunch repurposed, as required by the necessities of winter in the Fold. The Friendly Men ate their meal, cranky and smelly with manure, and at the end of the meal Rufus, as big across as any two of them, came over and clapped his hands together with the crack that made them jump and squeal with fearful delight. The official handyman, maker, and fixer of the Fold, he had several years ago been convinced by Martin to agree to be a substitute Shepherd, covering illness and time off, a concession that still bewildered Rufus.

"That man is some kind of warlock," he would often complain to Micah. "How he convinced me to agree to this, why I *keep* doing it . . ." But the answer to these questions was obvious to anyone who had seen Rufus with the Friendly Men. They adored him, and he could not help but reciprocate their affection.

"All right, you maggots. Playtime is over. Nice Mr. Gault is off duty. You're stuck with me til bedtime." He scooped little Jonathan up in his massive arms to his eternal delight, and Donny roared with laughter, but Thomas had to be pried, weeping, off of his brother's arm and transferred finger by finger to Rufus'. With bellowed excitations Rufus hustled them off to help clear the tables for the evening games, and Micah took advantage of the confusion to slip out of the kitchen door. It closed behind him, the shouts and the screams and the laughter and the smells suddenly cut off, and Micah was alone for the first time that day; sweetly, deliciously alone. He ran down the empty street, the great leaping strides he only used when he was sure he was alone.

He sprinted up to the high-gabled farmhouse on the edge of the village that served as library and archives. The windows were lit with a warm and cozy glow.

2
Wisdom And Other Information

Lorne was at home, of course. He almost never left, sleeping and taking all of his meals among his charges: the Book Dragon never left his hoard. Micah knocked on the solid oak door beneath the sign the Cool Guys had made in Woodshop ("Welcome To The Library Books"). There was a sound of muffled cursing and a hurried thump-thump-thump and then the door was jerked abruptly open, and a bearded face thrust through the opening. It bore an expression of such perfectly practiced disgust that Micah had to choke down his laughter.

"Micah Gault you are interrupting me when I am reading and reading is a quiet activity and when people interrupt me I cannot focus and if I can't focus on my reading I can't be expected to be successful in my endeavors, can I now?" stammered the man behind the beard.

"Hello, Lorne. I'm sorry to bother you when you are reading. I was wondering if I could borrow a book from you, if I promise to be very quiet while I select it?" This was the prescribed coda for negotiating with Lorne Heemskirk. He could never quite be made to understand the precise boundaries of his duties as librarian, but nobody in the world could have kept the Fold's library and archives better organized or more securely preserved. If you could get in the door, you could find almost anything, and you would find it filed exactly where it should be according to the Dewey Decimal System. In the tangle of wilderness the world had returned to, there was something almost impossibly comforting about visiting the library on a winter's evening, to wander in the warm, clean silence among the ordered shelves, to browse the thousands of volumes gathered there. There and, perhaps, nowhere else.

Micah submitted to the usual search of his pockets for pens, liquids, or any kind of food, all strictly forbidden, and underwent interrogation as to his purpose and intentions. His darkest suspicions at least mollified, Lorne reluctantly issued Micah the regulation candle (very small) in the shielded holder he had designed himself to be sure that no flame or dripping wax came near his precious charges.

Candle in hand and rules repeated once more, Micah was cleared to browse. He made his way slowly through the first floor of the farmhouse and up the stairs. The first floor contained no books, at Lorne's insistence: far too great a risk of flooding in the spring. Instead it housed his living quarters. Carefully hand-lettered signs lined the hallway and urged the visitor upstairs: "This Way To The Books." "No Food, No Drinks, Not Even Water, Nothing." "You Better Wash Your Hands." "You Better Not Rip Or Fold Any Pages."

Up the creaking staircase on the second floor the silence became absolute, except for groaning of the old wooden house in the March wind. "Second Floor: Wisdom and Other Information," proclaimed Lorne's spidery handwriting over the doorway on the landing.

The many rooms of the second and third stories of the old farmhouse were packed with books. Tall wooden shelves ran from floor to ceiling on every inch of available wall space, and every shelf was packed tight with books of every conceivable form and description, from soft ancient molding hardcover tomes, to cheap glossy paperbacks peeling before their time. Fashion magazines, phonebooks, instruction booklets for toasters and vacuum cleaners, it was all here, the ancient treasure and the ancient trash, gathered alike, repaired and preserved and set here to rest until the words within were again required. It was local lore that Wayne and Robert had had to reinforce the floors and load bearing walls lest Lorne be buried beneath his hoard.

Micah ran his fingers along the rows of faded spines and felt the familiar shiver that always came over him in this place. The scouts of the Fold had searched the counties around the village in every direction for decades, and had never come across anything like this. Other settlements were small and rare, and generally vicious in their desperation. The only thing that had mattered for the last forty years was survival, and there was no indication that anywhere in the former nation the story was any different. The wisdom, art, and science of man had been gathered here, welcomed by Martin and then by those who followed him. The accumulated knowledge and craft of the human species that could be contained within the covers of a book were safeguarded here, in a ramshackle farmhouse by an old man with Asperger's syndrome.

Was there no other remnant? Surely not. The unbidden words in the notebook returned to him, and the feeling that had arisen as he had reached the boundary. There was more out there than wilderness and dead cities. There had to be. And more than merely danger. Surely the fall of an empire had left more trace than this upon the Earth. They knew so little here in the Fold, just the going-out of the lights, and the burning that had followed it, and the unbroken silence that had followed that. But here, gathered into five rooms on the second floor of Lorne's house, was nearly a full record of what had come before, and Micah had pored over it, awe-stricken, since he was old enough to sit up.

It was all here, from the clear and concise histories of the nation from prehistory up until the year of its collapse, to technical manuals for the machinery that made it run. There were full print runs of glossy gossip magazines tracing the rise and fall of celebrities and their fashion that spanned fifty years. A walk-in closet on the second floor was filled from floor to ceiling with car magazines that marked the progression of the automobile from 1982 until the last year the factories produced them.

As a young teenager Micah had become as obsessed with cars as young children will be with dinosaurs, and had read every single issue from cover to cover multiple times. That was before his ordination, when he still had more than two hours of time to call his own in a week, but he still peeked into Lorne's collection of owner's manuals from time to time. He loved the manuals, and the small comforting glimpses they gave into a world with other priorities than survival. The manuals with their casual discussion of oil changes and shift patterns were like finding the tracks of a mythological beast in the winter forest. There was one engine still running in the valley, reworked to run on kitchen grease, and Micah had memorized everything he could from these texts to contribute what he could to its working. But these machines were once so common that more pages were devoted, strangely, to their aesthetics than their technical function. The images were strange and very wonderful, but they were not what continued to draw Micah here, nearly every hour he had off, year after year.

No, that was the third floor. "Just Stories," read Lorne's dismissive label. Lorne was famously contemptuous of fiction, but never in a thousand years could he bring himself to dispose of even the most fallacious text. The alleyways between the shelves were narrower here, and in places neat stacks of books sat on the floor, a necessary practice that Lorne abhorred. It was a tight-packed warren of shelves and books, always cold in the winter (being as it was two floors above the potbellied wood stove), but Micah had dressed for it. He wound his way through the labyrinth of shelves, reveling in the smell of the place, the warm musk of slowly rotting paper and cardboard and leather and paste, to his favorite place in the world.

It had taken a bargaining process that lasted four years, but at last Lorne had agreed to allow Micah to move an old armchair up the stairs to the third floor. Lorne did not see the purpose of a comfortable sitting place in what he referred to as "The Stacks."

"It's a repository, not some bankside café! What will you do there? You sign the books out, and you take the books home! You return the books! That is how a library works." But because he had been coming there since he was a toddler, and because the library only had three or four other visitors a week, and because deep in his heart Lorne loved Micah like a son, he relented at long last.

Micah had placed the chair in the gable-nook of the third floor, where a window would light his pages and he could look out at the fields beyond the edge of town. He retrieved his copy of *A Prayer For Owen Meany* from where he had carefully returned it, according to the Dewey Decimal System (Lorne had made him take a course, taught by Lorne himself), placed his candle on the windowsill, and eased his aching body down into the familiar creak of the chair. He retrieved his thick wool blanket from beneath it, pulled it around himself, and began to read. Usually two hours in the chair with a book passed in a blissful heartbeat, marked by Deb's carefully timed ringing of the hour from the belltower of St. Stephen. But this afternoon was different. Whatever the voice was that had compelled him to write his farewell in his journal on the cliff continued to disturb him.

Surely, the voice began to whisper, all this is being squandered. What were they doing with all this accrued knowledge? Nothing at all. There was no time for them to apply any of this wisdom (and other information), no time to be improved or refined by it. All their time and all their energy belonged to the Brothers and Sisters. The princes, as Micah had dubbed them long ago in the privacy of his mind, for the sense of entitlement with which they claimed the days and hours of his life, these meek that had inherited all the Earth that Micah had ever known.

The more he thought about it, the more this seemed the inevitable conclusion: the Fold was a waste. A noble and a beautiful waste, but a waste nonetheless. A door had opened within Micah, and he found himself unable to keep out the cold. All the long-repressed, too-swiftly-countered objections were in him.

I never chose this, came the echoes of resentment. *I was born into it. I don't have to be here. It's unfair. I owe these people nothing. It's immoral. It's bullshit. It's a waste of time and resources. Of my life.* Micah sat silently, waiting for these objections to be answered. He knew they were selfish. He knew that they weren't strictly true, that surely none of the princes had chosen their circumstances either. But he needed more of an answer than that to the question of why he remained, and this time, no compelling answer came.

He found himself sitting alone in the library window with the overwhelming knowledge that the life he had known had ended. He stared blindly out the window for a minute. Then he carefully tore a blank page out of his journal and began to write a letter.

The bell rang four times, and Micah folded the completed letter into the copy of *The Wind in the Willows* he planned to read to the Friendly Men tonight, and after submitting to Lorne's arcane sign-out process, he walked back through the snow to the attic over the kitchens in a state of quiet disbelief.

Philip and Donny and Sam and Jonathan were waiting for him with Rufus, who went off-duty as he always did, with a weary shake of his grizzled head and a mutter of "I don't know how you do this everyday."

Thomas rushed to Micah and took up his rightful place on his left arm, a look of utter relief on his face, and Micah was plunged into a familiar hell of guilt. Jonathan was asleep, as he always was by this time. Donny began the evening with a bombardment of questions. Sam was pacing in nervous circles around the room, flapping his arms. And Philip had screwed shut his blind eyes and begun to scream, as he always did. As always. As always.

Micah took his place against the west wall, lit the candle, took the book out of his bag, and began to read aloud. Gradually, Philip's keening began to lower in volume and intensity before petering out. The reading also helped the ever-anxious Thomas to sleep, but more than anything, it helped keep Micah from losing himself to the terrible blend of tension and monotony that defined his days. He opened the book to where the newly written letter marked the page.

"Chapter Six," he began, "'The Piper At The Gates of Dawn.'" Around the attic the night grew colder. The letter, removed from the insulating pages of the book, absorbed the cold. It contained his formal resignation.

3
Kindly Endure

The sun was still an hour from its rising when Philip's dawn-wail brought Micah crashing into wakefulness. He stared at the timbers of the ceiling for a moment, trying to summon the strength to throw back the blankets and reenter the world of mud and feces and biting cold air. And then, with a sudden rush of relief, he remembered that it was Sunday. Once he had gathered the men for breakfast and taken them to church and attended the weekly Shepherds' meeting, he was free for the rest of the day, clear through to the evening sleep-watch.

Hard on the heels of this relief came the recollection of yesterday's decision, and of the letter it had engendered. Micah was filled with a wild and reckless joy at the thought. Removed from the contemplative state he had known in the library, it seemed insane, the actions of an individual with no relation to Micah himself. But that individual's actions, now recalled, filled him with a white hot excitement unlike any he had known before. There was a future in that letter, and the unimagined novelty of unguessed possibilities. For the first time in his life, the future seemed unknown.

Micah's heart pounded in his chest as he pulled on the rough woolen habit that served as a Shepherds uniform: medical scrubs, apron, and on Sundays, a symbol of holy orders taken. It had been washed and dried the night before by Karen, then folded and placed outside his door as it was every morning. The Shepherd's habits were the only garments washed daily in the Fold, in an attempt to protect the Brothers and Sisters from the worst ravages of contagious disease. But Martin insisted they also be worn to church on Sundays, even if the Shepherd was off duty.

He dropped Thomas off with the ladies in the kitchen and took Philip down to the pump to be washed off, then back up to the attic for clean clothes. Philip struggled and scratched, as he did every morning. He never seemed to mind the smell or the sensation of the nightsoil on his body, but he hated the cold. The water was almost unendurable, even to someone without sensory issues. There could be no choice when it came to hygiene, however. Disease and the fear of disease were an ever-looming specter in the Fold. A dozen past epidemics had caused the little cemetery beside St. Stephen to overflow into the field beyond it.

Micah and the other Shepherds followed the Guidelines for a Healthy Fold, written twenty years ago by the long departed and greatly missed Dr. Chatterjee, and the Guidelines were posted in every building in the village. Before his passing, Dr. Chatterjee had trained every working Shepherd in the basics of field medicine.

But as Rufus was fond of saying, "Napoleonic Wars, man. It's like the fucking Napoleonic Wars around here." So Philip had to be washed of his excrement in the predawn darkness, with cold water, every morning, while he shrieked and clawed at Micah's hands.

Once a semblance of hygiene had been reimposed upon the Friendly Men, however, there was never any trouble getting them down to the Hall on a Sunday. It was the day of the vaunted porridge and pig sausage. Everyone ate their fill and were glad in the good-smelling warmth of the place. At nine o'clock a bell began to ring and everyone walked and wheeled and stumbled and limped and leapt out of the doors and down the street, to St. Stephen-in-the-Fields.

The church of St. Stephen-in-the-Fields had never been intended to serve a parish of this size, not even in the glory days of 19th-century Canadian Anglicanism. Every scarred and splintering pew was now packed and groaning. Roaring and crying and laughing and loudly shushing one another, the mass of men and women filed through the old blue doors beneath the weathered Agnus Dei, and past Lou-Anne, swinging joyfully from her bell-ringer's rope. It took twenty minutes and every effort of all three Shepherds to get everyone more-or-less seated. No attempt was made to keep the men and women quiet. Church was not a place for silence, not during service, not in the Fold. Surely, as Martin was fond of saying, the very rocks would cry out if the Brothers and Sisters were shushed in their praising.

Once inside the building, the Shepherds returned their Friendly-Pretty-Cool folk to the care of their waiting families. Sunday was Family Day for those who still had living relatives. Those who did not found a place with one of the volunteer families not directly connected to the caregiving at the heart of the community. These were mostly elderly farming couples, whose own departed childen had once been in the care of the Shepherds. Everyone had a family on Family Sunday. Thomas and Micah found their mother Joanna in the pew she always waited for them in, and she hugged her youngest before the eldest put his arm around her, where it would stay all day.

As the excited congregation shouted out its joy and consternation, Martin Safarian detached himself from the mob and took his place. He stood at the lectern, beneath where the high arch of the roof-beams was carved with the seventh verse of the fourth chapter of the book of Micah. Martin was wearing his spring vestments for the first time, which caused much excitement among a certain faction of the gathered. They were a light brown and embroidered with budding trees, embroidered by Nelle before her passing, as all his vestments had been.

Martin raised his hands and Lorne rushed forward with the Book of Common Prayer and placed it on the lectern, opening it to the correct reading. He sang out the liturgy over the broken men and women and their broken helpers, who sang out together in response. The pews were still lined with tattered prayer books and hymnals, despite Lorne's tearful protestations and repeated attempts to liberate

26

them for safekeeping in his house. Martin kept the collect and the homily short, out of necessity, then sang out the benediction while Rosie Meech broke the bread and poured the wine into the bowls. Martin raised his calloused old hands again and blessed them in the old words, as he always did. "The gifts of God, for the people of God." And the people of God bellowed out, as they always did, "Thanks be to God!"

Then the whole village came pouring up the aisle to the altar, carrying and being carried. Some took too much and some took none at all and some threw what they took on the ground but when everyone who wanted to had eaten and drank until the bread and the wine were gone, Martin spoke his blessing of farewell:

"Let us go to love and serve the Lord."

Then it was over, not twenty minutes after it had begun, and the men and women hurried back out of the doors, to the library and to the woods, to the fields and the workshop and the stables, to firesides and family time. The Shepherds remained. Sunday was the Shepherds meeting, in the quiet after. The letter was in Micah's breast pocket; foreboding was in his heart.

The full-time Shepherds took their long-accustomed positions in a rough circle: Micah sitting on the steps of the chancel, the older ones preferring the first row of pews. There were only three fully ordained Shepherds, though in the past there had been as many as six. There were eight others (including Rufus) who held other roles within the Fold but who stepped in during illness (frequent) and on days off (rare). Micah led the Friendly Men. Bethlehem Manassi was responsible for the Pretty Girls, and old Rosie Meech mothered over the Cool Guys, of whom her son Barry had been a founding member.

Martin settled heavily down into his place near Micah on the worn steps of the chancel, below the altar. He took off his vestments, now that Lorne had left, and folded them on the faded carpet. He spoke softly, but not a word was lost.

"And how are we all?" he began, as he always did. One by one the three Shepherds opened their journals and gave a summary of the little victories and large disasters of the week that had been. Samuel's ongoing dysentery and consequent weight loss. Emma's losing battle with self-injury. Barry's record-breaking two weeks without a serious aggression. Jessica's successful care and feeding of an orphaned barn-cat, the fulfillment of a lifelong dream. The appearance of gangrene in Joseph's badly broken leg, the result of his refusal to rest it. When the three had finished, the eight corroborated and expanded upon each tale.

It was an exhausting litany, delivered by exhausted celebrants, but to speak of exhaustion in the Fold was an exercise in redundancy. Nobody there could remember what it was like to live or work in any other state.

It had been a relatively quiet week, the long slow emergencies proceeding at their usual pace without an overabundance of interruptions. When the silences grew long enough, Martin closed with a prayer and dismissed Rufus and the rest of the Relief. The core stayed bowed in their circle, silent for a few minutes, and then one by one began to speak.

They spoke of the same events of the same week, but in very different tones. The cheerful professionalism was gone, and the Shepherds unpacked their secret hearts. Rosie began to cry, softly first and then openly, loudly weeping, as she described the long, slow and still ongoing death by suffocation of Aaron Peterson. Her thin body, seventy-two years old, shook violently with sobs as she talked of all those she had seen grow sick and die, all the Brothers and Sisters she had buried. They placed their hands on her and prayed silently. When her sobs quieted, Bethlehem began.

Bethlehem was angry, filled with a hot and unresolvable fury. She spoke of the cruelty of her Sisters to one another, the bullying and the little violences, the strong among the weak pushing down the weaker still. She raged against the limitations of their situation, of the unfairness of it all, of the seeming silence of God. Bethlehem's voice reached a crescendo as she cursed out her rage. It subsided, and she began to laugh as they prayed for her, though the tears ran down her cheeks.

Finally it was Micah's turn. He had fully intended to tell them about his unexpected revelation. He meant to present his letter, aware of the disaster it would herald for the community. He had been growing increasingly anxious throughout the course of the meeting, and now his heart was pounding again. He took a deep breath. He looked at Rosie and Bethlehem, hollow eyes red for weeping for sorrow and for rage. He looked at old Martin, studied and practiced in his compassionate composure, and he swallowed the words back down. He couldn't add that to their already crushing burdens. He couldn't abandon them. Not yet.

Micah quickly searched his brain for some lesser vexation. He quickly found one, and expounded on the difficulties associated with caring for his brother, of always having taken care of his brother, to the exclusion of all else since childhood. It was a familiar theme, one performed many times before, and he riffed easily now.

He stole a quick look around. The other Shepherds were nodding silently. Martin was staring at the floor, as he often did when listening intently. No one seemed to have sniffed out any inconsistency between his initial intention and his public statements. But there was a fresh wound in his weary soul. Micah couldn't remember ever being anything less than entirely truthful in a Shepherd meeting before, and certainly not with Martin there. He felt sick, but it was a sickness that he would have to bear. There were only three of them. Only three who could, and would, do the job.

Rosie Meech was already walking with a cane, and seemed more bent and lined every Sunday. Bethlehem Manassi had three children of her own. Micah was the young man, the strong man, the hope for the future. There was no room for anything less than complete service in the vocation of the Shepherd, and Micah knew it. This was not the world of fifty years before, when people could live as they wanted. If he chose to go his own way, every man, woman, and child in the Fold would pay a blood price for his autonomy. He shut his mouth, and kept it that way.

The long silence that always marked the meeting's conclusion came and went, and then they ended as they always did. Martin placed his hand on the head of each of them in turn and gave his benediction, the motto of the Shepherds: "Kindly endure." One by one, they repeated it back to him: "Kindly endure."

Martin put his hand on Micah's shoulder, gave a double pat, and went out to the barn, and then Micah was alone. He closed his eyes and took a deep inhalation of the musty air, filled with the smell of hot beeswax and the lingering funk of homemade incense, and he asked Jesus what he should do, and how he was supposed to do it. And he sighed and got up, Jesus not being forthcoming with His answer, and went to his mother's house.

4

The Sport Of Kings

It was the small schoolhouse on the edge of town, although nearly every building in the Fold was on the edge of town. It was the house in which Micah had been born and had lived with his mother and brother, until his sixteenth birthday, when he had been ordained as a Shepherd and had begun his ministry.

The house was empty, his mother out with Thomas for several hours still. These rooms were memory incarnate, the smell of the place and the sounds it made as he moved through were utterly unchanged in any detail from his earliest memories.

Here he lived when he wasn't working. His old bedroom had been kept for him, the old pictures he had drawn still on the wall, every margin filled to make the paper last. He lay down in his bed in the old way, half propped against the wall, and read until he fell asleep. It didn't take long.

Micah was awakened by a banging on the door. He wiped the drool from his mouth and tried to shake off the sick fog that always accompanied him after waking from an unplanned nap.

"Hello? Anybody home? Any grown-ass men still living at their mom's house, perhaps?" came a booming baritone from two floors below. Micah smiled to himself as he listened to his mother answer the door and merrily berate Rufus for his language as he pulled his pants on and stumbled down.

His mother was sitting at the kitchen table with Thomas, marking a stack of spelling tests and gently chastising Rufus, whom she loved. "I'm just saying, Mr. Castle, that any young lady who happens to hear you using that sort of language is not going to be interested, not one bit."

Rufus was grinning through the wild black tangle of his beard, peering out of the hood of the ancient black sweatshirt he never seemed to take off, like a bear peering out of its den. "And just where exactly are these young ladies meant to be arriving from? Do they often arrive unannounced out of the bush on a Sunday afternoon?"

"Stranger things have been known to happen, Mr. Castle. But they won't hang around long if they hear you taking that tone with a woman of advanced years."

"Not so advanced as all that, Mrs. Gault. And since we're on the topic, don't you think Micah would be a bit less moody and weird if he had a good solid father figure?"

Joanna Gault mockingly appraised Rufus over her cracked reading glasses. "Solid, certainly." They both dissolved into laughter, which Micah was happy to interrupt.

"I've asked you both to please not make those kinds of jokes when I'm around."

"Your mom won't let me make the other kind," rumbled Rufus. "It's the Sabbath, brother. Let's get the f . . . frig out of here."

"Have fun, boys!" called Micah's mother from the door. "Don't let him pressure you into smoking that horrible stuff he grows. It's of very poor quality."

One step out the door and Rufus took his familiar swig from his canteen. They took two bikes from the well-maintained fleet behind the old general store, waving off the Cleland family's pleas to stay and play horseshoes with a kind but firm denial, and rode on down the road.

At the usual place they left the road and rode along the dirt path on the edge of the pastures, past the herds recently let out into the early spring, to Rufus' house by the creek. It was a cabin, not much more than a shack, but Rufus had built it himself, and it hung together with the same air of practiced indifference that Rufus did.

Rufus built a lot of things, and fixed a lot of other things when they broke (or when the Brothers and Sisters broke them), and although he would never admit it he had become a pillar of the community, if a creaking, crazy-angled pillar who drank too much homemade moonshine.

They leaned their bikes against the wall and Rufus unlocked the splintery door with a rusty key he wore around his neck. He lit a fire against the musty darkness and fell groaning onto a moldy, overstuffed couch like a ship making harbor. He filled his pipe with cannabis, took a deep inhalation, and for the thousandth time offered it to Micah. For the thousandth time, Micah refused, and felt guilty refusing.

"You know that breaks my heart, sir. I grow this myself, you know. These plants are my children. When you reject my kush, you are rejecting my children." It was a familiar script.

"Yes, Rufus. Once again I reject your dank stinky children. When are Martin and Bethlehem getting here?"

"Soon enough, young man, soon enough. But maybe long enough to sober up." Rufus offered his canteen, Micah took a polite sip, and then there was the expected knock at the door. "Our guests!" He made his lumbering way to the door, cracked it open, and sang out "Who is it?" in a lilting falsetto. Martin and Bethlehem were welcomed into the dark little room. The Stroop family had given Bethlehem a clutch of sandwiches for all, and as the messenger, she was rewarded with a crushing embrace and a wet, whiskery kiss.

When everyone was seated and the food equally portioned, when Martin had accepted his own pipe and everyone their mug of well-vintaged cider (also Rufus' handiwork), and when the initial relieved conversation of relaxation had subsided, Rufus stretched expansively and said, "And now, the Sport of Kings." From behind the couch he pulled an old piece of plywood drawn over with a grid, and a stack of books. From a box on the bookcase emerged three small, hand-carved wooden figures and a small leather bag, oddly shaped.

31

Rufus opened his Dungeon Master's Guide and bellowed "When last we met, you had just glimpsed the Crown of the Skaftafell on the cursed hill of Amon Myrgancyr. Ladies and Gentlemen, what do you do?"

"I prepare a Fireball spell and run up the hill," said Martin.

"Easy, Father. You have no power here. Here I'm the boss, or the warlord, or the high priest, or whatever it was we decided to make you. Here you gotta roll for initiative."

And so they spent their Sunday night playing ancient games of make-believe until the bedtime bell rang from the church. By then the conversation had strayed from the invented scenarios of the game to the more perplexing details of their actual circumstances. A debate was playing out that had been argued a dozen times to Micah's certain memory, and had no doubt been ongoing since the founding of the Fold before his birth: Why? What? How?

Bethlehem argued first and loudest, in passionately accented tones, that the continued existence of the Fold was incontrovertibly miraculous. Only God could have brought them all together in this place, and only God could have kept them there for so long, while so many other similar experiments in survival had failed. "We are the Lord's anointed. He bring us here, He keep us safe. For the little ones," the term she invariably used for the Brothers and Sisters. "We take care of them, He take care of us. We don't?" She gave her characteristic dismissive shrug. "See how well it goes for us then."

Rufus retaliated with his trademark blend of benevolent condescension. "Oh Bethlehem, how I love your stories. You are so gifted at remaining in character. This isn't *Lord of the Rings*, and it's not the book of Revelation. We're alive and well and through the worst of the shit for the same reason anybody else is who is still out there. We're smart, and organized, and we work our fucking asses off twenty-four hours of each and every day. That, and we're lucky, of course. Very lucky." He took a deep drag. "And one day we won't be. And raiders will find us, or a drought will, or tuberculosis will stage a comeback tour, and then we're gone the way of our dearly departeds."

"Bah!" answered Bethlehem, with a dismissive flip of her hand. "The boy here doesn't know."

"And when our luck turns, my dear," continued Rufus, undisturbed, "we'll see how much your God cares for His little ones. I love them as much as you do, and don't you dare deny it, but they're not a magic talisman of protection. They give us purpose, and a common goal, and that's magic enough. But they won't save us in the end."

"That's blasphemy, my boy, and you'd best be repenting of it, whenever it is you sober up. But you do love them, I'll give you that, and for that I'll love you, and because my Jesus told me I had to." And they laughed together, at each other and at themselves.

Micah recused himself from the debate, as he always did, but the dueling narratives buzzed and swarmed like insects in his head and made his heart beat fast and the anxiety bubble in his stomach, for he knew the question was key, and that he had no answer.

Martin leaned his chair back up on two legs against the wall, and smoked his pipe, and smiled to himself.

Soon enough their time was up, and Bethlehem and Rufus had to return to their duties, Bethlehem to her Pretty Girls, and Rufus to the Friendly Men. Micah still had an entire evening and night gloriously alone. When they had left, he walked in the forest beneath the stars for a little while, and then rode back home along the rumbling wooden boardwalks to revel in the rare luxury of sleeping in a silent house.

At dawn he got up to find that his mother had made him breakfast. They ate together in the old kitchen, trading stories about the Brothers and Sisters and those who cared for them. Again the urge arose in Micah to confess his revelation, to tell his mother that he was done, that he was leaving. But she looked older than he had ever seen her look that morning in the early light, and the house around her seemed so large and empty. He swallowed the words again, told another anecdote, drained his tea, and left to relieve Rufus in the Hall.

5
The Glow

Micah fell almost immediately back into the rhythms of chaos and routine that marked his Shepherd's life. He and the Friendly Men fed the horses and mucked out the stables until lunch, then spent the afternoon doing their own laundry with well water warmed over a blazing fire, then wrung out to dry. It was a long and involved process, and soon the bells were ringing for supper. All of the Brothers and Sisters stayed in the hall after the meal as Rosie Meech led Music Time, banging out ABBA and Elvis songs resurrected from the old world by her battered six string and everyone roared along with vast enthusiasm. Micah was on dish duty with Thomas and Donny, a daunting task but a warm one.

After the piles of warped plastic dishes were dried, Micah delivered the Friendly Men back to Rufus' grudging care, because it was Monday night, and that meant Night Watch. It was not a pleasant station at the ragged end of winter. A hut containing a woodstove was provided, perched on the edge of the escarpment, but out of necessity most of the night was spent patrolling the borders of the village, monitoring the roads that came from the south and from the east, and, most important of all, keeping the sheep, the chickens, and the cows from predators.

The famous story, the one every night watchman couldn't help but consider whenever their turn came to walk the borders of the town, had occurred twenty-seven years before. On a warm night in August, six armed men, wandering bandits as far as anyone could figure it, had entered the village. They had murdered Ken Reed, as he was mucking out the barn by lamplight, and they had stolen almost every horse the community possessed. Nothing of the kind had occurred since, but once was more than enough to ensure the job was taken seriously. For that reason, the person on Night Watch always kept their bow strung, and their quiver full of arrows.

Micah took his seat in the door of the hut and looked up at the sky through the bare arms of the trees. Sometimes, among the thick cold stars, one could be seen to move, to trace a perfect line from horizon to horizon. When Micah was a child he had been told it was a satellite, launched before the darkness fell, remaining obedient to its orbit. Whether it was still broadcasting a signal, and whether that signal was still being received in some place still capable of doing so, had been the course of much debate in earlier years. But the debate had grown cold and then ceased altogether. It simply wasn't relevant. Once, high enough to barely be, a plane could be seen flying over. Perhaps over the whole country, to and from places that hadn't descended into darkness.

Tonight there were only the eternal markers of the night sky. There were fewer clouds, but a deeper cold. It was March, and still bitter, and the stars were laid out across the perfect blackness of the sky like a map, the Milky Way running like a river through the center of the night.

After an hour in the hut, Micah made his slow, steady way around the borders of the village, checking the sanctity of the gates, peering down the empty roads that ran west and south, down to where the City once had stood. It was a silent night, except for the usual ruckus coming from the homes where some of the more vocal Brothers and Sisters were unable or unwilling to sleep. In the stables the horses were calm, the sheep and the cows were mostly sleeping in the moist barn-warmth of animals. Out beyond the little ring of light cast by the few wakeful houses, the land stretched out in darkness, with only the white patches of snowy field visible, and the hills were black where they rose against the stars.

Micah turned and made his long circuitous way back through the center of the village to where it met its abrupt western edge against the cliff face. He climbed the switchback trail to the top, to look out over the dark blue tapestry of the sleeping fields. Out here above the edge of town there was no sound but the creak of the trees in the wind and the crunching of his boots on the old hard snow. He turned to go back to the watchhouse, to warm his fingers by the fire, to drink a little hot tea out of the precious, ancient, battered thermos they all shared.

Suddenly his shadow leapt into being before him. It was faint but distinct, his shape on the snow in front of him, snow that was lit with a faint orange light. It stood for a moment, then the shadow and light that had revealed it disappeared. Micah turned around, confused, to find its source. Nothing. The same black night of stars. And then to the southeast, a silent bloom of light. Luridly orange, it leaped into the utter blackness of the sky like an explosion and remained there, static, unshifting, as if it were painted on the night, as if it had always been there. It was like no illumination Micah had ever seen. It was not the cold mystery of the moon or the stars, or the enveloping promise of sunrise. It was not the familiar dance of firelight. It was something else.

Micah stood, mouth open, staring without believing. He had never seen it, but he had read it described in a hundred novels, and it couldn't be anything but electric light. Hundreds, thousands of electric lights. Someone in the old, dead City had found a way to power it again.

He stood there alone, looking out through the silhouettes of the trees, black against the orange light. It was three o'clock in the morning. The village below slept, undisturbed. He was alone in the knowledge that the world had begun again.

Micah stood like a statue for a full minute, then two, unmoving, waiting for the light to disappear again. It clung to the belly of the long low layer of cloud on the southeastern horizon and the Earth was silent. Micah hesitated for another moment, then turned and walked deliberately through the silent village to the church. The creaking doors were never locked. Within the sanctuary he could smell the incense, see the small red flicker of the votive burning on the altar. He said a prayer for the moment after, seized the rope in the carillon in his mittened hands, and began to pull. The great bronze bell boomed out from its tower to shatter the still of the night's silence, as the light in the south had broken its darkness.

It seemed almost too loud to be believed. The tolling of the bell cascaded out over the town, bouncing back off the limestone walls of the escarpment to fill the valley with its voice. Lights began to appear in the windows of the town, and then shapes could be seen, running through the streets to the doors of the church where Micah waited, bearing the news they had already read for themselves in the sky.

Emmanuel was the first to reach St. Stephen, with Wayne and Bethlehem close behind. By the time they reached the doors of the church their questions had died on their lips, and they stood with Micah on the steps and stared into the orange glow in the southeast sky. No one spoke for several minutes. The Brothers and Sisters began to be heard, shouting questions, crying out in the language of fear and protest and excitement, calling in tongues that could not be translated. A few had followed their Shepherds out of their homes and were beginning to gather beneath the bell tower, some jumping with excitement, some crying with terror, some completely indifferent. Thomas, wheezing, wormed his way through the crowd and latched on to Micah's arm, his eyes wide with fear, gesturing for Micah to look, look at the sky! "I see it, Thomas. Lights." The buzz of the crowd began to grow into a roar, when a low voice intoned at his shoulder, curious, but betraying no alarm.

"This is an interesting development," murmured Martin, "isn't it?" Micah turned. Martin, still gazing at the light, had a sad smile on his lips. Then he climbed the ramp of the church and spoke to the gathering crowd.

"Everyone! I think we can all see what has happened here. Someone to the south has found a way to turn their lights back on. Obviously this means many things will be changing for all of us here, but I don't think any of those changes are going to occur tonight. So I suggest we all go back to bed and get some rest so we are not too sleepy to discuss it together in the morning. How does that sound to everyone?"

It sounded reasonable enough. Rufus came up and punched Micah in the arm. "What the fuck, man. You couldn't wait until morning? No, Micah needs his big dramatic moment. Micah needs to ring the bell. You think Philip is gonna let me sleep after this?"

Micah chuckled dutifully, but his thoughts were far away. Rufus turned and together they stared at the glow. Neither spoke for a long, long time. Finally, Rufus rumbled, "You know what this means, right?" Silence for a moment, and then: "Me neither, man. Me neither." He sighed heavily, gathered his scattered charges, and herded them back down the street with his massive arms and a few loving curses.

Micah began walking slowly back to the Watch Tree as the town returned to its familiar silence. He couldn't take his eyes off of that glow in the sky. It seemed to dominate his vision, constantly calling his gaze back to itself. The stars above him suddenly seemed weak and transient, barely lights at all in the presence of the looming luminescence to the south. It was a strange and lonely wait for the dawn, but in its time it came, to swallow up the glow and end his watch. Micah stumbled home to bed, and dreamed a strange and troubling dream. In it, the tree he always scribbled in his journals had somehow come to life to tower above him, forty feet high. It was beautiful, but somehow freighted with horror. It rocked and swayed in the March winds, its inky bark backlit by a lurid orange glow.

6
Pig-Watch

The next morning at breakfast, the Hall roared with talk of the light in the sky. The Shepherds were generally a conscientious and professional order, but this morning there was no pretending it was an ordinary day. Guiltily checking over their shoulders periodically for signs of choking or fights or elopement, they gathered at the back of the Hall, deep in conversation with each other.

Electricity had returned to the world. The thing they had all dreamed of, theorized about, prayed for, for so very long. Strong, steady light in the night. Water you didn't have to pump by hand, hot water you didn't have to heat in a kettle over a fire. The return of recorded music, maybe even movies (Lorne had hundreds preserved in his library, just in case). Electric heat in the winter, air conditioning in the summer, the internal combustion engine becoming commonplace (at the mere thought Micah's heart began to pound). One day, the fabled Internet? Nothing was impossible. Nothing could ever be the same.

And then, when this rabid speculation had run its course, the inevitable next question arose: Who? Who had found the means, long thought impossible, of recreating and restoring the wiring and the breakers and the bulbs, not to mention the plants that powered them? Was it hydro, wind, solar? Nuclear? It spoke of a monumental turning point in the story of their world, but there was no immediate consensus on who the light-bringers were. There was no way of knowing how far the darkness had spread forty years before, nor was there any clarity to the extent it had now retreated.

Of course, the light-bringers, whoever they were, would have no idea that the Fold existed. What should the Shepherds do? Should they wait for the reborn city to discover them? Or should they go down to meet them, to present themselves, swear allegiance, beg for electricity? No one knew, and the uncertainty was agonizing. Luckily, in the Fold there was always something to be done, immediately, which tended to preserve one from the perils of overthinking the unanswerable questions of the future.

Sure enough, the Friendly Men were already finishing the breakfast they had begun not five minutes previous. What came next was always coming quickly, whether you were ready for it or not. Though in one sense everything had changed, in another practically nothing had. The real world, the world of living and struggling and caring, went on. The imagination would have to take care of itself.

By Wednesday, the lunchtime conversations had exhausted their novelty, and routine had resumed its tiresome reign. After lunch was Pig-Watch, and after the usual tedious struggle, everyone was in their winter jackets, maneuvering out into the March wind and up the road to the pens. There the Friendly Men were issued their staves by Bill and the pigs were released and guided out to the forest where they began their daily search for winter forage in the leaf-mold, newly uncovered by the receding snow.

While on Pig-Watch, the Friendly Men were charged with chasing back any hog that might stray too close to where the escarpment dropped into the valley, and with watching for packs of coywolves and feral dogs. If one was seen, they were to shout "DOG!" as loud as they could, regardless of species. Then Micah would use the bow he carried in his Thomas-free hand. That was the theory, anyway.

Donny loved Pig-Watching and took his duty seriously. He had long since bullied Jonathan into patrolling the cliff-edge with him. Thomas, who never left his station on his brother's arm, joined Micah in patrolling the more dangerous open forest on the other side of the foraging area, watching for predators. Philip, who hated the forest, knelt by the path back to the barns and rocked back and forth, crying softly to himself. It broke Micah's heart, even after so many identical years. But no one could be spared to sit with him, and he couldn't be left alone back in the attic bedroom. There was too much to be done just to maintain the Fold's precarious status quo.

The Friendly Men had been on the job for an hour when Martin came strolling out of the woods, dressed as always in his old chore coat and wool toque. His appearance was not unexpected, as Martin's love of the pathless forest was well-documented.

He greeted each of the Friendly Men in turn, a hug for the gregarious Donny, a long-distance handshake with Jonathan, a hand placed on the sobbing Philip's head, and an acceptance of Thomas' bone-crushing embrace of his bicep. When the excitement of the unexpected visit had subsided, Martin turned to Micah and said, "The brothers Gault. I wondered if I might walk with you a while."

"Ahhh . . . ummm . . . yeah. Certainly. Of course. Yes," Micah stammered in reply, unconsciously affecting the grownup tone he always used when speaking with the founder of the Fold. He heard the change in his voice and despised himself for it, but the deep need to appear in control, in charge, worthy of the responsibilities given him, overrode his sense of shame. Speaking to Martin always made Micah acutely aware of his position as the youngest Shepherd by a significant margin. And now this new restlessness and his as-yet-undisclosed decision made him feel like a traitor as well as a child. He knew these feelings were foolish. He talked to Martin every day. Everyone did. Martin was everywhere, all the time, always working, always involved in every piece of the daily life of the Fold, always giving guidance and advice.

But Martin was also Martin; Martin had discovered this valley, and he had run the community alone for two years, caring for the first of the Brothers and Sisters single-handedly. He was the one that spread the word in those early, brutal days that there was a place like this: a place that wanted things, and people, that no one else did. Martin had built this place up from nothing, though he would deny it vehemently if accused. "God built this place. I was just the first person to get here," he would say.

Micah had grown up hearing stories about Martin from his mother and from the other Shepherds who had served as his aunts and uncles. Martin was a legend, *the* legend of the Fold, and he had never asked Micah to come and talk to him alone like this before. Illogically, his mind flashed to his last entry in the notes, and he unconsciously felt for the journal in the satchel that hung at his side, and the letter still in his breast pocket. He knows, thought Micah. Somehow, he knows. Stranger stories had been told about the man.

Thomas detached from Micah's arm and made the transition to Martin's. Martin was the only person outside of his family he would touch. He put his hand gently on top of Thomas'.

"Come. Let us watch pigs together."

The pigs were foraging in an old forest of oak trees for the troves of acorns hidden beneath the rich brown shining carpet of leaves. The sun, still weak but gaining strength with each passing day, came shining down through the bare branches. The thin hungry pigs were ruthless in their rummaging, filled with reckless delight to be set loose to forage again, and the Friendly Men had their hands full. Donny was chasing a pig away from the cliff edge, screaming "Be careful pig! You'll fall!" Philip's keening echoed through the forest, but the long-accustomed pigs went about their business unperturbed.

For ten minutes they walked the borders of the forage-forest, simply attending to the task at hand. Martin answered Jonathan's questions, the same questions, patiently, as he always did. Thomas hung from Martin's arm in ecstasy. Micah gave Philip his snack, early, and the keening briefly ceased. The resulting silence was blissful. Finally, just when Micah was about to ask the obvious question, Martin began to speak in his low scratchy voice.

"I saw it go out, you know. It was the most awful thing I have ever seen. Like watching a ship go down, a ship the size of a nation.

"I hated that light when I lived in the City. It was always worse in the winter. The streetlights reflected off the snow, you know. Blotted out the stars. Made the sky look dirty and orange. But when it went out, the dark was worse. We think we know what it is we want. When I was young, we all thought we wanted the untamed wilderness. But it was tamed for a reason.

"Now that dirty orange light's back. What does that mean to you, Micah?" Micah was silent for a long time, then answered in a quiet but steady voice.

"It means we have to go there. It means we have to go back to the City."

Martin gazed at the southeast horizon and sighed. "Yes, I'm afraid it does."

A long pause. That hawklike stare again. "You are the rarest thing in this village, Micah. Do you know that?"

Micah had not been expecting this. He looked at Martin, furtively, trying to gauge his expression, looked away, looked back, and looked away again. "I don't know what you mean."

"I mean that of all the extraordinary people that make up this extraordinary place, you are unique, though you may not think so. Do you know why?"

Micah began to shake his head, "no," when he realized he did know. He didn't want to say it, didn't want to haul the awkward words out of his mouth, but Martin deserved more than that. Martin deserved his entire unpacked brain and heart.

"I was born here. I'm the only Shepherd who was born here."

Martin smiled. "That is correct. You are the true and natural-born child of the Fold. This is your home, and the only home you have ever known. You are of this place in a way that none of the rest of us are."

And then, in classically Martin fashion, he stopped speaking as though all their business had been concluded. They continued their patrol. Donny screamed out a warning: there was a coywolf on the western border. Micah, mechanically, put his whistle to his lips and blew a short blast, and the ears in the brush disappeared. It might as well have been a gunshot to the creatures of the valley, conditioned as they were to expect a deadly accurate arrow to follow within five seconds of that sound. They continued their rounds. They helped Jonathan, who was struggling with his water bottle. The sun climbed higher in the sky.

"Do you know what that means, Micah?" said Martin, suddenly but without haste, as if no time had passed since their last exchange. This time Micah did not know how to respond. It meant many things. It meant nothing. He shook his head.

"It means that of everyone who lives, or has lived here, you are the only member of this community who did not choose to make your home here. Have you ever thought about that?"

Micah nodded, and Martin smiled. "I thought you might have, and perhaps recently. It is not an easy distinction to bear." Another long pause.

"I was there the day you were born. Not a day of your life has passed on which we have not had some contact. I have watched you grow up, day by day these twenty-two years, and have often wondered what kind of person you would become. The Fold was founded to provide refuge, to preserve the good that existed when the world went black. Often I've wondered what kind of a child the Fold would prove to produce, what kind of adolescent, what kind of man or woman it would raise up for itself. And I have to tell you, Micah, that the answer you have proven to be is perhaps the greatest of the accomplishments of this place." Martin seemed to have caught some internal current, and was riding it now. There were no more pauses in his monologue.

41

"Micah, I waited for you to complain, as a child, that your playmates weren't the children of the village, but the Brothers and Sisters. I waited with greater dread for your teenage years. I waited for you to perceive the seeming injustice of your position, of the brutal nature of the service you were born into. I waited for your disappointment and your rage at the long hours you labor. I watched with bated breath as others of your generation came to the Fold and left it again, while you remained the servant of the Brothers and Sisters. I waited for you to cry out against the unfairness of it, to blame Thomas, or your mother, or me. I waited for you to come to despise and resent the Brothers and Sisters. I waited for you to run away.

"But you didn't, and not because you were stupid, and not because you had been so thoroughly indoctrinated. You are far too intelligent for that. You grew up into this life of service. You studied it and you understood it and you made it your own, though no duty ties you to this place. For this you are to be commended. You are a true son of the Fold, and we are all deeply in your debt." And Martin stood, and bowed to Micah, who sat, wide-eyed, in something resembling a state of shock.

"And I suppose I just wanted to tell you this, this morning, because I think we both know what that light in the sky means. It means you might soon at last have a choice to make. And I also want to say that I do not know what the right choice will be, but I know that in the Holy Spirit you will make it.

"Micah, I will tell this to you and to Thomas, and to no one else: I am afraid. I am more afraid than I have been since the day those lights went out. I am sick with fear."

Micah stared at the man before him, this living saint, this legend. It was not rhetoric. There were things in that old familiar face he had never seen there before, things he had never dreamt could ever be seen there. Terror. Helplessness. Need. Thomas sensed the new and awful mood, and clung to Micah's arm so tight that it began to go numb.

Then the expression was gone, or rather transformed into something else. The fear remained, but not the panic. Martin looked up from his shaking hands to stare out into the borders of the forage-wood, eyes flicking back and forth, as if he expected a pack to appear at any moment. And he began to speak again, and his voice rang with steel.

"For all the years since this place came into being, we who have been burdened with the responsibility for it have been reasonably assured that we are providing for the Brothers and Sisters, and for one another, the best life that could be given in the world we find ourselves in. We took comfort in this, when those under our care sickened and died. When they died from seizures, and influenza, and from infection."

Micah was silent. The labored wheezing of Thomas' lungs filled the pause in the conversation as if to accentuate the point. Martin caught his eye, and nodded slightly, acknowledging the unspoken.

"We left the City, left the insulated towers, and the straight, flat roads, because without electricity and infrastructure, the City was worse than wilderness. We came here, because here we could win what comfort or security there was to be had.

"But now it seems order has returned to that wilderness, enough to turn the lights back on and all that it entails. If there is power, there will also be production of things we need here: antibiotics, medical equipment, electric heat, a second, better tractor. A hundred other things. We will need to talk about it, all of us together, but it seems clear to me that we cannot allow those in our care to suffer and die for lack of things that exist a few miles to the south." There was a long silence, as Martin and Micah very carefully did not look at Thomas. The rattle in his lungs suddenly seemed very loud indeed.

"Nor should we deny these newcomers the peculiar blessings hidden in this place. It is my belief, and has always been so, that the world needs our Brothers and Sisters just as much as they need the world. The Fold was not founded as a hiding place, and it will not become one now.

"This is why I came to talk to you. You know this place better than any of us. You are *of* it. I know you've been curious to leave. How could you not be? You, alone among us all, have never seen the world beyond our borders, and that is not fair. So I am asking you to go, for us: to be our herald. Go there, as us, as the Fold, and judge these newcomers and the world they have built. Show the light-bringers who we are. Show them our particular light. No one could be a better representative. Place this village before them, and let them choose what to make of us.

"And then, make your choice. This is my charge to you, as your leader and your priest. My request—and it is a request only, not a command—is that you return to us, if you will, if you can: return, and tell us what you have seen. Tell us if the age of the Fold has indeed come to its end. And we will support your choice as we helped raise you up to make it."

Silence fell on the forage-woods. "Come, Thomas, let's give your brother a moment," said Martin, gently detaching his arm from Micah's and offering his own in its place. Thomas acquiesced, and Micah walked on alone towards the border of the forest, arms wrapped tight around himself, hands in his armpits. He reached the line of ancient boulders that lined the pasture and stopped, staring out from the shadow of the hardwood bush, to the light of the open land beyond that came streaming through the tangle of the branches. He stood there until Thomas began to call, then turned and walked back to the waiting pair.

Thomas turned his face away from his brother's approach. On Martin's arm, tears were running down Thomas' red cheeks.

"I'll take that as a yes, then," rumbled Martin, and it was only then that Micah realized that his face had split into a wild and joyful grin.

7
Strange People In A Strange Time

The sun was going down and the lamps were being lit in the village when the bells rang and Micah and the Friendly Men began herding the pigs back to their pen. As they returned to the Hall Rufus came out to meet him on the road outside, his arms crossed. "You want to tell me what's going on here, buddy? Starting Friday, I'm stuck covering for you with the Friendly Men. Indefinitely. Do you know how much extra work that is going to be? Who's gonna watch my plants?" Rufus stuck his fists in his eyes and rumbled like a wounded bear at the thought. "So what's going on, man? What did Martin say to you?"

"He...uh...he wants me to go to the City. To see what's up. With the lights."

Rufus' eyes went wide for a moment before he was able to push down his surprise into his characteristic nonchalance. "'To see what's up with the lights,'" he repeated to himself in mumbled tones. A great sight, and then to Micah: "Well, I guess I can hold down the fort for a few weeks. But you have to bring me a wife. And a helicopter. And a lot of booze. And your mom has to watch my plants." They helped each other wrangle their stragglers into the Hall. As he entered, Karen, Emmanuel and Rosie immediately converged on him. "Word spreads fast," muttered Rufus.

"Is it true?" demanded Karen. "Martin's asked you to go to the City for us?" Micah nodded, embarrassed and strangely ashamed. "And you said you would?" Another nod.

"Are you crazy? Do you know what it's like down there? You wouldn't catch me down there, not for all the hot baths and air conditioning in the world. Who knows what those people are like? Murderers, rapists, cannibals, and that's just the stuff I've seen myself. Mark my words, it'll be something worse. It always is. You're crazy to go, Micah. And your poor mother's going to have a fit when she hears. I don't suppose you've seen fit to inform her yet."

"Don't listen to her, Micah," interrupted Emmanuel. "It's a good thing that you're doing. Brave thing. I wish it were me going, but Beanka wouldn't ever stand for it. It's the City, man. The City. Stuff nobody's ever seen." And he laughed, his deep, careless laugh. Rosie Meech said nothing, just bit her lip, then turned and made her way back to the Nice Ladies.

"When are you leaving?" The question came, again and again. Asking, asking, asking. "I don't know," he replied, "I need to talk to Martin more. I need to talk to my mom. I need to pack. I need to plan."

He knew they shouldn't be talking about this here, but there were no secrets in the Fold for long. Soon enough, Ellen could be heard announcing to anyone who would listen, "Micah's leavin' us! Leavin' us. Micah why you leavin' us? Micah's leavin' us! Running away! Not comin' back!"

Several of the girls began to cry. Donny wheeled around as if he had been shot, then ran up and began peppering Micah with furious questions. Dinner was quickly descending into a howling pit of anarchy when Martin quietly entered the hall, letting the door slam behind him. The Brothers and Sisters immediately fell silent, staring with that blend of wonder and fear with which they beheld no other person in the village.

"Peace, brothers and sisters. Peace! Why all this commotion?"

Donny ran up to him and said "Micah's leaving, Martin! She said so, Karen said so!" and he began to cry. Martin put an arm around him, let him sob into his coat. Then he addressed the room.

"Donny is right. Micah is leaving. He is leaving because I have asked him to. I have asked him to go down to the City, and to find out how they have turned the lights on, and what sort of folks 'they' are. I have asked him to return to us when he has answered these questions. I have released him from his duties until he leaves, which will be soon, so that he can prepare for the journey. The Friendly Men will be joining with the Cool Guys until his return. Please coin a suitable name.

"Soon it will be Sunday. We will all be together at church together, all of us there with Jesus. We can discuss this there, together, in a matter befitting the grownups I know you to be, not like birds at a feeder. I'm asking that you allow Micah to live his life and to do his job until then. Is that something you can do for me? Now please, everyone, finish your dinners, and take your plates to the kitchen."

There was silence, for a moment. Then Donny turned to Micah and asked in a loud, matter-of-fact tone, "Do you think you'll come back or do you think you'll probably die?"

"I don't know, Donny," Micah replied, and sat down to eat his supper.

The rest of the week was subsumed into the unaltered tides of routine. But despite Martin's placating words, he was clearly feeling a sense of urgency, and an emergency service was called for Friday morning after breakfast.

The day came, and when the meal was finished and the dishes were soaking in their tubs, the people of the Fold paraded down the main street to St. Stephen. They packed the old brick church and washed up against its walls like a restless sea. Church was always chaotic, as was any occasion that found all the Brothers and Sisters gathered together, but there was a special tinge in the air this morning, anticipation or panic or glee or some mixture thereof, that possessed even the most stoic of the old farmers.

Martin prayed, Lorne called out, and the Fold sang back their responses as they always did. Micah bent his head and closed his eyes and let it sweep over him and surround him. His lips began to move, but not to the words of plainchant psalm.

The hymn and the howling that accompanied it, some sounds of joy, some of pain and confusion, the prayers of the church crested over him like a wave. He loved this place and these people. But he had already left it in his heart. He looked up through the crowd and caught Martin's eye, his falcon-gaze. Martin nodded. Micah nodded back.

The hymn came to an end. Martin took his place at the lectern. He stood, silent, for a minute, searching the rumbling congregation restless in their pews. Finally he spoke.

"I'm not going to preach to you as if nothing at all has happened. I'm not going to give a homily filled with veiled references to our situation. I'm going to talk to you, and you're going to talk to me and to each other, in an orderly and mannerly fashion ..." The congregation laughed. "... And then we're all going to talk to God, and then maybe He'll talk to us.

"Friends! We live in strange times. But we are a strange people, so it is perhaps fitting. The light of the City has reappeared. Some of us remember it. We remember what happened when that light went out. We know what God did then. He made this place for us. He brought us here. And who can say He's not good, and that He hasn't blessed us? We're the folks He said that sermon on the mount about." Martin's voice boomed out, the cries and the howling making a counterpoint, a harmony, a chorus to his words.

"We know what He did. We've been kept. He hasn't changed. And now, one of us must go down to see what this new thing is that he is doing. We don't know what we are sending him to find. He doesn't know himself. He'll go alone, and he'll be serving God and us in his going, as he has done here since he could stand. God has done a lot of good through him. That God holds us still. We are His flock, and the sheep of His hand.

"Micah! Will you come out from your hiding spot so that we can pray for you?"

It was what he'd been dreading. Sick to his stomach and grinning like an idiot, Micah made his way up the aisle, past the people who had raised him, past the people he had helped to raise, past everyone he had ever known. A lot of them were crying, and reaching out to touch him as he passed. Little pats, hard loving slaps, grabs at his sweater, pinches, from hands with feces under the fingernails and hands scoured OCD clean.

Micah stood at the front with his eyes on the floor. Martin put his hand on Micah's shoulder and said "Everybody up!" The Shepherds and the Brothers and Sisters stood up and jumped up and pulled themselves to their feet and surged around him. He was covered in hands, the same hands, gentle and rough, steady and trembling, blessing and pinching. The familiar incense of their bodies settled upon him, and Martin began to pray.

"Lord Jesus! We ask that You would go with Your servant Micah, that You would protect him, the cloak around his shoulders, the fire he sleeps by in the night.

Be his only weapon. We ask that You be with him and carry him down the old roads safely to the City. We ask that You give him wisdom in dealing with whatever he finds there. We ask that You bring him back safely to us. We ask that Your will would be done with him and with all of us. Bless him, and keep him, and cause Your face to shine upon him, and give him peace. In the name of the Father and the Son and the Holy Spirit, Amen!"

The "Amen" echoed back through the old church, in voices clear and voices stuttering and labored, but all of them loud, and all of them earnest.

8
Mom and Pack

Attending to the Friendly Men during the service had been Micah's last duty as a Shepherd. They left the church with Martin at their head, in awe of the old man. After a seemingly endless litany of farewells (solemn and tearful and even jealous), advice, and admonitions, everyone went back to their work, their suffering, and their kind endurance.

To Micah's surprise and delight, he found himself alone in the chapel, without responsibilities. The depth and purity of the silence was absolute and he sat there drinking it in, staring blankly at the woven hangings the Good Girls had made one long winter twenty years past. He was drunk and stoned on the silence, and seven minutes passed before he realized he had been sitting there with his mouth slightly open, out of his body.

Micah rose and left the church. The center of town was quiet, everyone busy at their various activities. He stuffed his hands in his pockets and began to walk, feeling lost. Suddenly, as if by instinct, his feet gained their direction. They took him to the quarry where Rufus and the Friendly Men were engaged in a rock finding and throwing contest. Micah disengaged Thomas from Rufus' arm and together the brothers walked back down the road to the old school house. It was a time for mothers.

The schoolhouse was well over two hundred years old, first the township school and then a converted dwelling and now, in these latter days, returned to its original purpose. Its one classroom was shining, spotlessly clean as always and smelling of childhood. The adult-sized desks were empty today, Fridays being an "all hands on deck" workday necessary to maintain the community's precarious grip on survival.

"Mom?" yelled Micah, more out of habit than necessity. A hundred thousand times he must have yelled that word, in that interrogatory tone, in that spot, in the voice of a child and in the voice of a young man. And the cry was answered, as it invariably was, "I'm here in the back, boys. Take your shoes off, please."

They did so and made their way across the shining hardwood floor to the door beside the teacher's desk, his mother's desk, piled with books and writing utensils and pictures of him and his brother.

Joanna Gault was sitting at a little table in the little kitchen she maintained in the back of the schoolhouse, with a book and a cup of tea. She was wrapped in an old brown robe, her graying hair pulled back into a braid. She put her book down as he entered, took a long sip of serviceberry tea, and said, "So?" She was not smiling.

Micah grinned, sheepishly, and sat down at the table with her. Wordlessly, she pushed a tin of biscuits towards him. He took one, more to have something to do with his hands than for any other reason. He munched it slowly, looking around the little apartment as if he hadn't spent most of his life in the building. It was a warm little room, clean and spare, the essence of a kitchen in the same way that her classroom was the essence of a school.

His mother stared at her cup of tea, an unreadable look on her face. Joanna Gault was a master of unreadable looks, her expression and her tone utterly neutral. "You've agreed?"

"I said yes. I said I'd go. I'm going."

The statement of intention came out of his mouth, and his mother's expression became her own. "Martin is a wise man," she said, tears in her eyes now, "and I hate him so much right now. Oh God, Micah. Oh my God." She wrapped her arms around him tightly, and Thomas wrapped his arms around them, and she and Thomas wept together, and then she got up and made another pot of tea.

"I'm glad, really I am, underneath all this," she said, gesturing to her tear-streaked face. "He's right, of course. It needs to be you, for your sake as much as for the rest of us. You can't just stay here forever, not when Thomas is . . . is gone." She paused and lovingly rubbed Thomas' shoulder with a long ragged sigh. "At the very least Micah, you deserve a bit of a vacation."

"I don't! It's not that. I just . . . I don't know," Micah replied.

"Oh shut up. Of course you do. And you'll be living here until you go, I hope you know, both of you. There are some things for your trip I put in your room too. Just some old things I found that I thought maybe you could use. Your dad's."

Micah and Joanna looked at each other in silence for a moment. Then his mother launched into a story about the hilariously vulgar thing Sanjay Chatterjee had said in his reading class the previous Tuesday. They talked together until the sun began to go down behind the cliff, the three survivors of their family, each soon to be alone in their own particular way.

When the bell rang for dinner, Micah and Thomas walked their mother to the Hall. It felt very strange indeed to see Rufus there, fresh from his ordination as a Shepherd and very awkward in his new habit, eating with the Friendly Men. Micah felt horribly guilty to be sitting with his mother, not watching for choke hazards or monitoring for bullying or theft, but simply to be eating dinner. It seemed an insane luxury. The Friendly Men, as fickle in their affections as ever, were in raptures of joy and awe that the legendary Rufus Castle was eating with them. Rufus who they worshiped and adored, Rufus who was known to sometimes sneak seconds of pudding for them and to give piggy-back rides. And Rufus would now be spending every day with them. Minds had been blown. Rufus himself looked almost as overjoyed, if a little overwhelmed, at the prospect.

Midway through the meal, Martin came sidling over in his unobtrusive way and said, "Can I meet with you tomorrow after breakfast, Micah? At the library? Talk this thing over a little bit?"

Micah nodded foolishly, his mouth full of food.

"Great! Tomorrow then."

Tonight there was Singing and Stories at the church for those who wanted to go. Micah accompanied Rufus and the Friendly Men, to give Rufus the chance to ask him any questions and to impart as much of his hard-won understanding of the strange and seemingly arbitrary ways of Philip, Jonathan, Donny, Thomas, and Sam.

When it was over he returned to the schoolhouse, was kissed goodnight by his mother, and climbed the creaking stairs to his bedroom in the attic above the classroom. The floorboards were warm from the glowing stove. He sat down in his old cold bed and lit the wick of the tallow candle that sat by the bed. The room slowly rose up around him in the glow. Every shape in it was imprinted in his memory, a room he could navigate in the dark.

And then, suddenly, not. A shape on the old dresser, unfamiliar geometry as jarring as a missing step. He carried the candle over and placed it on the dresser. He knew every object in this house, but not these. The strange smell of it was sharp in his nostrils.

It was a backpack, made of a material he had rarely seen, but recognized to be nylon. The forest green material was smooth beneath his fingers, slippery even. It smelled nothing at all like the wool and leather and wood and tallow and manure scents that suffused the world he knew. He put his right arm through a strap and swung it on to his back, and gasped. It was packed full of unknown objects, but it still seemed almost supernaturally light. He could feel a metal frame between his back and the load he bore, but what kind of metal could weigh so little? He swung it back down onto the bed and stared at it in awe. This was an object from another age, a traveler from a future that was in fact the past.

With the light of the candle he examined it more closely and saw that it was patched and sewn in several places. He recognized his mother's hand in the tiny careful stitching. It was strangely decorated: An embroidered patch depicting the former Canadian flag. A button that read "Not all who wander are lost," corroded now, rust staining the material beneath it. Another button, a rendering of a man with a large black mustache that read "Ubermensch" below it. A tingling came into his hands, an uneasiness in his stomach. As if on cue, there came his mother's knock at the door.

"Come in," Micah croaked, his mouth dry. He had not swallowed in several minutes. Joanna closed the door quietly behind her. Micah turned and asked, "Is this . . .?" in a low, husky voice. His mother nodded sadly.

"He carried your brother twenty kilometers in that pack. To here." A pause.

"Your dad wasn't always like the stories you've heard about him. About the Forge, and all that." There were tears in her eyes.

50

"Anyway, it's yours now. I don't need it, and you will. You won't find another one like that, at least not that anybody's willing to part with. There're a few surprises inside, too." She sat down on the bed beside him, unspeaking, and watched him open the pack.

There was a pot and pan of clever design that nested within each other. They were scorched and pitted but whole, and unbelievably light. They hid a cup, knife, and fork within. Metal cutlery! Almost every utensil of any metal had been pounded into an arrowhead in the early days, but these had been saved from all those years of hunting, to accompany him now.

There was a compass in a green plastic case. There was a water bottle, bright orange and made of an incredibly hard and smooth plastic. There was a strange nylon tube, like a parachute in a bag that he could not identify until his mother told him it was his tent. There was a down-filled sleeping bag that rolled to impossible slimness. There was a knife that when folded out was revealed to be many tools in one.

"The things inside were mine," said his mother with a smile, "but the bag and the tent was your Dad's. He was very proud of it. Even the stupid buttons and patches.

"Micah, you know that I am proud of you. What mother would not be? And I'm happy for you, also, though my heart is broken. I'm glad you're going. I know what you've given up to stay here. We all do. We've seen it. We chose this life, but you didn't. This light in the sky, whatever else it is, is an answer to my prayers for you. This light gives you a choice at last.

"But please be careful. They will offer you things there, I'm sure of it. You are a strong, smart, young person. You are what every community needs and desires. They will try to buy you for themselves, and if they can turn the lights on, they can offer you things you can't imagine. Make a home there, Micah, if you find a good one, but do not let them buy your soul. They bought your father's, and he never was never able to get it back."

She kissed him on the forehead, and closed the door behind her as she left. Micah lay awake for a long time before sleep would come. The simple unease in his heart was gone, replaced by more concrete anxieties.

The next morning Micah ate breakfast with Rufus and the Friendly Men. The Men, with the exception of Thomas, barely seemed to notice him, their devotion given entirely over to the novelty of Rufus. Rufus himself was looking decidedly less sleek and cocky then usual and kept catching Micah's eye with exasperated stares coupled with silently mouthed expletives and elaborately-mimed suicides while they ate, before Micah slipped away guiltily and made his way to the Library.

They were waiting for him, sitting together around a large circular dining-room table in what had been the kitchen of the farmhouse. Martin Safarian, Arthur Colpitts and Rosie Meech: The Presbyter.

9

The Presbyter and the Masterpiece

The kitchen was drenched with the morning sunlight that came streaming through the eastward windows. The scarred table was stacked high with books and maps and Lorne was fretting about, berating Arthur for using a mug without a coaster. Rosie Meech creaked to her feet and tottered over to Micah as he entered, her seamed and ancient face split into a wide delighted grin that showed every one of her rotted teeth. She embraced him, then took his hand in her warm withered paw and led him to the table. Martin smiled. "Lorne here has been kind enough to allow us the use of his kitchen, though he admits that it is highly irregular."

"Highly irregular, resulting in a far higher chance of spillage, mess, and destruction of valuable documents!" croaked Lorne, his face a mask of disapproval.

"We are grateful for your help, Lorne," returned Martin. "And I'm sure Micah will be more than amenable to your requests."

Lorne spun around and fixed Micah with his single blazing eye. "When you go to the South, you will bring me books. Books I don't have already. Books, magazines and newspapers. And maps. And manuals. And comic books. Primary sources. You will write down what you see and you will give your notes to me and I will transcribe them properly, for the archives."

Micah smiled, deliberately. "Yes. I would be happy to do that, Lorne. As much as I can fit in my pack." Lorne relaxed visibly, and scuttled out of the room, grinning madly.

"Now," said Martin, "if you will join us."

He gestured to the last empty place at the table. Micah took it, exceedingly uncomfortable in the presence of these three. It was these three who together had founded this community, who had made it strong enough to stand these long decades alone in the wilderness, who had carried it on their backs to this day. The eyes in those weathered faces were fixed on his: Martin's bright and dancing, peering out from the tangle of his hair, Arthur's laser stare, the judge, the appraiser and quantifier of all things, Rosie Meech, her tiny black mouse-eyes so full of kindness and wisdom that it might as well have been the mother of God sitting there, offering him sumac tea in a chipped mug out of the old brown pot.

Micah sat down and wrapped his hands around the warm mug, stared at the hard-scrubbed table, took a sip, looked out the window, before finally stealing a glance at the three of them. They were all gazing at him, still.

It was Arthur who spoke first, in his strangely high voice with that unexpected

Irish lilt. "We're not here to judge you, so don't be afraid. We're here to look at the maps with you, and to try to prepare you for the journey, as best we can. You brought your journal, I see? Good. There's a lot of preparations that need to be made. Your expectations will need some management."

Martin chimed in: "What Arthur means is, you're going to the City. But not the city we knew, and not the city you've read about. Of that you may be sure. Study the reports of what it was like in its prime, and the journals about the fall. Read my old notes, and Rosie's, and Arthur's. Talk to your mother.

"But be ready for anything, especially the unexpected. What's happening there could not have come from within that same city. It's fall was too complete. Someone has come to it and brought it back to life. No book and no man or woman here can tell you who these people are, or what else they may have accomplished. You'll be the first of us to know. You go into the utter unknown."

Rosie Meech hopped down out of her chair and tottered over to Micah, to take his hand in both of hers and kiss him on the cheek. "May the Lord bless you and keep you, Micah Gault."

Red in the face, he stared at the floor and muttered "Thank you." Arthur harrumphed loudly.

"To the business at hand. If the two of you are finished being esoteric and impractical, let's speak concretely. We don't know much, but here are the basics:

"We know from our hunters and from the last few groups of refugees to arrive that the lands around the City are largely empty. In the first collapse, people fled and brought their problems with them.

"What those problems were depends on whom you ask. There were the several financial collapses, the increasing political divides, and of course the virus, all dancing a tarantella together. There was the government, either doing too much or not enough. There were the protests and the counter-protests, then the riots and the riot police. In a word, division. Everyone's fault, and no one's. You grew up among survivors of those years, and I'm sure you've heard a different theory from every one of them. I don't intend to burden you with another. God knows there's blame enough to go around. God knows we've all paid for our part in it.

"But whatever the cause, once the imports stopped, the trouble really started. Whether by command, or just another infrastructure failure, the water and the power went out. People turned on one another almost immediately, as if they'd been waiting for a signal. A lot of people died those first few dark nights.

'Then there were the snowbirds: Huge caravans of people who tried going south to escape winter without electric heat. We never heard back from any of them. We don't know if things were worse in the States, but they certainly weren't better; a good measure of the chaos started there in the first place. Those that stayed, the ones that locked themselves in and hoped for the best, they froze, or starved.

"Only far enough out of the city, in the places where people grew their own food, did anyone have a chance at surviving. We know some of the towns between us and the city are still there, and those we can confirm we've marked on this." Arthur produced a worn leather case. He placed it on the table and undid its leather ties. He pulled out a map Micah had never seen before.

"Lorne made this for you. He's worked night and day, although we told him to pace himself. He's not a young man anymore. He calls it his masterpiece. He was too shy to give it to you himself." But when Micah leaned back in his chair, he could see Lorne peeking around the corner, smiling with his whole mouth.

It was beautiful, hand-drawn with perfect scale and precision on thick, creamy paper. It was enormous, portraying the Fold and the lands south towards the city, the ripples of topography in black ink, the wandering paths and long straight roads in red. The detail was incredible: landforms, forests, rivers, streams, and swamps all rendered perfectly.

"This is as accurate as possible in regards to the current state of the lands to the south, based on our most recent report. Lorne has taken the liberty of tracing out what he believes to be your best and safest route, and we concur with his judgment." He leaned over the map and traced the dashed and winding line that ran red down the length of the map with a gnarled finger.

"Take the deer path that crosses the pastures to the south. You have taken it as far as Tenth Sideroad, I believe. Do you remember what it looks like?"

Micah nodded. He had been filled with wonder and curiosity by the old road since childhood, grass grown long through the gravel, the straight wide path through the overhanging trees, so unnatural, so strangely comforting. He had longed to follow it all his life, to wade through the long soft grass down that strange southbound avenue.

"I must tell you your old friend Wayne is making you a pair of skis, though he will never forgive me for ruining the surprise. They are, however, a relevant variable in our calculations and so I must disclose. They'll help you cover twice as much distance in a day.

"Once you reach Tenth, you'll make good time, but you must be careful. We're not the only ones out there with maps. Although of course," he corrected hastily at a throat-clearing from Lorne in the hallway, "their maps will not be so accurate nor so beautiful as ours. Be wary. Keep your weapon close by. They lit that tower at night to call people, I'm sure. Any folks you meet along the road will be desperate. There are other ways to survive than our own, but they do damage to the soul.

"Tenth Sideroad will take you to the town of Burrows. Last we heard, their settlement was a stable one. A huge extended family lives there, more like a Highlander clan than anything else. They keep to themselves, but make sure that you declare yourself early and often. They've never been the sort of people you want to catch by surprise. They might give you food and lodging, should you need it. Unfortunately, we don't really know. This is piecemeal intelligence from at least six summers back.

"But you can't avoid Burrows, because that's where Tenth meets Highway 87, or did, once upon a time. Eighty-seven isn't anything special, just a paved version of our roads up here, but after you follow it for twenty or thirty kilometers, it turns into the 487: four to six lanes, straight as an arrow, right into the heart of the city. It runs the whole length of the old province, lake to lake. If any piece of infrastructure has survived, it's the 487. It's monstrous, like the dried bed of a river bigger than you've ever seen. You've never seen anything like it.

"You'd travel fast on the 487. It's flat, hard and straight. But it's extremely dangerous. No cover, nowhere to hide, naked beneath the sky. And for that reason, we would advise you not to take it. Lorne, together with the rest of us, has plotted a route for you that runs parallel to the highway, through the old suburbs. It won't be as easy or as fast, but you're much less likely to be seen. You'll be taking the side streets, going house to house. Lots of places to hide, should it come to that.

"You might need to leave your skis at that point, unless you want to carry them. If you can, find a landmark, mark it on the map, and stash them there so you can find them on the way back. Make your way through the suburbs and the industrial parks that come after them and then the City will be in sight. New roads might be laid. Old ones might be blocked up with dead cars. Buildings may have fallen. New ones might have been built. Who knows what any of that looks like now?"

The strain of the hardening reality of the journey to come was showing on Micah's face. Rosie put a hand on his arm.

"Use your head, and your heart, Micah, and your legs of course. He will do the rest. Give the bad things you see and feel back to God. Pray. Rest assured we will be praying for you. You will know what to do, and what to say. Tell the truth of this place to the people there. The Fold has never been a secret."

Martin continued, "Please remember, this is a reconnaissance expedition only. Don't worry about bringing back supplies, but please bring yourself back to us. If they are friendly, willing to help and to trade, we'll return with wagons. You are our ambassador and our scout."

"And our spy!" yelled Lorne from the kitchen. Martin shrugged, with a grin.

Micah was silent for a long minute, staring at the map without seeing it, until the mass of red and black lines began to swim in his vision.

Arthur cleared his throat. "Rosie believes that they're a community not unlike ours, though with less . . . pressing responsibilities then we have. More time and resources to focus on practicalities, but not so different from ourselves. I'm less optimistic."

"Which brings us to our final point," said Martin. "After your return, by unanimous agreement of this Presbyter, you may be honorably discharged from your duties as a Shepherd of the Fold, if you so choose. You will have done your duty, and more. It isn't fair that you should be expected to live the life of a Shepherd if a new life is available to you. You will be free to return to the city, if you wish.

"Celebrate tomorrow with us as any other Sunday. We'd like to send you off Sunday next, after church. Take the next week for yourself. Lorne has made a reading list for you, begrudgingly." Sure enough, Lorne was there, scowling at Micah's elbow with a cartful of books, maps and pamphlets.

"The entire community has been instructed to provide you with whatever you might need by way of supplies. I think," he said with a small grin, "you will not need to concern yourself with food. Your only challenge will lie in carrying what Karen and Bola will burden you with. Please make an effort to bring all the food they give you, even if you need to feed some of the pies to a bear somewhere. They are already angry enough with me for letting you go."

Arthur inserted himself, the way he always did. "Listen to the stories the people can tell you. Ask every silly question you can, and write down the answers. They might save your life."

"Micah," began Rosie, and she stood up and rushed to him and wrapped her arms around him, weeping softly and kissing his cheeks. It was a little like being kissed by a raccoon. Arthur raised his mug in solemn salute, his eyes twinkling within his eternally grave expression.

"Kindly Endure," intoned Martin.

"Kindly Endure," echoed the rest of the Presbyter. Micah gave a small awkward wave and fled as politely as he was able to.

As he made his way out of the kitchen, Lorne grabbed him by the arm. "The books I've collected for you are upstairs, in your usual place. No dogears, drinks, or underlining."

"Thanks, Lorne," said Micah, desperately happy for some direction, some specific starting point in the massive and seemingly impenetrable task of preparing for a journey into a new world.

He made his way upstairs to the sagging armchair in the dormer window. Beside it, Lorne had placed a plastic crate with an interlocking lid. Micah collapsed into the chair, his body letting go of its tension now that he was at last alone, away from the scrutinizing eyes of the great lords and ladies of the Fold.

10
Like A Ghost

The box Lorne had prepared stood before Micah, looking for all the world like a treasure chest. Micah stared at it for a moment as the possibilities of what it might contain began to swirl and billow in his mind, then cracked open the lid. It was filled, of course, with books and maps. A note in Lorne's meticulous copperplate script informed Micah that they had been ordered by relevance in the interests of time. Micah smiled to himself, but the smile was quickly replaced with an expression of awe as he began to leaf through the top book of the pile. It was a battered notebook of a different kind from the one he himself carried. At first he couldn't believe what he was looking at, couldn't believe that it had been entrusted to him. But it had been.

It could only be Martin's original logbook, his first handwritten account of the last days before the collapse and of his journey to the Fold, that first cruel spring. A large note fixed to the cover read "WASH YOUR HANDS FIRST" in Lorne's precise hand. Micah hesitated, then put down the book, descended the stairs, and made his way to the pump behind Lorne's house where he scrubbed as if in ritual preparation. Lorne gave an approving nod upon his reentry, and Micah returned to his roost and began to read:

Date: March 8ᵗʰ
Shift: 7:30 AM-10:30 PM
Staff On Shift: Beanka Peterson, Rex Olenko, Susan Raikonssen. Recording Staff: Martin Safarian
Six new clients (Rajesh L., Glen P., Janine R., Philip A., Erica B., Donavan A.) joined program today. Clients arrived together in Ministry van at 7:30 AM, showing obvious distress.

Micah read until the dinner bell rang. He went to the hall and ate with Rufus and the Friendly Men, missing them already. He then returned to the library and read late into the night by the flicker of the shielded candle. He returned to his cold bed and slept in the alien silence, his mind filled with images of sidewalks impossibly smooth, straight, and clean, jarringly intercut with the chaotic scribble of Martin's exhausted hand.

Micah spent most of the next day after Church reading, finishing Martin's account of the journey and moving on to Rosie's, and then the deceased Bill

Thompson's. He read of the founding of the Fold, of the desperate early days, the backbreaking process of reclaiming the land, the failure of the second harvest. He struggled through Bill's agricultural explanations of the crop failures of the early years, the discovery that the seeds had been designed only to germinate a single season so that they would have to be purchased anew every spring, and the role this had played in the leanness of those years. He skipped through page after page on Bill's quest for heirloom seeds and his eventual triumph. He read of the years spent building up the herds, relearning the old skills of agriculture and animal husbandry.

With more interest, Micah studied Rosie's accounts of the establishment of the Order of Shepherds, the writing of their Rule by Martin and Nelle and Rosie and Bill, the growing pains and failed experiments. He finished broken-spined journal after broken-spined journal and stacked them neatly, knowing Lorne would be watching.

By lunchtime he had reached Emancipation Years in the chronicle, when the Shepherds began to ride out throughout the province in search of the rest of the old institutions where those with disabilities had been gathered again as the economy failed and support systems withered. He read with vicarious triumph of their return to the Fold with wagons full of souls liberated from incarceration, often with their haggard staff converted and ordained, jailers redeemed as Shepherds.

These were the Troy-tales of the Fold, stories he had heard on the knees of the grizzled veterans themselves. He finished Francis' account of the raid on the Oneida Regional Center and closed the ancient exercise book that contained it. Micah sat, curled up in the chair, and read as it grew dark outside.

After the Emancipations followed a period of relative peace, when each member of the constellation of surviving communities reached a wary equilibrium. There was trade between them, and the Fold let its purpose be known throughout the region. Soon those in need of Martin's brand of mercy were dribbling in from the south and the east, in search of refuge from an unkind world, for their children or their siblings or themselves. Careful records were kept of all these newcomers, among them Micah's own parents, bearing Thomas in the backpack that was now his. In a separate ledger were recorded the names given to all anonymous infants and children left at the borders of the village in the night. According to the dates next to these names, some lived only a few days, and some did not survive their first night. But some of the names belonged to grown men and women he knew very well.

Others had come to the Fold perceiving its mercy as weakness and seeking to take advantage of it, by guile or by force. These scenarios tended to resolve in one of two ways: Martin let the interlopers take whatever they could carry, based on his interpretation of the New Testament, or the loose confederacy of farmers who surrounded the village would mete out justice based on their interpretation of the Old. The two responses seemed to alternate in a rough sine wave.

He read until late into the night, until after even Lorne had gone to bed with a stern admonition not to fall asleep with a candle burning. The old house creaked in the wind, and an owl was calling outside the black window as he closed the last of the logbooks. The archive was almost complete. Lorne had made sure of that. Every one of the retired Shepherds were represented in these logs, and a few who were only names to him, Shepherds who had lived and served and died in his childhood or before, legends. The more recent logs were kept in the Shepherd's Hall, containing as they did information about living Brothers and Sisters, relevant and confidential.

But there had been a chapter missing. He had made sure of it, searched through the relevant years again and again. It was the chapter he had both longed for and dreaded reading, but it was not here. It had been carefully excised, redacted, by . . . someone. The records were present for every member of the Fold, from Martin on down, all complete, except for one family: his own. There had been no direct mention at all of his father. But there was still one book remaining in the bottom of the box.

The last volume was not a logbook at all. It was a novel: a yellowed and dogeared edition of John Steinbeck's *East of Eden*. A note reading "FOR EXTENDED LOAN" in Lorne's meticulous hand was affixed to the tattered cover.

This was baffling. Lorne did not condone fiction, only consenting to keep it in his library after long negotiations with Martin, and he never recommended it. But the reading list had been carefully curated. This was not an accident. So when it grew too cold by the dormer window, and when he heard the night-howl of Philip Ramirez that signaled midnight, he returned all the books but one to the crate. *East of Eden* was nestled safely at the bottom of Micah's pack as he climbed the stairs back down to the door. Lorne awoke at the sound of movement and was awake and watchful at his desk by the time Micah reached it. He gave Micah a long, searching look as he left, then said, "Please take good care of the Steinbeck. It belonged to . . . to a friend of mine." There were strange, unaccountable tears in his eyes, and Micah hurried out for Lorne's sake.

The next five days sped by in a whirl of preparation that was half glorious vacation, half grim, war-room strategizing. Most of the time was spent in research, poring over every old travel guide, newspaper and trashy magazine he could find that discussed the city as it had been. The rest was spent talking to those who had last made the journey: Bethlehem, and Bola, and Rufus. Rufus had been the very last to come up that road. Micah spent hours each day assisting him with the Friendly Men, using the opportunity to train him for his coming absence while he asked every question he could think of.

"It's crazy out there, man," said Rufus on the Wednesday before Micah was to leave, as they helped the Friendly Men muck out the stables. "It's like, you know, the wild, but it's like, a human wild? A lot of people died, and a lot of people went south, but a lot of people didn't, and the ones who survived and stayed mostly did because they were nuts. Look at Martin. Nuts.

"And let me tell you, the fall of civilization has not improved their mental health, any. The world is not well, man. And that was, what, how many years ago? God knows what it's like now. My advice? Ask our craziest farmers until you find one that's kept a loaded gun all these years. Beg, borrow or steal it, and keep the safety off. Wish I still had mine to give you."

Micah began to receive gifts. Karen and Adi had promised him all the food he could carry before Martin had even confirmed he was going anywhere. Jon the smith presented him with a belt-knife in a newly-tooled leather scabbard. His mother gave him a new wool sweater, and five pairs of thick rough socks she had knitted. Bertram gave him his own pair of cross-country skis, which he had made himself from birchwood. Micah had known Bertram his whole life, and had not understood that there was anything different about him until he was almost twelve years old. He was quite angry at Martin for having ruined the surprise, but accepted Micah's explanation that it had been necessary for planning the expedition. "So much faster than walking, in the snow," he conceded. "Then you come back sooner."

Finally, Micah was summoned by Gord. Gord went by the grand title of Quartermaster but was in reality responsible for the hunting and trapping that supplemented the Fold's supply of meat, leather and fur. He had been running traplines through these woods since the days when there had been laws against it. Gord was a gruff and formidable man, and the Brothers and Sisters feared him and his wild family, and Micah suspected that the feeling was mutual. He refused to live within the town, citing safety concerns, and the Fold's one small gunlocker slept with him in a cabin two kilometers to the west. Micah had never seen the inside of that locker, but he knew from the legends what was kept inside it: four semi-automatic rifles, maintained in prime condition, and a supply of ammunition that could only be described as priceless.

Martin had long forbidden the Shepherds to carry weapons, making a grudging concession to bows for the purposes of hunting and shooting the coywolves that regularly threatened their livestock. Gord had taught Micah how to shoot the bows he handcrafted for the village, and had proven an excellent teacher. Now he advocated that Micah be given one of the rifles for his journey: "Not to be used," cautioned Gord, "except when absolutely necessary."

"Extreme eventualities," Martin had muttered, through gritted teeth. The debate had gone on for hours, until eventually Gord threw his hands up in surrender. As a compromise Micah was outfitted with four of the precious remaining carbon-fiber broadhead hunting arrows, a new set of muskrat gloves, and one of Gord's own composite hunting bows.

Micah spent the ragged remnants of the week alternating between attempts to assure his mother that he would not surely die, and training the increasingly desperate Rufus to the unique ways of the Friendly Men. The rest of the time he spent alone, reading, breaking in his new skis, and trying desperately to think of everything he could possibly need for the journey.

At last the fateful Sunday arrived. It was the 25th of March, a bright, hard, cold morning. The weary old snow was still hard-packed four feet deep in the valley, but the breeze bore the faint musk of mud and meltwater. Spring would be in the valley in a week, two at the most. Micah, awake and alone in his old bedroom, checked over his pack for the last time.

The last of his food had been delivered last night by Karen and Bethlehem, given over to him with an embarrassment of tears and blessings. He strapped his parents' ancient tent, impossibly small in its blue nylon tube, to the frame of the pack and fixed the unstrung bow to the quick-release harness that Wayne had made for him. He checked the case of books, water-and-crush proof, crafted by Wayne to Lorne's exacting specifications especially for this journey, in which slept Lorne's map, two yellowed guide books, his Bible, two journals, and *East of Eden*.

On top of the books Micah packed four sweaters, four pairs of pants, four shirts, and as many pairs of socks and underwear as he could fit into an oilskin bag. At the bottom of the bag was his Shepherd's habit, which Martin had asked him to wear if and when he was asked to speak for the Fold in an official capacity. On top of his clothes he pushed down his old orange sleeping bag, arranged the food (in yet another oilskin bag) on top of that, then strapped the pack shut. He pulled his parka over his mother-made sweater and strapped his ancient fannypack diagonally across his chest, packed full nuts, strips of dried beef and pork, and dried fruit.

He tied the long awkward laces of his boots and then it was finished, and he was sitting there on his old bed, staring at the door. Down the road, the bell of St. Stephen-in-the-Fields was ringing out through the valley, calling the Brothers, the Sisters, and their Shepherds to worship and farewell.

As Micah neared the church he could hear the hooting and calling and crying out of the Brothers and Sisters already inside the ancient red-brick walls, like a flock of strange and varied birds. There was no sound on earth like it, like bells and battle-cries and the roar of a mob and the singing of a choir all at once. Micah opened the big wooden door a crack and peered in. Inside it was the usual Sunday morning scene, nearly deafening, everyone together, nearly the entire population of the valley. The separate groups disappeared here, and everyone looked back at everyone else. Martin in his vestments took his place in front of the altar and a relative hush fell. He read from Second Kings, the story of the four desperate starving lepers.

"And they said to one another, 'Why are we sitting here until we die? If we say, 'Let us enter the city,' the famine is in the city, and we shall die there. And if we sit here, we die also. So now come, let us go over to the camp of the Syrians. If they spare our lives we shall live, and if they kill us we shall but die.'"

Micah recoiled. Martin was simply following the readings for the day from the Lectionary, but the words were ugly and unsettling and not at all the comforting benediction he craved before leaving. Suddenly, with a deep and absolute certainty, he knew that he would not be able to abide what was coming next: the public blessing, the prayer at the front with the elders laying on hands, the rounds and rounds of handshaking and advice-giving and well-wishing and heartiness and tears. Micah opened the door a little wider, to meet the gentle eye of the Agnus Dei above the altar, and then carefully shut it without a sound. He was alone in the silent village.

He shouldered his father's pack and took his skis from where they waited, propped against the old stone wall. He tightened the leather straps around his boots, and with swift sure strokes he slid; he passed through the town like a ghost.

11
The True Goodbye

The sun was bright on the snow-buried pastures that hemmed the village in. The cattle and the sheep were still in their winter lodgings and the bare fields were hidden deep under a white, unbroken crust. The brief thaws and refreezing of the past two weeks had hardened the top layers enough to bear his weight, and Micah flew across the fields on his skis with his heart split in two. The deep wild joy of freedom and the dark vast dread of the unknown were staring at one another across the center of himself.

This was his country, the land of his earliest memories, where he had learned to stand and to walk and to speak. This was where he had played as a child, where he had sweated and brooded and wept and raged away his adolescence. He knew every rock and tree, hill and hollow, pond and stream and marsh to its bottom. For two days he flew across the hard white back of his homeland, the passage easy, the skis well-made, his body young, and made strong by the hard tending of the Princes.

Micah spent his first night in one of Gord's hunting camps, well-chosen and well-maintained, sheltered from the wind and close to water. He made his fire large and bright without fear of who might see it, ate his bannock and his jerky warm, and prepared to read by the brave light of the high blaze.

He reveled in his solitude, and he rejoiced in his strength and his skill, that he could live so well alone in the land, even the thin ravaged land of winter's end. Micah reached into his pack for his journal with the intention of recording this rare, pleasant mental state, but his fingers closed instead around an unfamiliar paperback with a broken spine. He pulled it out, puzzled, and held the cover up to the firelight. *East of Eden*. With a delicious sense of mystery, he opened it. Why had Lorne chosen it for him? Why had he insisted he bring it on the journey?

Micah had read *Of Mice and Men* and hadn't much cared for it, so he began hesitantly. It was not what he would have picked for a time like this. The writing was poetic and compelling, the story engrossing, but it was written in a cold voice full of sorrow and fury. He flipped through the pages, looking for an inscription, an annotation, for any sort of clue. A sharply-creased sheaf of lined paper slid into his lap.

Full of curiosity, Micah unfolded it eagerly. It was a letter, written in an untidy, crowded scrawl, a hand he did not recognize. "*To my children,*" it began, "*Thomas, and the Unknown One.*"

He dropped the letter as if it were burning, and sat staring down at it as the melting snow began to soak through the paper. He picked it up, folded it back tight, and buried it and *East of Eden* deep in his pack. Not tonight. Not tonight. He sat by the fire, all his new peace stolen away, until exhaustion overcame him and he retreated to his tent and the sleeping bag within.

By the middle of the next morning Micah had reached the Tenth Sideroad of what had been Monora Township. It had been an important local thoroughfare once, unpaved but well-used and lined with mature maples. The road was all but gone now, the maples ancient and collapsing, the rutted space between them alive with their children. Tenth marked the unofficial border of the Fold's lands. No one from the community had passed beyond it in the last three years, even while hunting. There had been no good reason to do so, and many not to. Micah had himself been here four or five times in his life, usually on hunting expeditions with Gord or Jon or Rufus, but several times just to see the border itself. He had loved to stand on the edge of the known world and look beyond it, and then to turn for home with a chill running up his spine. He had loved that sense of being watched by the unknown, from the unknown.

That chill returned as he stood leaning on his poles, staring through the skeleton fence of maples. This was the true goodbye. Anyone to be found beyond this old east-west road was as strange as a stranger could be. He swallowed hard and pushed off, slowly into the spider-shadows of the naked trees. The road had grown in on the edges, but an path still remained open and smooth down its center. He turned left onto it, and began pushing east towards where the town of Burrows should be, and the highway that ran south through it.

Micah glided through a silent world. There was no trace of the present age of man, no smoke on the horizon, no track but that of rabbit, coywolf, and deer. These lands had been deserted by his species for nearly a half-century. Only remnants of a human past remained, here in the hollow stare of a burnt-out farmhouse, there in the snowy barrow that marked another collapsed barn.

Micah was amazed at the speed of his progress down the former county roads. He had assumed that beyond the maple garth, past where the Fold maintained the trails, the ways would be overgrown to impassibility. But the Fold had not made the trails. They followed the roads of the old order, the roads the nation had made while it lasted, hundreds of years old and graded and resurfaced every spring. Hills had been carved through to make way for them, and forty years of neglect could not erase their memory from the land. He made twenty kilometers the first day.

That night by the fire Micah studied Lorne's map. By the crumbling bridge across the Nottawasaga river that he had crossed that afternoon, he estimated that he would reach Burrows within three days, four at most. Easy passage, if the road held true. He returned the map to its case, and with a deep sense of trepidation withdrew *East of Eden*.

The yellowed glue of the spine cracked as he opened it, and he winced involuntarily at the thought of Lorne's reaction to such a sound. Slowly, unwillingly, he flipped through the pages toward the hidden letter. He stopped suddenly with a sharp intake of breath. Drawn in the margins of the text, starting at the roots and winding up and out into curving branches, was a scribbled image of a tree. But not just any tree: It was *the* tree, the same tree that Micah drew, that he was always drawing. The implications turned his belly cold, and he quickly flipped forward through the pages to where the letter lay.

He took it out and spread the letter flat against the cover of the book, angled so the light of the campfire spilled across it. In the red and fitful dancing of that glow he could see the imprint of each character, how his father's pen had been pressed into the paper by the weight of his father's hand. The letters were deep, etched almost, the paper torn in places. His heart pounded as he smoothed the crumpled creases of the evening before and began to read:

To my Children, Thomas and the Unknown One:

If ever you should come read this, it will be because I am gone. Dead or alive, I do not know. But I will not be with you anymore, and I believe that to be for the best.

The world is full of cruelty: The cruelty of nature and the cruelty of chance and the cruelty of women and men. It has always been thus. Don't be fooled by the old lie that things were better back then, before the lights went out. I was there, and I remember. I have lived in both worlds, and I will tell you they are one and the same.

Do not be fooled by this place in which you live. It does not reflect reality. It is a soap bubble on hot pavement, living but a moment before its inevitable end. The world, the true world, is of the strong and not the weak, whatever Martin and your mother may have told you. And sooner or later, we are all the weak, and then there is no longer a place for us in it. For me, that time has come. But before I go, let me tell you the story of my strength, and how I lost it. Then judge me, as you must, and judge the part of me that lives in each of you.

Hot tears stinging his eyes, Micah gripped the edges of the paper in his fists and stared into the dying heart of the fire. He felt the old wound of fatherlessness opening again, and he longed to hurl the letter into the fire. But he knew that if he did, he would go on imagining an infinite number of endings forever unless he knew the one that was scratched into the paper. That wound would never close again. The only way out was through, so he cursed Lorne for his meddling, wiped his bleary eyes on his coat sleeve, and forced them back to the page.

I was happy with my small place in the world, and I was not ready when it began to end. In those days, I was allowed to be who I was, and to live as I wished. This has not been true for a very long time.

I spent the last days of the old world working in the City's university library. I read as much as I wanted to, which was constantly. I wrote when I had something to say. I watched the pretty girls come and go. Sometimes, when they needed something, they would come over and talk to me.

But the days began to go bad. If you are able to read this, then you will have heard the theories and the arguments, about who asked for too much and who would not share their abundance, about who was the victim and who the perpetrator, ad infinitum.

The news was compelling and fascinating at the time, and fuel for conversation with the pretty girls, but in those days it was still far away and unable to touch me in my youth and strength. We would all live forever in institutions too mighty and venerable to fail.

And then it wasn't far away anymore, and then the "why" didn't matter because the "what" left no space for anything but itself. The bickering on the bus and subway, the hypocrites in City Hall, and Queens Park, and Ottawa, the apartments locked down like filing cabinets full of rats, the masks and the riots and the people coughing their way through the mall. It drove the pretty girls back to the small towns they came from and closed the businesses and hushed the city streets I walked home at night. There was no longer music coming from the bars, just the news and the anxious, urgent discussion it engendered. Then the bars were closed and there was only the shouting and crying behind the well-locked doors of private homes.

I cared about as little as anyone in that city. I had never had much time for music or dancing or conversation. I lived alone in a small apartment, and I wasn't afraid. I had nothing worth stealing, and no one to lose. My parents, your Oma and Papa, lived far to the north, in a run-down town I had no interest in returning to. I had few friends, and in those fat and easy days I had also the luxury of believing I did not need them. My treasure was the library, and I cared about nothing else.

As the days darkened, I immersed myself more and more completely in that treasure, chasing feelings of safety, security, permanence. Outside, the institutions were erased one by one. I stayed longer and longer after the end of each shift. The books were my teachers and my comforters, the walls between me and the ever-crueler realities of the world outside. I read endlessly. I was changed by the words. I believed that the words that indwelled me would save me. And one day they would, for a while.

Everyone stopped coming to the library, and I stopped going anywhere else. My paychecks stopped arriving, I didn't care. My coworkers and supervisors stopped showing up, but that was only a relief to me. The library was my citadel. In the lone silence it was all the more mine, and I came to believe that I owned it, that I had a right to it, as if I had somehow built it and written the books within. I had started sleeping there, stockpiling my food and supplies in the stacks. One afternoon I emptied my apartment of the little I owned and left the door unlocked. It was a time for leaving the old patterns behind and creating new ones. It was thrilling.

The university, and the library that served it, stayed open for a long time after most of its students and faculty had deserted it. The halls fell silent, but the lights stayed on and the furnace kept humming. I think it was a symbol to someone who had the power to make those decisions; a symbol of something they weren't ready to admit had already left the world. It was an impulse I understood very well.

I sat in my familiar spot, on the fifth floor by the bank of windows that lined the north side, overlooking the gates of the campus. I had sat there for the better part of five years, all through my undergrad and the few months of my stillborn degree. I sat there when I needed to focus, to work, to hide from the entirety of the rest of my life. My back fit against the support pillar, the side of the carrel hemmed me in, and I could not be seen unless the observer looked down one long specific row of bookshelves. I could see without being seen, and that is what I needed.

What I saw from that window I will never forget. Beyond the decorative gates of the campus the world was burning down. From my roost I could see down most of the length of the wide avenue that ran from the gates down to the lake, and every intersection between. I watched as the looting began, the armed robberies, the rapes, the pitched street battles between the mobs and the police. I watched as the military arrived to support the police, and saw the two become indistinguishable. I saw the workers come and take the bodies away in city-branded sanitation trucks. I watched, and read through the never-ending stack of books in my carrel. I fixed my gaze on Marx and Engels, Machiavelli, Burke, Paine, Camus, Arendt and Zizek, in the world of form and theory and abstraction. When the sights became unbearable I closed the blinds and slept in a muffled, fluorescent womb.

Soon the library, like so much else, was locked and boarded up. I was gleeful to be left inside. They searched for me fruitlessly, and soon I was left alone at last. I had clothes, a bed, far more food and water than I would ever need, and I had books. I had all of the books, and nothing else much mattered, even then. My disconnection was almost complete.

They put up a wall around the campus, in the hopes that it could be preserved for when life could return to it, but it was just plywood and barbed wire, and soon it was breached in a dozen places. The looters came and went from time to time, looking for valuables. I have always been good at hiding, and they never came close to finding me. They took the computers and the fixtures, but they left the books. Why wouldn't they? They believed that in a month this would all be over, order would be restored, and there would be a market for stolen electronics again.

I lived there alone for six weeks, and in many ways they were the best six weeks of my life. But then the lawless men came back. This time, they didn't have a plan. They didn't want to take anything to eat, or use, or sell. The survivors were beyond pragmatism. This time they came to burn.

Their motive was unknowable. I don't believe they could name it themselves. But there was something within them, some impulse or feeling or instinct that demanded a sacrifice vast and of great value. On the night of March 21st, that sacrifice was the university library.

I tried to stop it. I emptied every extinguisher in the stockpile. But there was too much fuel for the fires they started. There were too many books. I burned with them that night.

In the end I saved only seven volumes in my melted nylon backpack, as I fled into the bitter air of the outside.

I have never been the same since that night. Seeing the collected intellectual wealth of a species consumed by the dull, drunken inclination of a handful of thugs is something I have never recovered from. The mind is nothing without the strength to defend it.

Except for East of Eden, which I was reading at the time on the recommendation of one of the pretty girls, the books I saved were not literature or philosophy. They were survival texts: first aid, woodcraft, guides to edible plants, knots. I vowed to memorize them, to internalize those skills until they were a part of my muscle memory. I vowed to become strong. I vowed never again to be the boy hiding in the library. It is a vow I have kept.

I left the city, fleeing from and with everyone else. I stole the things I needed: tent, water filter, clothing, boots. A gun, then another, and another as the opportunities arose. I wrapped them in oilcloth and kept them in a secret place. My aim improved. There were lots of opportunities and I have always been a quick learner.

I lived in the fields and forests that surrounded the suburbs for those first weeks, raiding for food and supplies, surviving mostly on canned food heated over a fire. I continued my role as silent witness. I watched from the treeline and the empty second stories of houses while the weak and unprepared were robbed and raped and enslaved and murdered by the ready and strong. I read the collapse of that civilization like a textbook. I learned those lessons well. I have never been able to unlearn them.

I lived in the forest that spring and summer. My learning curve was steep, and I nearly died in that first season, but as the summer passed I went from strength to strength until I could hardly believe I had ever been anything else. The strength of my hand was my glory, and the strength of my intellect was my pride. I came to believe that my survival was due to my own indwelling superiority, and not the blind luck it had been. I turned from a weak man into a strong man, and in the autumn I met Julian and my fate was sealed.

But Micah was too exhausted to allow whoever Julian might be into his psyche tonight. Micah returned the letter to its place and the book to its, doused the fire, and crawled into the shelter of his father's stolen tent.

12
The Silo and The Gleam

Micah awoke to the raucous orison of the birds, sung out to the barest smudge of orange in the eastern sky. He thought of Philip and smiled. He quickly ate his breakfast of bread and cheese curds and cold water and was moving before the rim of the rising sun broke the horizon.

The day was revealing itself to be the warmest of the year thus far, and Micah was sweating through the sweater beneath his parka. Soon he had taken it off and was feeling the cool and glorious air on his unprotected skin for the first time since the previous fall as he flew across the snow.

The mildness of the weather lent a delirious joy to what was already a state of extreme anxious excitement. He was nearing the first marked town along his route, a tiny dot called Camilla. It sat on the mapped line of Tenth and betrayed nothing of itself, except that when the last maps had been made, it had been small. But the idea of it made his heart pound with fear and delight in ever-varying concentrations. In all likelihood it would be abandoned, the inhabitants gone in search of safety in numbers. But there was really no telling what, or who remained.

Micah came upon it sooner than he had anticipated, cresting a mercifully unobstructed hilltop. The road ran down into a river valley below, and there it was, ten or twelve red brick buildings huddled around the concrete bridge that spanned the Nottawasaga. His hunting instincts came into play, late, and he strung his bow and dropped into a squat at the foot of a large tree to the side of the road so as not to be silhouetted against the sky. He leaned back against the trunk of the tree and kept as still as he could as he searched the town below for movement. One, two, three minutes he waited, barely breathing, with an arrow ready to be pulled back.

The arrows were for animals, everyone had said, all agreeing on the same lie. "This is an age of desperate men," Martin had said to him, "and there is little to separate a desperate man from an animal save that to kill one is murder and a danger to your soul. You know your Aquinas, what is permitted in self-defense. You also know my opinions on Aquinas on that matter. But I pray it will not come to that."

Four minutes passed without the slightest sound or movement, only March roaring in the trees and the rush of a river newly released from ice and full with snowmelt and runoff. A sudden flash of reddish-brown, and Micah pulled the forty-five-pound draw of the bow back to his ear in a heartbeat. A fox, making its careful way down the main street. He sighed audibly, relaxing the tension without releasing the arrow. The fox vanished. Micah made his way down the hill.

The population sign was still there (250), but Camilla was not. The eyes of the houses were dark, the windows long since shattered, living rooms and kitchens drifted in with snow. An eroded gas station stood at the crossroads at the center of the town and Micah stared in wonder at the corpse of a Chevy Cobalt where it lay dead in the service bay. He knew it immediately and after a quick scan for motion, ran across the wide main street to examine it. This particular specimen would never run again, but the clean steel and aluminum lines still quickened his heart. He stepped in through the shattered doorway in search of salvage, but he succeeded only in disturbing a very large and well-organized family of raccoons.

A half-dozen other cars and trucks, half rust and half moss, littered the main street. It had taken an hour and a half to drive from the Fold to the City in former times. "What a waste," Micah muttered out loud. His voice sounded ugly in his ears.

He had thought to spend the rest of the day here, exploring, but after a few minutes of examining the ruins of Camilla his curiosity had exhausted itself, leaving only a strange urgency to cross the bridge and make the tree line, to leave this place behind him. The town was less than uninhabited. It was a dead thing, an emptiness.

Micah stopped in the middle of the bridge and looked down into the roaring brown rush of the Nottawasaga. Great rafts of ice were tearing away from the banks, borne away west before curving south to the lake, the same lake to which he was traveling, the lake on whose shores the city stood. With the sun on his back and the freed river singing joyfully in its banks, it was hard to believe that city could be anything less than the fulfillment of all his wildest dreams.

Once making the ridge, Micah flew again over the white landscape. This was a country made for skis, a country of blinding purity and stillness. A country without motion beyond his own, until suddenly, there was. Seven dark shapes, laid out in loose formation. Coywolves, the hybrid breed that had taken the crown of the food chain since the decline of the human population. Not generally aggressive towards man, though there were stories, and this was a desperate time of year. They circled slowly, and he drew his still strung bow and sighted the leader. At a signal invisible to Micah, the pack melted away.

He was grateful for this response, but troubled by it. These were animals familiar with human weapons, and he brooded over the implications for the rest of the day's journey. But though he carefully watched the horizon and the road, there was no further sign of a human presence.

That night he made his camp in the empty concrete circle of a broken silo, in case the coywolves should return. The roof had blown off in some long-ago storm and he sat with his back to the far wall with the fire between him and the doorway. He watched the stars wink into being in the perfect ring of sky above him. He stared up at the dark blue-spangled dome, the same beloved stars. He had known their names since the age of five, those ancient names for old friends, coming and going with the seasons, but always returning again, the same pattern on the same night each year.

But as the last light of the sun bled from the western horizon of the ring, another light began to grow from the southeast, creeping across the starry disk until a third of the stars were consumed by it. A light like, yet utterly unlike, the setting sun. A dead orange glow, a lurid gleam that illuminated nothing. He found himself afraid, imbuing the glow with supernatural properties though he knew exactly what kind of bulb produced it and in what quantities they must exist. He had the strangest feeling that the glow was watching him, and he suddenly wished he had chosen a building with a roof.

Fortunately he'd still need his tent tonight. The temperature was dropping as quickly as it had climbed, and though the silo still retained some warmth of the day, the winter demanded respect. With relief he assembled the tent and took shelter from the cold, and the light in the sky.

Once safely ensconced in his sleeping bag Micah retrieved the Steinbeck from the depths of his pack with the sense as if fulfilling an unpleasant duty, and once again opened the pages of his father's letter to the firelight.

I was gathering roots and mushrooms with my book in the woods. I had picked up a fistful of morels and was about to devour them when a voice barked, "Drop it!"

There was Julian with a shotgun trained on me. He let me crouch there in front of him, frozen, with the mushrooms in my hand, for a long minute. Then he broke into a grin and then a laugh as if I had told a joke.

"You think I'm going to shoot you? Think I'm going to take your mushrooms?" He laughed again, as if he were not holding a gun to my head. "Those are false morels. Poisonous. If I wanted to watch you die I just would have . . . kept watching." He stood grinning down at me for another long moment, clearly enjoying the power dynamic.

"I'm Julian," he said, offering a hand. "You look like you could use some help."

I babbled a counterargument from my mushroom book on bushcraft but he easily batted it aside with his experience. "A true morel, little gatherer, will be hollow inside from the tip of the cap to the bottom of the stem."

He was right, and he was armed, and I owed him. That unsettling smile still in his teeth, he gestured with the barrel of the shotgun. "Come on, then." I followed him through the woods. What else could I do?

Soon, we were approaching a circle of brightly-colored nylon tents, pallet huts, and plastic supply crates. They were mostly men and mostly heavily armed. Seeing us, one of them broke off from the group and approached, casually stropping a bush knife.

"What are we thinking," he called to Julian, "this one a slave or a steak?" Julian glared at him and said to me, "You'll have to forgive us for Owen. He fancies himself a comedian." He gave me a friendly shove in the lower back with the shotgun and announced to Owen, "I've got a good feeling about this one, if he can keep from killing himself long enough to learn how to survive." Owen gave a cold smile and replied, "We'll see, then."

And just like that, I found my place in the new world. I became Julian's protégé (not that I was given any choice in the matter), and once it was clear I was under his protection, I was welcomed by the others. They were survivalists mostly, doomsday preppers delighted at having been proven right. They had a smug sense of self-satisfaction that made me despise them immediately. In retrospect, they merely held up a mirror in which I finally saw myself as I truly was.

I settled easily among them. We had all learned our skills and our philosophy from the same books. We were a homogenous community, more or less. Over time the community began to transform from a gathering of the like-minded into something else. The survivalist mindset involves setting one's self apart from the normal, regular folk. But those folks were dead and gone. The fantasy had come true. They had been proven right, smart, stronger, better, but now there was nothing left to oppose, resist, or prove. Except one thing: that we could once again make chaos submit to the will of man. To our will, specifically.

We found an old lime kiln and forge that had been used in pioneer times to fire bricks and forge tools. Its carcass had become the highlight of a provincial park, but now we lit its fires again and built our city around it. Julian, charismatic, physically dominating and subtle in his cunning, was already the de facto leader, and no one could supplant him. There were challengers in those early days, but he cut them down with a smile on his face.

Only Owen remained as a viable opponent, but he was intelligent enough to know his shortcomings, namely his inability to express himself in a charismatic and convincing way. By way of redressing this, he set about becoming my friend and making me into his mouthpiece. I already had Julian's ear, and was therefore useful. In those days I was stupid enough to believe these men were my friends, but I was fearful enough to take on any role that made me appear useful to them.

Wear a mask for long enough, and eventually the face beneath it conforms to that shape. The boy in the library was almost gone and only here, only now, do I begin to understand what was lost when he was. It was my turn to be powerful, to do unto others rather than have done unto me, and together Julian and I consolidated power within the community. There was little opposition to our rule after the first violent days. After revolution, everyone is weary of struggle and happy to have a strongman to make decisions.

Julian was a loving tyrant. I have never met another person like him, except perhaps Martin. They are the same, in many ways, each a photonegative of the other. Julian kept me safe, and let me believe that I had a part in creating that safety. He made me feel strong. Martin's opinion of himself is that he is weak and fallen and kept alive only by the grace and forbearance of an unseen god. If such an obviously great man as Martin is depraved, what little must he think of me, of any of us?

We were many things, but weak was not among them. We were strongmen leading strongmen, and we built ourselves a little kingdom around the kiln and the forge. The name seemed apt, and so we took it for ourselves. The Forge: thirty souls on the quarried summit of a limestone hill to the northwest of the city. It was a silly, pretentious name

72

(as is another, similar name), but we believed we deserved it. We believed that we would hammer a new world from the molten remnants of the old. We had nothing to fear and nothing to learn from a society that had choked to death on its own terror.

There was excellent hunting there, and clean water was plentiful. But more than anything it was defensible, and nothing was more important to us in those days. We lit bright fires and feasted, unafraid in our strength, awaiting the challengers who would come to test it.

Many came to us, seeing the smoke of kiln and forge billowing in the sky, hoping to warm themselves at the fire. Most were sent away freezing. In those early days, our only business was survival. We were not a refuge or a charity, and despite my long immersion in the doctrine of the Fold, nothing I have seen or heard has shaken my belief that if we had welcomed the panicked, starving hordes that gathered at our fences, none of us would have survived. There would be nothing but hungry corpses on that mountain.

There were corpses enough, as it was. We shot the ones that climbed or cut the fence, more and more of them as the winter set in, until the message was received that only death awaited them on the mountain.

We were grateful for Julian, and served him without question, with the exception of Owen, but his opposition was only in whispers. Those were the days of my great sins, the things I cannot forget or forgive myself for, the things I have never confessed to anyone. I regret the lives I took, but then again I am alive to regret them, and consequently you are also alive.

One of my first tasks after the organization of the Forge as a permanent entity was to personally organize a series of rubrics and tests to decide who would be deemed worthy to join us. I held the keys of heaven and hell. I sat in judgment over the world, and chose who would live and who starved that first winter. It was a cold document, but its pragmatism is the reason you are alive to hate me for it. If there is a god, he will judge me by what I wrote there.

The true cruelty of the Agreement, as we called it, was that it was ongoing. The test you passed to be deemed worthy had not to be passed once, but passed every day. Weaknesses revealed a week, a month, a year after first admission were grounds for exile. You were never safe. This was Julian's amendment. I objected at first, but he convinced me.

So it was that the day came that Jack, one of our founding members, was sent hobbling down the mountain alone, leaning on a crutch made from a tree branch. He had misjudged a blow from his ax while chopping firewood and we had no patience for the time he'd take to recover. Jack found himself on the wrong side of the ledger I kept in my office.

We were not totally without mercy. There was an appeals process. But Owen had weaseled his way into a position that swayed that process one way or the other, and Jack had recently undermined a policy set forth by Owen. So Jack went down the mountain, and did not return.

The rigid brutality of our defense of the purity of the Forge was relaxed after the first

73

two years. We had stabilized our food supplies and built permanent structures able to withstand the winter. We were farming, and beginning to have surpluses. The rubrics were relaxed to an extent, and more and more newcomers were welcome. Especially, and to my delight, if they were female. So it was that Joanna was welcomed to the Forge. But who would not have welcomed her?

Micah had long suspected his father to be a bad person of some description, but his mother had refused to give him the evidence to damn him, always replying to his outbursts with "You didn't know him, Micah. You weren't there." This letter seemed to be that evidence. These were the words of a bad, fearful, selfish man, a man who had killed because he was afraid.

But then Micah remembered the fox in Camilla, and how quickly he had nocked his arrow, and how ready he had been to send it towards a human target. He would have aimed for the throat. He would not have missed.

He didn't know how to feel now towards his father, except sick, and sad. The hate was gone, and he missed it. It had been a clean and simple way to feel. Micah lay down in his turmoil and waited for his exhaustion to overtake him in the tent, within the silo, underneath the glow.

13
The Dam Between Worlds

It was a Micah much less inclined to adventure and journeys-into-the-unknown that awoke in the gray light of the following morning. His ancient tent had proven far less waterproof than its attached booklet had claimed, and he woke up frost-rimed and deeply discouraged. The new day held no memory of the beauty of the one before. He ate his cold breakfast of jerky and bannock and thought of all the years he had taken the ladies of the kitchen for granted. He packed up his sodden camp and began to break a path through the broken brush and the hard stale drifts.

For most of the morning Micah flew, ski-shod, along the county road. He had just finished excitedly recalculating his estimated day of arrival in the City when he was stopped in his tracks and forced to revise those estimations. He slid to a halt, and leaned on his poles with gritted teeth.

The smooth, flat, arrow-shot way east had come to a sudden end at the dark green bottom of a beaver pond. Sometime during the empty decades since the road had last been maintained, the local colony had dammed the culvert that channeled the stream beneath the road. Soon it had pooled and spilled over, and many generations of beavers had lived out their days by the still waters that had once been the county road.

With a sigh, Micah sat on a fallen tree, removed his skis, and strapped them to his pack. A week earlier he would have glided across the frozen surface, losing not a minute. He'd known he would come across a barrier such as this sooner or later. It was the reason he had not simply ridden a horse and reached the City in a few short days. No domesticated animal would be able to navigate the tangled and half-frozen morass he now tripped and stumbled through. A man alone could barely do it. Soon his feet were soaked and frozen and the mud was up to his knees, but he was unwilling to risk heading deeper into the woods in search of hard ground, and losing the road that must resume on the other side of the swamp.

In the end it took nearly two hours for Micah to fight his way around the soggy margins of the swamp to where the track resumed, and when he finally did he was exhausted and thoroughly drenched. For the first time he felt a twinge of discouragement as, shivering, he retrieved his second pair of pants from his pack and removed the mud-soaked ones, already freezing stiff in the wind.

From there the journey remained difficult. The previously open road became a woven net of fallen trees, the casualties of a dozen ice storms. He was constantly required to remove his skis, to climb over the tangle where possible and to trudge through the lingering drifts where not, sometimes walking twenty minutes out until he managed to find a way through the bush. The weather was fitful, the sun slipping in and out from behind the steel-gray cloud cover, and he found himself alternately sweating and freezing.

It was later that afternoon that he began to find the traps. Gord ran several traplines in the forests around the Fold, and Micah was familiar with the cruel necessities of the business. But these were far beyond the furthest borders of Gord's territory. After so many miles of exclusively natural forms, their sudden appearance seemed deeply sinister. Micah was forced to slow his pace even further to avoid them, and any sense of peaceful solitude was gone from the woods. They were no longer on his side, hiding not only animals that must be assumed to be dangerous, but also men who must be assumed to be enemies.

In the late afternoon, Micah was climbing a trail that curved up out of another river valley and was startled by a sudden movement in the brush. There came the sound of snapping branches and the crunching of snow. He crept closer to investigate, bow out and arrow nocked before he realized he had done so.

A deer had caught its leg in one of the traps and was frantically attempting to free itself without drawing the attention of predators. Even from this distance, Micah could see the panic in the animal's movements. It was a horrible scene, and he knew that to involve himself would mean risking his detection by the unknown trappers. Still, the fastest route would be straight past it.

As he began to move towards the deer, two figures materialized out of the forest. Micah was experienced in tracking prey that did not wish to be seen, but he had not spotted even the slightest trace of movement in the forest from which the two men emerged. Men they must be, but men so obscured by camouflage that even in the steady light of the afternoon it was difficult to be certain.

They moved with an unnatural silent swiftness, one wrenching the deer's head back while the other slit its throat without a moment's pause. A steady stream of blood began to flow down the hill as the men skinned and butchered the deer with terrifying efficiency. Micah, not daring to move, could only watch as the deer was reduced to its component parts and carefully stowed onto a camouflaged toboggan. They were focused utterly on their work, as sure of their solitude as Micah had been.

Before the shadows could grow much longer, the men and their prey had melted back into the forest. Micah remained unmoving for a long time, watching as the steaming blood cooled, then congealed, then froze on the snow. His heart was pounding and his body was cold with sweat, and he realized that he had not been afraid, not really afraid, until this moment.

This was also the moment in which he remembered how to pray. Prayer had been everywhere in the Fold, and all the time. Karen and Adi sang blessings into the food they prepared. The old Shepherds worn out in their labors went every day to St. Stephen, and their prayers were not for themselves. Many of the Brothers and Sisters talked to God, yelled at Him throughout the day as much as they yelled at Micah. And of course his mother was always praying for him and Thomas, and always telling them so. But he had fallen out of the habit himself. It seemed redundant in a place like the Fold, a place full of professionals, as it were.

But Micah was praying now, and had been since the man-shapes had appeared, praying with every quick ragged breath, praying that his cover would obscure him just enough, that his tracks would not be seen, praying that he could be allowed to move away from this place and to keep moving until the dusk came and hid him.

His prayers were answered, and by the time evening fell Micah had climbed the bloody path and made his camp on a bare section of old road far from the killing-place and the last of the traps. He had given up on his skis, leaving them tied to his pack, and was scratched and scraped from climbing through the bush. This country was forty years' wilderness, forty years removed from modern man and his machinery, and he felt every year in his body.

Though still afraid of the unseen eyes of the unfriendly forest, Micah lit a small smokeless fire to dry his boots, and to study Lorne's map. After checking and rechecking what landmarks he could discern, he came to the unwelcome conclusion that he had traveled only a quarter of the distance he had covered the previous day.

The shadows completed their conquest, and the last of the light left the sky. That night was very unlike the one that had preceded it: a late winter's night on the borders of those familiar woods and pastures had been like a night in his own bedroom, with a fire burning bright and unashamed and a view of the stars. He had crossed an unseen border when he crossed that dreadful dam, and another when he had watched the taking of the deer. It was as if the beavers had been given the task of building a border as well as a dam, and made it to mark the end of one world and the beginning of another. On the one side of the dam had been all he knew and understood, and on the other was everything else.

One year when game had been scarce, Micah had explored north of the Fold, gone out five days on an expedition, but this was a different sort of wild than that had been. That land had never been tamed or settled. Men and women had lived where he was now, not just deer and squirrels and coyotes. They had lived here, and then they had all died. He searched for a word for this new sort of wilderness, so he could write it precisely in his journal and rob it of some of its fearful power.

He searched for the sensation that caused the rivulets of cold to run up and down his spine. And then he found it, and wrote it down in the darkness. The word, of course, was "haunted." He looked at the light in the south, lurid behind the skeleton of the winter branches. A haunted forest, with what beyond it? A city of ghosts, perhaps.

At the thought of ghosts and haunting, with again a reluctant sense of duty, he pulled the letter out of *East of Eden*. He blew the embers bright and piled on enough sticks to read what he could endure tonight.

I was in the Scriptorium (as I insisted on calling it in those ridiculous days), hammering out a new constitution for the Forge. Like Robespierre, we seemed to be writing a new constitution every week, as some new dogma arose and was contended over and decided upon with blood. I remember I was recalibrating the rubrics to solve some question of admission for those with technical expertise but also debilitating physical injury. I remember deciding that such a person should be allowed to enter, and live. I remember feeling myself merciful, and full of grace.

I heard the watchman's bell ringing to announce another newcomer at the gates, and ignored it. It was ringing several times a day by this point, and though I hid it from Julian, it deeply disturbed me to see the supplicants rejected (as nearly all of them were). At best, there were scenes of desperate pleading and bargaining followed by heartbreaking despair. At worst, there were attempts to breach the fence, and the merciless and unwavering response to any such attempt. The quick work the bullets did was a thing of the past, replaced by the slow writhing business of death by arrow.

After a few minutes I heard the rusty gate creak open and shut again, and knew with vague surprise that the penitent's request had been granted. I caught a glimpse of your mother as she passed the open window, and that was it. You probably won't believe that I could love anyone, but I can, and I did in that moment and I've loved her ever since. And, while we're on the subject, you should know that I have loved you also, the best that I've known how.

She didn't want to come to the Forge. By now we were known throughout the surrounding townships, feared by some, hated by many, but envied by all. Her brother, your uncle Calvin, had convinced her to follow him there. He decided he was going, with or without her, and she came to keep him safe. She was right to do so. Calvin would never have been allowed inside the Forge without Joanna's intervention. He was too much body without enough brain. It was obvious to us, and to the rubrics, that he was a problem waiting to happen. But we let him in, because we wanted her. Joanna was worth any price. I saw that immediately, just as Martin later did.

She openly despised us, and it is a mark of her desperation and the love she had for Calvin that she condescended to add her name to the Agreement. Though she would never admit it, she was a perfect fit for the Forge. Your mother was, and is, the most proficient person I have ever met. She has no match for skill acquisition. She delights in mastering tasks, and nothing is too complicated or too mundane for her attention, be it crop rotation or field medicine. She is smart and strong and focused and disciplined. She is the sort of person upon whom cities are built. But that is only half of who, and what, Joanna is. Julian feared and hated her with his cold and dangerous fury, but me she conquered utterly. That is what saved me, for a while.

Calvin, as foreseen, did not last. He was utterly lacking in wisdom and forever picking fights with people who outmatched him in every way. Finally, he got himself into a situation not even Joanna could extricate him from. Bound by the laws of the Forge to enter into a duel with a gaunt but deadly old man named Samuel by his own foolishness, he got a blade in his left eye one cold October morning, to the surprise of no one but himself.

By this time there was nowhere left to go for a woman on her own. And, by some miracle that seems an impossible fantasy even as I write it now, Joanna had come to find in herself more love and pity for me than hatred. I do not claim to understand it, but the years between have spoken for themselves.

We were not married, as the Forge saw no purpose in such rituals, but we swore our own oaths to one another. We built a cabin together on the outer edge of the settlement, and nothing in this new world has been as sweet as those years.

The unaccountable love of Joanna began to have a strange effect on me. My conscience, calloused and cauterized nearly out of existence, began to experience a most inconvenient resurrection. So long blinded to the cost of the daily function of the Forge, to the foundation of misery on which it was built, I began to see it again.

Your mother did not preach or even criticize. That has never been her way. You know how she is. She simply was, then as now, and her existence itself was a devastating rejoinder to Julian and I and what we had built. I began to have difficulty sleeping. I wondered about the state of the survivors beyond our fence, of those my documents had rejected. I remembered my parents, and my sister, and worried if they were alive.

I swallowed my shame and my guilt and my uncertainty and watched as they slowly turned to rage. I accused Joanna of self-righteousness and hypocrisy. I called her terrible names. She remained calm, saying nothing, waiting patiently for me to repent of my own volition, which I always did.

I hit her only once. She hit me back so quick and so fast and so hard I didn't even feel it, until I did. I was a dangerous child, though I had been given charge of a city, and she treated me like a child, and loved me like one. She still does, I think. It's a strange thing, that being loved as a child is loved, I at last became a man. I longed to be the person she seemed to think I could be, and so it began to happen. We become the masks we wear.

Julian appreciated Joanna's usefulness, first to the community and then to himself. She was the weakness he had been waiting for me to reveal. Our long partnership had served its purpose. The Forge had grown strong and sustainable. The crisis of origin had passed. It had become a kingdom, and there can only be one king.

I never wanted to be that king. But even less did I want Julian seated on the throne. By then I knew him better than anyone, and what I knew was darkness. So I fought to keep my seat at the table. For ten years we lead together, always in conflict, always attempting to outmaneuver the other. I did many ruthless things, things I know Joanna will never forgive me for. I hid what I could from her, and to this day I don't know how much she knows of what I did in those years. But if I had not done them, Julian would have been allowed to do worse. This is what I tell myself, what I have been telling myself for years. Sometimes I catch myself saying it aloud as I go about my daily business.

If the end of my time in the Forge began with Joanna's arrival, it was completed with the birth of Thomas. Procreation was of course strongly encouraged, even mandatory

79

(had it ever been necessary to enforce), and to have a son and heir seemed somehow a confirmation of the strange feudal fantasy in which we were living. It meant an immediate increase in status in the Forge, and an immediate advantage in my undeclared power struggle with Owen. Though Julian would suffer no rivals while breath was still in his body, he was known to be impotent, and had named me as heir if I could provide proof of succession. Owen had a daughter, and so his hatred for me grew every day. With a confirmed heir in Thomas I had reached the apex of my power, and my happiness.

But it became evident soon enough that Thomas was who he was. We had no way of knowing why, but there was talk of a genetic disorder, which of course no one could disprove. Owen did not act immediately. He was nothing if not patient, and he waited for five years, until it was clear to everyone that Thomas would not be of sufficient use. And then, without warning, he called a meeting before Julian and the entire community. His case against me: Thomas had no place in the Forge. I must either exile my son, or be revealed as a hypocrite and be exiled with him. Had I not done the same to so many for much less? Had I not written the rubrics of exclusion myself?

I had not a word to say in my defense. I still don't. My own words were read out in judgment over my Thomas and he wept in Joanna's lap because she was weeping and it made me sick. It felt as if half of me were a disease that the other half was attempting to expel, and the very air of the Forge stank in my nostrils. In an attempt to be the better half and not the disease, I packed our things that night.

The fading fire would need more fuel to call any further secrets from the darkening pages, but Micah couldn't bear to read another word. He stuffed the Steinbeck back down into the bag, and put his numb and aching hands up to the dying embers of the fire.

There was a quality of malevolence to these woods he had never imagined a forest could hold. It was only the usual night music: the crackling of raccoons in the underbrush, the rustling of squirrels overhead, the low moaning wind-song. But now those familiar sounds filled his heart with dread, and he had to fight not to spin around and search the darkness with each new disturbance. He found himself longing for the night-cries and the endless questioning of Philip and Donny, and most of all for his brother's arms wrapped around his own, as they had been nearly all the nights of his life. He felt the distant thunder of a panic attack building within his chest, and knew he must master it if he would sleep tonight. Unable to think of a better mantra, he began to speak their names into the dark: "Thomas. Donny. Sam. Jonathan. Philip Ramirez. Thomas. Donny. Sam. Jonathan. Philip Ramirez. Thomas. Donny. Sam. Jonathan. Philip Ramirez . . ." The names spiraled up through the raised and naked arms of the trees like an incantation, and slowly his breathing steadied, and soon the Shepherd slept.

14
Name and Intention

The next day was one long trudge. Micah hauled his body down twenty more kilometers of frozen road, raised a shelter for it in the woods behind a dead Tim Hortons, then threw it down on the ground to rest. There was no need to look at the map, for the town of Burrows was as directly south as it was the last time he checked. *East of Eden* stayed in its place at the bottom of his pack. Too much of that letter was in his bones now, building up in his marrow like radiation. His exhaustion had been intentional, if only subconsciously so: he had pushed himself as far and as hard as he possibly could so that weariness would take him before curiosity could. He had wondered all day who he was, what he was doing. His father's words would only multiply those questions.

The next day came, warmer, a moisture in the air that spoke of spring. By sunrise, Micah had already been traveling for an hour and a half through mixed woodland, when they suddenly ceased and he emerged into a wider country of open fields. He could sense an immediate change in the atmosphere.

It was not just the absence of saplings returned to decolonize the cleared land. It was not just the long row of boulders demarcating the geometry of the fallow soil. The scent of chaos, of natural desperation that had permeated the wildwood was not present here. There was a quietness and peace nearly tangible, a feeling he had been born into and raised up in and recognized instantly. This land was tended, stewarded, husbanded land. It was a cared-for country. It was a garden.

Immediately, Micah retreated into the tangle of brush to stare out on the white and brown patchwork of the fields. They were silent, a still, bright expanse broken only by the crow that made its way from fencepost to fencepost, croaking its guttural cry. He tracked it with narrowed eyes. Fencepost. Fencepost. Field. The bare branches of an oak tree standing by the road. Then with an excited croak the crow stooped and landed beside . . . something. A small, dark shape in the center of the road the crow pecked fiercely. Joined by one, then three more. Micah's heartbeat quickened in his chest. It was probably an animal, a dead squirrel or mouse. But he found himself watching the white horizon where it swelled up to meet the sky several kilometers ahead. No shapes. Unbroken, except for the line of maples along the road.

He would have to cross the field eventually. The nearest cover was far to the south, through deep, unbroken snow. He set off towards the crows and their mystery with steady thrusts of his ski poles. It took two tense minutes to cross the distance.

The sun was beautifully warm on his shoulders and he was quickly sweating, from the sun and from the deep uneasiness that had now set his heart to pounding. The crows scattered at his approach. He leaned over on his poles, biting his lip until it bled. It was the burnt heel of a loaf of bread. Leading back up the road from it where it lay were the tracks of a shod horse.

The animal response of his body came immediately: the pounding heart, the flood of perspiration, the instant and overwhelming desire to find cover. With deep breaths and shaking hands, he mastered the instinct. He was a hundred meters from the nearest hiding place. Anything that was going to see him had already done so and anyone who intended to shoot him would have by now. He knelt beside the tracks. Fresh. He sniffed the bread, and it smelled good beneath the charcoal. The unseen horse had defecated and the scat was cold, but not yet frozen. No more than two hours old. He wrapped his fists around his poles and pushed off as hard as he could and herringboned to the top of the hill.

Below him lay what appeared to be another river valley. The alluvial curves were the familiar shape, and at its bottom lay a vast and gently curving presence, so flat and smooth as ice. Except it couldn't be ice, because it was arrayed, row on row, with the remains of rusted-out vehicles of every size and description. And Micah knew that he was looking for the first time at what had been King's Highway Number 87.

The town of Burrows, however, which every map and account had led him to expect at the crossroads, was nowhere to be found. It seemed to have been erased, and in its place a valley, beautifully cultivated and bearing the unmistakable marks of husbandry: well-kept fields, well-fed herds. The road passed through the fields to the edge of the valley, and then leapt like a miracle across the hollow in the land, a perfect parabola of concrete and steel. Or so it once had been.

Now the great arc was broken at its apex, the ragged edge hanging fifty feet above the valley floor. Micah had seen pictures of these ramps before, of overpasses and cloverleafs. But none of it had prepared him for the sheer colossal reality of it. He forgot all about cover and his silhouette against the sky. He stood and stared, with his mouth hanging open, at the works of man.

So in awe was he that he wondered for a moment what that sharp crack had been and why he knew the sound. Then something bit into the frozen soil at his feet and he remembered and threw himself onto the ground and with a great and awkward struggle wrestled his bow from his back and an arrow to its string.

Ten seconds passed as the crack echoed around the valley, and then another sounded. The second bullet kicked up a clod of frozen earth a foot ahead of his face, a splinter of rock cutting across his cheek.

"Name and intention!" came a high, clear voice from somewhere above him. Micah opened his eyes and peered out from between his outstretched arms. He saw the glint of sun on glass from the rim of the ramp that curved across the valley. A masked and goggled face appeared above the guardrail, and the cry came again.

"Name and intention!"

With the loudest voice he could muster while flat on his face he shouted "No harm! Micah Gault, investigation of electric light to the southeast!" There was silence for half a minute.

"Unstring that bow and approach the gate with your hands in the air! If you try anything else, I will shoot you in the head."

It was a girl. Certainly a girl, though this revelation did not assuage his terror in the slightest. With shaking hands, Micah returned the bow to its place on his back and strapped his skis on top of them in a show of good faith. Then he got up, hands in the air as instructed, and walked down the hill. The small black shape did not move, and he knew that his every movement was being tracked through what must be a very powerful hunter's scope, and that the rifle to which it was attached could certainly match the range of its vision. But the first sensation that arose in Micah, bizarrely, was not fear but social anxiety. His old introverted self-consciousness came welling back up inside him like a sickness, after his long freedom from it, hidden in the untroubled bush. Suddenly he was painfully aware of the tangled growth of his beard, the length of his greasy hair under his wool toque, the mud and deer's blood on his jeans.

It was a long and strangely tedious walk down the hill and over the fields, around to the highway and the unbroken southern ascent of the overpass. The highway was massive, unnaturally smooth and black against the snow on either side. It was nearly fifty meters across and lined with concrete abutments two meters tall. Halfway up the overpass a wall had been built of pine logs, sharpened at the top like pencils. In the center of the wall was a gate, and above it hung an impressive wood-burned sign that read "Burrows."

As Micah waited for the sniper to open the gate, he turned and looked down the wide smooth road to the south. It rose as clean as the frozen river he had first taken it to be, up to the lip of the valley. For a minute he stared at the road and considered whether it might not be better to just keep going, to leave the very many potential dangers of this strange little settlement behind him and press on toward the goal, which now seemed so close. But the shape on the overpass was the first new contact he had ever made, and he knew that if he retreated into his inviting solitude now it would be twice as hard to make contact when he finally encountered the light-bringers.

He waited for a long time, until he heard the crunch of snow on the other side of the wall. A small panel built into the larger gate slid back, and he was startled by his own haggard reflection in the lenses of a pair of scratched aviator sunglasses far too large for the face that wore them. A voice, high with tension, but unwavering: "If you want to come in and rest, you can, as long as it's just the one of you. But first you need to pass your weapons through the hole. I'll give it back to you when you leave, if you don't try anything. If you give me half a reason to, I'll kill you where you stand."

83

There was nothing in her voice or expression to discourage Micah from believing every word she said.

He couldn't think of anything to say in response to this, so he slid his bow and arrows and knife through the hole. He felt the hand on the other side grab it and pull it through. It was only after they disappeared through the hole did it occur to Micah that he may have just been robbed, and was maybe about to be robbed some more, but then the gate creaked open.

15
September of the Overpass

She stood four meters back from the gate, her back straight and her feet planted wide apart. In her hands she held a scoped rifle unlike any Micah had ever seen. The cold utility of its design suggested that it was not a weapon built for any civilian purpose, but its designer would find no fault in its current handling. The girl's finger was steady on the trigger, and the gleaming barrel did not waver an inch despite its obvious weight.

She stood as still as a rendering of Artemis for one long minute, and Micah found that he had time to examine the scene in detail as he stood waiting for her to speak, or to lower the rifle, or to blow his head clean off with it.

The surface of the highway overpass, forty feet across, had been covered over with earth and then planted with grass, bushes, and even small trees until it resembled an elevated park. In the center of this park stood a wooden longhouse, built on a stone foundation and covered over with a thatched roof. A rusted yellow school bus leaned as if asleep along one side of the structure. It was a structure from another place and time, but it had clearly been built by a generation not yet passed from the earth, and was very much inhabited by at least one person.

That person was young, not older than twenty. Her dirty blonde hair was tied back in a blue bandana, and her face, where it emerged from a voluminous army jacket, was hidden by those huge sunglasses. The lips below them were white and pinched, and he could tell from his long experience with the non-verbal that she was afraid, and dangerous in her fear.

"Place of origin?" she called out, in a high, ragged voice.

Micah, hands still on his head, stared at the reflection of the valley in her sunglasses and replied in what he desperately hoped was a calm, friendly, sane voice, "The Fold. A few days to the northwest. Formerly the village of Monora." He paused, wondering once more whether it would not be better to just get far away from here as quickly as possible. But if not now, then when? How many encounters would he run from? Screwing up his courage, he pushed on:

"May I rest here for a few minutes, maybe fill my water bottle? You're the first settlement I've seen." A long silence, the face behind the sunglasses unmoving, impenetrable. Then she nodded, her jaw visibly clenched, and swung her rifle onto her back with an easy, practiced motion. Micah had just relaxed a single degree when she pulled an enormous handgun from the holster on her belt, cocked it, and motioned with the barrel toward the longhouse. His previous state of anxiety reasserted itself.

She stared him down through the blank bug-eyes of her aviators for a long minute. The dead eye of the gun barrel wavered a fraction. "Are you going to try to hurt me?"

"No! Of course not. I promise," said Micah, desperately willing that his face produce as harmless an expression as possible.

She said nothing for another minute, her finger unmoving from the trigger. Then she sighed, and gestured with the barrel for him to walk in front of her, up the shoveled path that led to the house. "Come on then. You can try, if you want too. But I'll hurt you worse." Micah nodded vehemently, eager to convey his absolute belief. Awkwardly, fearfully, he shuffled up to and past the girl and her weapon, and walked towards the fantastic house waiting for the bullet. But it continued not to come.

"This is amazing, what you've done here," Micah ventured, exceedingly anxious to change the subject from assault. "Did you build this?"

She was silent for a moment, as if weighing the question. "I helped. My family built it. When I was a baby, mostly. You know my family? The Burrows? Seven generations on this land, before they took it for the bypass. But then we took it back."

Micah indicated that he had heard of the town of Burrows, if not the family of that name, and was about to ask if her family was here with her when he realized that the answer was self-evident. Except for the harsh voices of the crows, the valley was as silent as a tomb.

With no apparent exertion and a long rumbling clang, the girl slid the massive steel door of the great house back on its track. A great rush of warmth greeted him, and the smell of cooking meat. His mouth immediately filled with saliva.

The longhouse was very dark and extremely warm inside. A large fire burned in a stone hearth on the far wall. A shape lay on a table in front of it, silhouetted in the firelight, and something about it filled Micah with disquiet as he strained to make out what it was. He took a few steps closer, then stopped dead. It was the body of an old man, milky eyes open to stare without seeing through the smoke that coiled about the ceiling, his long white beard stained yellow with nicotine. Micah's eyes flicked to the girl and her weapons. She caught his gaze and shook her head firmly.

"I didn't kill him, if that's what you're wondering. That's my granddad. He died two days ago. Too much shit in his lungs."

Micah relaxed. The body itself did not bother him. Death was never far from the Fold. Micah followed the girl up the length of the house, towards the fire and the corpse, and the sense of unreality grew and grew. He felt as if he had passed into some ancient, northern dream.

The walls of the main hall were lined with doors, four on each side, rooms that shared the outside wall. Many people had built this place, and lived here after. For all its ancient sense and feeling, it had been built by human hands holding modern tools, hands that had known their business. The vaulted ribs of the high roof were not wood but steel, great curved girders, unpainted, rusting but sound. The walls were squared and insulated.

The girl reached the end of the long hall and gestured to the several torn vinyl La-Z-Boys that sat a little to the side, next to the massive hearth. Micah took the one furthest from the body on the table and sat on the edge of it, hands clenched tight to thwart their desire to nervously wander.

After Micah had shimmied out of his coat and sat down, the girl lingered a moment beside the table. He saw her hand dart out, briefly, to touch the dead man's shoulder, and then she took off her sunglasses and turned to Micah.

"You want some sumac tea? There's moonshine too but I'm not drinking that with you till I know you better." Her eyes were green, and weary.

"Yes, please," said Micah. "I would like that very much. The tea. Please."

She nodded, more to herself than to her guest, her brow furrowed, her eyes on the floor. The girl filled an old bronze kettle with water from a blue plastic rain barrel and hung it over the fire that blazed on the hearth. She sat down in the tattered recliner closest to the table and the dead man and tucked her legs up under her chin. The handgun lay on the vinyl armrest beside her, the dead eye still watching him. Only then did she push the sunglasses up onto the top of her head, and he saw that her eyes were green and bleary with sleeplessness and grief. She pulled a long-stemmed wooden pipe from somewhere in her garments and began to pack it with something brown before lighting it with a thin stick from a lamp nearby. She took a deep drag, exhaled, and her eyes met his. Micah found himself fixed in her unblinking stare, those green eyes wide as a cat at dusk. Locked in that gaze, he forgot all about the gun. She blew out a blue ring of smoke and said, "You talk first."

He took a deep breath, choked on the smoke, and began to cough uncontrollably. Finally clearing his throat, he began. "My name is Micah Gault. I've been walking for four days. From the Fold, northwest of here. We saw the glow in the sky from the City. You must have seen it." She volunteered nothing, her face remaining resolutely without expression.

"I was asked to go and see what it was. I'm hoping to take the highway straight down, and I was told this town, or I guess this family, was where I turned south."

"Burrows. This is Burrows. But it's not a town anymore. Or a family. It's just me now." Her hand crept over to the gun. Then her brow furrowed. "Did you say northwest? Three or four days?"

Micah nodded. "Yeah. Four, I guess, now that I think about it."

The girl was shaking her head, the suspicion returning to her face. "No, you're not. You can't be. People don't live up there. They can't."

"Why not? I do. I mean, we do. Me and a whole village of people. Why don't you think people can live up there?"

She looked embarrassed, unwilling to answer. Finally, she ventured: "Because that's where the valley is. The valley of ghosts. My grandad told me stories about it. It's haunted, it's been haunted ever since the lights went out. Ghosts of all the people who died or something. My brothers went up there a couple of years ago, on a dare. They heard screaming, and howls, but it wasn't coyotes. It was people's voices, except making sounds people can't make. They spent a whole day in that valley, hunting, and the screaming never stopped."

Micah found himself laughing, unexpectedly. "Yep, that's us. That's the Fold. A lot of our people are . . . different. Some of them are . . . they do a lot of strange things. Some of them scream all day, sometimes. But they're not ghosts or monsters or anything, just people who need more taking care of than most. That's what I do, me and some of the others there. We're called Shepherds, and we give the people the help they need.

"A lot of those need medicine, medical equipment, stuff you can't get anymore up here. We thought that maybe they would have some in the City, now that the lights are back on."

She was staring at him blankly. A long pause, then: "Retards, you mean? You look after a bunch of retards?" Her tone was disbelieving and accusatory.

He was expecting this. It was a common response among those who stumbled upon their valley or heard of its mission. "Some people call them that. But we don't."

"What do you call them then?"

"Their names, mostly. Brothers and Sisters, if we have to talk about them as a group. Sometimes I call them the Princes, because they act like they own the place, like they own me. But that's just a joke. My brother is one of them, my actual brother. They're just people, and some of them scream sometimes. It's a terrible sound, I know, but it's just their way of communicating, when they don't have words. Usually it just means someone is hungry, or hurt, or just worried."

She had been silent, listening like a deer and staring at the mug in her hands. Suddenly her head snapped back up and she snarled, "You lying to me? You trying to sound nice so that I'll trust you?"

"No, I'm not. That's the truth. That's what we do. That's who we are. Who we try to be, anyway."

The girl's vulpine gaze left him and wandered over to the body on the table, where it lingered for a long moment. "How? How do you feed them all? Take care of them when they're sick? It's impossible."

"It's not impossible. It's just a lot more work. It sucks, honestly. But what else are we supposed to do?"

Suddenly he was staring into the barrel of the handgun again. "Prove it. Prove that place exists, that you're not just another outlaw here to rape me, and kill me, and take my house, because I'm so fucking *stupid* that I let you in here. Prove it, or I'll take you outside and shoot you in the head. I've done it before." She was on her feet now, finger on the trigger, safety off.

"I believe you!" protested Micah. "But I can't prove it. I don't have anything, just a letter from our elders."

"Letter's no good. Doesn't make it true just because somebody wrote it down somewhere. So you better come up with something else, quick."

Micah sat in his chair, hands out, palms up, mouth open, at a loss. And then it came to him. As slowly and steadily as he could, he pulled his arm out of his coat and pulled up the sleeve of his sweater. He held his bare forearm up in the firelight. Even now, two weeks since leaving Philip Ramirez with Rufus, the distinctive puncture and bruise pattern was unmistakable, the red and black and purple and yellow crescents, each print clearly discernible.

"These are human bites. And these are fingernail scratches. Repeated over time. You can see how the older ones are more healed. It's from one of the guys I look after. Where else would I get these?"

She came closer and grasped his forearm, holding it nearer to the hearth. Her hand was very warm and a little moist. Her eyes flickered over the pattern, the varying colors of the marks, each dating the bite, red for the newest, down through dark blue to purple to green to yellow.

She let go of his arm. "And this," he continued, pointing to the wide leather bracelet on the wrist below the marks. "It's our . . . sign, I guess. We all wear them, the Shepherds."

She studied it suspiciously. "Is that a dog? Is that what it says?"

He ran his fingers over the image Rosie Meech had tooled into the leather, a blocky, stylized creature bearing a shepherd's crook. "It's a lamb," Micah said. "Or it's supposed to be, anyway. We wear them so that the blind folks can know the arm of a Shepherd. The words are in Latin. They mean 'Kindly Endure.' It's our motto."

"I'm not an idiot. I can read. Just not Latin," said the girl, a little too quickly. "I'm sorry. I believe you now. I think you're crazy, you and all those Shepherd people, but you're honest crazy and probably harmless crazy too. I'm sorry. It's been a bad couple of weeks around here." Their eyes moved, in unison, to the corpse that lay on the table not four feet away.

"Why do you let them bite you? Why do you let them live with you, if they're doing crazy shit like that? Does your family make you? Are you a slave there?"

He stood for a moment with his mouth open. The questions, the obvious questions no one in the Fold ever thought to ask anymore, hit him like a thunderbolt, and he found all the old, studied answers from Jesus and Vanier and Nouwen were gone from his mind and left nothing in their place.

"I'm not a slave. I do it for lots of reasons." Alarmingly, Micah found himself unable to think of a single one of those reasons, other than the obvious one: "My brother needs help with almost everything." But he knew in his heart that that was not the true answer.

89

It seemed answer enough for the girl, however, who gave a brisk nod and sighed, a deep, ragged sound. "Sit down, please. I promise I won't point any more guns at you. You want some stew?" Micah wanted some stew very much indeed.

When she had served out two bowls of mutton and lentil stew from the vast cauldron that simmered on the fire, she sighed one more time and said, "I guess I owe you some information, after all that." His mouth was too full to reply. Meat had been for feast-days only in the Fold, and the stew was delicious.

"My name is September. My family, the Burrows, farmed and hunted and lived on this land since long before the lights went out. The government took it from us for the highway, for a while. But when the city fell apart, we were ready to take it back, and we did. Then some other people tried to take it away from us again, after that. But we didn't let them, this time. We took good care of the land. We took good care of each other. We were a good family. At least I thought we were, until that goddamn light came on.

"When the lights came back on, we did what you're doing now, just a whole lot better. My brothers and my father went down on horseback to check things out. When they came back, two days later, they said it was a miracle. All the nice stuff had come back. And they were looking for people to live there. 'People just like us,' they said. We'd have power, running water, toilets, fridges, screens. All of it. Like in the old stories." She stopped, and her eyes grew hard.

"They were looking for healthy people. There was a lot of work to do. We were welcome there, but only if we could help rebuild. That's fair. That's how a farm works, except . . . except Granddad was sick. And old. With the winter and everything he had worked a lot harder than he should've. He got a thing in his lungs, couldn't stop coughing. He couldn't walk far, couldn't work more than an hour at a time. It wasn't that big of a deal. He could still ride a horse. They could've taken care of him there, easily. We could've taken care of him here. We had been taking care of him.

"But the City wouldn't even let him inside the gates. My family had to choose, and they chose the City. And they left Granddad here to die, he that cleared this land and built this house. But he got old, they said. Got weak. There's no room for weakness here, even in a family. That's our motto down here, I guess. Don't know how you'd say it in the Latin.

"They were gonna leave him to ride back here from the City alone. They told me to leave him, to come with them, and I probably should've listened, but I just couldn't make it sit right. We had a fight. They threatened me, and then begged me to come with them.

"But I left them. I took Granddad back here. I tried to help him get better. But he didn't get better. He died yesterday, and I've just been sitting here, trying to figure out what to do, and then you came along." She let out a long, ragged sigh. "I don't know why I let you in. Fucking stupid, crazy thing to do. Maybe I wanted you to kill me. Maybe I just didn't want to be alone, even if you were bad. World seems a pretty horrible place to be alone in lately."

They sat together in silence for a long time before Micah realized that September was crying. She wept in utter silence, the tears rolling down her cheeks like rain down a statue, her expression unchanged. Micah said nothing, but fixed his eyes on the fire as if he hadn't noticed.

When the silence became intolerable, he ventured: "I think you did the right thing, if that matters any." September smiled, faintly. Another silence, longer. "Are you going to go down there now that he's . . . gone?"

September shook her head fiercely. "Never. They wouldn't take Granddad, they're not getting me. That family's not my family anymore. Buncha fucking traitors." The silence resumed, and stretched on. Micah finished his stew and scraped the bowl clean and then just sat, unsure of what to do or what to say.

It was September who broke that silence, finally: "Tell me about that place you came from." So Micah did. He told her everything he could think of, about the valley and the cedars on the cliffs, and about his mother, and about his brother, and about the Friendly Men, and Rufus and Lorne and the library and the workshop and the church and Martin and Rosie Meech and everything else he could think of. When he ran out of things to talk about she began asking questions, and he answered them until the sun set behind the escarpment in the west and cast its last red light on the broken overpass and the house that stood there.

Eventually the silence returned, and lengthened. The spring was blowing in outside, and the wind picked up and set the walls to creaking as the fire began to burn down. September got up and fetched several split logs from the immense pile of immaculately stacked firewood that covered one wall. When the fire had blazed up again, Micah said, "I can help you bury your Granddad, if you want."

She nodded, wiped her face with the sleeve of the filthy army jacket she never seemed to take off, and swallowed hard. "You don't have to do that. But thank you." A long pause. "We're going to have to burn him, though. Ground's still frozen, and I won't let the coywolves have him. I was gonna do it in the morning. Would appreciate the help, if you're willing." Micah gave his nervous assent.

"You can sleep here tonight, if you want to." Full dark had fallen and the fire had burned down to a red landscape of glowing embers. "God knows we got room enough. Are you leaving tomorrow?"

"Thank you. And yes. I better, I mean. Sleep here. And leave tomorrow." After a minute's hesitation, "I would really like to stay longer, though." All of a sudden a change came over her features and she was desperate again, her eyes wild.

"You shouldn't go. There's people down there, so many people, thousands. They're all so smart and strong and beautiful and . . . not like you. Or maybe they are. They know everything. They always have an answer. They talk until you join them or you run. My family said they would come back. But they didn't and maybe you won't either." She stood up. "Would you come outside with me?" He followed

91

her like a dog. She smelled like woodsmoke.

Night had fallen outside. They walked to the broken edge of the overpass, behind the longhouse. September sat down on the end of it, dangling her legs fifty feet above the dark valley below. "It's OK. It's safe here." He sat down beside her, and they looked south to the rim of the valley where the orange glow burned its corona against the night.

"I'll never go back there," she said. "And you shouldn't either. You shouldn't even go near it. There's something there, a . . . spirit. It wrecked my family and then it stole them from me. It ruined them. And it'll ruin you too."

Micah considered his answer a long time. "I think . . . the Fold was ruining me, too. Making me bitter inside, or something. I think I have to go south. I think I'm called, and if I refuse it I'll become something . . . bad. That spirit, it's already inside me.

"And anyway, my brother can't breathe. If there's something they have that can help him, I need to try and get it." She nodded, and he knew she understood that at least.

They sat there for a long time, legs dangling from the end of the ancient road, and talked much, and were silent much, and the one was as sweet as the other and for the first time that year the air truly smelled like spring.

When the chill of the night began to bite they went back inside. Lantern in hand, she showed him to one of the many empty bedrooms off of the main hall of the longhouse. The walls were covered in pictures torn out of old magazines, yellow with age. "One of my brothers' rooms. Sorry if the blanket smells." He thanked her, and she nodded and closed the door behind her.

Micah dropped his pack, kicked off his boots, lay down on the bed and groaned contentedly in the beautiful indoor silence, so welcome after the roar of the March wind. He stared up at the glossy ragged-edged photos. Cars, warplanes, girls without their shirts on. He tried to focus on the cars and the jets.

He stared up for a moment, then pulled the now-familiar letter from his pack in an effort to distract himself. This had become his ritual before sleeping, a restless liturgy he longed to reach the end of.

Your mother had a plan to save us, of course. She always has a plan ready for when my careful machinations collapse into ruin, as she is always correctly convinced they will. And her plan, of course, was the Fold.

We had heard of the Fold, of course. It was a running joke among us. We assumed it would fail, as so many less-ridiculously premised communities had. It was too far away for us to take its resources for ourselves, as we surely would have had it been closer. Instead, we waited and even made bets on how long it would be until we'd hear word of its implosion, when cripples and retards (as we put it at the time) would come groping at our walls for us to laugh away. But the Fold remained, still holding to its insane mission. And now we were to become a part of that mission.

We had left before morning. I had no doubt that Julian would kill us if we stayed. Your mother had organized everything in advance, weeks before. She had even contacted Martin through a system of dead-drops as soon as she began to suspect something was wrong. I was furious when I learned of this, but swallowed my rage, and my jealousy that someone else was more prepared, and my shame in being forced to rely on the charity of others. What I swallowed has been poisoning me ever since.

We left with Thomas and whatever else we could carry. We walked all night to get there, Thomas weeping in my backpack the entire time. We came to the Fold in the morning and Martin met us at the gate like a patriarch acting so kind and patient and wise. I hated him for it, because I hated myself. Because I had been wrong about the Forge, been made a fool of when I had thought I was a king. But I had no place else to go, so I swallowed down the rest of the poison, and this has been our home for ten years. It has been a torment. There are people who can bear this life, who can bear these people, but I am not one of them.

I tried, and no one can say I did not. I tried to become like them, and was rejected. I tried to embrace the smallness and meanness and filthiness of the life here, and have failed again and again. I am not for this life and I do not understand those who are. They have sold themselves away, even Martin. I've been owned before, and I could not, cannot, go back to that. Something is required to make a life here, either a goodness or an ignorance, and I can find neither within me. I did not, cannot choose this life.

In their kindness, or their charity, or their pity (and I cannot say which is worse), they have made a place for me. They know I cannot, or will not, or should not be what they call a Shepherd, so they have made me their librarian. They have tried to give me back my life before this all happened. I have done my best, and it is the one good thing I've been able to pull from these years. The library of the Fold is probably the largest, and certainly the best organized, remaining in these lands. They gave me an autistic protégé, and I suppose in that sense I have been a Shepherd with a flock of one. To my surprise, Lorne and I have come to love one another, and he has been a good student, to everyone's surprise. The greater miracle is that I have been able to be a good teacher.

But although I have been able to train Lorne to be what I once was, I have not been able to find that person within myself again. The years of survival, of the implementation of force upon others in order to achieve my will, of holding in myself the power of life and death over others, has changed me. I have been a prince, if of a small and ugly princedom, and I am no longer at peace among the books. I have been changed, and I cannot find a way to go back. And the person I have become has no place here.

So for these past ten years I have become increasingly isolated, with no exercise for my skills or my desires: a murderer among the pacifists, a heretic in a monastery, a human man among the so-called saints. My own son is a torment to me. I love you, but you took everything from me, and you take it afresh every day.

And now she's pregnant again. There is a strong possibility that whatever is wrong *with Thomas is genetic, and I simply can't bear to do this all again. So this is my goodbye. But I have one last request for you, the child I will never know. If you are reading this, if you have that ability, I ask that you do what I could not. I ask that you use the years of your life and the words of your mouth and whatever it may take to make Thomas understand that the failure, the weakness, was not in him but in myself. Make him understand that I loved him, that I still love him with what little aptitude I possess. It is a frail and feeble offering, but I ask that you make it on my behalf.*

Sincerely,
Your Father

Hate and understanding combined to form an acid in Micah's gut, where it churned and settled deep within. He closed *East of Eden* around the letter like a lead-lined coffin around a radioactive corpse, and looked up again at the posters on the ceiling. In spite of the deeply personal and upsetting nature of his reading, Micah found his mind wandering from his father's revelations.

There was a person under this same roof who was completely unlike anyone he had ever met. The image of her burned in his mind's eye like the after-image of the sun, and he found himself holding his breath to increase his chances of hearing the slightest sound she might be making elsewhere in the hall. His eyes stared through the posters without seeing them, his mind's eye taken up entirely with the face of the girl.

16
A Kind of Death

Micah came awake, staring at a yellowed poster of a person he knew from past research to be named Katy Perry, and trying desperately to remember where he was. It all came rushing back: The overpass, the rifle shot, the corpse on the table. The face of the girl.

The great house was silent except for the crackle of the fire in the hearth, where he found September making porridge in a cast iron pot.

"G'morning," she muttered, shoving a bowl into his hand without meeting his eyes. She dumped a liberal amount of maple sugar onto hers, offered him the jar, and they ate together in silence. As soon as she finished her last bite she said, as if after great deliberation, "I think I need to do this thing now."

Without a word he followed her over to the corpse-table. Together they wrapped her grandfather's body in a torn gray woolen blanket. September stared down at the graying, tattooed face with an unreadable expression in her unblinking eyes, then put a hand on its cheek before pulling the blanket over it. Her eyes were hard and bright.

They carried the heavy, rigid bundle to the broken edge of the overpass where they had sat the night before. September had built a pyre there sometime in the night, a massive structure of oil-soaked wood with fuel to spare stacked beside it. Micah suspected that she had not slept at all. They carefully laid the shrouded body on the wood, and then stood together beside it as the rising of the late-winter sun reddened the valley. The sense of unreality, of saga, returned.

"Do you want to say something? A prayer?" he asked her, desperately searching his memories of the many, many funerals he had attended in the Fold for an appropriate statement. She shook her head quickly.

"You can if you want to. But not out loud. Please."

He did so, while September picked up a long branch topped with a bundle of rags soaked in what smelled like moonshine and set it aflame with flint and steel. Then, without ceremony, she thrust the burning end into the dry wood beneath the body. The pyre lit with a *whoompf* of ignition, and they retreated back to the stone steps of the house as the flames spread. When the blanket that wrapped the body caught and began to burn away, September turned and went inside, Micah following closely behind.

Back inside, September gave no further invitation of hospitality. She returned his bow, arrows, and knife without a word. Then she shook his hand, a strange, strained gesture, and they walked to the gate in their now-familiar awkward silence.

"Before you go . . . do you know anything about engines?" ventured September.

"Like, from a car?"

She nodded.

"Not . . . practically." Micah said. "But where I'm from we have stacks and stacks of old car magazines, and I've read them all. So theoretically, sort of. Yes."

"Would you take a look at our bus? I can't get it to start."

"It runs?" Micah exclaimed, delighted. "On what?"

"Used to, for short runs. On biodiesel. Grease, mostly. It's been a while since we've needed it though. I tried to start it a couple of days ago, trying to distract myself I guess, but it won't start."

He followed her away from the blazing pyre, around the west side of the house, where the bus was parked. September pulled the huge hood down with no apparent effort, revealing the engine beneath. Micah, praying beneath his breath that there was something within that steel and plastic tangle that he would recognize, stared into the engine bay and tried to look knowledgeable. He stood and stared for several minutes, shuffling through decades of *Road & Track* magazine in his mind and hoping against hope that something would connect the memory to the reality.

"Spark plug!" he all but shouted with relief. "That's a spark plug. I remember that they don't work when they're dirty."

September reached a small hand into the greasy guts of the bus and pulled the component out. "Looks pretty dirty to me. And you know what? My brother Matt has a box of these, in the shed. I used to ask him what they were, and he'd tell me to shut up and go away." She ran off into the house and came back a moment later, a clean white replacement in her hand.

The new spark plug was installed with a minimum of trouble, and soon September was in the driver's seat of the bus, turning the key. With a piercing squeal and a rumble that echoed around the silent valley and scared the crows off the roof of the longhouse, the engine roared to life. September howled with delight, and called out, "Screw you, Matt!"

Micah, still unable to believe he had been useful in the endeavor, found himself wishing the repair had taken longer. But soon September was out of the bus and walking him to the gate again.

"I hope everything goes OK for you down there," she said. "Sorry I can't give you a ride. Got work to do here," she nodded at the still-burning pyre. "You're not far now, anyway, and it's best you go unseen for the last bit. Little guy like you, not so good in a fight, you're better off sneaking through. And the bus ain't sneaky."

Micah, devastated by this description of himself but trying hard not to show it, replied, "Thank you. Do you want me to give a message to your family, if I see them?"

She shook her head once, jaw clenched. Micah waved half-heartedly and closed the gate behind him. He passed beneath the underpass and made his way up the lip of the valley. Every few steps he turned to look behind him. September was standing on the high bastion of the overpass, watching him, silhouetted against the blaze of her grandfather's pyre like a monument to some forgotten war.

That day was the worst of the journey thus far. His body knew that it had not been compelled to leave its comforts, and was rebelling. He could still feel the warmth of the hearth. He could still taste the meat in his mouth, and the lumpy softness of the brother's bed. Most of all, he could see those barely-glimpsed instances when the girl had smiled, and hear the warmth as it had crept into her voice.

But he was not there with her. He was back in the March wilderness instead, in a wide empty land of abandoned pasture grown up in bitter groves of crab-apple trees and weedy poplars. A cold wind blew endlessly through the gray monotony of the rotten end of winter, resisted only by the sad-eyed ruins of the burnt-out farms he passed. The sky was a dead, flat gray and the rain came howling down the fields uncontested to buffet him with bits of squall until he was soaked through.

Micah could feel a cold creeping into his chest, and though the road here was even and unobstructed, it had begun to rise steadily upwards out of the valley. Outwardly, the day's journey was much the same as the ones that had passed before. The snow was patchy here further south and those patches were shrinking quickly in the rain. He abandoned his skis, burying them beside the road with a little cairn of stones to mark the place, thanking Bertram beneath his breath, and continued on foot. The abandoned farmland stretched on and on through endless variations of brown and gray with the white of the snow clinging on in the hollows. Here and there a copse of birch had reclaimed the cleared land, but for the most part it was simple walking along a hard straight road.

The land was silent but for the crying of the crows, and now, for the first time, of the seagulls. But Micah was full of noise within. He had never known anything like what he now felt inside of him as he ran over every detail of the previous day and night, over and over again. Every word she had said, and the tone and timbre of her voice as she had said it. The firelight in her hair. The smell of her as they had sat side by side on the edge of the broken highway, the same highway he now was walking down. And above all, the fierce hard torment, sharp in his chest, at the thought of her alone in that dark house, and of all the hundred thousand terrible things that could befall her there. It was all that he could do not to turn around and run back north.

For the first time, Micah considered abandoning his journey. But this was foolishness, of course. Had he ever in his life met anyone as capable as her? She had already proved to him that she could kill any living thing that entered her valley without leaving her front porch. But he could not quell the urge to protect her, no matter what logic had to say about it. The memory of her lived inside him like a warm star and he found himself speaking out loud to her, reenacting conversations from the night before. He found himself singing, and giggling madly to himself.

He caught himself, stopped himself, told himself that he was an idiot, pure and simple. There had been girls in the Fold, of course, though never many and only a few who had stayed long enough to make any sort of connection. Of those, none had been willing to get close to a boy so obviously fated to live and die a Shepherd. For to be a Shepherd was a kind of death: the responsibilities of the vocation precluded nearly all others. While it did not require celibacy or anything like it, it was a life few were willing to sign on to share. Not in return for the dubious delights of marriage to Micah Gault, at any rate.

But Micah Gault was no longer a Shepherd, and was far away from the Fold. Meeting September in his current unattached state had been like meeting a unicorn, a mythical creature that could grant him his dearest wish. She had not seen him burdened with a hundred unbreakable attachments. She had not viewed him as the stone that would drown her in an unfathomable sea of human misery. She had not looked at him as a curse to be avoided. She had looked at him as a reasonably attractive, if stringy, young man, perhaps even as a Prospect, and this was something he had certainly never experienced before. He told himself he was being stupid, and that the odds of a healthy relationship with the first available girl he had ever met were astronomical. The old saying about the last girl on Earth came to mind.

But with it came the realization that she surely was not. There would be other girls in the City, similarly unattached as he so newly found himself. Amazingly, this was the first time the thought had occurred to him. Excitement quickened within him, then soured. Something in these thoughts had called to mind his father's letter, the girls in the library. He tried to clear his mind, to think of nothing, ahead or behind, and failed utterly. He missed the Fold, felt guilty at the thoughts of the undoubtedly more enjoyable, if not better, life that lay ahead. He longed to reach the end of his journey, to discover those as-yet-formless delights. He wanted most of all to race back down the hill to Burrows, to bang on the rusted steel door, to kiss the gun-wielding unicorn on her mouth.

But Micah was still under orders, if not holy orders, and so it was with heavy steps and a reeling, divided mind that made his way down the wide cracked highway, south towards the city that called him like siren songs and filled him with arousal and revulsion and fear and want until each was indistinguishable from the other.

He had still not reached the top of the high moor that edged the southern wall of the valley when nightfall overtook him. Micah made his camp in the ruins of an old tire storage facility where a dry corner could still be found beneath a bit of shattered roof. He made a fire on the exposed foundation and wrapped his sleeping bag around himself. It smelled as it had always smelt, the nighttime sweat of his own body laid over the old sour smell which he could only assume was the inherited odor of his dead father. The bedding was the best the Fold could provide. But last night's bed had spoiled it for him, and now he found himself deeply dissatisfied with his shelter. A lot of things had been ruined by September Burrows, he realized. A deep

99

and childish unhappiness settled within him, and he made no effort to renounce it as he sat and stared at the fire. He did not retrieve his father's letter from its hiding place. There were enough unsettling voices in his head already without adding that most unwelcome one.

That night the glow in the southeast seemed very close indeed, and Micah slept uneasily in its light. September had said he would be able to see it from the top of this interminable hill. September.

Micah awoke to another colorless morning, as miserable as he had ever been. The chill had returned to the air, and he shivered as he emerged, damp with condensation, from his sleeping bag. He broke his sodden camp and continued the climb up the moor. He reached the crest an hour before noon, bent and trudging beneath his pack, feet and knees sore and unaccustomed to walking on pavement. He looked out from the top of the ridge, and sank down onto his haunches.

The fields rolled over and down the far side of the ridge for several kilometers. But beyond them the familiar arable tones were replaced by a uniform concrete gray, and he could make out sharp-edged geometric shapes in the haze of the humid air. Not the scattering of farms and little towns, but a sight he had never beheld, a thick forest of squares and rectangles, miles and miles of concrete trees. His brain, unaccustomed to the mass terraforming of the late Anthropocene, struggled and failed to comprehend what his eyes were seeing. But that was not the end of it.

Beyond the monochrome expanse, through the hanging mists at the limit of his sight, was something else. It was barely the size of his thumb from this distance, but his breath caught in his throat when he saw it. He had seen a thousand pictures of it at every stage of its construction, had memorized its vital statistics in childhood, had drawn it over and over again as a child. He had known it was real, but that knowledge did not live anywhere in his body, certainly not his eyes. Nothing had prepared him for the sheer nightmare scale of the Tower.

The highest manmade point in the Fold was the cross at the top of St. Stephen-in-the-Fields, a marvel to his ignorant eyes, but the lesser structures that huddled about the Tower's base would all but dwarf that old cross many times over. There were fewer of them than there had been in the old photographs. In the pictures, the tower stood as a Nephilim queen among an entourage of giants. He had known many of them by name. At least half of them were missing now, brought down by some unknown and unspeakable violence, now lying in a confusion of rubble. But while most of the differences between the photos and the skyline as it was were deletions, there was one unmistakable addition: a wall encircled the central high rises, even and white as a snowdrift.

Micah crouched there on the ridge until his thighs began to cramp and his calves to tremor. He had never felt so small or so alone or so ill-equipped for a task than now, finally in sight of the Tower and the Wall. He wanted nothing more than to turn and slink back down the hill, to go back to Burrows and find September and

100

take her hand if she would let him.

But then he thought of Philip Ramirez, and then of Donny and Jonathan and Sam, and most of all Thomas struggling to breathe, and he gripped his ski pole walking stick and started down the hill.

The highway ran down broad and straight before him, straight and unwavering as a line of longitude, down the slope and onto the plain and across it into the heart of the City. If the snow and his skis had remained it would have been nothing at all, but it was easy enough on foot. His hunter's instincts told him that the road was dangerous, but he could think of no better option. Lorne's map had nothing to say of this transformed country. He made his bow ready to hand, though he knew it would not be enough to save him. He would be at the mercy of denizens of the gray land, just as he had been at September's. He searched the margins of the highway for the slightest movement, and he prayed.

Once he was down off of the hill and onto the plain below, the world around him began changing quickly. First came the billboards, looming out of the fog like giants, the tracts of their paper gospels long since torn away by the wind that came roaring up from the lake. They stood by the dead highway in mute alien groves, and at first Micah could not begin to guess their purpose. They seemed to be pure structure, unattached to any communicative intention. For a long time he believed them to be sculptures, until he came to one that still bore the indistinct after-image of a large bald man offering him legal counsel in the event of his arrest on charges of impaired driving, and then his reading brought the word back to him.

At first he was fascinated. He climbed the steel ladder of the first he came to, standing above the plain on the little wire platform under the wide blank face of it, until some ominous groaning sounds brought him scampering down like a squirrel. But as their march continued, one after the next, hour after hour, he came to hate them, dripping rust, faceless, purposeless, yet eternal. A hundred more lined the road south as far as he could see, each as meaningless as the last, the ones with images the most meaningless of them all.

As evening fell it began to rain, and Micah sought shelter beneath a fallen image of seven immaculate faces, terrible in their faded beauty. It was dark and dry beneath the great wing of metal, though it warped and rattled in the wind. That night his sparse dreams were of enormous flying things that swooped down upon him as he ran to a refuge that he knew was out of reach. Sleepless, he made mute prayers in his mind to the God beyond the sky for the courage and wisdom to do what he must do, and to do it well. He waited for a warm feeling or a strong feeling or any new feeling at all to enter him, some confirmation that his prayer had been heard, that he was not walking alone into the unknown. No such answer came, but he was not so young as to be much discouraged by that.

When at last the light of dawn crept beneath the collapsed advertisement, Micah discovered that he had not spent the night as alone as he had believed. Five feet away from him lay the naked corpse of an old man, stiff and blue with rigor mortis. He seemed uninjured, his body lined and ravaged with hunger, but unmarked. He lay beneath a blanket of leaves and a torn tarp as if sleeping, as he no doubt had been when cold and malnutrition and age had taken him.

Micah stared at the body, trying to imagine why on Earth the man would have taken off his clothes. He conjured up stories of hypothermia victims doing so in their death agonies, before the truth, too obvious to be seen at first, came to him. The man had of course been robbed, forced to remove his clothes and left to freeze, with no Samaritan to find him here in this empty place between ages. Micah pulled the tarp up to cover the man's face, and scuttled out from under the billboard like a startled mouse.

The late and unexpected discovery of the dead man had disturbed Micah deeply, and he was possessed by an animal requirement to see as far and as wide as possible. He made his panicked way to the next standing billboard, climbed the ladder built into its stalk, and crept out onto the wire mesh catwalk and looked out across the world.

A thousand acres of rotting boxes met his eyes; the work places and dwellings of dead men. The morning sky was gray and the boxes were gray and the earth beneath him was not earth at all but the cold cracked gray of the dead concrete highway. The highway was no longer a strip of death running through a brown and breathing world. Here it had spread like a dammed stream flooded over, and the blight of it ran between the boxes and smothered the soil and its children. What bits that still grew up grew like the seed cast among thorns, choked by the cares of this world.

Micah remained alone, the only living soul to be seen, though he knew the safety of his loneliness would soon end. He climbed down and continued his journey, traveling now through the endless ranks of empty geometry. He could no longer see the towers of the city to the south, and the land lost all sense of meaning and perspective. There were only the next dozen acres of featureless cinder block walls, hollow-eyed and naked beneath the skies.

Forty years is not so long a span in the cosmic scheme of things, but it is plenty of time to lay waste to an untended subdivision. Everything of material value had been stripped from the homes, down to the copper pipes and the wiring in the walls, but a hundred thousand other precious things remained. Pictures still hung on the walls, the faces in them still recognizable through sun-bleach and water damage. Books remained on their shelves, the pages mostly destroyed but the titles remaining on their withered spines. Dead electronic devices lay everywhere, empty screens, now only reflecting. But most prevalent of all were the children's things. They seemed to have had so much, so very many objects, and almost all of them seemed to have been left behind. In many of the houses it seemed that all that was left were drifts of plastic toys, primary colors faded and spotted with mold but otherwise incorruptible. As the day passed the eerie perception began to grow that this had been a land where only children had lived, that only children had disappeared from. That night it was a child's bedroom he slept in, in the second story of one of the more robust ruins, a corner room from which he could watch the road as it ran from east to west, as well as south. He did not sleep well that night, the deep silence bearing as it did what could only be described as a haunted quality.

On the morning of the next day he passed through the last rank of broken boxes. The highway rose above the houses on long concrete legs, a graceful sweeping rise and fall, like Arthur had said, like a sauropod's spine. He made his way up the long, smooth ramp as the houses grew smaller beneath him and then gave way to more boxes, but larger, with flat roofs, structures so massive in their square-footage that he could hardly believe that he was seeing them. From his maps and photographs he was able to recognize the abstract arrangement of squares and rectangles that had been the Cloverdale shopping mall. Half the roof had rotted and collapsed in on itself, and now a small forest grew out of the center of the vast ruins.

At the apex of the overpass, overcome by the childish and overwhelming urge, he unzipped his pants and relieved himself through a gap in the guardrail. This silence was so total that he could hear the splash of his urine fifty feet below. He giggled, his laughter echoing into the void. He looked down to see the arc of the flow, and stopped giggling abruptly. On the curb next to his feet sat a neatly coiled pile of fecal matter, unmistakably human.

His lightness of spirit departed as swiftly as it had arrived, and now he only wanted to put the dead land behind him as quickly as possible. But first he had to finish what he started. He did, suddenly ashamed of his nakedness, as quickly as he could. He covered himself, and hurried over the bridge. Soon there would be no cover. Soon there would be eyes.

By the end of the day he had reached the end of the halo of factories and warehouses that ringed the City. The City, the true City, was close now, its towers rising above that unaccountable wall. The sun was setting as Micah found a doorless convenience store at the convergence of two streets, chased out a squalling family of raccoons, and laid his sleeping bag out in a mildewed corner. He didn't know how long he'd been sleeping when the voices woke him.

17
City of God, City of Man

It was a group, a fairly large one from the sounds of it, converging on his location from another of the cleared streets. The voices he heard were happy ones, unafraid, shouting and laughing, even breaking into song.

Micah bolted awake and quickly and noiselessly rolled up his sleeping bag and slipped it into his pack. He crept up the flight of stairs at the back to the second story into what had clearly been the proprietor's home. He dropped to his hands and knees and crawled to the empty window to peer down at the adjacent street.

A procession was making its way down the avenue. He counted twenty-one people: old people, young people, children. They were dressed in bright colors, singing as they made their way up the street. One woman played a tambourine as they walked, and the children shook old plastic containers filled with stones.

Their leader was a tall man in a hat hung with brightly colored ribbons. The empty left sleeve of his bright green jacket was pinned up against his chest. In his right hand he held a penny whistle to his lips. His fingers danced as he played, and no one in the group seemed to be carrying a weapon of any kind. The sight and sound filled Micah with joy, but his own imagination was filled with danger, and he wondered at their boldness. The old man beneath the billboard had not been dead long. His robbers could be close and looking for more victims to despoil.

As the procession passed beneath him and the laughing voices of the children rose to his window, he could keep silent no longer. Micah got to his feet and called down out of the broken window, "Hello!"

The procession stopped, and the one-armed man took the penny whistle from his lips and raised it in welcome. "Peace to you!" There was no fear in his face, or in the faces of those who followed him. They seemed not to have entertained the possibility that Micah could be a danger to them. "Won't you come down and join us?"

At a complete loss for words, Micah made his numb, astonished way down the stairs and out to the street and was immediately surrounded by smiling faces. A child ran up and threw her arms around his knees, nearly bringing him to the ground. The group began to laugh, and Micah, caught up in the sudden happy absurdity of the situation, found himself laughing also.

"Who are you?" he finally managed to say.

"Pilgrims, like you," said the one-armed man, "on our way to the City of God. By way of the City of Man. My name is Benjamin, and these are my family and friends. Join us!" he repeated.

Micah did not, in fact, wish to join them, though due more to his social anxiety than any threat he perceived from the group. He had known and loved many charismatic fellow travelers in his life, but was by nature an introverted Anglican and found their enthusiasm exhausting. But he could think of no polite way to explain this, and so he fell into step beside Benjamin, to the cheers of his followers.

As they made their way through the outer suburbs of the City, Micah was told the story of the Anawim, as the pilgrims named themselves. "It's Aramaic, you know," Benjamin explained, although Micah has not asked. "The language Jesus spoke, you know? Means 'The Small Belonging to God.' And that's us, isn't it guys?" The group agreed loudly and with a joy that seemed surprisingly genuine.

Micah was actually very familiar with the concept of the Anawim, as it was an oft-recycled theme in Martin's homilies, but was given no time to explain this to Benjamin. Their story was remarkably similar to that of the Fold. Benjamin and the fellow founders of their community had originally been counselors at a Pentecostal youth camp in the Muskokas during the last days of the former order and had retreated there after its collapse. There they had lived and reproduced and grown over the past decades in the belief that they, a faithful remnant, were enduring the end times (and who could argue the point?) in anticipation of the final return of Jesus Christ to the Earth and the ushering in of His eternal kingdom. At the end of the narrative, the group exclaimed as one, "Maranatha!"

"Come quickly, Lord," translated the overstimulated Micah, repeating the prayer for himself. The Anawim exploded with delight at this, immediately conferring the title of Brother in Christ upon him. They continued expounding their own theology for the next several hours, while Micah nodded like a bobblehead doll, agreed with everything he reasonably could, and tried to obscure the fact that he had never spoken in tongues.

Where the resurrected City stood in the eschatology of the Anawim was unclear, but it was definitely an important part of it, and no doubt more would be revealed in the proper time. After several hours they got around to asking Micah where he had come from, and they listened with polite interest as Micah haltingly explained the purpose and origins of the Fold, but didn't seem to find its existence relevant to "the story we find ourselves in," as they put it. They did, however, offer to pray for an outpouring of the Spirit on that community, then proceeded to do so, loudly and at length.

The Anawim were strange and emotionally exhausting, but they carried no weapons, and their young seemed happy and healthy. Benjamin was undoubtedly their leader, but seemed to hold his authority lightly. The word "cult" came often and again to Micah's mind, but as cults went it seemed relatively innocuous, and people who lived in glass houses (or strange religious communities) had long been warned against throwing stones.

As the sun went down, they made their camp in the open compartments of a scorched storage unit, one of the hundred that lined the highway. The Anawim made a large fire, and three or four acoustic guitars appeared as if by magic. Micah knew most of the songs, "Awesome God" and "All In All" and "Days of Elijah," and sang along, to the delight of his new traveling companions. But he could not partake in their casual fearlessness, and couldn't keep from turning around during the worship, to look into the dark, to wonder who else was watching, listening, waiting for the right moment. The blue corpse beneath the billboard was always before his eyes.

In the morning the group continued deeper into the suburbs. Excitement grew among the pilgrims as they approached the city. It was not clear exactly what they expected to happen when they arrived, but the overall impression was that it would be wonderful, a blessing, and, most emphatically of all, the will of God. Their excitement was contagious and Micah found it growing within himself as well, though trepidation grew with it.

As they walked, he talked with Benjamin. Micah was dumbfounded by his faith, characterized by a lack of preparation and concern that could only be described as childlike, and with his confidence in a warm welcome to the City.

"As Anawim," he repeated, "everything belongs to us. That City belongs to us. It will be given to us." Micah, no stranger to this brand of charismatic enthusiasm, kept his mouth shut and his eyes open. He had heard Arthur and Bethlehem hash out this particular point of doctrine a thousand times and had never come any closer to a position, other than that he hated theological arguments.

The suburbs slowly gave way to the business parks, and then the smashed office buildings and gaping warehouses gave way to something new, and Micah knew Lorne's map had reached the end of its usefulness.

The pilgrims came through a gap between two strip malls into a vast emptiness. For half a kilometer, in a great ring, the city had been razed, burnt, and cleared. They were suddenly flooded with light from an unobscured sky, and were instantly, completely, and unavoidably exposed. Across the great cleared space stood the white wall Micah had seen from the ridge at Burrows. But it was not the smooth, even edifice it had seemed from that distance. It was less a wall than a great, heaped mound of everything.

Micah saw now what had become of the towers missing from the skyline. Fallen, collapsed in on themselves, they had been converted to heaps of rubble by what force he could not imagine. They had formed a barrier where they had fallen, and then the resulting debris fields had been shored up around them until the ruins formed an unbroken perimeter around the undamaged core of the City. The ruins had been painted white, giving the impression of purity from far off, but up close the effect was ghastly, a parapet of broken bone. A long straight path had been cleared through the rubble, up to what appeared to be a gate. He could see human figures there, busy at some unguessed task.

Micah stared, aghast at the scale of the wall of ruins, but the Anawim seemed unabashed, and went singing up the road, their caravan rattling behind them. Benjamin gestured to him with his arm and declared, with a wide grin, "I was happy when they said, 'Let us go up to the House of the Lord!'" Micah opened his mouth to reply he knew not what, but Benjamin was already gone, flute in hand.

At the gate were more people, great crowds of people, coming in and walking out. Micah had anticipated this moment for so long, had expected a crippling social anxiety, but the Anawim had broken the ice. What he felt now, more than anything, was a certain embarrassment to be arriving as part of their singing, dancing, tambourine-playing entourage.

There were guards at the gate, armed not with bows but with rifles. They were not exactly wearing uniforms, but the ironed crispness of their clean, well-fitted clothing bore an air of competence and authority intimidating in its own right.

To the left and right of the guarded gate, and stretching into the distance around the perimeter of the great wall, men and women were working. They were clearing rubble, stacking stone and broken concrete onto the wall. The word that first came to Micah's fearful mind was "slaves," but closer observation disabused him of this notion. They were not guarded or even watched closely. They worked hard and quickly, but not fearfully. Instead, there was an eagerness and an excitement in their labors. The workers kept glancing over at the guards at the gate, like teenagers eager to be seen as adults, not working to avoid punishment, but to gain approval and acceptance. It was all becoming clear to Micah when the guards approached their group to make the situation explicit. Benjamin had begun a long-prepared speech when the guards cut him off abruptly with a speech of their own:

"Hello and thank you for joining us here. You're welcome here, but let's get something straight, right off the bat: We need workers, but that's all we need. We're building something here, something big and strong and good, and if you want to be a part of it, you're going to help us build it. You'll each be compensated for the work you do, each of you individually. First you work outside the wall. After that, we'll see. You might be let in to work in the second ring, and maybe even the third, but that's based on individual, observed merit and ability. Nothing else. I'm sure you're a great leader," the guard said, looking Benjamin up and down doubtfully, "but that's neither here nor there. Those hierarchies end here."

"Christ is our leader!" replied Benjamin, after a moment's unguarded consternation.

The guard nodded, clearly having heard it all, and stranger, before. "Well, if you folks will just follow Christ over here to this little table by the wall, Sarah will get some information and then Grant will get you set up with the tools you'll need". He pointed with a gloved hand through the crowd of busy, grubby strangers to where a neat white table sat beneath a neat white tent. At the table sat a small neat white person, immaculate among the filth. Micah and Benjamin and the rest of the Anawim made their way over to it.

"Good morning! Welcome to the Welcome Table!" exclaimed the person, a young woman with the whitest, cleanest teeth Micah had ever seen. Her black hair shone in the early sun. He could smell it and it smelled good.

"My name is Sarah. Might I ask you for your names and your dates of birth, as accurately as you can give them?" They answered, one by one. Micah knew his birthday, but several of the Anawim could only give a year, and some of the years given seemed very unlikely indeed. Benjamin, Micah was surprised to learn, was only five years older than himself, despite his air of confidence and missing arm.

More questions followed, bewildering in number and variety: Parents' names, living still, cause of death if deceased? Level of education? Special skills training? Had they ever seen visions or been spoken to by an unseen voice? (Here Benjamin perked up, visibly.) Had they experienced respiratory difficulty? Would they consent to testing of blood and urine? A cheek swab? How much weight did they think they could lift? How much could they carry for 250 meters? Five hundred? How many fingers and toes did they possess, and would they consent for them to be counted? Any history of mental illness? Suicidal ideation, self-harm, eating disorders? Any history of congenital disability in the family? For the women present, an entire series of separate questions concerning menstrual and reproductive health followed, at which Micah reddened.

Then a written portion. A booklet was distributed among them, a series of sentences to read concerning the actions of a brown dog and his counterpart, the gray wolf, questions to answer with the little pencil (attached).

"No sharing your work, please!" remarked Sarah, cheerfully. Then a math portion, at which Micah began to sweat. Was he going to fail in his mission because he couldn't remember BEDMAS? He tried to imagine the conversation with his mother, the teacher, and shuddered. But it turned out to be a fairly simple algebraic equation, and he finished the booklet and returned it to Sarah's table, rewarded with another bright smile.

"Thank you, everyone!" chirped Sarah when every booklet had been returned. "This will be processed and collated and the results will be taken into account when it comes time for your next bracelet.

"That reminds me! I haven't given you your bracelets." She produced a sheave of green plastic strips from a box beneath the table. "These are the green ones, obviously!" She giggled.

"Green is for beginnings, for growth. It's our first tier here. If you have a green bracelet, it means you've been through our initial screening and are welcomed to work in the area around our walls. The guards will keep you safe while you work, and you'll be fed and sheltered and compensated based on the work you do. Just make sure you have someone scan your bracelet every time you bring a load in!"

"A load of what?" came a voice from the group.

"Whatever you want!" exclaimed Sarah brightly. "Steel, copper, any precious metal. Circuit boards, computer chips, rubber, catalytic converters, batteries, spark plugs! You'll find the current exchange rates posted at the processing site just over there." She pointed down the wall a few hundred meters, where a series of steel bins were lined up, labeled and heavily guarded. "You'll be compensated based on what you bring, and how much."

"Compensated how?" came the same voice.

"Again, the board has all the details. But food, obviously, and firewood! Repair kits, alternative shelters should you require them. Medical supplies." Micah's heart caught in his throat, the sound of Thomas' labored breathing suddenly loud in his ears. He had been forgetting.

"Just show us you're willing and able to help, and in a few days I'm sure you'll all be welcome inside!" Sarah exclaimed, but Micah saw her eyes shift to the empty sleeve pinned to Benjamin's chest, and saw her smile become just the smallest bit fixed. "Any questions?"

There were many, but none on the topic of the process that had just been outlined. The process was straightforward and it quickly became clear there was not going to be any negotiation between the empty-handed pilgrims and the walled and rifled city they wished to enter.

They made their way over to the processing center. There a guard motioned to a variety of tools laid out next to the wall. "Take your pick. Just give us a hand here and you'll be welcome to stay." The Anawim, clearly no strangers to obedient manual labor, dutifully took up their tools and began to help the dozen or so ragged mendicants who had preceded them.

Micah didn't know what he had been expecting, but it wasn't this. He had expected close interrogation of his motives, and for speeches to have to be made to authorities in his role as ambassador. This was much easier than that. He removed his pack and placed it carefully in the pile of others watched over by the guard, then chose a pair of heavy work gloves and set of bolt cutters and set off to harvest what he could from the fallow acres of abandoned vehicles that sprawled to the east of Sarah and her little white table.

As he searched for items and materials from the approved list, other travelers trickled in from every direction. There were hardened survivalists and dangerous-looking paramilitary groups. There was a group of Sikhs and a pair of Eastern Orthodox monks. There were large farm families and what appeared to be the cast of a preserved pioneer village who had survived the ensuing decades by an extreme form of method acting. All were welcomed warmly by Sarah at her welcome desk, given green bracelets, and directed to their work.

Micah had been working for an hour, fruitlessly searching the ruins of a Mack truck, a Toyota Tercel, and a Chevy Suburban for the materials listed on the board, when he heard a hesitant tapping from the other side of the SUV. It didn't sound like any sort of efficient labor process, more like a message in Morse code, and so he went to investigate.

He found Benjamin there, hammering hopelessly away at the rear bumper with a mallet. Benjamin looked up, sheepishly. "Guess it'll be prayer and fasting for a while," he said.

"Come with me," said Micah, trying not to embarrass the man. "There's nothing worth taking here."

They walked out through the scrap fields, away from the efficient dismantling of the more experienced scavengers, out beyond the range of the guards' guns, until they found the red and white hulk of a decommissioned TTC bus that seemed relatively unmolested. The two developed a system, Micah cutting through the hide of the beast with the bolt cutters, Benjamin clamping on with a vice grip and ripping long strips back with the overdeveloped muscles of his right arm to reveal the bright copper wiring beneath.

They worked until dark, rummaging through the detritus of empire in search of the precious little precious metals that remained. As the sun set, Micah left Benjamin to guard the meager fruits of their labor while he returned to the wall for a wheelbarrow and to retrieve their packs. They returned it to the processing center together, Micah insisting to the clearly skeptical guard that it had been a mutual effort and that compensation be equally divided. Grudgingly he agreed, and after weighing the copper, he produced what Micah thought was a gun. The guard laughed as Micah put up his hands in a gesture of surrender. "It's a scanner, hick. Hold out your wrist." He held up the scanner to the pattern of black and white squares printed on the green plastic that Micah had taken to be decorative. "This is good for dinner tonight for each of you, a bag of firewood, and a bag of kindling. Hope you brought a tent."

"I did!" Micah answered excitedly, to the impressive indifference of the guard. He and Benjamin joined the line of oil-and-sweat-stained laborers. When they reached the head of the line, their bracelets were scanned by a smiling young man who could have been (and perhaps was) Sarah's brother.

"Peanut allergy?" he asked brightly. Micah stared at him blankly.

After a moment the correlation between the two became clear, and he shook his head and was handed a peanut butter and jam sandwich, a ziplock bag half-filled with raisins and granola, a small hard apple, and a plastic bottle of water. The promised firewood followed, contained within a web of plastic mesh that Micah picked at in fascination.

"Could we have some of the beans, please?" asked Benjamin, pointing to steaming bowls the hulking laborer ahead of them in line had received.

The young man's smile became fixed. "I'm sorry, sir. Your bracelets indicate you haven't earned quite enough for the beans yet. Maybe tomorrow! Enjoy your sandwich!"

As they made their way back to where the Anawim were eating in the shadow of a gutted dump truck, Benjamin said to Micah, "I bet if you weren't working with me today you'd have earned beans."

"I don't really like beans anyway," responded Micah, untruthfully.

They were greeted by the Anawim, but their reception now seemed muted. Many of Benjamin's followers seemed unwilling to meet his eyes, and their greetings were mumbled. When Benjamin began to loudly pray the blessing over the meal, there were a lot of open eyes and uncomfortable diggings in the dirt with feet. Micah noticed that though several of the Anawim appeared to have earned beans, none offered to share. Benjamin, for his part, appeared not to notice. He ate his sandwich and drank his water enthusiastically and with many apparently genuine breaks to "Praise the Lord, who gives His children bread in the wilderness!" But the Amens in response were mumbled.

After the meal, Benjamin produced his flute and began to play "Seek Ye First." By the time he transitioned into "Shine, Jesus, Shine," the Anawim were singing and clapping, the new tensions apparently forgotten. They sang into the night, until one by one they fell asleep by the light of the roaring consumption of the hard-earned firewood.

18
Moths of the Second Ring

It felt very strange to Micah to walk up in a place and not immediately walk away from it. After they had breakfasted on the last of their remaining provisions, the Anawim quickly dispersed to their work, leaving Micah and Benjamin by the smoldering embers of last night's fire. Benjamin gave Micah a furtive sidelong glance. "Come on, man," said Micah. "Same plan as yesterday."

A grateful smile broke across Benjamin's face. "How sweet it is when brothers live together in harmony! Like oil running down the beard of Aaron." Micah understood the reference, but it still made him very uncomfortable. He broke the awkward silence with an improvised discourse on which tools had worked well yesterday, and which needed to be swapped out.

They finished stripping the bus and moved on to a misplaced combine, and then a wheelchair van which provided an uncorroded battery and two intake catalytic converters. That night they would eat beans, with credit left over for more.

Around noon on the third day, as Micah and Benjamin steadily eviscerated an OPP Durango, the gate in the white wall creaked and scraped open, and a great sound emerged. It was a guttural, choking roar, and with it came a terrible smell that burnt the eyes and the throat. For the first time, Micah understood all the descriptions of diesel exhaust he had read over the years.

From out of the gate came the huge, hulking shape of a salter plough, the great blade shining in the silver sun, the exhaust belching black from the pipes behind the cab. An air horn sounded three times, easily the loudest sound Micah's ears had ever translated to his brain. He stood, transfixed by this total assault on his senses.

Benjamin broke the trance. "Micah, look: he wants us to come over." It was true. The driver was gesturing, and from the wreck fields the workers began to converge.

The driver was shouting over the rumble of the plough. "I need some big strong guys to come in and help me clear for the day. Anybody want to be blue for the day? See how we do it in the second ring?"

Micah's stomach lurched. He needed to get inside that ring. His eyes flickered to Benjamin's empty sleeve. Benjamin caught the glance, grinned a sad grin. "One noble gesture at a time, man. Put your hand up. They don't want me, and that's OK. But you need to get in there, and you're big and the Lord has blessed you with two arms. He has given me other gifts. Perhaps the crown of martyrdom among them."

Micah looked at Benjamin with incredulous horror. Benjamin laughed again. "I'm kidding. Or you know, maybe not. But either way." He grabbed Micah's wrist with his one very strong hand and raised it high in the air.

The driver of the plough caught the movement and pointed down at Micah. "Yup, you'll do, buddy. Climb on up. You can bring your bag, but no projectile weapons. The bow's gotta stay."

Micah slowly drew the bow out of its cradle on the side of his pack. He held it in his hands for a moment, remembering the hands that had made it for him, and why, and at what cost. He handed it to Benjamin, realizing even as he did so the absurdity of the gesture. But Benjamin only grinned and saluted him with it.

"The Lord bless you and keep you, and cause His face to shine upon you," he said, and before he realized what was happening, Micah was up on the running board, clinging to the passenger's side mirror with four others. With an ear-splitting beeping, the plough reversed through the gate into the second ring of the City. As the gate ground shut Micah caught one final glimpse of Benjamin among the rejected, his right arm raised in farewell. The glimpse was swift: the machine was incredibly fast for its bulk and Micah had the unsettling sensation of being sucked backwards into the City as a fly is into the mouth of a frog. The unfamiliar fug of diesel fumes filled his unready lungs, combining with the vertiginous reverse motion to create an immediate and overwhelming nausea. It was not at all how he had imagined his first experience on a motorized vehicle.

"My name's Dustin," screamed the driver over din of the diesel engine. "I'm Foreman, Second Ring. Pleasure to meet you, gentlemen! Now," he concluded, throwing the plough into neutral and bringing a blessed end to the infernal beeping, "kindly disembark and see Sarah for processing."

There, by the gate, was Sarah, at an identical white table under an identical white tent. "Hi guys. Me again!" She waved, unnecessarily, and they lined up at her table. "Just a couple more tests!" A nasal swab. A quick stab from a needle, a bright red vial labeled with their names and put in a cooler with a few dozen others. A scan from what Micah again thought was a gun aimed at his forehead but turned out this time to be a thermometer. New wristbands issued: blue.

The City of the second ring was a study in contrasts. Immediately in front of him was a dense interlocking labyrinth of row houses and mid-rise apartment blocks. It felt horribly claustrophobic after the wide open spaces of the wreck fields. The Wall rose behind him, the rubble that formed it unpainted on this side. The tight grid of streets cut their way through the tower blocks, mostly empty and dead-eyed with broken windows. As he watched, Dustin spun the plough as easily as if it were a motorcycle, lowered the blade, and began to clear a side street of rubble and dead cars with a metal scream and a foaming bow-wave of sparks. Directly ahead, a long straight avenue ran down from the gate, already cleared by Dustin's plough. Far down, at least two or three kilometers, he could see it come to an end at another wall, smaller, neater, cleaner, but no less definite. Behind that wall were the true towers, the true City, from which the light came, from where the shadows were cast by the rising sun.

His examinations were interrupted by another engine, another honking horn. "That'll be Arlo!" chirped Sarah. "He takes the new folks. He needs your help, and he's waiting for you!"

Micah and his fellow chosen wandered vaguely eastward towards the sound, climbing over uncleared rubble and around unbroken barricades. As they moved east, the apartments and townhouses failed and the prospect opened up. Ahead was a wide open acreage he recognized from the old tourist guides as one of the city's largest parks, now transformed into an expanse of rich farmland between the wall and the towers. Beyond the field, he saw vast expanses of glass glittering in the morning light: the greenhouses had kept the harvest going all winter long.

On the margins of the nearest field chugged a shining blue tractor, ridden by a weathered man in a Bass Pro cap, presumably Arlo.

"Morning, fellas. I don't want to know your names, and you don't need to know mine, except I'm sure that perky young miss who works the door has blabbed it all ready. There's nothing much for us to talk about, so let's get to the point: this field needs to get plowed and planted or we'll all starve to death. But it's full of shit. Not the good kind of shit, not cow shit or pig shit or chicken shit, but the bad kind. Your garden variety rocks, but all sorts of other shit as well, just about anything you can imagine. I need it out, and soon. It's very heavy. If you can get the shit out of my field without breaking yourselves, you can sleep on this side of the wall tonight. Do we have ourselves an accord?" Uncertain responses came, all to the affirmative. "Good! Then get to it, if you please. Sledges are in wheelbarrows by the wall, if you'd like to avail yourselves."

So Micah spent the day in the fields of the second ring, levering out the bad shit. It was heavy: not just rock (though there was plenty of that) but slabs of broken concrete, paving stones, shattered rebar, sheets of torn and twisted metal. The sledges proved invaluable: once levered onto one, it could be pulled rather than carried to the piles on the edge of the potentially arable land. The other chosen ones seemed unwilling to work together, and Micah didn't push for cooperation. He missed working with Benjamin, strange as he was. Micah hoped he was OK, and said a quick and silent prayer for him. He knew Benjamin would be praying for him, probably out loud, probably using the most uncomfortable language possible.

When the sun was high overhead, they heard a bell ringing and saw Sarah, white on the edge of the brown field. As they started wearily towards her, Arlo chugged by and commented, "That's not blue bracelet food. She's brought that special for you Moths, God knows why. Any of you touch her I'll cut your fucking nuts off."

Sarah had set up a table and chairs on the edge of the field, and when they were seated produced what Micah knew from his reading to be some kind of sandwich from a brown paper sack, wrapped in aluminum foil. Aluminum foil! It was genuinely shocking, to be presented with evidence of such a surplus of such a precious material, made delicate as paper, used to keep a sandwich warm and then thrown away.

"Here you go, gentlemen! Courtesy of the Mission. Day One on the blue bracelet only gets you peasoup, but I've seen how hard you've been working and I thought you deserved something extra! Hope you enjoy it!" They did enjoy it, wolfing down the meat and cheese and hot white bread while studiously avoiding looking in Sarah's direction, while Arlo chugged ominously back and forth behind them, plowing and replowing the same stretch of cleared earth, and watching.

Finally, Micah broke the silence. "Sarah," he began, after carefully swallowing the last of his sandwich and making sure his beard was free of cheese. "Why did Arlo call us Moths?"

She laughed, a high clear pure sound. "Oh, that's just a silly name for . . . for you folks who've been coming because we turned the lights on. Moth? Get it?" She giggled again, less certainly this time, clearly afraid now that she had given offense.

Micah forced a laugh for her sake. "That's . . . funny. I guess we are like moths. In that way." They smiled at each other, stupidly.

Arlo gunned the tractor's idling engine behind them. "Lunch's over, boys! If I break a disc on some piece of bad shit you missed, I'll kick you right back over that wall and there'll be no meatball sandwiches with Miss Sarah there, I assure you."

"It's OK, Arlo, I brought one for you too!" She skipped prettily over the furrows, kissing him on the check and pressing a silver-wrapped package into his hand.

His gnarled face broke into a toothless grin. "Thank you, Miss." Then, turning to the others, "Moths, back to work!"

It was that afternoon, as the sun began to wester behind the apartment blocks and the shadows stretched out long and cold, that Micah began to find the bones. At first he thought they were dirty white PVC piping, and then he thought they were maybe deer, and then he found the pelvis and knew. He called Arlo down from his tractor, who stumped over angrily. He softened when Micah showed him the discovery.

"Lots of those out here. At least five or six a day, if we don't find a mass grave. Took a lotta dying to clear this land, though that's always been the story. Take whatever you find to the south edge. You'll see the pile there. We bury what we find as decent as we can. Ain't enough, but it's the best we can do."

Micah recovered the rest of the skeleton, thankfully cleansed of any soft tissue by the secret ministry of the worms, and then he found two more. He stacked the bones together, as neatly as he could, in the ossuary on the southern edge. By the time he had finished recovering the third skeleton, Arlo was leaning on the tractor horn.

"Decent work today, Moths! Go find Sarah and she'll let you know where you're sleeping tonight. Hope to see you again tomorrow! Plenty more shit in the fields," he finished, with the air of someone quoting a well-known aphorism.

Sarah met them at the edge of the field. "Good work today, guys! Micah, thank

116

you for being so careful with the bones. I'm so sorry you had to deal with that!" Micah could not summon an appropriate response.

"How would you all feel about sleeping in a bed tonight?" The weary, filthy men nodded, tiredly. "Wonderful! Why don't you follow me?" She paused. "I'm sorry Carlos, Ted, you're not on my list. Head back to the gate and the guards will let you out, OK? The work you've done will be added to your credit." She pointed to the bracelet on her own wrist (yellow) with an incongruent smile.

She turned back to Micah and the two other chosen ones and wrinkled her nose. "I hate doing that, but we've got to follow the rules. It's the best we can do, right now." For a moment, it looked like Carlos and Ted were going to follow behind them, but a guard approached and they turned away back towards the gate. As he looked back, he saw the guard snip their blue bracelets from their wrists. He remembered Benjamin, then, and a spasm of guilt tore through him, but he comforted himself with Benjamin's parting words. He had to get further in, for his family, and this was clearly the only way. Benjamin had his own family to look after. Micah had to follow the rules. It was the best he could do.

Sarah led them down the cleared but darkening streets to a well-lit former Costco location, now an immense dormitory for his fellow Blues. Inside, it was several acres of bare metal bunk beds with thin polyvinyl mattresses of the kind most easily disinfected. Sarah turned, a look of embarrassed distaste crossing her face.

"I almost forgot! Sorry guys, but if you choose to stay the night we have to shave your heads. Too many lice outbreaks. That OK with you? We'll get you straight in for dinner afterward!"

Micah was familiar with this method of coercion, having used it himself many times, and agreed. The buzzing of the shears on his scalp sent shivers down his spine, and his head was cold. Sarah distributed woolen toques to the newly shorn workers. "Donations, from the inner ring. Very high quality! Very warm and soft!"

The new Blues made their way to the nearest in a series of long metal tables, where they were served hot meatloaf, corn, and mashed potatoes. Micah noticed that there was no scanning of the code on the blue bracelet. It seemed that entrance to the second ring conferred a level of trust and a level of privilege that didn't need to be as carefully monitored, once earned.

Micah tried to savor his meal, but found himself devouring it in a manner that could only be described as *wolfing*. The meatloaf contained more ground beef than he would ordinarily have consumed in a month. He finished it far too soon, brought his tray to the window, and was directed to a bunk with a blanket folded on it. With a sense of overwhelming unreality he pulled his sleeping bag from his pack and rolled it out on the bunk. He put the folded blanket on his pack and laid his head back on it and listened to the breathing of a hundred restless strangers. It sounded the way people had described the breaking of waves on a beach, and before they turned the lights out he had joined his snoring to the chorus.

19
Our Lady of the Pretty Girls

Micah was awoken by the blast of the air horn. He packed his sleeping bag back into the pack he had used as a pillow, and took a moment to brush away the dirt he had left on the vinyl mattress. Breakfast was served from a window by an unsmiling woman with gray hair, and Micah was struck by the parallels to the morning routine in the Fold, except now he was the recipient of care and the one being monitored for signs of disruptive behavior. He was the one who needed to be kept and managed. She slopped out of a large bowl of oatmeal porridge, and Micah resisted the urge to ask for pig sausage, if only out of tradition. Belly full of porridge, he hurried out into the morning light, where Arlo lounged indolently on the salter plow.

"First one out! Lucky boy." He tossed Micah a set of keys. "Follow me."

What followed was the most enjoyable day of Micah's life. The keys were for a Bobcat, described by Arlo as a "fun-sized bulldozer," and after a five-minute primer he was set loose to clear the tight grid of streets that formed the second ring, following Arlo's example on the much larger plow. The Bobcat was tracked and not particularly fast, but to Micah it felt like flying, flying and then colliding with a dead Corolla and then feeling it *move* and then he was *pushing a car* with the miraculous machine strength he had been granted. He was flushed, his heart pounding. He tried to name the feeling and its source, and four cars later he realized the name was Power.

Further in, the streets ended at a high steel wall. Over the wall loomed the true towers, impossibly tall, burnished and glowing in the afternoon sun. It was in their shadow that he worked his mechanized power, clearing the street of vehicles and rubble, pushing his loads out to the end of the side streets where the buildings ended. Before Micah knew it, the sun was going down behind the apartments to the west. It grew cold, quickly.

He heard three blasts on Arlo's air horn and followed the echoes back toward the dormitory, where his wrist was scanned again, adding the day's labors to his invisible credit score. As the scanner did its work, Arlo roared up and screeched to a halt.

"Nice work today, Moth. I want to see you out here tomorrow for more of the same." He rumbled off in a cloud of diesel fumes.

That night proved more eventful than the previous had. Micah was, by training, a light sleeper. He was well-accustomed to being awoken by any sound of distress, to being instantly alert and ready to respond to whatever the emergency might be, whether seizure, choking incident, or act of aggression.

It was the latter that woke Micah. It was two in the morning by the battery-powered clock on the dormitory wall, and a very large man that Micah remembered as Taylor from their intake together was attempting to relieve a smaller newcomer (Charles? Michael?) of the fanny pack around his waist. The owner of the fanny pack was attempting to defend it, unsuccessfully, and this defense seemed to offend Taylor, who began to beat the owner's head against the cinderblock wall.

Micah was not sure why he decided to intervene. He was by disposition extremely opposed to confrontation, particularly with large strangers in the dead of night. Later on he decided that it must have been the fanny pack, which was the same battered threadbare model that was Donny's pride and joy, a gift from his deceased mother.

Whatever his motivation, Micah leapt to assist the smaller man (Paul? Andrew?) in the defense of his fanny pack before he fully realized what he was doing. The would-be thief turned his attention to Micah, and began to throw punches. And then a strange thing happened: Micah, who had never been in what could properly be called a "fight" in his life, found his body knew exactly what to do. The fists came, and he blocked them with open palms. The feet came, and he was suddenly no longer within range. The aggressor tried to hit him, and simply could not. Micah had been hit and slapped and kicked so many times that his body knew how not to be, even, especially perhaps, at two in the morning.

Before sixty seconds had passed, the door of the dormitory burst open and two guards in blue shirts restrained, handcuffed, and escorted the man away. A third guard stayed to explain, in a voice that ensured that the entire dormitory heard: "You break the peace like that and you're out. Out of the second ring, out of the first. And when you go outside that wall, you don't come back in.

"And you," he continued, to Micah now, "that was some excellent intervention there. Where'd you learn that?" Micah sputtered, trying and failing to find an explanation that would not sound ridiculous. Fortunately, the guard took his blank stare for manly reticence and moved on. "Anyway, nice work buddy. I'll be adding that skill to your file." He scanned Micah's code and left with the protesting thief.

Micah turned back to the fanny pack man with what he hoped would be an encouraging smile, but the man had already laid down in his bunk again, his face to the wall, his fanny pack wrapped tightly in his arms. Micah followed suit. He lay awake a long time, the adrenaline still roaring through his veins.

The next day was much like the one before it, with everyone on the labor team on their best behavior, the events of the night before very much on everyone's mind. That afternoon, while Micah was absorbed in clearing a drift of shattered bicycles that blocked an alleyway he became aware of a small white shape in his peripheral vision. It was Sarah, waving.

"Want to take a break? Dustin and Arlo said it's OK!" Micah nodded bewilderedly. "Can I ride with you? I know a nice place, I'll show you how to get there!" More bewildered nodding, and Sarah was climbing up onto the running board, one arm slung around the roll bar, the other hanging loose. The Bobcat was small, a single-seater, and she was very close to him. He was immediately very aware of her scent, which was lovely. Her leg pressed up against his, but she didn't seem to notice.

"This way!" she pointed the way with her free arm, hanging from the roll bars like a pirate. She directed him deeper into the heart of the City, through already-cleared streets to a mostly restored neighborhood. It was demarcated by a thin but menacing line of silver wire. They passed through a checkpoint, Sarah waving perkily to the guard, whose stone-faced countenance opened into an indulgent grin at the sight of her. The stony expression returned as his gaze shifted to Micah, however, with a cold glimmer of steel in the eyes. He was here by Sarah's good pleasure, and by extension the good pleasure of her protectors, who were clearly legion in the inner rings. The Bobcat grumbled past cafés and storefronts, the same delighted greetings for Sarah, the same guarded glares for Micah. But there was too much wonder in these streets for the lack of welcome to penetrate. He had just spied a library, a library that contained books he hadn't read a dozen times, and his heart was leaping in his chest. He suddenly recalled his promise to Lorne.

"Here! Park here!" cried Sarah. Thankfully, there was lots of space, and Micah was not called upon to demonstrate his parallel parking skills, or lack thereof.

The hand-painted sign above their destination read "The Mission." A variety of rough-looking characters were gathered around it, smoking things and drinking things. Sarah hopped down, greeted several of them by name, and held the door for Micah.

He was greeted by light and warmth and a wonderful smell. The café was full of men and women who looked like Micah, served by men and women who looked like Sarah. She was greeted loudly and warmly by both.

"Everyone, this is Micah! He's new to the second ring. Please make him feel at home!" Over-wide smiles from the staff, looks of suspicion and jealousy from the clientele.

Micah waved, lamely. "What's that smell?" he asked.

Sarah smiled. "That's coffee, Micah! Doesn't it smell good?" she asked, as if to a child. Micah nodded, like a child. "Do you have it, where . . . where you come from?" He shook his head, and Sarah immediately ran to the counter and retrieved a steaming mug from a girl behind the counter who could have been her sister. She returned to Micah, who took the porcelain mug in his hands obediently.

He had many times read the smell of coffee described in books, and had longed one day to experience it. Now that he could judge for himself, he knew that even the purplest of prose had not captured the reality of the fragrance that rose before him.

But more so even than the smell, he was entranced by the heat of it. He was almost entirely certain that the beverage had been heated by electricity, and he could not have found that more enchanting than if it had been heated by a dragon's breath. He lifted the mug to his lips, closed his eyes, and drank deeply of the mythical brew. He immediately choked and very nearly avoided spewing it all over Sarah's white woolen coat. Coffee did not taste the way it smelled.

"Maybe some cream and sugar?" Sarah inquired benevolently, and then began to giggle, and then Micah began to laugh, and things were easier after that. The sugar and cream had transformed his beverage from an undrinkable bitter acid to an undrinkable sweet decoction, but he bravely choked it down as his heartbeat accelerated and he heard the singing of his blood in his ears. Sarah retrieved a green tea for herself and returned to the table.

"Is there anything you'd like to see in the City, particularly?" she asked. The library, came the immediate answer to Micah's mind. A swimming pool. A movie theater. A flush toilet. He choked these answers down with another swig of coffee. He was getting distracted. He needed to regain his focus. Micah cleared his throat.

"Sarah, I need to see a doctor."

Concern flashed across her face. "Are you . . . are you sick?"

"No, no . . . I'm fine. It's my brother. He has trouble breathing. He always has, but it's getting worse. I thought you might have something here that could help him."

"Is there someone looking after him, where you're from?"

"Well . . . yes. There's a bunch of people looking after him. That's what we do. It's why we exist, I guess, the Fold. That's what the community is called. And I'm a Shepherd, a . . . caregiver, I guess you'd say. For people. With, you know, disabilities. Of different kinds."

Sarah's eyes grew wide as her comprehension dawned. "That's amazing! Such good work you're doing. Like what we do here at the Mission, but . . . maybe harder. Different, anyway.

"I can see why you would want to see a doctor. But unfortunately everything outside of the Mission costs something. We have Roberta. She's a nurse. She's here three times a week but she's not going to be able to give you what your brother needs. You'll have to see one of the doctors, and that's going to cost . . . more than you've earned so far." She looked down at the table, clearly ashamed not to be able to help. Then, with false cheerfulness, "But I'm sure you'll earn enough soon! Arlo says you learned how to drive quicker than anyone he's trained, and that you clearly know a thing or two about machines. And . . . I heard a rumor that you stood up for a man who was attacked in the dormitory the other night." She turned red.

"I heard you fought the man who was attacking him. And not just that, but you were really good at it. In fact, that's why they let me let you in here. I've been . . . asking." She got up from the table, blushing furiously, turned, then turned back again.

"There's a service on Sunday morning, at the chapel at Dufferin and Eglinton." Micah stared blankly. "Two blocks that way!" she pointed. "It's at ten. In the morning. On Sunday. In . . . two days. I don't know how up on the days of the week you are, where you come from. Anyway, hope I . . . we . . . see you there!" She rushed off almost at a run, leaving Micah to sit alone with his undrinkable beverage, withering beneath the glares of the other patrons of the Mission.

He worked through the next two days with the incredulous but steadily growing understanding that he was good at what he was doing. The others who had entered in with him seemed to struggle, some with physical weakness, some with technical aptitude, and some with a strange, unnameable psychological inability to adapt to their surroundings. But Micah was coming alive in ways he had never experienced. Every morning he leapt out of bed with the airhorn that awoke the laborers, threw on his clothes, and all but sprinted to the works yard, where Arlo threw him the keys to the Bobcat with less and less trepidation.

When Sunday came, it was with an unfamiliar measure of disappointment that he left his coveralls folded by his cot and instead pulled on his Shepherd's habit. The habit was always worn to services in the Fold, as Martin would say (more to himself to anyone else), "to invest the garment, and therefore the role, with a sacral quality." It was also almost always the cleanest garment Micah possessed at a given time, as the habits were washed nightly to prevent the spread of contagions.

In the Fold, Sunday had genuinely been a day of rest, but today Micah found himself wishing he were heading for the works yard instead of the battered and smoke-greased chapel that stood on the corner of two recently cleared streets. The church was fairly busy, a stream of ragged men and women filing silently through the doors and across the stained linoleum floors to find their place in one of a hundred folding chairs carefully positioned for the purpose. His coreligionists took their seats and the fluorescent-lit sanctuary echoed with the squeaks and creaks of uncomfortable people shuffling awkwardly.

They had not scanned wrists at the door of the church, but Micah was sure that someone was taking note of who was in attendance, and was equally sure that that was the reason for the capacity crowd. He did wonder how exactly being counted among the faithful worked into the metrics of those gathering such data, and if it was in the end beneficial. But he was more or less there to seek the face of God. And maybe also the face of Sarah.

And soon enough there she was, among the worship band that took the stage to put the uncomfortably silent parishioners out of their misery. Sarah played tambourine and sang backup to the worship leader, who played old hymns with new verses on an acoustic guitar. He seemed encouraged when the congregation sang loudly along with the centuries-old bits, and visibly and unaccountably confused when the singing petered out when they came to the verses he had clearly written himself. They muscled their way through "This Is the Day" and "On Christ the Solid Rock I Stand" and "I Could Sing of Your Love Forever," and then a man took the carpeted riser at the front of the sanctuary under the pull-down screen.

He was a kind-featured man in his late fifties with a well-groomed beard, wearing vestments Micah recognized as coming from the Anglican tradition. A bishop's crozier leaned in the corner, but remained there.

"Good morning, everyone!" he called out in a delighted voice booming out of a beaming face that seemed terribly out of place among that congregation. "I'm Father Dan, and I'm glad you're here! We've all been working so hard, and it's good to take a rest together. That's what the Sabbath is for, after all!" There was something familiar about his cadence and delivery, though Micah couldn't quite put his finger on it.

The sense of familiarity continued as Father Dan launched into his exuberant homily, an exegesis on the parable of the laborers in the vineyard from Matthew 20. Micah had heard a fair few exegeses from a fair few itinerant preachers who had seen the Fold as their mission field, some of whom had to be forcefully seen to the boundaries of the village by Rufus, and he listened skeptically.

Father Dan knew his craft and his audience well enough not to push it past ten minutes, however, and soon Sarah and her team were back up on stage leading a rousing and mercifully orthodox rendition of "Shine, Jesus, Shine," and then coffee and muffins were served at the back to the long and orderly line of grateful parishioners.

Father Dan caught Micah in the coffee line like a predator at a waterhole, as Micah had dreaded he would. "Hey! I love your outfit! That's the Agnus Dei, right? The Lamb of God?" he inquired loudly and enthusiastically, pointing to the sheep Rosie Meech had embroidered on the left arm of the habit, many decades ago. "Are they vestments of some kind? A habit? Are you from a religious community?"

"Yeah, sorta. Yes, I guess," mumbled Micah, his endless anxiety concerning such questions in no way having prepared him for when they actually came.

"Well, I would love to talk to you more about it. Maybe at the service here next month, if you're here? Or if you make the next ring, you can find me at St. James' Cathedral, the other three Sundays of the month. Make sure you wear that outfit! I just love it!" And then Father Dan was gone, accosting other bewildered souls along the coffee and muffin line.

With coffee (creamed and sugared to within an inch of its life) and muffin in hand, Micah burst out through the doors of the church and took a deep, relieved breath of air that did not smell of mildewed carpet and old linoleum.

"Micah! You came!" came a too-loud voice and a touch at his elbow from behind, causing him to jump and spill half his hard-won beverage on the habit he now sincerely regretted wearing. It was Sarah, who had clearly been waiting for him. "What did you think?"

"I really liked the music," began Micah, lamely. "You're really good at the

123

tambourine." Sarah blushed furiously, again.

"I really like your . . . habit," she stammered, by way of answer. "Is it a habit?"

"It is a habit! Nobody gets that right. It's . . . kind of silly looking, but it gets the job done. We always wear them to church where I come from. Seemed too weird not to. And," he chuckled awkwardly, "I wouldn't want to come across as weird!" Sarah laughed, somehow even more awkwardly, and then a silence more awkward still then the laughter settled in.

"I better get back to the yard," broke in Micah, eventually. "I'm hoping to still get some hours in."

"Can I walk you there?"

"Sure. I mean yes. I mean thank you." They walked back the two blocks to the works yard, talking easier with every step. Soon Micah, riding a wave of sugar and caffeine and the novelty of a pretty girl who would listen to him, began to share his thoughts about Father Dan's exegesis.

"I just don't think that's what Jesus was talking about, you know? It's like Father Dan thought to himself, 'I'm talking to a bunch of laborers today,' then looked up 'laborers' in the concordance and thought, 'They're laborers, they'll like this one.' I'm not trying to be critical of the system here, but isn't the whole point of that parable that you don't have to earn your way in? I get that Father Dan's talking about heaven, but don't you think there's some . . . applicability here that he's missing?"

Sarah seemed very taken aback by this, and had no response but a furrowed brow. An awkward silence fell, thankfully broken by Arlo's rough voice.

"Back to do some work, are ya boy? Done praying at Our Lady of the Pretty Girls?" Sarah disappeared as quickly as she had appeared outside the church, and Micah was left alone with Arlo.

"No Bobcat for you today, boy. You're late so I gave it to Keith. You get a shovel. Time to get some dirt on your dress." And he threw Micah said shovel. Micah carefully removed his habit, folded it, placed it on the top of a wall of crumbled brickwork, and began to dig.

◆ ◆ ◆

Micah continued that work through the rest of the week. Sarah's previous praise had not been flattery alone. Micah had proven himself more than proficient on the Bobcat, earning even Arlo's gruff nod of respect, and spent many delightful hours clearing sidestreets, glorying in the easy strength of the machine. He thought of Thomas, and the Fold, and of September, and Benjamin, all fleetingly, and felt guilty when he did. But he told himself that he was working his way into the center, the place from which he could actually help them.

He saw Sarah occasionally throughout that week, though always from a distance. He would find himself loitering around the mission on his lunch breaks and after dinner but before the strict curfew imposed on all guests of the outer ring, ostensibly to ask the nurse a question about respiratory tract infections, but really in the hopes of catching a glimpse of her. When he did, she would smile and wave, and he would wave lamely back, and then she would move on to her business. There were always newcomers to process, although not many entered the second ring. He felt a flame of pride blossom within himself, then a cold drench of shame douse it as he remembered what he was celebrating.

At the end of the Friday afternoon of that week, Sarah caught him as he made his way from the works yard to the dormitory. She was dressed in white again and seemed to glow in the dirty brown dusk of the second ring.

"Micah, I was wondering . . . I was wondering if you would like to come to a party?" The request from the incandescently clean girl to Micah, still in his filthy City-issue coveralls, seemed absurd to both of them, and she laughed even as she made it. Before Micah could answer she began to qualify.

"Not as like, like a date or anything. But it's in the third ring and I know you've been wanting to get there. If you go through the next gate you could get to see a doctor. You'll have to, actually," she trailed off awkwardly. Before Micah had a chance to respond she began speaking again in a rush.

"My parents are going to the party, so I'm expected to be there. But I'm encouraged to bring a guest. They want to meet new, interesting people, and I think you're very new and very interesting." She trailed off again, red in the face.

Micah was also blushing, but found the words. This was clearly the opportunity he had been waiting for. "Thank you, Sarah. I'd love to go. It's very kind of you to think of me. When is it?"

"Tomorrow night. I'll let the guards know and they'll come and get you for medical screening when it's time. Um, see you then?" She trailed off a third time, then gave a strange little wave and turned and skipped awkwardly away.

Micah, flushed and glowing and humming again with adrenaline, returned to the dormitory for dinner.

20
The View From The Rectory

Working on Saturdays was optional, but strongly encouraged, and Micah needed both the credit and the distraction. He was taking nothing as a given, and knew that others needed to know his keenness. He had also fallen deeply in love with the Bobcat, and rose early in the morning every day to be there as soon as the works yards opened. He had blown straight through lunch and completely lost track of time when he turned the corner of a narrow street to find two men in uniform waiting for him.

"Micah Gault?"

He nodded overenthusiastically in an attempt to appear nonthreatening. A scan of his wrist confirmed his identity.

"Your presence is requested at . . . a party." The speaker, clearly ex-military, seemed very unimpressed with the task he had been given and with the thin, dirty recipient of his invitation.

"OK! Let me just park this!" Micah drove the Bobcat back to the works yards and came running back to where the men waited, disgustedly. "Here I am!"

Micah followed the men down the main avenue. The route had clearly been made a priority and cleared of debris long before Micah's arrival. The glass in the storefronts had been restored, clean and new, and the stone and concrete facings of the buildings did not bear the scars of the outer precincts. The avenue ended at the wall of the third ring.

The third ring was markedly different from the first two. It was taller, cleaner, and made of steel panels painted a matte white. At first it appeared to have no gate at all, until at their approach a high section of steel swung back without a sound, moved by unseen hands or unguessed technology. Through the gate, Micah had a glimpse of glass and polished metal rising in impossible glories before he was gruffly escorted into a structure to the right of the gate, flush against the wall.

Inside he was met by a slight man in his sixties with a neat mustache and thick spectacles. "Ah, an invitee," he addressed Micah in crisp but not unkind tones as he scanned the mark on the bracelet.

"You are Micah Barnabas Gault, late of the northern marches. I am Dr. Peter Zaretsky, and I'll be conducting your pre-entry medical examination. I hope you understand that no insult or implication is intended. We need to run a pretty tight ship here in the third ring. The wider world has been a bit of a viral wilderness these last few decades. Lots of strange and wondrous beasts living and moving and having their being in the lungs and hearts and intestinal tracts of the folks out there. Quite a few miraculous reappearances of creatures long extinct. We don't want any nasty little surprises reversing our own reappearance here, do we?"

Micah mumbled that no, he wouldn't want that. Dr. Zaretsky pulled what appeared to be a rectangle of dark gray cardboard from his satchel. He touched its surface, and it blossomed into brilliant color and light, surprising Micah very much. The doctor made some complicated motions over the rectangle with his fingers before grunting in a satisfied way.

"Ah, here we are. Your bloodwork came back from the first gate and was entirely satisfactory. Seems they've been feeding you well wherever you came from, though not quite enough for my taste. A boy your age shouldn't be so thin, but I suppose there are extenuating circumstances," he chuckled, gesturing at the tableau that surrounded them.

"You don't seem to be carrying anything too nasty, but I am going to have to perform a brief physical, if you don't mind. Can't be too careful these days, especially with Regis' daughter."

Micah had no idea how to take this final remark, not knowing who Regis might be but assuming it must be Sarah's father. Thankfully, there was no time for a response. Dr. Zaretsky directed Micah to strip behind a white divider where a brisk and businesslike examination was conducted. "Nothing out of the ordinary, young man. Some better clothing and you'll fit right in in the third ring. Now, let's get you moving further up and further in."

"Wait! Dr. Zaretsky?" Micah called to the doctor, who was already on his way to his next patient.

"Yes, Micah?"

"Do you . . . do you sell medicine?"

Dr. Zaretsky gave a quizzical look. "Occasionally. What do you need? But I'll warn you, I can't give opioids. Under pain of banishment."

"No, nothing like that. It's for my brother. He lives . . . where we're from, and he has a lung . . . thing. It's getting worse." Micah described Thomas' condition, repeating the diagnosis Dr. Chatterjee had given so many years ago, when they were boys.

Dr. Zaretsky's brow furrowed. "And you . . . you walked all the way here . . . for a puffer for your brother? And now you're going to put it in your bag and . . . walk back?"

"Well . . . um . . . that's part of it. There are others, with needs. A lot of others, with a lot of needs. Probably more than you have supplies for. So I was hoping to talk to . . . you know . . . the people in charge." Here Micah gestured aimlessly at the towers further down the avenue. "And I thought I could get help for, you know, all of them."

The doctor stared at Micah blankly. "More people with serious medical needs? Why so many? How are they still alive?"

"Because we take care of them."

"You . . . take care of them. They are your family?"

"Yes. Well, some of them. I mean all of them. I mean in different ways. But we need a lot of medical help. That's why I'm here, officially."

"A lot of medical help," Dr. Zaretsky said slowly, giving Micah a long stare. "And where did your brother get his diagnosis, if I might ask? It's very specific."

"We had a doctor, a good doctor, Dr. Chatterjee. He delivered my brother and I, and diagnosed him. But he died about five years ago."

"Not Sujoy Chatterjee? Ob/Gyn?"

Micah shrugged.

"We went to school together. I wondered where he'd gotten to. Some sort of leper colony out in the woods, eh? Well, that tracks. So officially, you're here looking for supplies and medical aid? Well, you'll have to go deeper in and higher up for that, I'm afraid."

"Yes," stammered Micah, "but unofficially, I mean personally, I was wondering if you have anything that would help my brother, that I could buy for this?" He offered the QR code on his wrist. Dr. Zaretsky pulled a scanner from an external pocket of his satchel and scanned the code.

"No, I don't. You'll come to understand the economics of this place in time, but it's enough to say that you're not even close. But never mind their nonsense." He reached into the bag and retrieved a small plastic bottle with a plunger on top. "You can't afford Ventolin, and it won't fix anything long-term anyway. But I can give you this. It's a nitrous inhaler. He might not have heart trouble now, but I can pretty much guarantee he will sooner or later, or someone else will, and this will save their life. Just better bang for your buck. Buy you time to get down here and earn some real medical care. Dosage and instructions are written on it . . . don't tell anyone where you got it. And don't sell it to anyone. If you do, I will hear about it, and you'll be out of here so fast it'll make your head spin. And I'll be in 'trouble' too, I guess, although I'm not exactly sure what they'll do to me. Fire one of their two doctors? The med schools aren't exactly churning us out these days."

He handed the triangle to Micah. "Good luck to you and your brother. My medical advice? Use the doses in this to get him here, and to do the work to get a couple of rings in, where we can take care of him."

Micah nodded, trying to keep his expression neutral. He knew exactly how many rings in Thomas would get, based on the rubrics of acceptance he'd seen in action. "Thank you, Dr. Zaretsky," was all he said.

The doctor nodded curtly, adjusted a setting on his scanner, and ran it over Micah's bracelet again. "There you go. Medically cleared for entrance to the third ring. Remember, money can't buy happiness, but it's more comfortable crying in a

Benz than on a bicycle, as we used to say."

Micah nodded again, unsure how to respond to this. The doctor winked at him, then gestured with a flourish towards the door of the building. "The city awaits."

Sarah was waiting outside the medical building with her own scanner. "Congratulations, Micah! I'm so glad you made it in. Can I show you around?"

Of course she could. Who else was going to? She made as if to take him by the hand, then, seeming to catch herself, withdrew it.

"Follow me!" she said, red-faced and brightly.

It was the city of his childhood imagination come to life. It was the city of the faded advertisements and the yellowed National Geographics and the Junior Novelization of the Film With Twelve Pages of Stills From The Movie, but it was more. All the familiar, obsessed-over details were there, preserved, but were fleshed out with a hundred thousand smaller details. It poured into his eyes and ears and filled his open mouth and throat. He drank it in and sweated it out through the blood in the cracks of his chapped hands.

Everything he saw was sharp and clean as a blade, the streets running straight and swept through stenciled tower block canyons as defined as if they had been digitally rendered, each building striking and unique. This was architecture, mankind considering the permanent mark he wished to make upon the face of the earth and then making it, correctly and precisely and eternally. This was not the rough wooden bulwarks against oblivion he had been born and spent his days in. This was real craftsmanship, and real artistry, and nowhere had any expense in treasure, toil or time been spared.

Micah stood at the gates of it all with his head thrown back and his mouth gaping open, trying and failing to process what he saw. For four full minutes he forgot himself and stared in wonder at the pure geometric beauty of it. For four full minutes he forgot about everything that lay behind the stainless gate and the high white wall.

Then his fingers found the plastic triangle in his pocket, and it all came rushing back to him. There was so much here, a lifetime's worth of new-discovered experience, but it was evident even from those four minutes all that was *not* here, and for the first time Micah understood what the Fold really was. He wished beyond any longing he had ever known that he had never left it.

It was very quiet within the great white walls. The shouts of the clearance teams, the roar of rubble pushed across pavement, the reverse-beep and rumble of the dump trucks emptying their loads was suddenly gone. In their place was a scraped-clean silence that felt like pressure on Micah's eardrums.

"It is pretty wonderful, isn't it?" Sarah's voice broke through his reverie. "It's hard for me to see it. I was only three when my parents brought me here, so it's all I've ever known. For which I'm very grateful, of course. My mom and dad were in the first wave of resettlers, up from a community in Wisconsin. Missionaries. They were with the group that rebuilt Milwaukee, and then spent some time in Chicago before they were recruited for the Mission here. You'll meet them at the party. I've told them all about you." The blush again.

"Speaking of which, I've had your . . . your habit brought from the second ring. I hope you don't mind, I've had it, um, sterilized. Would you wear it tonight? We are always so interested in the different cultures that have developed over the last . . . period of history. And yours is so unique. It's at our apartment, which is where the party is, so I thought we could go there early. If you wanted to you could, uh, have a shower before you get dressed." Now they were both blushing. Micah nodded furiously, and followed Sarah from the gate.

Sarah led him on swept sidewalks through gleaming streets, past well-stocked shop windows and immaculate galleries to a grove of mirrored-glass towers that grew where the Wall curved south toward the shores of the lake. He followed her to the megalith that she unselfconsciously pointed out as "home." As they approached the entrance, the weight of the tower above him became more and more oppressive, a vertiginous nightmare of displaced matter. It was simply too big, too heavy, too high. His animal brain began to panic. He would be crushed, must bolt before the trap was sprung.

Micah froze before the tower, unable to look away from the tapering immensity of geometric mass that had replaced the sky above his head. Sarah looked back to see what the trouble was, and a look of compassionate condescension crossed her face.

"It's OK, Micah. This sometimes happens to people the first time they see the big buildings up close. Just take my hand and look at me."

He did so. Her eyes were blue, and he soon forgot his existential dread. Slowly she led him up the sidewalk to where the tower met the earth. Glass doors slid open as they approached, startling Micah entirely, and then he was inside of it.

Within Sarah's tower was a second universe of silent hermetic warmth. The air within seemed not to move at all. He could hear their footsteps land on the carpet. He could hear the buzzing of the fluorescent lights. He could smell a variety of different fragrances, but all of them were pleasant, and all were intentional. Somebody had designed *smells*. The level of control over the environment was dizzying.

Everyone in the building seemed to know, and love, Sarah. In every corridor she was warmly greeted by every member of the uniformed staff and every well-dressed resident the same. Micah was met with suspicion and an undertone of protective menace that Sarah seemed oblivious to. They came to another sliding door, this one of brass, and Micah followed Sarah into a mirrored box. Micah had begun to speculate about what the box might be when a vertiginous rush of upward motion staggered him and left his stomach swimming about the soles of his feet. "It's an elevator!" he shouted, and Sarah began to laugh uncontrollably, and then he was laughing likewise.

They were still laughing when the elevator reached its requested altitude with a muted chime and the door slid open again. Down the carpeted hallway they went to the last door on the right. Sarah opened the door and called in, "Mom? Dad? I'm home, with a friend!"

Micah removed his muddy boots and Sarah led him down a white-carpeted hall to a wide living room. A man and a woman, older, well-dressed, and obviously Sarah's parents, sat in comfortable chairs across from one another with books on their laps and cups of tea in hand, framed by a wide picture window that looked out on empty blue sky. On the clean white walls were hung icons from a variety of traditions: Renaissance Madonnas, bearded Orthodox fathers, Christ Pantocrators of every shade and hue. At the sight of their daughter and her guest, they returned their books to the stacks that rose by each chair, and rose from their repose with wide, welcoming smiles. The woman Micah had never seen before, but the man was Father Dan.

"Sarah," he intoned. "Welcome home, Daughter. And Micah, if I recall correctly? My fellow vestment enthusiast?" The woman smacked him on the arm as Sarah turned her brightest red yet and stared fixedly at the ground.

"Uh, hi, again. I didn't know you were Sarah's dad."

"Evidently! But I'm sure my daughter has her own perfectly legitimate reasons to obscure her patrimony." He laughed. Sarah didn't.

"Micah. Ignore my husband, please," said the woman. "We all do our best to distance ourselves from him when we can. He's just so loud and . . . liturgical." She was tall and elegant and buried in a very large sweater.

"My name is Diana," she said, taking his hands in her soft warm ones. He could feel the bones beneath her crepe-paper skin. They reminded him of his own mother's hands. "And welcome to our home. This rude man is Daniel, as you know, and you should by no means feel compelled to call him Father. He enjoys it altogether too much.

"Thank you for having me to your home," began Micah tentatively. "It is very beautiful."

"Thank you, Micah. The Rectory, we call it. The city council lets us stay here as part of my compensation for services rendered. Weddings and baby dedications and funerals, mostly, and the former more than the latter for the first time in ages, I'm happy to report. I work out of St. James these days, the big pointy one downtown. Father Regis by name and vocation, though you can call me Dan. No Father is necessary, as Diana has made clear and certainly no Archbishop." The guffaw, the titter, and the uncomfortable look again. "Although that is technically the title." The women of the family rolled their eyes.

"By default, of course. But you must join us down there this Sunday. Absolutely magnificent building, a real miracle that it was spared during all the unpleasantness.

"Little bits have been passed on to me, but I was hoping to hear some more about where you come from. You consider yourself a Christian community, do you not? An offshoot of the New Monasticism school perhaps, from what Sarah tells me, a survival of the L'Arche movement, most likely. Looking after . . . um . . . disabled folks? Very commendable stuff." Father Dan paused, finally, and looked to Micah for a response.

"I guess you could call us that. We're kind of our own thing, I guess. Martin was an Anglican, before, and he set up our church along those lines. That's what you are, right?"

Dan grinned. "Close. Transplanted Episcopalian, to be technical. No kings and queens involved."

"Well, we have to be pretty . . . adaptable with our liturgies. We just sort of do our best, I guess. But yes, Martin started the Fold in order to take care of the people he rescued from the institution he was working at when the lights went out. And it's grown from there. Maybe you'd like to come and visit some time, see St. Stephen? Since I guess you are our . . . archbishop." Sarah's face brightened at this suggestion, while a shadow crossed Father Dan's.

"That's something I'll have to consider. I'm afraid you come to us at a moment of some uncertainty in the story of our city. I think my presence will be required by the flock here for the foreseeable season. But I appreciate the invitation!"

Diana strode forward again. "If you've heard quite enough of *that* sort of talk, please be welcomed to our home. Would you like some coffee?"

"Yes please! With some cream and sugar, if you have any."

"Certainly."

Micah spent a very pleasant afternoon with the Regis family. In many ways their home, and the work their Mission was doing, seemed very much in the spirit of the Fold. Dan and Diana were kind, compassionate and extremely well educated, as was Sarah.

After a breakfast of almost supernatural flavor, they sat on the thickly carpeted floor and drank sweet coffee while eating something called cheesecake that made his heart rate spike and his blood sing in his veins.

The Regis family had a gift for conversation and drew out the story of the Fold and Micah's journey even as they told their own family saga. There were tears, and more laughter, and the laughter grew more genuine as the day wore on. For all of Father Dan's bluster and pretense, it was clear that he was a man who genuinely cared for others, a comfortable man who wanted others to be comfortable.

Diana was something else entirely. "Dan is a natural insider," she exclaimed, with an exasperated but loving glance at her husband, "but I'm an Outsider. Like you, Micah. That's what they call anyone who arrived after the Wall went up. Although you enjoy the added designation of Moth, arriving after the lights came on. Lucky you," she grinned ironically.

"But didn't Sarah say she moved here when she was three? From Wisconsin?"

"My mom died. Was killed. On the journey," said Sarah.

"Killed by a band of desperate men," amended Dan. "And that was during the refounding of Cleveland." He smiled sadly, tiredly. "This is not, as they say, our first rodeo. We're part of a mission by the folks out west. The spiritual arm, you might say. This City is our second phase. It's going . . . much smoother this time. And of course it's here that I found my Diana."

"Yes, I came into the Regis story much later," Diana confirmed. "My sisters and my elderly parents came west from the maritimes about ten years back, up the seaway and around the falls. The Wall, or should I say the Fence, as it was then, had just gone up." Diana was guarded where Father Dan was gregarious, but when her confidences came, they were the more meaningful for it.

Sarah remained mostly silent, answering questions when they were posed to her and assisting her parents when necessary, but mostly just stared at Micah while trying to make it appear as if she wasn't. A tension had inhabited her body that he had not seen in her before, and she seemed increasingly uncomfortable as the day wore on. As Micah began to discuss in greater and greater detail the origins and purpose of the Fold, and his own reasons for making the journey to the City, he noticed her eyes flickering periodically towards the east-facing window, but thought not more of it.

The discussion branched off into increasingly esoteric territory, when sometime during the second hour (theology of the body), Sarah suddenly got up and pulled her mother into the kitchen, where a muted but obviously strained conversation took place. They soon returned, Diana smiling widely and perhaps a little falsely, Sarah's expression troubled. She crossed the room and pulled the blinds on the window.

"Gets pretty hot in here when the sun shines in directly!" she announced by way of explanation, although Micah had not noticed any discomfort and the sun had been fitful at best. Father Dan appeared not to have noticed anything strange about his daughter's behavior, and only pressed Micah further on his thoughts concerning the resurrection of the disabled body.

"You'll have dinner with us, of course?" broke in Diana. "You can also have a shower, if you like, and then dress for the party. It's just up a floor, in the penthouse. We can all go up together, and then you can stay in the guest room tonight, if you'd like."

Micah stammered his acceptance and gratitude. He wolfed down the dinner of prime rib and roast potatoes, and could not refuse the proffered second helping.

While he helped Sarah with the dishes, Diana left and returned with Micah's habit, crisply folded and a different color than he had always believed it to be. This immediately triggered a lengthy interrogation from Father Dan about its liturgical purposes and their implication. Micah held the garment up for examination, explaining that it wasn't really a habit, but more of a combination between an apron and a long hooded sweater.

"When Martin started the Order of Shepherds, he wanted it to have a strong

134

liturgical component, to remind the Shepherd of why they were doing what they were doing, that it was holy work, that they were dying to all the other lives they could have lived, just like monks and nuns do. So he made himself a habit to wear, and encouraged the other Shepherds to wear them, too. And then they realized that it was a good idea to have one shirt to wear while doing personal care, that could be washed regularly, in the river, to keep from spreading illness. Sort of like the scrubs that nurses used to wear. We have lighter, short-sleeved ones for summer."

The Regis family passed around the habit as if it were a sacred relic. It was of rough canvas softened by repeated washings, long in the arms and waist and with a deep hood and pockets. It had been passed down from his predecessors in the Order, hemmed and mended many times. On the breast the embroidered symbol of the lamb was a brighter white than it had been for a long time; the old familiar brownish stains were gone.

Micah felt a sudden and unexpected rush of anger at their expurgation. Those stains had been made by human beings: Thomas' saliva where he habitually rested his head, Donnie's mucus from when he had used Micah's sleeve to blow his nose so many times, in spite of Micah's repeated requests that he not. Philip's blood from the time he cut himself when in revenge he had broken the window for Micah's lack of attention. That physical evidence of the Princes was gone, replaced by a clean, pressed garment; a museum piece, an item in a reliquary.

Micah held his sudden anger down and forced what he hoped would be perceived as a grateful smile. "Where should I change?"

"In the bathroom, of course! I'm sure you can figure out the shower. Guest towels are all set out."

The revelation that was Micah's first hot shower was more than sufficient to drive all thoughts of stain-removal as a metaphor both positive and negative, and the mystery of the east-facing window, from his mind. The water, almost but not quite unbearably hot, pounded on his crowded skull and his knotted muscles, and he wondered without answer how he would ever come back from this.

After forty-five minutes he was finally able to force himself out of the shower and into the soft expanse of the waiting towel. Beside the towel had been placed a clean t-shirt, underwear, socks, and a pair of jeans ("Donated to the Mission, Micah, don't worry about it!" Sarah called through the door, when he had asked how much credit they would cost). He put them on, then pulled on the habit over the red scrubbed skin of his arms. It seemed coarse and harsh, and he wondered how he had borne it all these years. He stuffed his traveling clothes, which now seemed fit only for the burn barrel, into his satchel next to Martin's letter. He considered whether he should give the letter to Father Dan with a request that he purvey it to the higher levels of the council, but decided he would hold on to it a little while longer.

Micah emerged from the dripping bathroom into the good-natured laughter of the Regis family. They were dressed and ready for the party, Sarah extremely beautiful and extremely flushed in a white dress.

Together they left the apartment and padded down the carpeted hallway to the elevator. As the brass doors opened on the penthouse floor a rhythmic, muffled pounding suffused the air. Micah could feel it in his lungs and in stomach, and it filled him with consternation. He began to sweat, and his heart seemed to pound in time with the sound behind the door. He was having trouble breathing.

"Micah . . . are you OK?" came Sarah's voice from somewhere to his left.

"What is that sound? I can feel it in my guts."

"It's music. Just loud music. It's OK. This is the party. Here, let's go inside. It's OK, you'll see."

Micah did not see. Inside the enormous penthouse apartment it was much worse. It was very dark except for where it was very bright, lit with strange, unsettling lights that strobed and spiraled and made it impossible to tell how many people were crammed into the penthouse, or what they were doing, or if they were even human at all. Micah felt like he was spinning, and then like he was drowning. All through the maelstrom of sight and sound shape after roughly human shape kept approaching and introducing itself and shaking his hand and shouting questions over the music, questions he could not begin to answer. When an island in his vertigo briefly appeared, Micah would search the faces and costumes that approached him for some clue as to who might hold authority here, to whom he might give Martin's letter, of whom he might beg an audience, to achieve his goal and then get as far away from this room as possible. But no very likely candidate recommended themselves. They all seemed equally glorious, equally important, to behold him equally with the same curious and amused benevolence. And then the spinning and the breathless nausea returned.

Micah was not the only object of interest for the glorious and important ones. Others began to enter the apartment, clearly outsiders. A young Buddhist monk in saffron robes. A woman with a shaved head and haunted eyes that gave credence to her mumbled claim, when pressed by her hosts, that she saw visions. A man dressed, if Micah's historical reading was correct, as Elvis Presley, who sang strange, unsettling songs at the slightest provocation. All these and a dozen others were greeted and admired with the same brand of detached interest with which he was being questioned, and Micah began to understand that he had not been invited here as an ambassador for a diplomatic audience, but as something else entirely. The panic attack swelled to its crescendo, and soon most of his attention was paid toward his attempts not to vomit on any of the ever-changing shapes around him.

At some point in the nightmare, one of the shapes pressed a glass into his hand. Desperate for some mutually human activity to take part in, he threw it back and swallowed it in a single gulp. It was not water, as he had believed it to be, and it burnt his throat as it went down. He had drunk alcohol before, but never anything Rufus had not made in his cabin. These drinks were not like those drinks.

Almost immediately the panic began to subside and his heart rate began to slow. He was suffused with a warm glow, and time seemed to pass at a more leisurely pace. All seemed suddenly to be more or less OK. He forgot his troubles and his anxieties. He wished all mankind well, and knew in his heart that mankind wished *him* well. He had entered the warm womb at the heart of all things and was cradled in the hand of all that had been and was and would be.

Everyone around him was beautiful, and kind, and unaccountably interested in him. Figures shining like gods approached him and asked questions about the mundane details of his life. A widely impressive man in a tuxedo approached and began quizzing Micah about infrastructure in the Fold. Micah stammered through some clearly unsatisfactory answers about drainage and repurposed septic tanks.

A woman in a ballgown began to cry while telling him about her long-dead brother, who had had cerebral palsy. Micah awkwardly accepted her embrace but could find nothing to say but "I'm so sorry" over and over again until he was able to extricate himself.

He had passed through half a dozen similar encounters, searching for Sarah and her parents, when suddenly Father Dan was in the center of the room, lit from above and tapping his glass.

"Thank you all for coming! If I may be forgiven my eccentricities, I would like to make a toast!" He raised his glass, and the rest of the guests did the same.

"To our Lord, on this His Good Friday! Who suffered in our stead, that we might not. Amen!" The crowd echoed the Amen with varying degrees of irony. Micah's head was reeling again. It was Good Friday? That much time had passed? Back in the Fold Martin would be holding his midnight vigil for any who cared to join, and the altar at St. Stephen would be covered in the old black bedsheet they used every year. June Hayward would be crying as they read the story of the Passion, as she did every year.

The revelation of the day horrified Micah for reasons he could not have readily named, and as the music and the vertiginous lights resumed, his sense of nightmare doubled.

Seeing his obvious discomfort, Father Dan approached and offered Micah a glass with something brown in it. He took a deep swallow of his own and sighed.

"It's a lot, isn't it, son? It's a new world. But it's the old world too. This is not how I want to be marking today. But it's what they can stomach, for now. There'll be time for more, and better, later. In the meantime, drink that down. It'll help."

Micah obeyed. He was surprised to find that it was full of bubbles that danced in his mouth and his throat and his stomach. He chased the bubbles with more bubbles. It was a delightful sensation. There was ice in the drink too, as well as the lovely bubbles, and he began to giggle at the notion. Just like the advertisements in the old car magazines he had memorized. He drank the rest of the bubbles down, crunched the ice in his teeth. Father Dan was gone, replaced by someone claiming the title of hospital administrator who was asking pointed questions about triage strategies in the Fold. His reticence and anxiety gone, Micah began to enunciate and elucidate as he had never done before. He answered every question posed to him with a confidence he had never known before, oblivious to the look of increasing horror on the hospital administrator's face. All that talking made him thirsty, but fortunately relief came readily to hand.

He heard himself expostulating the philosophy of the Fold to a passing professor, how that philosophy was expressed in policy and action, flaws in its execution, plans for the future. A crowd of gods gathered around him, apparently hanging on his every word, transfixed by the glory of his language and the utopia of virtue they described. He saw Sarah behind them, staring at him intently. The look on her face was surprising, more consternation and concern, even horror, than admiration.

He was momentarily taken aback by this, but the gods around him seemed so enraptured and delighted by all he had to say that he put this anomaly out of his mind and continued on, in more and more detail, at greater and greater volume. He felt wonderful. He would have so many helpful notes for Rufus when he returned, who clearly had much to learn about the art of fermentation.

He was reaching the climax of his dramatic account of the time Doug McKeen had fallen through the ice while skating when he began to stagger and sway. Sarah swooped in and, with a firm hand on his elbow, guided him away from the main body of the party and out onto the balcony, ignoring his protestations that his audience would never learn how the story ended. The night air was cold, the spangled constellation of the city lights below dazzling and disorienting.

"Micah, I think you should get out of here and find some place to lie down before you hurt yourself. Also I don't think you should be telling some of these stories to these people."

"I can't lie down here! I don't know whose house this is. What if they get mad?"

"I don't mean lie down here. Come with me, you can have a rest in our spare bedroom."

Micah, ever obedient, took her proffered hand and let her lead him out of the party room, down the hall to the elevator, and back to the Regis apartment. She pushed him into the spare bedroom and closed the door while he collapsed onto the bed and slid sidewise into sleep.

He was awoken the next morning by the sun lancing painfully in through the east-facing windows. He was alone. At some point, likely during one of the many half-conscious trips he recalled taking to the washroom in the night, he had changed (been changed?) into a pair of soft cotton pajamas. He remembered the lights, the wonderful lights, out the bathroom window next to the toilet. A city of stars. Micah looked around the room, and found his habit cleaned and folded on the bedside table and his satchel hanging from a hook on the door.

He dressed quickly with a pounding head. He needed to use that beautiful washroom again, very badly. He stumbled out of the spare bedroom and down the hall to the kitchen, where he found Sarah making scrambled eggs. She jumped and spun around, wide-eyed and strangely guilty, when he cleared his throat. "I'm, umm . . . up. I'm just going to use the washroom."

Sarah did not respond. Her jaw clenched and her lips pursed until they formed a dead white line in her face. Several seconds passed, until finally with great effort she nodded. There were tears in her eyes.

Micah was baffled by this response, but the urgency of his need overruled any further questions. He hurried down the hall, and was soon enjoying the warm clean glories of the washroom.

The porcelain seat was warm, the door locked (never a possibility in the Fold due to safety concerns), and the room was silent. No one would bother him here. He could take his time, do what he needed to do, and flush it away. No one would know. It would be his own, private business. He shivered with delight at the novelty of it.

Lost in the experience, Micah's gaze wandered out of the window that opened next to the toilet. The light that poured in was intoxicating, the view spectacular. From this height, the rings of the city were laid out like heraldry. Another dozen or so towers sprang up around the Regis', rising in a gleaming grove, a copse of trees young and vibrant and shining in the morning sun. The inner barricade ringed them round like a walled garden. Beyond it, the tight geometry of the streets of the second ring spelled out its statement of order into chaos. He recognized the pattern of those streets, and gave a little "Ha!" when he spied the tiny white and orange shape of the Bobcat working its way along one horizontal arm of the grid. He looked for the three or four streets that he himself had cleared, then realized the window looked east, across a section of the city he had not yet visited.

From this elevation he could see beyond the eastern stretch of the Wall, to where it met the waters of the lake, shining and magnificent in the early afternoon sun. Beyond the outer ring was a wide, gray waste written with an endlessly repeating arrangement of geometric shapes, the same illegible hieroglyphic phrase written out again and again across the face of the land. But between the wall and the wasteland was something he could not account for.

At first glance, it looked as if something were growing on the perfect curve of the outer wall, some fungus or rust that had gathered there. It was made up of different shades of brown and gray, with the odd flash of bright primary color, and the growth was moving and shifting as he watched, as if it were alive. Micah's hand moved to his satchel on the floor beside the toilet, and withdrew his ancient binoculars.

Cognizant of the absurdity of his situation, but too curious to be bothered by it, he raised the binoculars to his eyes, his pants around his ankles on the toilet where he sat.

They were definitely people; seemingly another collection of wanderers such as he had joined at the northern gate. But this was a gathering of an entirely different nature. There was no order here, no organization. No one seemed to be coming in or out. He looked closer, adjusted the focus on the binoculars. There was no gate at that eastern edge, no little white tent. There was just a mass of bodies where the wall met the lake, and as he examined them, he could see that many of the bodies lay unmoving on the ground.

What motion there was were chaotic and confused; the movements of people used to guidance, accustomed to being led, who are suddenly without the care they have been taught to require. There was a pattern to the motion of the masses on the eastern wall that was horribly familiar. And suddenly he knew what he was looking at.

Micah put the binoculars down, got up from the toilet, pulled up his pants. He felt no anger, no sadness, no disappointment. He felt nothing but a dull awareness that he had always known that this would be the case. It always was, always had been. But now the anger was rising, and he was grateful for it.

21
Penance

Sarah was sobbing. "You don't understand, Micah. It's just for a while. There's no other way. Not yet."

The blood roaring in his ears and hot tears filling his eyes, Micah gave himself over to his anger: "You sit here, eating and drinking and talking about Jesus, while they starve to death, while they freeze!" He turned to Father Dan. "You're an . . . an Archbishop! You're allowing this here? Within sight of your window? How?"

Father Dan put out his hands in a conciliatory gesture.

"I've tried, Micah. I've spoken to the council so many times. There's a plan for this place, a plan that's worked in other cities. But it has to be adhered to extremely carefully. You can't rush things, or the whole system falls apart. The council has promised to help them, to let them in, just not yet. We don't have the infrastructure yet. We haven't reached that stage of the plan. We'd all starve. You must see. You must listen to reason. In the meantime, we do what we can. We keep order, even there. And we have done so much good. Saved so many lives. Sarah and her friends, down at the gate every day . . ."

"Is that all you're willing to do, then? Enough to let you sleep at night? Enough to keep the wrath from your door? This isn't faith, Dan. It's just . . . playing dress up."

Father Dan squeezed the bridge of his nose between his tented fingers.

"Micah. You are young. You are so, so young. You don't have children. You don't have the same kind of responsibilities we do here. You have your ideals, which are pure and right and holy, but . . . you're young. You don't understand. You just don't understand," he repeated, his voice trailing off weakly.

"No," said Micah. "I don't. And I don't think I want to. Thank you for taking care of me last night when I was drunk. I'm sorry I threw up on your carpet. I have to go now." He pulled on his boots and slammed the door behind him.

Down in the street below the building, he heard a voice calling his name from high above. It was Sarah, small, white, on her balcony. "Micah!" she called. "I'm sorry! I should have told you." He looked up at her for a moment, searching for the words, but found none.

He turned and made his way to the gate that would take him back into the outer ring. The guard scanned his bracelet and opened a passageway for him.

"Going out, eh?" the guard inquired with a distant curiosity. "You Moths don't usually go back that way, until you're made to." Micah had no answer to this. He walked through the half-cleared ruins of the outer ring, head down, the blood pounding in his brain. He came to the gate, where he was scanned again. This time the machine gave a "Bonk" instead of a "Beep," and the guard shook his head. "No go, buddy. There's a block on your pass. Can't let you out."

"What?" stammered Micah. "Why?"

"Dunno," shrugged the guard. "Never seen this before, if I'm being candid with ya. We're here to keep folks out, not in. But somebody in the Inner wants to keep you here. You steal something?" His face suddenly darkened, and he put a hand to the gun on his hip. "You kill somebody?"

"What? No!"

"Well, you're staying here with me until I hear otherwise."

Micah sat down miserably on the ground with his back to the wall, waiting for whatever was coming next.

After several awkwards minutes, the silence was broken by Sarah, flushed and panting, running up the street without a coat on, her feet slipping out of her shoes.

"It's OK, Russell!" she was shouting. "I put the block on him. I just need to talk to him before he goes." She took Micah by the hand and pulled him into a cleared alleyway, away from Russell, who nonetheless continued to listen and watch, his hand on the gun on his hip.

"Micah," Sarah gasped, "I'm sorry. I'm sorry about my dad. I'm sorry about what you saw from the bathroom. I'm sorry about . . . how it is. And I know that's just words. But come with me." She took him by the hand and pulled him away from the gate, towards a white building near the dormitory. Her former reticent bashfulness had disappeared now, replaced by a cool, distant anger, and he was not its object.

Sarah swiped a piece of plastic past a reader by the door and pushed it open. "This is the Mission's supply depot. We have everything here, and we have discretion to give it out to those who come to the gate hungry, as we see fit. That is also my father's doing, so please remember that, too, when you leave here."

She pulled Micah inside and down the aisles lined with tall metal shelves. The shelves were loaded and groaning with the necessaries of life: dry goods, canned soup and fruits and vegetables, flats of water bottles. The next aisle revealed sleeping bags, winter coats, rows of footwear in different sizes. Then, first aid supplies.

"Micah, you need to look at this. This is all that we have. This is the entirety of our surplus. If we give it all away, it might help some of those people. But then it's gone, and it'll take years to restock. Meanwhile, we have a hundred more refugees arriving every day. Shouldn't we have something to give them?" Micah sputtered and rumbled, but could not find a response acceptable to himself. Sarah cut off his attempts:

"Nevertheless, I'm giving it to you, by way of penance. I stole the key from my dad, although I think he would have given it to you himself if you gave him a little more time. Take whatever you can carry, and give it to the people you saw out our window. It won't be enough, so you'll have to decide just like we did, but I suppose you need to try. Take care of them."

Micah stood and gawped at the priceless horde in front of him for a minute, then turned to Sarah.

"Come with me. Come and help them with me."

A look of longing crossed Sarah's face, and for a moment he could see the affirmation on her lips. But it passed, and was replaced by an expression of profound sadness. "I'm sorry, Micah. My life is here, and I can't leave it."

"You don't have to leave then. Tell them to open the gates. Let them in. Make your dad do something."

"It's just not that simple. We've tried. We've talked to the leadership. But my family's place here is . . . precarious. We could be kicked out for what I've already done to help you. You don't know these people. They're frightened. Traumatized. They won't allow anything to threaten what they've got here.

"Everything here is a lot more fragile than it seems. There are cracks in the foundations, and believe it or not, my parents put a lot of them there. They want what you want, but they've got me and a lot more to think about. They're as radical as they can afford to be, but they have a lot to lose. And I'm worried, no, terrified, about what my dad is going to do. He hides it very well, but he yelled at you because everything you said was already inside of him. He was already on the edge of doing something, and you come into his living room, and start pushing him on the ledge."

Micah opened his mouth to object, but Sarah raised her hand and shook her head.

"No. Listen to me. Stop asking for impossible things you don't understand and let me help you in the way that I can." She led Micah deeper into the depot and began handing him items that he dumbly began packing into his backpack. As they reached the end of the aisle he broke in again.

"It can't be worth the price. Whatever you build here is going to have something dark at the heart of it. You'll all be implicated. It'll haunt this city forever."

Sarah turned, eyes full of angry tears. "You think I haven't heard all this before? You think you're the first? You think my parents haven't thought of this, that I haven't lain awake listening to them fighting about it? Tell me this, Micah, what thing built with human hands is not bloodstained back to its beginning? What have we ever made that's pure? Not this city, no, but I'd be willing to bet not your Fold either. We can only do what we can do. We can only do our best. And this is mine. And I'm sorry it's not more, but this is it. So fill up your bag, and go, before they realize what I'm doing. Please close the door when you're done."

She walked back to the door of the depot, then turned.

"I have to go now. I have to try to explain this to my parents, have to try to talk my dad out of shooting himself, or somebody else." Sarah took a deep ragged breath.

"Someone else is coming to help you. Wait here until they come. I can't be seen here with them. If we're linked to this, it's over for the Regises." She lingered in the doorway for a moment, studying Micah's face with an inexpressible sorrow in her eyes. "Goodbye," she said in a flat, dead voice, and then she was gone. The magnetic lock clicked behind her.

Micah was left in the silence of the depot, alone with the sound of his heart pounding in his ears and a strange static in his brain, waiting for his mysterious benefactor. Mechanically, he began a mental triage of needs, and began to fill the empty corners of his pack and the pockets of his coat accordingly. Food first, then first-aid supplies, then extra winter clothing. Socks. Toques. Mitts.

He heard a tone from the card reader on the other side of the door and the lock slid back. The door swung open, and Dr. Zaretsky slipped through and pulled it shut behind him.

"Mr. Gault. We meet again. Causing trouble for the Regises, I see? Which means trouble for us all. But anyway, that's neither here nor there now. Sarah has asked a favor of me, and I never could say no to that little girl. So here it is."

He began pulling pill bottles and packaged syringes out of the large square pockets of his frayed army coat. "Antibiotics, painkillers, sedatives, et cetera. Everything I'm not supposed to be giving away. Offenses worthy of exile, every single one. But it's the least I can do.

"Take them, and go. Put them to good use. Put yourself to good use. And pray for us here. We will need it." And with that he was gone, and Micah was alone again in the depot.

He removed his habit from his bag to make room for the medical supplies, and put it reluctantly on over his clothes. He removed his father's tent, as well. It would hold only two, and therefore would be of no use on the coming journey. He put it sadly on the tall metal shelf, wondering what they would make of it when it was discovered there. It felt like it should be buried, though it seemed just as poetic to be left unceremoniously.

When he was absolutely sure he couldn't fit a single item more into any of his repositories, he switched the light off and closed the door to the depot. The lock clicked behind him.

Slowly and with a bent and burdened back, Micah made his way to the gate of the outer ring. Halfway to the gate Arlo came rumbling up beside him on the backhoe.

"You headed out, kid? You got that look about you."

Micah simply nodded an exhausted acknowledgement, unable to bear the burden of another explanation, another debate with another person whose mind had already been made up long before Micah had arrived. They knew. They all knew the cost of entering the rings, and had decided it was a price they could afford to pay. He had nothing left to say to them.

But Arlo surprised him. "I get it, ya know. It's them folks out on the eastern edge, right? That's what they do to you. They get in your head, and they drive you crazy." He sighed heavily, staring himself with his washed-out blue eyes, out through the crags of his weather-ravaged face.

"I've seen a few like you. Not lots, but some. They go to try to help. I don't know if they do or not. But they don't come back." His face broke into the saddest grin Micah had ever seen.

"I'll give you a ride to the gates, though. I guess that'll have to be enough for my conscience today. C'mon up, kid." He reached down a gnarled hand and pulled Micah up into the cab, and they rumbled to the gate, where Russell waited. This time when he scanned Micah's bracelet, it beeped obediently.

"Can you do me a favor, Russell?" asked Micah.

"What's that, Micah?"

"Can you cut this bracelet off me? I don't have any scissors on me."

"You sure about that? Whatever you earned will be lost. You'll have to start over."

"Yeah. I don't think I'll need it again."

Russell shrugged. "If you insist . . ." he muttered, and passed a pair of snips from his uniform.

Micah cut through the durable plastic band and handed it to Arlo. "For the ride. And for letting me drive the Bobcat." Arlo barked a gruff "Thanks," his eyes suspiciously bright.

Russell pushed his button, and Micah was expelled by the City through its white-painted gate.

22
East of Eden

Benjamin was nowhere to be seen on the other side of the Wall, although he could see other former members of the Anawim, several of them, who carefully avoided his gaze. Without any other direction, Micah began to follow the Wall.

The whitewashed rubble curved slowly to the west as he followed it, cutting a smooth arc through the broken concrete flatlands. Slowly the curve revealed the blue expanse of the great lake by which the City lay.

Where the Wall met the lake in an unfinished causeway of broken rebar, Micah saw clearly what he had only dimly glimpsed from the washroom in the Regis' apartment: there on the frozen shore of the lake, in the lee of the high white Wall, was a second City.

The initial shock had already been processed. He had examined the scene carefully through his binoculars from his vantage point on the warm toilet seat, and he knew exactly what he would find. Micah didn't feel angry, or sad, or even disgusted. He felt nothing at all—just a cold, dead quiet that filled his heart and limbs and stopped up his ears until he seemed to be trudging through a silent world. He already knew what he was going to do. He had already come to the conclusion that there was no real decision to be made.

Without breaking stride, and without looking to the right or to the left, he pushed his way through the ragged ring of broken shacks and cardboard boxes, the plywood sheets propped up with sticks and the tents made of garbage bags—the dwellings of people who had not learned to keep themselves alive. In his peripheral vision he saw the corpses, the many, many corpses, and then he was surrounded by living men and women who looked like corpses but who grabbed at his hands and his clothes and pulled the pack from his back as he approached. He saw the ASL signs first—"Food" and "Eat" and "Hungry" and "Please"—and then came the voices, cracked and hoarse and weak.

"Please mister! Do you have food?"

"Have dinner soon?"

"Thirsty! Drink please!"

"Is it time for breakfast? Did they forget?"

There were dozens of them—men, women and children—all of them emaciated; all of them sick. Vomiting even as he watched. Some naked in the cold March wind. Those who were able crowded around making their weak and pleading demands,

146

but many simply wandered aimlessly, and many more than that lay unmoving on the cold earth. He recognized Down's syndrome and cerebral palsy, Parkinson's and Alzheimer's. He read the signs of dementia, of acquired brain injury and a dozen other disabilities he could name from experience. But those names meant nothing now.

Princes. His old private designator echoed in his head. Princes, without a Shepherd. Micah felt the panic rising now, his heart rate increasing, his breathing growing faster and shallower, deeply aware of the many unseen eyes undoubtedly watching from the walls behind. He remembered the exercises Dr. Chatterjee had forced him to practice, when he first began having panic attacks shortly after his ordination.

He inhaled deeply through his mouth, then pushed the air out and forced his mind to settle into that particular slot he reserved for extremely difficult situations in which there was no comfort or mitigation of circumstances to be had. Micah divorced his mind from anything but what was required for the completion of the task, a state of mind often necessary in the Fold. He forced himself into it, a sort of holding of the breath of the heart, and he began the first step of the task before him.

Micah began to survey the human wreckage strewn around the foot of the Wall. He walked its border: first along the Wall, then north along its flank, then east along its far side, then south again to the Wall. Then he walked through the center of it, stepping over corpses, pushing back the people who rushed him with a gentle but firm hand, counting. He could not think of them as people, not yet. They were a problem to be solved until he could come up with a plan of action. The irony of this mindset was not lost on him.

After twenty minutes' surveying, he came to understand that there was little point in making plans, in this time and this place. This was a task beyond what logistics or careful planning could accomplish. Logic, it seemed, was no longer his ally in this endeavor.

Because Micah was a Shepherd still, above and below and behind everything else, the oaths still held, and were binding. He was going home to the Fold, and those of the people here who would, and could, were coming with him. It was not a debate. The way of obedience was horribly clear.

Micah knew that even with Sarah's gifts he was not carrying enough food to keep himself alive on the journey back to the Fold without stopping to hunt and forage. From his initial estimate, at least thirty to forty of the hundred bodies he had counted were still alive. They would need to be fed before they could even begin the journey. They would need water. They would need better clothing than even the best dressed of them possessed. They would need tents and blankets against the cold nights of early spring. Most of them would need shoes. All these were to be had in excess on the other side of the Wall, but that might as well have been on the surface of the moon.

No, there was no preparation left to be done here. He had passed into what Martin had so many times called the Country of Miracles. He felt oddly light, and strangely free. He had never had a greater responsibility, and he had never felt less responsible for the outcome. He spoke to the God beyond the sky, and he asked for spring.

Micah stood there for a long time with his eyes closed, trying to find the will to open them. Suddenly, from somewhere in the wreckage he heard the twang of a bowstring and felt something pass his cheek at great velocity, followed quickly by the sound of an impact behind him. His eyes snapped open. Twenty feet away stood a young man holding a compound hunting bow. Before Micah had time to react, the man had pulled an arrow from the quiver that hung from his belt, and in one smooth motion nocked the arrow, drew it back to his ear, and released it. The arrow flew past Micah's head, this time on the other side. Almost before it found its mark the man was pulling a third arrow from its quiver.

Micah slowly raised his hands in the air without taking his eyes off of the young man, and held them high above his head. A moment passed, and the young man burst into unrestrained laughter.

"Not *you*!" he stammered. He pointed over Micah's shoulder. Hesitantly, Micah turned to look. Two coywolves, thin and no doubt desperate with hunger, lay dead on the ground behind him. Each had a single arrow in its throat. A third could be seen in the distance, running for the treeline.

"They come to eat the . . . the dead people," explained the young man, slinging the bow casually over one shoulder and closing the distance between them. "I don't let them do that. That's bad." He came closer and closer until he was only a foot away, and peered intently into Micah's face with a look of deep concern. "Are you OK?" asked the man again.

Taken completely by surprise, Micah's voice cracked into a chuckled "What?" at the absurdity of being himself found an object of concern amidst the surrounding horror. "Um. Yes, yes. I'm OK."

Relief blossomed across the man's creased and weary face. "Oh, good! I saw you stop and close your eyes for a long, long time and I thought you were having a seizure maybe. And I said to myself, 'That's why they kicked him out, that's why he's out here with us even though he looks normal and he's got that cool robe thing and stuff.' And then I saw those coyotes behind you and I thought they might try something. They do, you know. They took some of the others." A look of absolute hatred blackened the round, kindly face in which, for the first time, Micah noticed the familiar markings of Down's syndrome.

The dark expression passed as quickly as it had come, replaced by a wide and easy smile. The man grabbed Micah's hand and shook it vigorously. "My name is Alan. Did Scott send you? My brother Scott? He's in there," Alan nodded to the the Wall. When Micah shook his head "no," Alan shrugged philosophically. "Well, that's too bad. I was hoping maybe Scott had sent you.

"I'm trying to help out here. Some of these people are really not doing very well, and some of them are just dead. What's your name, anyway? Where'd you come from, before the City?"

"I'm Micah. I'm from a place north of here called the Fold. The people there, they . . . they try to help too, like you are. We saw the lights from the City and I came down here to see what was happening."

Alan nodded, wide-eyed. "The lights are so cool. I loved it when they came on, but after that they made us come and wait out here for a while." A frown crossed his face, briefly. "We've been waiting for a long time."

"Why did you have to come out here to wait, Alan? What are you waiting for?"

Alan's brow furrowed and his lips were set in a thin white line. "They said the doctors discovered some new thing. That it wasn't safe for us to be there. That we were going to make everybody sick." He closed his eyes. "They said our families would die. A lot of people said they were making it up. A lot of the moms and dads left, with their . . . special people. They didn't come back. But a lot of moms and dads let their kids get taken away. 'Doctors always know what's best, doctors never lie,'" he recited in a faraway singsong cadence.

"It was the doctors who took the special people away. They said they had a place for them, where it was safe for everybody, where they would take care of them. They said they just had to wait outside the City for a little while, until the doctors fixed what was wrong. They said that it was part of the Plan, and we *always* follow the Plan, right? The Plan takes care of us. That's how we got the lights back on, and the heat and showers and everything.

"By the way, have you had a shower yet? Showers are THE BEST. But I was really sad because I really liked a lot of the people that went with the doctors. A lot of them were my friends. We went to school together.

"So my brother Scott, he's an engineer you know, he said that he had talked to the doctors. You sure you didn't see Scott in there at all? Oh, you've got to meet Scott. He's the best. He's the one who taught me how to shoot. We used to go hunting together when we were kids, before we came here. Well, anyway, Scott said they said it was OK if I went with my friends, to help them out. He said they would let me work with them at the place where they were waiting until the doctors had figured things out. He said the doctors would give me a job to do, that I'd be helping the people who need help. He said he'd come and visit soon.

"But when I went outside with the doctors, I found out that they were just taking all those people outside the Wall, around to the side where nobody lives, the part you can't see from the walls. And then they wouldn't let anybody come back in. They wouldn't let me back in. I asked them what my job was, and they said my job was just to wait outside until it was safe again. But there wasn't any food, or any houses, or anything. We had to sleep on the ground.

149

"I kept waiting for the doctors to come back, but they never did. And you know what? I don't think they were really even doctors at all. Doctors help people, and this isn't helping anybody.

"But I am. I'm trying to look after the people who need help here, like it's my job. But I don't have what they need. A lot of them died. Terry died, and Anna, and Matthew died too. And it's my fault. It's my fault. I didn't do a good job. And I'm so hungry." Alan's round, cheerful face crumpled up, and tears began to spill out of his large blue eyes.

Micah grabbed his arm roughly, spun Alan around to face him, the anger suddenly flaring up white hot inside of himself.

"It's NOT. It's not your fault. It's their fault," he spat, stabbing a finger at the high white Wall. "It's the doctors' fault. It's Scott's fault. It's Father Dan. It's . . . it's my fault. Everybody who could have done something and didn't. Everybody who did something, and then stopped when they got scared."

Alan stared up at the Wall for a long time, his mouth open. Finally he said, in a small voice, "They had to send us away. We were going to make them sick."

Micah opened his mouth to contradict him but his soft heart intervened and he closed it again. "I'm sorry, Alan. I'm . . . upset. About a lot of stuff. But that's not your problem." He took a deep breath. "Can I help you with your job? I've got some supplies that will help a bit, and I know a place where we can go, where they have all the stuff to help . . . people who need help. There's good people there, who are good at taking care of people. There's food there. We'll all be OK, if we can get there. Do you think that's a good idea?"

Alan's eyes narrowed. "Are there doctors there?"

"No, not anymore. No doctors at all."

"What about Scott? How will he know where I've gone, if . . . when he comes back?"

"We can leave Scott a note. And I think he'll understand that you are helping people. Maybe he'll come meet us in the Fold. That's the name of the place."

"It's a weird name."

"Yeah, I know. Martin named it. You'll like Martin, I think. I know he'll like you."

"Well, OK then. If we can leave a note." The matter resolved, Alan quickly switched his focus in a manner Micah was coming to see as characteristic. "A bunch of the people started wandering away. I'm worried they're going to get lost and get hurt or something. I'll go get them and bring them back here, OK?"

Micah nodded and sighed raggedly as Alan ran eagerly away, yelling the good news to each haggard ghost of a human being he passed: "Hey! There's a guy here who's gonna take you to his house! He's got food and there's nice people!"

As Alan began to gather his fellow exiles, Micah finally allowed himself to really see them. He began to look into their hollow eyes and took the hands that were

150

stretched out towards him and gave what comfort he could. He began to listen to the thin, hoarse voices that had been beseeching him since he had opened the door in the wall. He listened to their cries for assistance, for information, for understanding. He began to accept the reality of their existence, with all of its implications. Then he took out his scarred black notebook and began taking down names.

Slowly he teased out what information he could gather. Names: Katherine. Rod. Dwayne Rutledge. Peter W. Mohammed "Mo" Abbas. Genevieve. Janice. Oliver. Robin. Travis. Jeremy. Sam. Scraps of biography here and there: My mom died and I had to go live here in the City and then they made me come out here. I used to live on a farm but now I have to live here. I was living with my brother, but I don't know where he's gone. His name is Tom. Do you know where he's gone? My favorite food is sausages, but there's no sausages out here. My cat is still inside the City, is somebody going to feed her? Diagnoses: I have diabetes and I know I'm low, I need to eat soon. Do you have any orange juice? I have seizures and I fall down when I don't get my pills, and I don't have any of my pills left. (Signed): I don't know where my mom and dad are. There was a big fight when they took us outside and they took them away. I'm hungry. Do you have any food?

For hours he circulated through the crowd, which grew ever larger as Alan rounded up the stragglers, the wanderers, and the fearful. Those who had the capacity had gathered around him first, asking him for something to eat, for something to drink for warmth, and again and again and again, to go home.

That had been the worst, and easiest part. He was trained for this, raised to it. Many of them could not or would not speak. Some of these had cards pinned to their shirts and stuffed into pockets. Micah knew what they would say and knew that the words would be enough to shatter what little self-control he still possessed. With a deepening and merciful sense of unreality he methodically collected the cards and letters in the pages of his logbook, scrawling a few adjectives to ensure that Lorne would be able to archive and match them to their owners, if they ever returned. There was still such a thing as professionalism.

He managed to get names out of most of those who could still speak, and a promise that they would follow him. He tore out pages from his book and made name tags for them. To those who asked for food he gave what he could spare. There was no point in rationing. There was not the slightest hope that the food he had left would feed them all, even for the day. But thanks to Sarah, they would at least eat today. He looked up at the Wall, where the sun continued to glint off of watchful glass. He raised a hand towards the reflections, his throat tight, and he said a prayer for a girl he would never see again.

When those who were responsive were gathered and made ready to go, Micah went to help Alan with those who could not. They were scattered through the camp, some lying among the corpses, too weary or hungry or sick to stand, some moving about intent on business of their own, some simply standing, unable to grasp the significance of Micah and Alan's presence, strong and healthy and speaking to them.

Their first task was to separate the living from the dead. Those who could understand his words and who had the strength to were already following. Next he went through the mass of prone and standing shapes, holding a bag of fragrant beef jerky aloft, and calling out "Food! Food if you're hungry!" Soon five or six gaunt shapes had shifted to their feet and were following him. He led them over to the people already gathered and divided the meat among them.

Then he went back through the children's village of garbage bags and cardboard boxes, and began to check each of the bodies that still lay there. He checked for warmth, and for a pulse. Most of them were clearly dead, and had been for some time. Several times he had to chase away vultures, and once a small pack of scavenging coyotes that would not shift until he hit their leader on the head with a large rock. And some bore signs of predation that could only have come from their fellow outcasts. After that, he sent Alan back to the group with the pretense of keeping any of the already organized from separating.

Micah counted thirty-three that he could confirm had died. He counted five that were prone and unresponsive but still alive. One by one he helped them to their feet and over to the waiting crowd, now growing restless and noisy. Some fought him as he carried them, scratching at his hands with long ragged nails. He tightened his grip on their arms with the practiced movements of long experience and guided them to the group.

The smell was unbelievable, even to one used to human waste in all its variety. The ground was thick with old feces and old vomit, and stuck to his boots like barnyard muck. From time to time he would look up to the clean white walls that rose out of the wrack like cliffs. There were people up there, small with height, but watching. But there was no sound from the City, only the flapping of garbage bags in the wind, and the cries of fear and anger and hunger of those waiting.

By early afternoon Micah was sure that there was no one left alive among the tide of corpses that washed about the feet of the City. There were a total of twenty-four survivors. Eighteen could walk without assistance. All of them were exhibiting varying degrees of illness.

Micah leaned against the Wall with Alan and ate a little bit of jerky, trying not to think. Thinking would mean coming to terms with the present and obvious truth that none of them were going to survive the journey. Below that truth was another, hypothetical one, equally grim: If he did manage to get them to the Fold, thirty-two new dependents would almost double the current population, a number that the Shepherds were already struggling to feed. He allowed himself the brief luxury of imagining a world in which he had accepted Sarah's invitation to stay, and immediately regretted it. There was no going back. Micah knew without a shadow of a doubt what Martin would want him to do, what the Fold would do in this situation. It was fundamental to what the Fold was—it was *their* Plan.

Desperate to distract himself from the implications of the situation, he turned to Alan and asked, "So tell me again how you get so good with that bow?"

A broad grin cracked Alan's face in half. "Me and my brother Scott—Scott that's an engineer—we had a farm with Mom and Dad, over that way," he said, gesturing to the east. "We had to be good at everything because there was nobody else to do it. I used to shoot coyotes and gophers, and the bad birds that ate the crop, and hunt too. When Mom and Dad died we were on our own for a while, until the City people came and invited us to come and live here. It was really good," he finished wistfully, "and then it was really bad."

"Well, I'm really glad you're here," said Micah. The two of them returned their gaze and their thoughts to the matter at hand. The sun was getting low and red in the west, the blue shadow of the Wall stretching away from their own.

Micah knew it broke every rule of wilderness travel to set out this late in the day, but most of those rules were no longer relevant anyway. There was no more food or shelter or safety here than there would be further back, up the hill. Their only chance was speed, to get back across that burnt plain of razed subdivisions and office tower stumps, back up into the hills where the shelter and the game were. Once they were there they could find a sound structure to shelter in, maybe a house with a functioning fireplace. He and Alan could take turns hunting, and build up a small surplus of food, and maybe, just maybe, have a shot at making the Fold, at which time a completely different set of insurmountable problems would come into effect.

He stole a glance at the restless men and women around him and tried not to wonder how many of them would still be alive when they reached the forest, tried not to think how much more possible this would seem if that number were smaller.

Micah turned his back to the bodies and the Wall and looked north, towards the darkening sky and the burnt flatland and the high brown hill that lay beyond it, and just visible beyond that the far-off snow-capped ridge, and the black line of the forest that crowned it. He tried not to think about the city behind him, of the warmth of the glassed-in lobbies, of the smell of food, memories which might as well have been of pictures in a book.

He walked over to Alan, who was speaking softly to a weeping middle-aged woman while he rubbed her back. *Anna: Forty-five years old, microcephaly, semi-verbal, mobile with assistance* summarized his Shepherd-brain, and he hated himself for it.

Micah took Alan aside and began to lay out his understanding of the situation to him. He hadn't known he was going to do this. It broke the rules of the Fold. Alan had a developmental disability: he had just suffered unimaginable trauma. Micah didn't know him, didn't know if this was information he could process right now, if he would panic or fall into despair or fly into a rage. He thought briefly of taking custody of Alan's bow before he spoke. But they weren't in the Fold. Micah had no authority here, and he didn't want any. Alan had the right to know.

Micah could see the fear filter into Alan's eyes, but he stuck out his bottom lip in a determined manner and Micah knew that he had done the right thing. They shook hands, and walked back towards the huddled knot of men and women sitting on the ground. Those who noticed Micah approach looked up expectantly as he drew near. Shepherd voice now.

"Hi everybody! We're ready to go home. We're going to walk for a while, until we get back to my house. It's warm there, and there's food." The gathering cheered, and clapped. And then Alan began to sing. His voice was strong and pure and carried over the wide frozen land and echoed up and off the Wall.

Skinnamarinky dinky dink
Skinnamarinky doo
I love you.
Skinnamarinky dinky dinky dink
Skinnamrinky doo
I love you.
I love you in the morning
and in the afternoon
I love you in the evening
And underneath the moon.
Skinnamarinky dinky dink
Skinnamarinky do
I love you.

As he sang, several others of their gathering began to join in. When he could resist it no longer, Micah joined, and together they raised their voices in a hoarse howl of joy. It was a strange, wild sound. But it was a joyful sound, a happy sound, a sound of hope. It rose up into the cold air, to the low roof of clouds, a sound much louder and stronger than it seemed such a thin and haggard choir could produce. They began to walk north, and as they walked they sang out the song again and again and again.

High above on the ramparts of the tall white wall, those who had gathered to observe heard the song rising up through the cold air. At first they were filled with wonder, and then they were filled with sorrow and wept, and then they were filled with a fear that they did not understand.

23
Easter Morning World

For two brutal hours Micah led the way up the hill, calling for them to follow him while Alan worked his way around the periphery of the group, gathering up the perpetual stragglers. Most of those who could understand them followed, glad for a sign of order in the individual hell of their personal chaos. But many of them just stood, growing anxious, growing afraid, beginning to panic. Some sat down on the ground. Some began to make their way back down the hill.

After the second hour of attempts, Micah knew he wasn't going to be able to avoid the inevitable solution anymore. He hated the idea, but it was that or nothing. He removed a coil of rope from his pack and cut it into lengths. By now it was clear who was going to follow, and who was going to have to be led. He separated those who needed to be led by the hand and tied a loop of rope around their waists and then tied the rope to the frame of his backpack. It would be agonizing, but it was always going to be agonizing. He helped Alan assemble an identical system of ropes attached to his own frayed blue nylon backpack, and then they began to walk north, up the highway, urging on those who could walk on their own, helping along and pulling along and finally dragging along those who could not. By nightfall they had traveled only two kilometers up the hill.

Jeremy Markson and Sam Wu were dead, and any lingering half-hope that remained in Micah's heart had died with them. It was just as impossible as it had originally seemed. All that he had accomplished was to arrange for these people to die in the ashes of a torched suburbia instead of beneath the walls that had rejected them. Maybe that was better. Maybe that was enough of an accomplishment. Maybe that was all the reason he had been sent here. Or maybe he hadn't been sent here at all, by anything more than circumstance and vanity and his own particular combination of savior and martyr complex. That was reason enough without bringing God into it.

The walls could still be seen below them from the shoulders of the great rise they had climbed. They were turning rosy in the soft evening light, and Micah was struck again by the serene beauty of them. They watched the lights in the city wink on in silence as they sat and ate the last of the food. To the north the road ran up to another wall: the starless, comfortless dark of night.

Micah had made the decision that afternoon that they would not stop at nightfall. They were on the open highway now, a road he knew to be wide and straight, mostly smooth and mostly clear of debris. It could be traveled in the dark with relative safety, and he knew also that if they stopped for the night that when the sun rose a large number of them would be dead. Better to be moving, to stay moving. That was the plan, in its entirety.

It was not a good plan, but there was nothing else that Micah could think to do. So he rallied them with false confidence and with empty promises of food and by taking them by their hands and by pulling on their ropes, and they continued their march, hour after hour, into the mouth of the dark.

By midnight he knew that he had done a terrible thing. The Brothers and Sisters of the Eastern Wall were simply too weak to walk any further. Already he was dragging Robin and Travis by their ropes, and soon he would be dragging their corpses. He had snapped at Alan twice when the young man had come to report that he simply couldn't get the stragglers moving. Alan had burst into tears, as Micah clumsily and exhaustedly apologized. But soon even those who were still relatively strong, those who understood where they were going and why, could not continue. When Dwayne tugged on his hand and said "Micah, I can' walk n'more" before fainting hard onto the concrete, Micah knew that it was over.

"OK everybody!" he croaked in the best Shepherd voice he could still muster, "we're gonna take a break now and have a bonfire." The army of ghosts that had marched about him all that day sank to the ground. Even the most vocal among them had long since ceased to make any sound, all lost in the same trackless waste of exhaustion. With numb and fumbling hands Micah built a fire and lit it and as the flames rose they revealed his charges, scattered unconscious in a wide constellation around the blaze in the center of the broken highway.

For a long time, Micah sat and stared into the heart of the fire, exhausted. Alan came and sat beside him. Neither of them said a word, and after a few minutes Micah heard soft snores coming from the man next to him.

He could barely move his arms and legs, but Micah's mind remained strangely alert. As his body relaxed, he allowed his mind to do the same. He began to pick through the numbed wreckage of his psyche, through the memories of the day and the knowledge of what was to come, searching for the final despair that he knew must be found beneath them.

Yet he could not. Try as he might, he could not find that sickly sweet sensation of self-pity and unfairness, the last poisoned comfort to be sucked from the marrow of his life. It simply was not there, and in its place he found a strange anticipation, a quiet certainty that something was coming. Whether good or bad he could not say, only that he found within himself the knowledge that these were not his final circumstances, and found himself waiting for that which would alter them.

Micah stood up, and turned from the fire, and looked up the rising highway to the black northern sky. He stared into it until he no longer knew what he was looking at, or how long he had been looking at it, or even who the "he" was who was looking at it. And then a single spark of light appeared in the middle of the dark, wide and deep and high. It danced unwinking in the void, slowly growing larger and larger.

Dwayne struggled to his feet and stood at Micah's side. For a long time neither said a word, simply watching the silent light slowly grow larger and larger, until Dwayne said in a quiet, raspy voice, "Here comes the bus."

And so it was. Slowly the light grew larger, and became a pair of headlights. Slowly the rattling roar of a struggling internal combustion engine became discernible. Slowly hope bloomed within his heart, and Micah began to yell, joyfully, incoherently, waking sleepers and chasing them off of the road. He unslung the hunting bow from his back, fitted an arrow to the string. Beside him, he heard Alan doing the same. It could be anyone, anyone at all. But it was not the Shepherds of the Fold.

It took ten minutes for the lights to reach them, ten minutes that felt like an hour. His heart was pounding in his chest, his hand growing sweaty on the grip of the bow. The men and women behind him began, in turn, to grow quieter than they had been during the journey thus far, and then suddenly to grow far noisier. They knew that something was happening, finally, something that was not walking. And then the lights were close, blindingly close, and the engine deafeningly loud after the long silence of the wasteland night.

For a moment Micah thought it was going to pass them by, to keep on going to the City and leave them to the dark, and for that moment he was relieved. But then came the squealing and the stench of corroded brake pads, and the sudden revelation of the ancient yellow school bus screeched to a halt in front of them. Before Micah could stop him, Alan had barrelled up to the door and was furiously knocking on it.

The cracked glass door folded back. Darkness within. The barrel of a high-caliber handgun emerging from the darkness, held in an unshaking hand.

"Excuse me! Excuse me! Can you help us?" Alan shouted into the weapon's maw, completely unphased. "We need a ride! My friends are sick and tired and they can't walk and we really really need a ride! We can pay you! I think Micah has money. Micah, you have lots of money, right?"

Micah hadn't moved, still standing, staring with his mouth open, when September came hurtling down the steps past Alan, tossed the gun to the ground, and threw her arms around him, tears pouring down her face. She felt like a thunderstorm in his arms.

"Holy shit, Micah, holy . . . holy . . . God . . . What are . . . what are you doing out here? Who are these people?" He watched the comprehension take hold. "You're walking back? All of you?" He nodded, too tired to explain, to meet the wild incredulity in her voice and in her face.

". . . Locked out . . ." he croaked, and it tore his desiccated throat. ". . . Left to starve. Going back . . . the Fold."

Wordlessly she fumbled in the pocket of her army surplus parka, many sizes too large for her, and brought out a metal canteen. Micah drained it in four ragged gulps and her eyes never left his face, wide with alarm, but steady.

"I'm sorry," he gasped. "Do you have more water? For them?" he gestured vaguely at the spectral flock gathered in the headlights' glow.

September nodded grimly, her eyes never leaving his. She did not seem to blink. He was reminded strongly of a wild animal surprised in its own territory. "Barrels and barrels. Food too, all I had left. This is Burrows now," she added, jerking a thumb back at the bus. Then she took her eyes from Micah's and began to survey the rest of the grim tableau.

September stood on the steps of the rumbling bus for a few moments, silent, her wide, unsettling eyes taking in the scene, the ravaged faces of the men and the women who had slowly come shuffling up out of the darkness, some of them pulling on Micah's arms now, seeking guidance and assurance, some of them seeking the warmth of the idling engine, others simply resting their hands on the sides of the bus, as if to test its reality.

"The City . . ." she said, in a low, calm voice, and closed her eyes.

"Is that where you're going?" asked Micah, his insides pleading with Heaven for mercy. Silence. And then:

"Not anymore. Get in. Get them all in." And September Burrows was smiling, a wide and reckless grin, for the first time in his experience. Micah found himself unable to look away. "Go!" she shouted, laughing, and then he was laughing, and their laughter rang from the scorched ruins of the sad old world.

The bus's stinking electric heater had been blasting away for hours and the shivering outcasts needed very little persuasion to take their seats in the warm, torn naugahyde womb of the bus. There was a seat for everyone, amongst September's gathered treasures and supplies. When all were safely ensconced, September showed Micah to her accessible supplies, and Micah portioned out a large handful of homemade granola and a withered but sound winter apple for each.

"Do you mind if I . . . stay in my seat here?" she asked Micah in a low voice. "I'm not quite ready for . . . them." He gave an encouraging nod, and got to work.

It took a long time, as some needed their apples cut, and a few needed water to be added to the granola, and the resulting gruel to be spoon-fed to them, but after the road this familiar labor was a joy. By the time everyone had something in their stomach, the sun was coming up on a cold, clear morning.

Micah climbed down out of the bus to where September was sitting on the bottom step, smoking her pipe and watching as the first rays lit the eastern wall of the City. He sat beside her on the step. The white Wall was red in the dawn light. He could just make out the wreckage that lay at its foot, and thought of the dead that slept among it, and of the living now sleeping in the bus behind him.

September took a long pull on her pipe and blew a smoke ring out over the scene. "Happy Easter, Micah. That's a big one for you guys, right?"

Micah felt a funny jolt in his stomach. He had forgotten. He grinned at the girl,

158

joyful, weary tears in his eyes. "Yeah, it is. The biggest one."

She grinned back. "I never really got it. Rabbits and eggs and chocolate and dead people coming out of caves or something. Pretty weird stuff."

"Pretty weird stuff," Micah agreed. "But all the best stuff is." He gestured around them, to the City, to the bus. "And I think you get it better than most." She knocked out her pipe, and got to her feet.

"Better get going. Running engine out here draws the scumbags out." He stood with her, put his hand hesitantly on hers.

"September, are you sure about this? You can go to the City. They would be glad to have you. You could be with your family." She shook her head. She was crying in her silent way, the tears cutting white trails through the engine grease that stained her cheeks.

"Not anymore. Not knowing this. I didn't have a choice before. But now I do. I need to know that there's a place left to . . . to not be OK sometimes. To be weak, once in a while. To need help. To fall down and not get left behind. So take me to your Fold, and we'll see if it's what you say. I'm not promising I'll stay, but I'll drive you there, if you show me the way."

Micah nodded and nodded, faster and faster, unable to think of anything to say. September turned and climbed up into the driver's seat, while Micah took a last long look at the City to the south before turning his back and following her. When she was sure that everyone was seated, she threw the monster into gear, and swung the wheel around and around until they were facing north again. "Ridin' the bus!" Dwayne roared from the back.

Micah put a hand on hers where it gripped the wheel with white knuckles. September wiped the tears and grease away with the sleeve of her coat, nodding also, and pushed the accelerator to the floor. The ancient idling engine roared to unsteady life, and the bus began to roll north up the dead highway, her belly filled with battered souls.

To have been transported from the grim, hopeless slog of the last twelve hours, with every mile begged and bargained and fought from his charges through the mud and the cold and the ash, to this strange, steady flight, warm and smooth and effortless, was like a good dream. But there are no smells in dreams. Here, there were: wonderful smells. The hot, powerful smell of the diesel engine; the sweet, rich smell of the bread and cheese and sausage and apples that September had directed him to, that he was now passing out to the dozens of grasping hands from the back of the dark bus; the altogether intoxicating smell of September's hair, so unique and so immediately recognized, as if they had spent a year together in Burrows and not a night.

Micah collapsed into the first ragged bench seat on the passenger side. He wanted to say something, anything to her of his gratitude and his relief and his joy, but the words would not come. It was not a time for words, or action. There was nothing to be done except to sink back into the seat, and to marvel at the hypnotic wonder of the Easter morning world slipping past through the cracked windscreen, at the yellow impossibility of the bus, its heavy rumbling effortless flight, and at the girl at the wheel, who had saved them.

24
Woodsmoke and Biodiesel

And so the long and solitary journey was played back in reverse at ten times the speed, in the joyous and howling company of the newfound Brothers and Sisters, high on velocity and biodiesel fumes and the fierce and sudden joy of a full belly. They came roaring back up through the wasteland of the burnt concrete boxes and up the high hill to Burrows. They stayed there for only an hour, long enough for September to retrieve her family's stockpile of rough woolen army surplus blankets and first aid kits, and for everyone to relieve themselves. Micah went with her as she shut the door of the house on the overpass for the last time, and again locked it behind her. They left the house on the overpass behind them, and September did not look back.

After Burrows the road began to worsen, and the easy flight of Easter Sunday became an increasingly difficult navigation of an increasingly difficult terrain. Micah, September, Alan and Dwayne spent two tedious hours hacking a path through an ancient fallen oak tree (September had an amazing collection of hatchets and axes, all of them kept incredibly sharp). But even when the road seemed clear, they were driving on tires that were little more than patched cloth, and by two o'clock the two spares had already been installed.

And even the fuel gauge in the bus dropped with alarming rapidity. September had strapped five jerrycans full of biodiesel to the roof of the bus, but that had been the last of her grandfather's carefully stewarded supply. By the time they had broached the third one, they were not yet home, and not yet near it.

But in the end it would not be the tires or the engine or the fuel supply that would bring their miraculous journey to a halt. As the sun rose on the third day of the journey back, they found themselves unable to continue to pretend that there was anything ahead that could still be called a road. Seven generations of the same family of beavers had turned the shallow valley before them into a black stagnant lake that rose to the shoulders of the drowned pine forest. They had reached the borders of the empty land that girdled the Fold, a country that the wilderness had ruled uncontested for three decades and counting. September eased the bus to a creaking halt where the pavement dipped beneath the still water and let it idle for a long time before finally killing the engine. Almost all of the Brothers and Sisters were asleep in their seats, and Micah, September and Alan soon joined them, utterly exhausted.

They awoke two hours later to the hunger-cries of their fellow-travelers. After the food was served out, they sat on the roof of the bus looking out at the gray tangle of bush as the Brothers and Sisters ate their breakfast rations. September stared at the black lake before them and spoke with a heavy heart:

"Nope. No way we're getting past that, over or around. This bus is staying here. We'll lock it up, set a couple traps, and come back for what we can't carry in a couple of days."

Micah nodded, grimly, pretending not to hear the part about the traps. "Listen, September," he replied, hesitantly, "the Fold isn't too far from here. Two days' walk, maybe. We can make it. It's going to be OK."

September sighed, and said, "Hey. Hey Micah. Stop it with that voice, please. You don't have to be the nicest guy or the hero or the martyr or whatever. You don't have to die for us, actually. Actually nobody has to die. I lived out here my whole life until yesterday, among some rough folks. I can handle this, if you'll let me.

"So please stop using that voice on me. Use it on yourself. I'm not the one who's freaking out. You had to get saved for once, yeah? It's not a big deal, if you can just get your head around it. And guess what? I get to save you, and I'm not quite done yet. So relax and let me think."

"She's right, Micah! You gotta keep it together! You gotta stay cool like me and September!" yelled Alan from below. Micah nodded, and nodded some more, and bit his tongue, and laughed.

"We're gonna have to walk it. It won't be that bad. It'll be rough on them," said September, gesturing to the Brothers and Sisters below, "really rough, but it's better than dying under that fucking Wall."

"Language!" shouted up Alan.

"At least it's April now, instead of fff . . . frigging March," said September, trying to avoid Alan's glare from below.

And indeed it was. The early sun that was shining down on them held an almost-forgotten warmth, and there was a gentle quality to the air that suggested that, at last, the warmth of true spring was coming to heal the old wounds of winter.

The Brothers and Sisters had become very fond of their bus and did not want to leave it, but Micah had dealt with similar scenarios a thousand times before. He applied the Shepherd's trademark blend of calm firmness and the promise of food until all were at last convinced that it was in their best interests to follow him. September hung back as they assembled by the bus. As the only one qualified to drive a bus, she had been very much occupied for the duration of their journey, and was only now for the first time really meeting the people whose lives she had saved.

September had never met a person with a developmental disability, and she exhibited the apprehension Micah had seen over and over again when a neurotypical person comes face to face with neurodiversity. She was visibly overwhelmed and afraid, but Alan was having none of it. He took her by the hand and pulled her into the crowd and began introducing her to each of the rescued, one by one. Alan,

162

in the role of protector, knew and was known by every one of them, and made it his business to make them known. Once out of the sacred driver's seat, September was mobbed by gregarious souls, taking her hands and asking her name and telling her theirs (Rod, Peter, Dwayne, Mo, Janice, Anna, Genevieve) and introducing those who could not give theirs (Robin, Sahi, Katherine, Oliver, Travis, and three men and one woman whose names he had not been able to determine). When the introductions had been made, they asked her every question they could think of, questions she could answer and questions she couldn't answer and questions that no one could answer. When Mo told her he loved her she began to cry, and at that time Micah interrupted and told them that they had better get moving or they were going to miss dinner at their new home.

Micah had been examining the condition of some of the other, less sociable Brothers and Sisters, and a fixed grimness had succeeded the relieved euphoria of the previous day. They were all far from healthy, but four of them were very sick. He recognized dysentery, fever, uncontrolled vomiting, and what looked like the beginning stages of tuberculosis. Many of the wounds he had dressed beneath the walls of the City had begun to stink. Gangrene was coming. They had to get back to the Fold, and soon.

Those who could carry packs were given them. Those who needed to be led were hitched to Micah and Alan and September, and they set off down the narrowing path around the pond, into the heart of the tangled wood, with many a longing glance back at the happy yellow shape of the bus. But the forest, so gray for so long, was not so monochrome as it had been on Micah's journey south. The early buds, little green suggestions of life, were scattered here and there throughout its tangled fastness.

All day they forced their way through the bush. September took the lead, following the trail when it was clear, consulting Micah when it was not. Alan patrolled the perimeter of the middle ranks, watching for predators of any species.

Micah took up the rear, herding the stragglers back onto the path again and again, prodding those forward who would not walk, steeling himself against the moans of protest and of pain. He had learned the art of this long ago, as any Shepherd must.

He kept a careful eye on September throughout the long, hard day. She was new to this, and clearly overwhelmed by the strange company she had found herself in. Her eyes were wide and her face pale and the strain was evident, but she was calm, and kind, and moved with a strong and steady pace through the bush. His insides gave a funny lurch when he looked at her, as if something of great mass, long secured, had broken loose of its restraints. He could feel it tumbling around inside of him, annihilating structures once thought eternal, altering landscapes assumed to be permanent.

As the sun began to set and the shadows grew deeper in the budding woods, the euphoria that had accompanied their miraculous rescue dissipated, and the old sense of the hopelessness of their situation settled over them again. There was enough food left for everyone to eat dinner, but not breakfast. Micah began to question the wisdom of leaving the bus behind. Night in the bush with an unknown flock of princes was a daunting proposition, and when it came it was deep and dark and cold and the Brothers and Sisters feared it.

But there were two luxuries afforded to them: an endless supply of firewood, and no further need to go unseen. So as the last light fled from the sky they built an enormous bonfire ten feet high in the empty pasture in which they had made their camp and gloried in the heat and the dancing light of it. The Brothers and Sisters gathered thick as moths around it and it became a matter of keeping the less wary among them from getting burned as they crowded as close as possible to the flames.

The last light in the west bled out of the sky, and the stars sprang into being in the great unbroken dome above them. They ate a reckless amount of September's carefully packaged and organized rations. Blankets and sleeping bags were shared as equally as could be managed, and as the Brothers and Sisters began to slip into exhausted sleep around them, Micah and September sat very close to one another and stared without speaking into the flames.

Sometime in the night Micah looked down and found his hand wrapped tightly around hers and felt her squeezing tightly back. Sometime later, he felt the soft weight of her head against his shoulder, and suddenly it didn't matter anymore how little food remained, or how many miles they still had left to go. There was the fire and the stars and the good thing that they had done today. And now there was September sleeping on his shoulder, and her hair smelling of woodsmoke and biodiesel.

25
No More Freaking Death Marches

The following morning dawned clear and bitingly cold. Soaked with dew, the sleeping travelers formed a corona curled tight around the still-hot embers of the smoldering fire. The Brothers and Sisters awoke cold and hungry and unhappy and became unhappier still when it was revealed that no breakfast would be coming. No one wanted to leave the fire, and no one wanted to go any further into the untamed woods.

They spent the day making their slow and tortuous way upward into the highlands that guarded the Fold, into denser and denser forest on a road that became more a trail with each passing mile. In late afternoon they broke through the wall of bush into an expanse of pasture the forest had not yet reclaimed, and Micah called a halt. He and Alan and September built another huge bonfire and the exhausted Brothers and Sisters tottered in from their scattering to collapse around it. When everyone had caught their breath, they shared the very last of the food, little more than a mouthful for each. There was much disappointment, and some anger: old habits and sleeping resentments that had been subdued by hunger and despair began to reawaken.

By the time order was restored, the sun had gone down and a hazy yellow moon was rising over the meadow. The Brothers and Sisters, exhausted by the day's travel, had begun to settle and drop off to sleep. Those still awake sat by the fire with Micah and September while Alan played forgotten tunes on his battered recorder. He knew a seemingly endless number of songs, most of which Micah and September had never heard, songs maybe no one else alive remembered. Alan had taught them the words to a few of them, and Micah and September were self-consciously struggling through "Yesterday" when suddenly there was a crashing sound in the treeline on the far side of the pasture.

Something large was breaking through the bush, and September and Alan had their weapons up and trained in a second, and then the sound of hooves came drumming out of the blackness beyond the ring of firelight. The nightmare-figure of a man on a horse materialized, shifting and eerie in the dim red glow of the coals.

Micah struggled to his feet, shouting in a cracking voice for Alan and September not to shoot, even as he fumbled for his own bow. Then suddenly the terrifying specter became his friend Rufus and the pasture was echoing with happy greetings and the wild laughter of desperate relief.

Rufus leapt off his horse and wrapped his huge frame around Micah, lifting him into the air while letting loose his rockslide laugh. His laughter continued to echo around the meadow as he fell silent and dropped Micah to the ground, suddenly taking in the rest of the firelit scene. The crowd of Brothers and Sisters, woken by the laughter, stepped out of the darkness into the firelight with wide eyes, one after another after another. Rufus stood there for a minute, nodding as he counted them. Then he sighed, and smiled a different kind of smile.

"Buddy," he said. "I think you may have misunderstood Martin's instructions a little bit there. But we'll make it work." He suddenly noticed September, standing in the shadows behind Micah, and Rufus drew up with a start.

"You know, I was kidding about bringing me a wife." September glared at him with her unblinking raptor gaze, and he blushed and turned away, stammering, "Sorry, miss, sorry. Not funny. Humor used as a defense. Not used to being around pretty . . . around girls. Stupid."

"September, this is Rufus. He is an idiot, and also my best friend. Rufus, this is September. She saved my life," broke in Micah, to put Rufus out of his misery. Still glaring suspiciously, September extended her hand. Rufus took it shyly, without meeting her gaze, and shook it. With obvious relief he took his leave of her and made his way through the crowd, shaking hands, getting names when he could, giving his own out to any who would receive it. When the Brothers and Sisters were finally satisfied, he sat down beside the fire, breathing heavily.

"Goddammit, Micah, where did they all come from? Who are they? And how in the *hell* did you get them up here?"

"We took the bus," called out Dwayne, from somewhere in the back of the crowd. Rufus roared with laugher.

"Never mind. Time for that later. You must be exhausted. Here, I've got buns and jerky and cider. Share it around. Haven't you been feeding them? They look like your fucking undead army."

"LANGUAGE!" roared Alan from his post.

"And who's *that* guy?" Rufus roared back.

"That's Alan. He saved my life, too. I'll introduce you. Where are we, Rufus? How far from town?"

"Three hours, on horseback. But I don't think your horse could get to the other end of this field in three hours. We'll stay here for the night. In the morning I'll head back and we'll send the wagons. No more of your fff . . . freaking death marches, brother." He looked around again at the ragged figures desperately feasting around him. Alan noted his self-correction and gave a curt nod of approval. Rufus nodded back manically and kept nodding.

"I can't believe this. I can't believe you did this. I mean, I'm sure you had your reasons, but . . . *shit*, Micah." Disconcertingly, Micah recognized fear in Rufus' eyes. He could not recall seeing that particular emotion there before, and it chilled him.

They spent the night by the fire, Rufus and September insisting that Micah sleep while they shared the watch. After a show of reluctance he agreed, after assuring September that she was safe with Rufus. She nodded, clearly unconvinced, and kept the pistol on her belt in prominent view.

Micah slept through the dark hours like a dead thing, while September and Rufus sat and asked one another careful questions. They quickly found common ground on the subject of firearms. Rufus loved guns the way Micah loved vehicles, and a functioning Desert Eagle was at least as wondrous to him as the Bobcat had been.

September was soon won over by the obviously genuine quality of his enthusiasm, and soon their conversation bled into more personal matters. He asked her about the world to the south, and she told him what she deemed prudent, which was little. She asked him about the Fold, generally, and then more and more specifically about Micah. Rufus gave easy, careless answers, very unlike the ones Micah would have given. And so September learned a very great deal more about Micah and his world than she would have from him, and this was very much to Micah's advantage.

As the sun came up they shared out what remained of their renewed food supply. Rufus, without any suggestion on their part, divided his own supplies among the Brothers and Sisters. Only Micah understood the extent of this sacrifice, never having known Rufus to willingly miss a meal for any reason. Lighter by two saddlebags of food, Rufus mounted his horse with a surprisingly easy motion, and rode back north across the pasture and into the woods.

That day was spent in what felt like unimaginable leisure after the ceaseless brutality of those preceding it. September and Alan explored the pasture and the surrounding birch woods with the more mobile Brothers and Sisters, while Micah cleaned and dressed the wounds of those who could not. Together they shot, dressed and cooked a rabbit and two squirrels, and found a stream free of ice from which they could fill their bottles. They spent several hours there with the Brothers and Sisters, washing their filthy feet and hands and faces together, slowly learning each other's names, and then moving beyond names.

There was Genevieve, gregarious and round, who had Williams syndrome and a self-described "huge crush" on Alan, who had come to the City three years before with her sister and her sister's family. "My brother-in-law, he never liked me. Always trying to get me to stop talking, saying I laugh too loud. My sister, she died having a baby, her third baby. And then Derek got his way."

There was Rod, who was blind and overwhelmed with a crippling anxiety that manifested itself in endlessly repeated phrases, mainly concerning the weather and the conditions of the roads. He assured Micah that it was not too late in the season for freezing rain, and that they would never get home then.

Rod was accompanied, always, by Janice. Janice had cerebral palsy and was unable to walk, and had been Rod's closest companion for the past five years. They had met when their families had arrived, and formed the nucleus of a day program started by theirs and several other families. Rod had pushed Janice's wheelchair, and Janice had directed him, while patiently answering his constant anxious queries. Rod had pushed that wheelchair up the broken road up the hill until the axles had broken, and then he had carried her on his back until the bus had come.

And there was Mo. Mo had been a structural engineer in a previous life, specializing in fluid dynamics, and it had been he who had helped the City, and three cities before it, to resurrect their sewage systems. But Mo had been t-boned by a joyriding teenager in a stolen Land Rover while on his way to investigate a broken water main one frigid morning thirteen months before the lights came on, and now Mo had a brain injury. He had exiled himself voluntarily to show solidarity with the Plan, and now spent his days in a depression so deep as to resemble a state of living death, remembering his previous life and vocation, but unable to remember how any of it had been accomplished. It was Alan who had persuaded Mo to join them in their exodus, and to Alan he had told his story, refusing outright even to speak to Micah.

By the time they had finished washing up, Micah felt reborn. The Brothers and Sisters, too, had quieted, their fear and anxiety passing away as order returned to the world.

September, too, was different. September in the forest clearing was very unlike September on the overpass. She met his gaze more readily, answered his questions more directly, and had begun to ask more and more of her own. She seemed to have removed six inches of armor plating. Micah suspected, correctly, that this was Rufus' doing, and he silently thanked him. September, it seemed, was a person who required proof of trustworthiness before confidences could be shared. Such had been the long and painful lesson of her life.

She asked him about the City, and he told her everything. When he spoke of Sarah and the Regis family he saw the hostility return to her eyes, but he kept talking until the story was told to the end, and when he had finished her eyes were soft again. "I wish you hadn't told me all that," she said. "I really liked hating them."

The sun broke through in the late morning and worked its alchemy on their pale winter hides and awakened those parts of their beings that had slept in hibernation since the last days of the previous October. The Canada geese were heralding their return north in long ragged chevrons, and as the warmth of the sun began to seep back into the body of the earth and up into the arms and hands and fingers of the trees, they heard the woods beginning to come alive again with the song of the red-winged blackbirds and the infinitesimal tree frogs.

The Brothers and Sisters felt it too. Micah could see the change slowly come over their thin and ragged faces. The desperation that had possessed them was draining away and the hard lines that cold and fear and hunger had left were beginning to soften. Francis had stopped biting at his hands quite so much. Ivy took some water for the first time since the previous morning, and Sahi's keening wail eased down into a low liquid burble. Micah began to catch glimpses of the people behind their symptoms, true personalities slowly emerging from the depths of their anxiety and terror and the attendant coping devices.

And Micah and September continued to talk, as naturally and as easily as either had ever done with anyone. They told one another the stories of their lives, hers as the Princess of Burrows, and his as the Shepherd of Princes. Their conversation flowed effortlessly in and out of the personal and the practical, trains of thought intertwining like swallows in flight. Something was emerging, something new that was more than either of them from which it grew, and it came rising up as inevitably as the buds from the red dogwoods that lined the meadow.

The woods were red with the setting sun when the two wagons came up the path, painted yellow and ringing with bear-bells. Rufus drove one, and Joanna and Thomas Gault the other. Rufus gave a whoop as they broke out of the woods and yelled, "There's your boy, Jo. And just look at what the crazy bastard did."

Joanna Gault made no sound, just drove the horses on ahead with unconscious skill, but as they drew closer Micah could see the silent tears running down her face. She leaped off of the wagon with Thomas on her arm and ran to him with the speed of a much younger woman and hugged him until his ribs cracked. "My boy . . . your hair." Out of the corner of his eye, he saw September turn away, her mouth a hard flat line again.

Thomas took up his place on Micah's free arm without a word, exerting considerably more pressure than was his custom. He led his brother over to the girl and said, "Thomas, I'd like you to meet September." Thomas turned his face to the sky and began to wail. Micah wrapped his arms around his brother as tight as he could, and knew enough to say nothing.

Rufus called out to the scattered Brothers and Sisters and led them to their places in the back of his wagon. Micah felt the burden begin to slip from his shoulders. The responsibility was no longer his alone. He had done something impossible and pride swelled within him, for about a second and a half, before his rationality and its legion of unanswerable questions reasserted itself.

"Micah," came his mother's voice, ending his anxious reverie. "Introduce me to this young lady before I have to do it myself."

"Sorry," he mumbled absurdly. "Um, Mom, Thomas, this is September Burrows. I, uh, met her on the road." He concluded with a lame gesture southward. September, eyes wide and shoulders hunched, stood as if turned to stone. Joanna walked up and embraced her.

"Thank you. I know it was you that got him back. Rufus told me all about it, and thank God. He could never have done this by himself. Not that I don't believe in you, of course, dear," she added, looking over her shoulder back at Micah. She released September, who immediately scuttled off to help Rufus water the horses.

It took a surprisingly short time to get everyone up and into the wagons. There was clean straw for sitting in and a bag of apples for the ride, and the Brothers and Sisters had not forgotten the wonder of the bus, and were excited to try this new permutation of the experience, this time with horses.

Within twenty minutes of their first arrival they were packed and seated, September with Rufus and Micah with his mother and brother, at her adamant insistence. With a "Gee" they were rolling out of the pasture of their deliverance and up the old gravel sideroad through the sunset woods.

"Now, Micah," began Joanna, "why don't you tell me how we all got here today. The real version, please, not the one you're going to tell Martin and Arthur and Rosie Meech." And Micah told her the story, omitting nearly nothing, as they passed through the old familiar woods and the dusk fell and Alan and Genevieve led the Brothers and Sisters in a rousing chorus of "My Heart Will Go On" behind them.

Joanna Gault was a wonderful listener, and interjected only to seek clarification. She was extremely interested in the events surrounding Burrows and its last inhabitant, managing to dig out every last pertinent detail despite Micah's determination to preserve September's privacy.

When Micah's narrative reached the moment of his decision to bring the Brothers and Sisters back to the Fold, he noticed a decidedly strained quality to his mother's expression. But of course there was. He had been sent out in the hopes that he could return with medical supplies, with new technology, with new hope for the Brothers and Sisters and their caretakers. He was returning with seventeen new souls to feed and care for, and nothing at all to aid in the undertaking except one inhaler, a nineteen-year-old girl of questionable mental and emotional stability, and Alan, who at least had the makings of a Shepherd. Micah was back, he was home safe, against all odds. But it seemed obvious, even to his exhausted mind, that all he had accomplished was to widen a tear in a quickly emptying sack of grain, while bringing nothing else with which to fill it.

She read his thoughts in his face, shook her head, the tears rolling now. "No, no, no, Micah. I'm only proud of you. I don't know what's going to happen after this, but I am only proud of you."

Suddenly another revelation, almost forgotten in the events of the few days, came rushing back to him.

"Mom," he said, "I read Dad's letter. The one he wrote to Thomas and I, before he . . . you know." She nodded, jaw set.

"Lorne told me he was going to give it to you. Didn't ask for my permission, but informed me, which I suppose I should be grateful for. They were very close, your dad and Lorne. Brought out the best in one another. That's why he lets you hang out in that library, you know. Your dad used to do the same thing."

"But why didn't you ever tell me about all that stuff?"

"I knew he'd written that letter, and that you'd read it eventually. I always got your dad wrong. I owed it to him to let him tell you himself. If he only would have allowed himself to, he could have been so much like you."

It was almost midnight when the wagons rolled across the borders of the Fold. There they were greeted by a chorus of yelps and shouts and howls, so reminiscent yet so unlike the cryings-out beneath the walls of the City, for this was a chorus in which Micah knew every voice. He was home. Several of the people in the wagons behind him sent up an answering refrain, the happy dins coming together in a strange and perfect harmony. Micah leapt down from the wagon and was met immediately by Martin, who shook him roughly and warmly by the hand, his weathered face cracked in two by a wide, sad smile.

"Well done, Shepherd."

The rest of the village had gathered, were helping the newcomers down from the cart and into the Hall. The benches had been moved back to the walls and bedding laid down in preparation. Micah could smell stew cooking. When he went back to help, Karen pushed him roughly back. "Nuh uh, buddy. You've had enough for one night. You take that bush girl you found and get her something to eat and a place to sleep, and start coming up with a way of paying her back for saving your life, if what I'm hearing is true at all."

Micah was too tired to protest the obvious lack of helping hands and merely nodded. He took the two battered tin bowls of stew Karen pressed into his hands, then found September in the crowd, looking lost and overwhelmed. He put a bowl into her hand, and without a word led her out of the Hall and down the old familiar road to the old familiar house. Their stomachs woken, roaring, by the scent of the stew, they ate as they walked, and by the time they reached the door their bowls were empty. The door was unlocked, as always, the house creaking with cold in the absence of its family. He closed the door behind them, closed out the noise and the night and the great dark masses of questions unanswered. He led her to his room, and offered his bed. She sat on it, looking up in a way that made his heart pound in his chest.

"This is my room, when I'm not with the guys. You can sleep here if you want."

She smiled. "Thank you, Micah."

"Well, we did it."

"We did."

Micah nodded, unsure how to respond.

He left and closed the door behind him and his insides were bright and fierce and his smile wild and wide. He gathered the cold folded blankets from the linen cupboard and made a bed for himself by the woodstove and was asleep before he knew he was lying down.

26
At The End of Platitudes

The next morning Micah awoke to a familiar sound. It was the meeting-bell, and he was in his old house, in such an extreme state of comfort after the cold aches of the road that he wondered how he would summon the will to leave it. But then he remembered September, who would soon be up and awake and set upon by curious and suspicious strangers with very little respect for personal space, and he leapt out of bed and quickly dressed in the nicest clothes he possessed.

He knocked on her bedroom door down the hall. When no answer came, he whispered, "It's Micah," and the door opened a few inches and a pair of eyes appeared. Reluctantly, the door swung open the rest of the way.

"Your mom found me some clothes," she said by way of explanation for the long woolen dress she wore. "I don't want to hurt her feelings."

"No, you look . . . you look good," said Micah, by way of understatement. Awkwardly, he stuck out his hand, and awkwardly she took it, and they walked without speaking towards the sound of the bell.

The Hall was packed and roaring with Brothers and Sisters, old and new, wild with disrupted routine and new acquaintances. Their shellshocked Shepherds, pitifully few, stared about in bewilderment. Martin stood on a box at the front and waved a hand to draw attention to himself and began to speak in his church-voice. Even the most bewildered among them seemed to understand that voice, and fell silent upon recognizing it.

"Brothers and Sisters!" he began. "We are all here today, packed in tight and warm, because the world we knew, the world we ate and drank and breathed and walked around in, has changed. Each of our little stories, and the big story that God is telling through all of us together, has already started a new chapter, and we have someone who can put this new direction into words. Micah, if you wouldn't very much mind, would you come up and tell us about what you saw down south, and what you did about it?"

Micah had known that this would be part of his task, and he had dreaded it perhaps more than any other. He walked the creaking boards to the front of the hall, feeling every eye on him. Once again, he wondered what it was that humans were supposed to do with their arms when they weren't using them, but as he passed by Thomas, his brother took his accustomed place on Micah's arm and accompanied him the rest of the way to stand beside him as he spoke.

Micah lacked Martin's gift for public speaking, and the Brothers and Sisters who were less mindful of the significance of the occasion began to complain loudly. They were in the Hall. It was mealtime. Where was the food? What did Micah think he was doing? This was preposterous. He was being boring, and, worse than that, he was not following the schedule. Micah should know better, even if he had been away.

So he raised his voice until he was almost yelling, and in that unlovely tone he began to tell his story. He described the roads to the City, and the condition of those roads. He told of Burrows and meeting September (a cheer from the Sisters, who had taken an instant liking to her) and her grandfather (cries of "It's sad when people die!"). He told of the Waste of Boxes and the burnt land and of the beauty and perfection of the city walls, and the Brothers and Sisters grew silent. He told of what he had seen within those walls, the stores and galleries, about the luxury and the beauty of it. He described the cars and gave a brief account of Arlo and the Bobcat. He gave a heavily abbreviated account of Sarah and her tour of the city and an even more edited version of the party (Rufus calling out "Tell the truth now, Micah!" from his place at the back).

He tried to give a true account of the kindness of the people he had met there, of Benjamin and of Arlo, and of Sarah, of the Regis family and their hospitality. But then, his voice suddenly growing in strength and volume, he told of what he had seen from the windows of their apartment, and of what he had found outside the eastern wall.

He could see the shock on the faces of the people who could understand. He saw fear on the faces of Brothers and Sisters, and black rage on those of the Shepherds. Adi shouted, "Those *assholes*!", and then apologized following Alan's admonition.

He told of Alan and his bow (here the Brothers and Sisters turned as one to stare at the newcomer with awe), of separating the living from the dead, of the death-march-turned-deliverance by September Burrows.

Here his voice ceased to quaver and grew loud and strong. He pointed to her, at the back of the Hall, and told the Fold what she had done, and she blushed furiously and stared at the floor as the crowd began to clap, deafeningly and solemnly, and several Brothers and Sisters ran to the back to hug and kiss her.

"And that's how we got here, and that's where these people came from. But I only came in at the end. I think that someone who was there for all of it should explain. Alan? Would you come up and tell everybody your story?"

Alan made his way shyly to the front, but when he spoke, it was with all the clarity and confidence that Micah lacked, and an awed silence met him as he told his tale. He told of how he and his brother ("Scott, who's an engineer") had come to the City during the days of its refounding after the death of his parents. He told of the doctor's lie, and of his brother's betrayal.

"They put us outside a few days after the lights came on. I'm glad it wasn't before the lights, anyway. I liked the lights. I used them to shoot squirrels. You should get some lights here. My brother Scott could help you," he continued, his voice loud and full of expression.

"I ate berries and the apples and granola I had in my backpack, but it wasn't enough. I shot some squirrels and one deer and I cooked them and I shared them with the other people outside, but it wasn't enough." His voice broke.

"I was scared of them. Some of them went crazy and tried to hurt me and hurt themselves. And then a lot of them died. Got sick, wouldn't eat, wouldn't drink the water I gave them. I don't know why they wouldn't. I tried really hard, but I couldn't help them. So I kept the fire going, and I shot the coywolves when they got too close.

"I asked the people on the Wall to let us in, but they wouldn't talk to me. Just pretended they couldn't hear, but I know they could. I don't know why they did that.

"I thought about leaving and trying to walk to another town, but I didn't want to miss my brother Scott if he came out looking for me. So I stayed, and then Micah came, and I helped him, and then September came, and she helped us." Alan finished awkwardly and shuffled back down to his seat, to thunderous applause. Martin took his place.

"Well, there it is, everyone. Everyone has always been welcome to leave at any time, but this morning I feel the need to extend that invitation once again. If any of you wish to leave this place, and go to the City, you heard Micah. You will be welcomed there, and no judgment will be passed upon you from this end of the room. It seems certain to be a much easier life, perhaps even a good one.

"To those of you who remain of your own choosing, the road before us is clear. As you are no doubt aware, the ratio of Shepherd to Brother and Sister has been altered significantly. We can no longer spare so many of the able-bodied to work the fields and care for the animals, and we have increased the number of mouths to feed by a third. Obviously, food supply is going to be a challenge, one of several. But these challenges will be overcome, together."

A voice arose in the crowd. It was Robert Sanderson, Cecilia's husband, a shepherd in the more traditional sense of the word. "Pardon me Martin, but how exactly? And don't give me any platitudes, I need a practical answer. We were barely getting by before, and we were at maximum yield for the hands we had. Now we've got fewer hands and more to feed? I can't do that arithmetic, Martin, and neither can you."

Martin chuckled. "Well, Bob, you know mathematics has never been a particular strength of mine. But you're right, of course. The numbers don't add up. Nothing about this place has ever made a terrible amount of sense. We don't live by the numbers here, do we? But somehow, it has always been found to work. There have always been variables we're not aware of at play, variables that make that kind of decision-making a fool's errand. Yes, it's all impossible, and now it's more impossible. But that is our business here."

Robert gave a gruff grunt of assent, shrugged, and sat down. Martin continued.

"Everyone who wishes can strike out on their own for the City, and leave those who can't. Or we all stay here, and keep doing what we've always done: Take care of each other, and do what Jesus told us to do.

"That's what this really comes down to. He told us to come here, and He brought every one of us, new friends included. Now . . . He'll do what He'll do. I don't know what that is. I don't need to. Our job is to follow where He leads today, and today I don't think his direction could be any clearer. I'm as scared as any of you, and I too want hot baths and fast food again, I promise you that. But He's giving me the strength not to do that, and so today I'll stay here.

"I'm an old man. I'll be dead soon either way; it doesn't matter very much to me, but I want you to look at that young man in the back, the one who brought all this trouble down on us. He's got his whole life ahead of him, and still he made his choice. That's the choice this place was founded on: that it's better to die in God's hand than to live outside of it.

"That's my choice, and I'll keep leading you if you want me to. You'll each have plenty of time to make yours. Kindly endure." The familiar blessing came echoing back. "Kindly endure."

The meetings went on for most of the rest of that day, and many things were discussed, with the Shepherds alternating in and out when they could be spared from their duties. But by the end of the day, no one had left, and no one had stated an intention to do so.

And then it was as if Micah's journey had never happened. Almost as soon as the meeting was over he was back to his old work, back to keeping and tending and watching and cleaning, back to the backbreaking days and the watchful, sleepless nights. Only now everything was so much harder, and now everything was so much better, because the Fold now contained September.

Hard times were now desperate times. The community had already been operating at its maximum capacity. The Shepherds already worked when they were sick, sweating and vomiting through their fevers with their Brothers and Sisters at their sides. There were no more reserves to be brought in, no standards that could be safely relaxed. September, despite her obvious trepidation, volunteered on her second day and was immediately pressed into service as Rosie's relief.

At his request, on the strength of Micah's recommendation and of the evidence of his actions below the Wall, Alan began his own service. He showed an immediate aptitude for the work, and on the fourth Sunday after his arrival, his apprenticeship with Micah complete, Alan became the last Shepherd the Fold would ever ordain.

27
Romantic Things

Micah's first night back on duty in the attic over the kitchens had not even ended before he began to seriously question his decision. When Philip Ramirez took up his keening, Sahi and Oliver, two of the new arrivals, began to join him in his cry. Donny, frightened and confused, had attacked them. Micah had had to restrain Donny for the first time in five years, and no one had gotten any sleep. The next morning, when the Brothers discovered their new, smaller portions at breakfast, Jonathan began to bite himself and spit at Micah, a behavior not seen for ten years. Jonathan had a point, thought Micah. The meal came and went, and he remained hungry.

Everywhere in the packed dining hall he could hear complaints from Brothers and Sisters in various levels of volume and violence. There had been three aggressions already this morning, which was unheard of. He could see the stress and the mounting desperation in the eyes of his friends. And this was all because of him, came the voice. He had returned to the Fold like the scourge of God, with ruin in his train. He found it hard to meet his friends' eyes.

But as breakfast was finished, all too soon, and the directing of princes to this activity or that began, Rufus socked Micah roughly on the arm with a massive paw and growled, "Snap out of it, asshole. No one blames you. This is not your fault. It's those fuckers who left them to die." Micah felt his spirits come flickering back to life. Across the yelling mob he saw September, neck-deep in her one day of volunteer training with Bethlehem and the Pretty Girls. Her eyes were wide with panic as a forty-year-old woman hung around her neck, yelling in her ear that she liked her yellow hair, while feebly trying to stop an immense young woman from stealing the shoes off the feet of a third. He succeeded in catching her eye, and made the biggest, happiest, most encouraging face he could, complete with a double thumbs up. He was answered with a beautifully mimed suicide by gunshot, but she was laughing, and that was like coffee with sugar in it.

Five days later, the first they could both be spared, Micah and September rode out to the bus to gather the rest of her supplies. After they had stripped it of all they could carry and use, she stood and stared at it for a long time, taking in the friendly yellow of the fuselage, the old brown vinyl of the seats, the patched but vital rubber of the tires, before turning abruptly and returning to the Fold. Upon their return, she stopped by the forge and gave Wayne its location.

"Anything you can salvage from it is yours. It was on its last legs before we pushed it here, so I think the engine is finished, and it's got a lot of rust on the body, but the frame is good. I hear you're good at repurposing stuff." The next day Jon took his tools out to the site and began the process of stripping it. When Micah tried to protest, she cut him off.

"I know what I'm doing. I made my choice. Not going nowhere anytime soon." He walked behind her that day, back to the pasture where the Friendly Men were ostensibly herding sheep, so that she would not observe the width and maniac nature of his grin.

Micah had given her a tour of the Fold that day, a twelve-hour furlough they had been afforded following their return. It was really a tour of his entire life: of his parents' house where he had been born and raised, of the schoolhouse where his mother taught, where he had attended what had passed as school in those days, of the library (after September had washed her hands, at Lorne's shrill insistence) where he had spent most of his spare evenings since. After September had signed the proper introductory forms, he took her up to his third floor roost, to the chair by the gable window. They sat there, soaking in one another's presence, until Lorne became suspicious and insisted they leave.

Finally he took her into the woods, and to all his favorite secret places. She was quiet, for the most part. She listened to him speak, when he did speak, but for the most part they simply walked together, listening to the language of the wind in the budding woods.

But when she did speak, it felt to Micah as if he had been living in a foreign land of foreign tongues all his life and for the first time heard a voice speaking his own.

Because she was new and untrained, inexperienced, and because Rosie had apparently insisted, and because Martin was a good friend, the next day September was moved from her temporary posting with the Pretty Girls to help Micah care for the Friendly Men, to learn from him the strange and unexpected ways of the Brothers and Sisters. Micah could almost weep with gratitude when he learned of the decision.

All their days were now entwined, and it was the purest happiness Micah had ever known, among the danger and the exhaustion and the smell of human waste and the eternal hunger in their bellies. It was wonderful, and terrible, and every day they laughed until their stomachs hurt, and every day they felt as if they could not bear the circumstances of their lives for another hour.

Thomas' initial heartbreak over September's intrusion soon turned to a sullen jealousy. This in turn gave way to a shy adoration, before taking its final form as a deeply protective and domineering big-brother love. He grudgingly gave up his constant place on Micah's arm, on occasion. His mother was very proud of him, and told him so.

Changes now came with every passing day, and the Brothers and Sisters did not countenance change happily. On Wednesday of the second week after Micah's return, an afternoon came when September had to inform the Friendly Men that there was no more beef jerky to be had for afternoon snack. Philip hit her in the face with the speed of a striking snake, leaving four bloody scratches across her cheek with long ragged nails no one had had time to trim. Micah, operating on three hours of sleep, lost control for a moment and hit Philip hard in the jaw. He cried for an hour, despite Micah's many apologies and extensive self-damnation.

He spent his precious fifteen-minute lunch debriefing with Martin, and he sat beside the old man and wept like a child. Nothing like this had ever happened before, in seven years of winters and night shifts. Things were turning a corner, entering a new normal, a sad and a dark one. Even Martin's ever-present humor was often missing now, replaced by a kind of quiet sorrow.

At the end of the debriefing, there was a knock at the door, and September entered shyly. Before either of them could speak she blurted out, needing both Martin and Micah to hear it, "I'm not a Shepherd."

"But you're doing great, everybody says so!" interrupted Micah.

"No. I'm not one, and I don't want to be one, and I won't be a good one if you make me be one. I can love these people in my own way, and I believe in what you're doing here, but it's just not in me to do what you do."

"Of course," replied Martin gently. "And Shepherds aren't conscripted, you know. They're called. And you are very wise to understand that you are called to something else. Do you have another role in mind for yourself?"

She nodded firmly. "I want to hunt. I'm a good shot, probably the best here. My rifle's the best, and in the best condition by far, and we need meat now more than anything. I've got ammunition I ain't turned over to Gord. It's mine to use, and I want to use it to feed us until the last round. I'm good with a bow, too, when the ammo's gone. Better than good, actually."

"It's settled then, Ms. Burrows," responded Martin with a smile. "I'll inform Gord that there is a new member of his little pack of wolves. He won't be happy about it, hating and fearing women as he unfortunately does, but I'm sure you'll win him over."

September turned to Micah. "Don't hate me. It's just not me, you know?"

Micah nodded his head vigorously. "Trust me, I understand." And so it was settled.

Micah's fifteen minutes were up, and he returned to the reconstituted Philip Ramirez and the Friendly Men. Donny was busily chirping out orders in his high voice, informing the ones he called "The New Men" of the day's schedule. He was assisted physically by Sam, who was busy arranging everyone in a line and trying to keep them there as they walked.

With much yelling and confusion, they made their slow and wandering way to their eventual destination, the bean field to the south of the village. They were met there by Bill, who was finishing up the plowing with his team of horses. The sun had broken through the clouds, and there was warmth to the air and the earth that had not been felt in half a year. It worked on everyone, and a little of the background panic and the sense of hopelessness that had dogged Micah throughout the day began to retreat. It was springtime, and they were here to plant a field with seeds that would grow into food that they could eat.

Bill explained the task in clear and simple terms to the assembled men, aided by the booming register of his voice and his sheer physical size. The Friendly Men had always been deeply impressed by Bill, and they stood still and stayed more or less quiet while he explained. Those who were able would be given sacks of seeds, which they were to plant in the furrows. Those less able were to chase any bird they saw, a task in which they delighted. This was considered the more desired of the two tasks, and much jealousy was evident in those who would merely be planting. Philip and Sahi, who were blind (Rodney, unwilling to be parted from Janice, had been made an honorary Pretty Girl), and Peter, who was new and had displayed a troubling disregard for physical danger, would be helping Micah. Bill finished his last furrow and drove the team back to the stables, and Philip Ramirez and the Friendly Men began to plant their field.

It was not a great success. Peter took a deep dislike to the task at hand and attempted continually to contrive his escape. Jonathan, still inconsolably outraged about the demise of afternoon snack (cut as part of the newly-recalculated rations), refused even to chase birds, and was later caught hand-feeding seed to them. Oliver, also new, simply stood, clearly overwhelmed and bewildered, staring at Micah and following him aimlessly wherever he went, nodding when spoken to but otherwise completely unresponsive.

What made the chaos more alarming was that the work was not optional busywork given simply to occupy the Friendly Men. The seeds had to be planted, or there wouldn't be enough food to eat. So Micah ended up doing most of it himself, continually interrupting his work to stop Sahi from wandering blindly into the forest, or Peter from scratching Sam when he attempted to coerce him into doing his work. Donny, thankfully, loved this job and had been doing it for fifteen years. He would keep working all night, if he were allowed.

Micah did what he could to hurry the process along, but when the bells began ringing for dinner, he couldn't help but notice that they'd only completed about two-thirds of what they usually accomplished. It was just another grim reminder in a day full of them. More Brothers meant less productivity, unfortunately. There was just no way around the fact, and he heard Father Dan's careful words echo up from his subconscious. The voice of accusation, of doubt and fear, began to speak again in the echo chambers of his heart.

The voice grew louder as the days went by and spring regained her mastery of the world. At the end of that first week, exhaustion was clearly setting in. Gabby

Morales had fallen down a flight of stairs and broken her hip while Rosie was occupied with her new Sisters. Rosie was inconsolable and had to be taken off duty for two days, compounding the situation.

On Sunday morning, Robert Sanderson announced at the end of the service that he was leaving the Fold. He denounced Micah's choices as the foolishness of youth, and Martin's acceptance of them as evidence of dotage. He announced, loudly, publicly, that the situation was unsustainable, and that if they kept to this course they would all starve to death when winter inevitably came.

"And I know you, Martin. Forty-five years I've kept sheep in this valley. I was here when you arrived. Shepherd to Shepherd: I know you. You'd doom the lot of us before you'd turn away a single one of these people. I can't follow you in that, and I can't stay here and watch you all die. It doesn't make any sense, what we're doing here. I'm sorry, everybody. I'm going to the City to see if they'll take me. I've done my part here. We all have." And without looking to the right or left he marched down the creaking floorboards and out the door. He was never seen again in that valley. His wife, Cecilia, remained, along with half of their flock of sheep.

Micah banished the very concept of free time and leisure from his psyche. All of his life became watching, tending, caring for someone. He was never off duty. He was never not smelling of urine and feces. He was never not responding to crises of some flavor or variety.

All that mitigated the sense of panic and despair that was growing within Micah was the warm and windy realities of spring, and of September. September, and how she smiled at him through the nearly-healed scratches that ran down her cheek and across her lips to the white point of her chin. September, and how she only seemed to grow brighter and fiercer as the pressure grew. September, and how to sit with her for a few minutes in silent exhaustion was better conversation than any conversation he had ever had.

Micah had never slept as little as he was sleeping now. His muscles had become like carved wood from supporting the Brothers who could not walk alone, from holding down those who would hurt themselves or others, from the long days in the fields. His arms were covered in scratches and bites from Barry, and his nose was healing crooked where Sahi had broken it during one of his frequent frightened outbursts. Micah had never eaten as little as he was eating now. He had never hurt the way he hurt. But he had never been so happy as he was, when September was there, dressing her kills and smoking venison in Gord's shed whenever he cared to see her.

On the first day of June when the world was green again, and September had joined the Friendly Men on a foraging expedition in the blossoming woods, Micah took her hand for the first time since their return. She did not refuse it, as he had feared, but instead gave it a reassuring squeeze. Minimal as the display of affection was, it did not go unnoticed by Donny, who raised a great hue and cry, very upset at

180

the sight of them doing "romantic things."

Thomas, sensing an affront to family honor, slapped Donny across the face, and Sam ordered him to shut up, informing him that he was "ruining everything" and that this development had come, indeed, at the proper time. Micah and September laughed, and squeezed each other's hands until it hurt and then ran frantically to stop Peter from pursuing a frog into the swift-running river.

September maintained her grip on his hand all the way back to the valley, though not a word was said of it, and nothing had ever felt as sweet as that reciprocal pressure beneath his fingers.

28
Summer's End

It was a hot, still evening towards the end of July when the word was passed quietly from Shepherd to Shepherd that there was to be a meeting for as many of them as could be spared. The cicadas were loud and the stars were fat and yellow in the misty darkness of the valley as Micah slipped away from the snoring of the Friendly Men and made his way through the village to the Hall. There he found Bethlehem, Alan, and Rosie Meech already gathered around a single tallow candle burning in the center of a long, scarred table. Martin acknowledged them with a nod, then began to address the gathered, his face somber.

"Hello everyone, and thank you for coming. I won't keep you long, but there's something you need, and deserve, to know. This is for Shepherds only, right now, so please keep it to yourselves. Bill is going to explain, as it's his area of expertise."

Old Bill Turnbull creaked slowly to his feet at the end of the table. He was extremely shy about speaking in public due to a pronounced stutter, but there was no better farmer left in those lands. No one knew the ways of soil and seed like Bill did. He had been the authority on agriculture in that valley since before Martin had arrived with his Brothers and Sisters.

Bill struggled with his voice for ten seconds before the words finally came.

"Ah . . . ah . . . as I'm sure you've all noticed, we've all been eating a lot less this summer than we did the last. Of course this is 'cause we can only grow as much food as our manpower allows, and that's less than it was, especially now that the sheep that left with Bob have taken their manure with 'em. What with watching all these new Brothers n' Sisters, there's only a few of us able to work the fields and care for the animals full-time, and that just ain't enough. I know you all help when you can, and the Brothers n' Sisters do their bit, but it just ain't, and nothing's gonna change that.

"On top of that, we've got about twenty more mouths to feed, three times every day. It's easy math to do, and you're not gonna like the sum anymore'n I do. Even with the rationing, we've already eaten through our reserves. Now I've worked this through every way I can think of, but the way I see it, we're not going to be able to set aside any reserves for next winter. There's just no food to spare. Everything we harvest we need to eat, just to keep everybody going." He took a deep breath, put his liver-spotted hands flat on the table.

"Now please, nobody panic. This is God's thing we're doing here, and God is just going to have to feed us if He wants us to keep on doing it. Remember Elijah and those ravens."

"Thank you, Bill. Quite right," broke in Martin. "As I have said so many times before, we are living in the country of miracles, friends. But we've been living here all our lives. It's just easier to see it now for what it's always been. Kindly endure." There was a chorus of Amens, but it was a visibly subdued group that stumbled back to their sleeping quarters that night.

Micah found himself unable to sleep. He climbed out the window and up to his accustomed spot on the roof, where he used to hide as a boy when he didn't want to be found, and sat there for a long time. The dead quiet of the middle night gave him nothing to distract himself from the long-dreaded news. It was out there now, a deadline, a question without an answer, the consummation of the doom he had chosen for himself, and everyone he loved. He remembered with guilt and longing the easy movements of the blue tractor, tilling the southern fields outside the City wall. There would be no hunger there.

Micah said the old panic-attack prayers and one by one brought up the old promises and the new reassurances he had received, that he had made the right choice, that there was a God who had demanded that it be made and who would be responsible for the consequences. But still the word "starvation" hung in the air and clung like a cloud of flies to the faces of his beloved throughout that night and many nights to come. If only he had given Martin that letter of resignation when he had the chance, before the lights had come on, he would be quitted of his now-hateful vows, divested of the Shepherd's habit, and all the burdens he put on with it. Someone else could have gone south, someone who would have made a wiser choice. He could be working the fields right now, content and useful and blissfully ignorant of the decisions made. He could be providing for the Fold, not the author of its ruin. He worried these thoughts like a dog with a rat until they were bloody and unrecognizable, and then he carried them back in the window to bed where sleep found him at last an hour before dawn.

Unlike Micah, brooding and pointless worry were not luxuries that September Burrows was accustomed to affording herself. The day after Micah had confided Bill's announcement to her, she confronted Gord. She demanded he give her free access to the remaining supply of .308 caliber ammunition to augment her dwindling supply. Gord was not given to responding to ultimatums, especially from "little raider girls from God knows where," and gruffly rebuffed her. September responded with a wager. Gord would give her seven rounds and one week. She would deliver to his hunting camp one freshly killed deer every day of that week. If she succeeded, he would give her a key to the ammo lockup. If not, she would submit to his authority. Gord laughed in her face and shook her small hand black with gun-grease.

September delivered her seventh deer, a six-point buck, on Sunday evening. She had also brought eight rabbits, six fat groundhogs, four possums, and a raccoon from the traplines she had set that same week. Gord shook his head and handed her the key. For a full month, Micah barely saw September. She was gone from morning til dusk, moving through the woods like a squirrel's shadow in the ragged green sweatshirt she invariably wore, rifle strapped tight to her back so as not to impede her movement. She came back after dark most days, trailing mud and leaves and splattered with blood. Many of the Brothers and Sisters began to be afraid of her, and tell dark stories, but the Friendly Men adopted her as their patron saint, and Donny had to be reprimanded for telling Edward of the Cool Guys that if he didn't speak in an inside voice, September was going to "get him." Edward had fled the dining hall in terror.

As the summer progressed, she begged special permission from Martin for Alan to be spared from his duties in the evenings and early mornings, and the two of them would hone their skills together. It was around this time that the pair began taking down the moose that had strayed south since the end of the great depopulations of the previous decades. They would mark their kills then have Gord bring his wagon to the site in order to bring in the massive carcasses.

September's kills were so numerous and so efficient that Bill grudgingly reassessed his estimates. She was moving the needle, buying them time. But time for what? Sooner or later, the game would be gone from the area. Sooner or later, winter would still come. Micah fell back into his anxiety, and the voice of doom returned, louder than it had been, more sure of its message.

Sooner still, however, it was time for the harvest, and there was simply no more time to be spared for dread. The last of the summer passed in a hot cyclical rush of heavy labor in the fields with the Brothers and Sisters, cut with fleeting moments of heartbreaking sweetness with September, as they drew nearer and nearer to what looked to be a last, loveliest sunset before the night.

One evening at the end of August, Micah was working with the Friendly Men to bring the few remaining sheep down from the high pasture. A spring fed a stream that fell down the tumbled limestone to become a river in the valley below. The Friendly Men and their little flock had stopped by the spring to water it and themselves before attempting the long switchback path down to the barns.

It had been a long day of fitful weather in the pastures, overcast with sudden squalls blowing in from time to time, soaking everyone and sending the Friendly Men running for the cover of the ancient barn that was all that remained of a prosperous farm. They were all tired, damp, and smelling of sheep, but as the sun began to set on the escarpment and the spring, a keen wind began to blow out of the west. Suddenly the high country was lit with a rich and wild red-winged light.

It had been a hot and muggy summer full of still, insect-filled heat, but the sudden western wind was cool and crisp and carried that first, undeniable breath of autumn. Suddenly, as if carried on that breeze, September emerged from the birch woods like a dryad, a dead muskrat slung over her shoulder. Without thinking and without the slightest reticence, Micah strode over to her and took her hand in his, and spoke with more certainty than he had ever known.

"I know winter's coming, and that nobody knows how we're going to get through it, but I don't care. I love you, and I want to marry you. I want you to be my wife for however long is left."

She grinned without the slightest indication of surprise, and said, "Of course. If we're going to die, I want to die with you. If we're gonna live, well—" And she nodded, and they kissed one another, gathered their flock, and made their way down into the valley with the end of the summer in their train.

29
Gloria In Excelsis Deo

Micah Gault and September Burrows were married in the old red brick church below the cliff on the last day of the month she was named for. It was a day blazing with light, the green of the leaves incandescent, the sky a dark and royal blue. While they stood in the sun, it seemed still to be summer, but the crisp bite of fall could be felt in the shade of the trees and the shadow of the cliffs.

September wore a plain white dress that Joanna had made her from a bedsheet, the only unstained material of that color available. Her hair hung down freely, washed and shining with the jealously guarded shampoos, hoarded for decades and never used except by brides on their wedding days and to wash the dead for burial.

Micah wore his Shepherd's habit, as had been tradition for the few such marriages that had taken place in the Fold. His mother had laundered it as clean as it would come. At his side stood Thomas in his office as Best Man along with Rufus and the Friendly Men, alternatingly proud and furious at having been scrubbed and dressed up and made to stand still when there was clearly a great deal of food nearby.

At noon the old cracked bell began to toll and Rufus began to play "All Creatures of Our God and King" on his battered, beloved guitar, accompanied by Alan on the recorder. September came through the doors of the church with the mingled summer sunshine and autumn cool, and the Brothers and Sisters sang and shouted and laughed and cheered for the two young people who had come to be married at the end of their world.

As September walked by them, Annie and Marge of the Good Girls leapt out of their pew to grab her by both hands and pull her the rest of the way to the altar where Micah waited under the cracked stained glass in the nave of the church. She followed them, pulled until running, laughing and weeping.

When the voices of joy could be quieted enough for him to be heard, Martin married Micah and September with the old words of the Book of Common Prayer and two rings hammered out of steel taken from the bus that had carried them home. When it was done, Thomas returned to his place on Micah's other arm, and the three walked back down the aisle. They were embraced by a howling herd of their beloved, and there was joy and celebration in the little church hidden in the fold of the land.

But, despite the sincerity of their rejoicing, September's beauty on that day seemed like the beauty of autumn itself: a last and lovely flowering before a long gray sleep. Though it rang with celebration, on their valley also lay the shadow of death.

They had already eaten three-quarters of the food supply that was required to see everyone through the winter, even on the strictest of rations. The facts were grim and irrevocable. There was a kind of freedom in this, to know that it could not be done. It was not a matter of working hard enough to make it through, of being swift or strong or wise enough. It would take something so far beyond effort to save the Fold, and in this there was peace and the possibility of rest, and the feast in the Hall that night was of a quality not known before, and the dancing went on with a fierce and desperate and deliberate joy late into the night, a night where laughter and tears met and married and gave birth to something beyond a feeling, something that lived on in their bellies and their bones long after the leaves fell and the snow came.

That night, as they danced and feasted, a killing frost fell early and hard. In the morning, when the village awoke on what was meant to be the day of the apple harvest, it was to find every apple in the orchard killed on the tree.

"There goes the cider and the sauce," muttered Bill. Apple cider was what kept them going through the winter, easy calories easily preserved, and this was a devastating loss. The drums of doom echoed louder in the already anxious nights.

Micah and September were given an old, sound farmhouse in the eastern pastures as a wedding gift, and three precious days alone together. On the morning of the fourth day, Thomas, Philip, Jonathan, Donny, Sahi, Barry, Peter, and Sam moved into the ground floor rooms. Micah and September kept their room on the second story to themselves, a difficult transition for all, but for Thomas in particular. But the Friendly Men loved Micah and September deeply, and surprised everyone with their flexibility and understanding. It was not the quiet home that the young Gaults might have chosen for their first married year, but the racket was a loving racket, and there was joy in their weariness.

So it was that autumn came. The sudden silent beauty of it swept across the Fold as it had every year of Micah's remembering, setting the valley ablaze with burnished red and gold. It hung like a tapestry behind their daily labors, which continued, unrelenting. Although the Shepherds struggled daily to discover new solutions to the ever-present question of food, their supplies steadily dwindled in lockstep with the pessimistic line on the chart that Lorne had carefully made to predict when there would be nothing left. His forecast, the accuracy of which no one thought to question, gave the 29th of December as the fatal date. He could not be dissuaded from referring to it loudly and publicly as Starvation Day.

Solution after solution was presented and discarded at the Shepherds Tuesday night meetings. There were simply too many mouths to feed, and not enough hands able to work the fields and tend the flocks. At every meeting, after Lorne gave his updated prediction of when the stores would be exhausted, a heavy silence fell, and then someone would say, in a quiet voice, "There's always the City."

And Martin would shake his head "no," and then he would say the closing prayer, and they would go back to their Brothers and Sisters sad and afraid. And as the leaves died in their glory and fell to earth in drifts of loveliness, the hearts of those that watched them fall grew heavy with dread.

On the first day of November, Harry and Diana Templeton left their house in the middle of the night without explanation, taking their son Pat with them. They took two horses from the paddock and left their house empty, the front door hanging open.

On the eleventh of that month, Scott Peters, a farrier by trade but assisting Rosie with the Cool Guys, was attacked from behind by Sydney Oosterman as he bathed another member of the group. Operating on a severe sleep deficit, he broke free from Sydney's grasp and then restrained him. Sydney spit in his face, and Scott began to punch and kick Sydney until he himself was restrained by two of his fellow Shepherds. Martin offered him absolution and two days' rest, but the next morning Scott was nowhere to be found.

On the 22nd of November, Melanie Patterson left her bed in the middle of the night clad only in an ancient Mickey Mouse t-shirt. Bethlehem, her Shepherd, slept through the bell placed on the doorframe to prevent this eventuality, and Melanie was found frozen to death outside of the kitchens the next morning when the kitchen ladies arrived to fire the ovens. Bethlehem, devastated, begged to be allowed exile, but after a long private conversation with Martin returned to her post. The situation was deteriorating, and everyone knew it. The Shepherds met constantly to attempt to remedy it, but no solution presented itself.

September and Alan and Gord began to shoot more and more deer to make up for the steadily dwindling supply of wheat and grain and vegetables. They dried and preserved what they could. This supplemented the food substantially, but Lorne had taken these measures into account in his prognostications, and Starvation Day held its place unyieldingly on December 29th. The steep spike in killings had decimated the local game, and the hunters could not be spared for expeditions further afield. By the gray death of November, the food supply was fixed, all options for expanding it exhausted. Rationing was increased to emergency level, and many of the Brothers and Sisters became aggressive in response: sleeping less and lashing out in uncomprehending rage. Injuries to the Shepherds and the more passive Brothers and Sisters began to rise. Exhaustion was epidemic, and morale sank lower every day. There was nothing to do but wait, and work, and pray.

For Micah it was the strangest season of his already strange life. His daily experience was of a mixture of the sweetest joy of his life, of the hardest labor of his life, and of the deep, aching sorrow that it would be ending soon. But for Micah and September, there was no question of leaving the Brothers and Sisters for a return to the City. It was not something to be discussed. They had made their choice. They had sworn oaths, to the Fold, to the Brothers and Sisters, to God, and to one another. And they could not forget the darkness beneath the walls the electric lights could not illuminate.

On the first Sunday of Advent, September woke Micah up before dawn. Through the crust of his exhaustion, he saw something in her eyes that he had never seen there before. She pulled him to his feet and pointed to the door. Together they put on their coats and crept between the beds of the Friendly Men, sleeping yet by some miracle, and eased the creaking door open.

It was breathtakingly cold outside, after the warmth of the farmhouse. The gray morning woods were thick with frost. The snow had not yet come, and the frost glowed eerily in the late starlight. In the cold clarity of the air, the hard bright stars seemed close enough to touch. September pulled him by the hand through the awakening town, away from the baking women, past the farrier's, where Wayne was lighting the forges, past the outskirts of the town to the trailhead. The silence of the woods was broken only by the crunch of the frost beneath their feet. The graceful bodies of the trees swung up towards Heaven around them and laced their fingers together above the path, and the burning bodies of the stars seemed to pulse between them. September took off her mittens and then his, and took his hands in hers, warm and rough from their labors. They stood there, unspeaking, the smoke of their exhalation rising up to the stars like incense.

"I know we have to get back, but I wanted to tell you something, somewhere like this, and this morning Jesus told me that he would watch the Brothers, so I could. I'm having a baby, Micah. Our baby's growing, right here. Can you believe that?" She took his bare hand and guided it up under her coat and the old green sweatshirt to place it on her stomach. It was not yet hinting at its secret, but he could count her ribs beneath the warmth of her skin.

Micah was filled with joy and terror in equal parts. He thought of his father and the last words of his letter, and chose the joy and dismissed the fear as best he could. He kissed September, and said his unnecessary words. They held each other for a time, a time, and half a time, and cried, and then they put their mittens back on and walked back to the village as the sky began to lighten in the east. The Brothers were still asleep when they returned, even Thomas.

After the breakfast, meager but hot (there was no lack of firewood), the young Gaults herded the Friendly Men down the road to St. Stephen, and heard Martin read the old words from Isaiah, and to watch the first candle of the four lit and to smell the incense, and to be warm together, singing. "For unto us, a child is born. Unto us a child is given. And the government shall be upon his shoulders, and he shall be called Counselor, and Prince of Peace.'"

Martin could barely be heard over the shouting and calling of the Brothers and Sisters. They were louder now than he had ever known them to be, always hungry now and generally furious about it. There was more hitting and scratching and biting, and September was not unique in her healing scars. Most of the Shepherds had taken to wearing thick deer hide gloves at all times, and most of the women had cut their hair short to make it more difficult to grab.

But Martin shouted out his call, and they yelled back their response, and the liturgy was completed, and Christmas came a day nearer. For that hour, it was easier to think about other things than the impending end of their food supply, about the end of their community, about the end of their lives. And it was easier to pray. So pray they did, alone and together, for deliverance and for sustenance, and for it all not to be for nothing, and for the City not to be right. They prayed, and then they went back to the hall, where they had taken to gathering in those days where there was so little to do but wait.

Micah continued to have trouble sleeping at night. Moral complexities he'd never imagined had begun to spiral into his daily reality, and he began to wonder if there was a conflict between his duties as a Shepherd and his duties as a husband and father.

Surely September and their baby must go south, and he must go with her. The thought when it came to him made his heart leap with sudden relief. But when he spoke to her, begged her, she simply shook her head, the old steel untarnished in her eyes. She had made her choice when her grandfather was still on the table in Burrows. But with the decision made, the sleep came no easier. All that he could do was to wrap his arms and legs around her and hold to the warmth of her doubled life like a saint's medal and pray to God and wait for sleep or morning.

The deep freeze came as Advent progressed, much earlier than usual, and the misery of hunger was compounded. As dark December hemmed them in, the people of the Fold compensated for what they lacked in food by luxuriating in their astonishing wealth of heat. They piled the fireplaces with fuel as high as was safe and lit them all, great glowing hearts of warmth. The Brothers and Sisters came and gathered around them with their keepers and were warm together and drank hot pine-needle tea.

The hall had long since been converted to accommodate a massive fire pit in its center, in the fashion of the mead-halls of Viking Scandinavia. It was an ingenious design, the work of Wayne and Rufus and Lorne, and included a special fence that ensured that no Brothers or Sisters overeager for warmth could get anywhere near the massive bed of coals that formed.

Books were read in the Hall, and stories were told. People slept when they were tired, and when the time for rations came they were passed around and eaten there. Rufus played his guitar, and September her fiddle, and they sang every song they knew. Alan became a sudden celebrity, teaching his adoring public four decades of lost pop music as played on the recorder. Lorne taught him musical notation and insisted he inscribe it all, even "California Girls."

There were entire days when no one left the fire at all. All the work of preparation had been done, and there was nothing much to do but wait. Wait for a miracle. Wait for Christmas. It had been decided, together, that on Christmas Day there was to be a great feast. They would have one last good meal together with all the stores that remained, and they would commit themselves to the keeping of the Lord.

When Christmas Eve came, the snow was as deep as the cold and broke sharp and clean beneath the feet of those making their way to the Hall. Not even Martin could recall a December as hard as this one, and the low iron-gray of the sky felt like the lid of a coffin sliding into place above the valley. Mae and Jessica lit the ovens early that day, for there was a feast to be prepared. The last feast.

The day was spent in rest and preparation. The Brothers and Sisters washed and were washed, dressed and were dressed in their finest. By lunchtime, their excitement, so long subdued, had reached a fever pitch. If there was something everyone among them understood, it was a feast. An air of celebration hung over the day, as was fitting, but there was something else there, too, in the background of everything, lingering in every heart and mind. A strange sense of anticipation had infused everything about that Christmas Eve, a joyful expectation. Micah found it within himself, and tried desperately not to examine it too closely, lest it flee like a deer. He simply let it exist, in the backdrop of the day, growing as the feast grew closer.

When the bells rang at three and they were making their way to the Hall, he mentioned the feeling to September. She nodded, quickly, looking excited, and troubled, and kissed his hand to quiet him. They followed the Brothers into the hall for the feast.

The sight that greeted them made their hearts hurt. Mae and Jessica, manic in their labors, had also decorated the hall for Christmas. Holly wreaths hung from the doors and pine boughs from the rafters. They had raided every attic in the town and had arranged every Christmas decoration they could find in a wild, concentric vortex of Yule. A dozen Christmas trees groaning with every long-hoarded decoration guarded the walls. Creches and nativity scenes told their ancient story on every flat surface. Garlands hung from the ceilings. And everywhere else were the candles, long regarded as sacrosanct and used only in times of desperate need. Now every candle they could find had been lit, and the length and breadth and height of the Hall glimmered and sang with dancing tongues of flame, a glow to answer that of the City.

When everyone was more or less seated and more or less quiet, Martin took his place at the front of the Hall beneath the yellowed photo of the last king, raised his hands as he had done at every meal for forty years, and prayed:

"Our Father, Who art in Heaven, hallowed be Thy name. Thank you for this food which we are about to receive. Thank you for all the food we have ever received from You. Oh Father, you have given us this day our daily bread, and that is enough. That is what you have promised. Thank you. Thank you. Thank you. Amen."

As the Amen faded, the last feast began, and the people of the Fold were riotous in their enjoyment. For two hours the troubles that lay on every soul in that valley were forgotten. There was only friendship, and music, and a long ecstatic dream of food.

For an hour, even Micah was able to forget his burdens, but while his Brothers and his wife were still heavily invested in their campaign against a battalion of meat pies, he was visited by a strange restlessness. The Hall suddenly seemed far too small and far too full. He was no longer hungry. Called by an invitation he did not fully understand, he leaned over to September and called over the roar, "I have to check on something, I'll be right back!" She gave him a quizzical look, but nodded.

No one else except Thomas noticed Micah slip away from the riotous feasting and out into the fading glow of the evening. His brother followed him out the door and took his place on Micah's arm, a right Micah did not argue. The two brothers stood in the empty street for a minute or two as Micah puzzled, trying to understand what his restlessness required. The empty town was not solitude enough. In the same absence in which he had once written a prophecy in his journal, he found himself led and in turn leading Thomas up the switchback trail that ran up the face of the escarpment. He knew every step, every limestone boulder and twisted cedar tree by heart, and his mind was far away, so it was to his surprise when they found themselves at the foot of the Watch Tree. There was no one on duty tonight, a dispensation for the last feast never before given in the history of the Fold.

For lack of any further direction, Micah climbed the wooden rungs nailed to the horny hide of the old oak tree and settled himself down on the weathered roost perched in the great arms of it. Thomas followed him up, and they set their backs against the trunk and stared out towards the southeastern horizon, out across the pastures and to the untamed bush beyond them. Five hundred nights he had sat here and wondered what lay beyond the far rim of that wilderness, and now he knew. The thought filled him with sorrow. It was a terrible thing for the hope that lies in the unknown to be lost, for it is lost forever.

As he looked across the silent lands below, the red ball of the setting sun slipped below the hem of the dark clouds that covered the Fold, and for a moment the valley was filled with the red glory of it. And then it sank below the known horizon and the world was a dusky pink and then a dusky blue and then an ever-deepening gray, and snow began to whisper down onto the earth.

Thomas began to shiver and snuggle closer to Micah. Micah put his arm around him and fixed his hat and scarf. Together they fixed their eyes on the southeast rim of the earth, and as the sunlight drained from the west, the glow of the city steadily bloomed to life and grew in reverse proportion.

Every night it reappeared, and every night the eyes of the Fold turned to it and were tempted and troubled by it. Every night it seemed larger and more irresistible, but tonight it was simply enormous, strangely magnified by the low clouds and the filter of snow, a monstrous bloom of sickly orange. It brought to mind a faded photograph of a long-ago nuclear test he had studied as a child, a fungal flame blooming in an alien desert.

Micah sat and stared at the lurid orange smear that had started it all, and he hated it, and loved it, and feared it, and longed for it. He recalled the next image in the magazine spread: a house, many miles away, torn into component molecules by the air displaced by the sudden appearance of the mushroom cloud. That light had ended his old familiar life. That light had given him September and the child that grew within her.

The bitter chill began to set in as the minutes went by, and they remained there, watching the light grow. It seemed as if it covered half the sky tonight, reaching out across the sky and eating up the darkness and the stars. Micah began to shiver, and he tried to remember why he had left the comfort of the final feast to drag his brother here.

Thomas didn't seem to mind at all. It was the first time they had been alone together in months, and he reveled in Micah's undivided attention. Micah turned and looked, really looked at his older brother, as he had not had the liberty to do in so long. He was shocked at how old Thomas looked. His hair and beard were flecked with gray, his face lined. Micah realized that the face he was looking at was probably very similar to that of his father's. Their mother had always said how much Thomas had looked like him. And with that realization, Micah understood that there was a duty still that had gone unfulfilled.

"Thomas, when I left, Lorne gave me a letter. From Dad." There was understanding in Thomas' eyes, and an old, old pain. "He talked about you in it. And you deserve to know what he said.

"Thomas, our dad loved you. I know it doesn't seem like it. I know it might not mean much to say it. But I believe he did, as much as he was able, which wasn't much. I don't think he was capable of loving the way you do, the way Mom does. I think that was his disability. And we have to try to make room for that kind of weakness also. So if you can, please believe me when I tell you that he loved you the best he could."

Thomas looked up to the stars and back at Micah and squeezed his arm and nodded once. Then he got up and pulled Micah roughly to his feet. They stood on the rough platform, joints complaining of the cold, and stood there for a moment, high above the valley, and tried to pray. But the cold and his weariness and the calm, cruel strength of the light in the sky filled his head and his heart. He could not find any words to say, except the tired old ones, almost meaningless on any other night, but he knew he must say something to the dark, sad valley and to the light that crept toward it.

"Gloria in excelsis Deo," he whispered, and then louder, "Gloria! In Excelsis Deo!" And then said it again, and again, and again, until Thomas beside him, eager to help, began to murmur also.

"Gor . . . selsy . . . do. Gor selsy do!"

They chanted together until the words lost all meaning and the brothers began to laugh. Their laughter grew and grew until it echoed across the valley and they could barely breathe and were in danger of falling out of the tree and then suddenly, silently, the light in the southeast flickered once, and went out.

They were alone in the dark winter's night, the lights of the village twinkling below, in a silence so profound they could hear the minute rustling of the snow falling on the branches around him. The washed-out stars were suddenly blazing overhead. For a full minute Micah held his breath, staring into the darkness, waiting. The light did not return. Beside him, Thomas whispered a single "Amen." Together they climbed down the rungs and made their way through the snowy forest and back down the switchback. The path was treacherous at night, in the snow, and they did not hurry.

When they reached the Hall, the feast was still in full and joyful swing. Quietly Micah opened the door, and they slipped inside. September immediately made her way over, her face full of worry. He took her hand, silently, and led her over to where Martin sat with the Friendly Men. In a low voice that surprised him with its calm, he told Martin what he had seen. Martin's face became exceedingly thoughtful, and he put his hand on Micah's shoulder and gripped it. "It's time to go back," he said, his eyes locked on Micah's. Martin's hand was trembling, the knuckles white. He rose to speak to the Hall, but the words never came. He gripped his chest and fell to the floor.

30
And They Rose Up At Twilight,
To Go Unto The Camp Of The Syrians

It was a stroke, Lorne assured them. He was the closest thing to a doctor they had since the passing of Dr. Chatterjee. It was Lorne who had kept his notes and medical texts and health records and read them all. But, as he kept reminding them, "I'm not actually a doctor. I've just read the doctor's books. I don't think that makes me a doctor. I've got it in my brain but not my hands." But nevertheless, it had been Lorne who had ripped Dr. Zaretsky's nitrous spray from Micah's stunned hands and administered it perfectly and in time. It was Lorne who had saved Martin's life.

Martin was alive, but he was paralyzed on his left side and could not speak. He joined the Friendly Men, at their insistence, and took his place among them as if he had never known another. But it was clear he was failing, and without the ministrations of a doctor, would soon die.

The Shepherds were unanimous in their agreement that Martin's last words should serve as their direction. He was leader of the Fold still, and he was insistent in the direction he had received, although he could not tell them from whence it had come. Too weak even to write, he responded to every question asked of him with the same gesture: one gnarled finger raised and pointed south. No doubt remained in his remaining eye. The other direction came from September.

"Burrows," she said to Arthur and the Shepherds, firmly, bluntly, brooking no argument. "Burrows first." She waved Micah's objection away. "I know I said I'd never go back. But this is different. There's still some rations there, maybe: the last emergency stock, buried under the floor. Nothing good, but it'll keep us alive for a day or two longer, and then we can march on the City. Get this man where he needs to go," she finished, jerking a thumb at Martin.

"I don't understand why he's so hellbent on getting down there, especially with the lights out, but if there's one thing I know about him, it's that he'd never lead these people anywhere he wasn't sure was better than the place they were. He's sure. And I'm sure 'cause he's sure. I owe him that much. I think we all do."

Arthur, Bethlehem, Rosie, Alan, and Micah sat in silence as she finished. Then Arthur stood, and said simply, "Let's go, then," and the Shepherds rose to return to their charges.

As Micah left the hall, he found Rufus leaning on the wall smoking.

"You hear all that?"

Rufus grinned. "Yup."

"What do you think?"

Rufus shrugged. "Why should anything we do here start making sense now?"

Micah grinned back, desperately, and went to find the Friendly Men.

It took the people of the Fold less than a day to pack the wagons for their last exodus, so few were their treasures. Most had only their clothes, a few beloved heirlooms, and the tools of their respective trades. It was hardest for Lorne, who cried bitterly when it was explained to him that he must leave his books behind, comforted only by Micah's solemn oath that they would, one day, return for them. The remains of the feast were wrapped up and rationed out equally for the journey. There was no more food to bring.

And so it was not yet noon on Christmas Day when every soul left in the valley beneath the limestone cliffs closed the unlocked doors to their homes and made their way to St. Stephen-in-the-Fields with all of their possessions on their backs. Five packed wagons waited there, the breath of the horses rising in the frozen air. Many of the Brothers and Sisters, faced with the utter ruin of their beloved routines and their precious familiarity, cried until their voices echoed from the cliffs.

But soon every last soul was packed into the little red-brick church for the last time. There they sang the old familiar carols of peace on Earth and second birth and Sammy read the story in the book of Luke, and then Rosie prayed for them, and for Martin. She asked for protection and for a safe journey. She asked for food enough to sustain them, and she asked for a good ending to all their stories.

After that there was a strange calm among the people that Christmas morning, a quiet assurance that they had already arrived safely, somehow, though they had not yet left. Even still, it took the better part of two hours for the Brothers and Sisters to become settled into the back of the wagons, each pulled by two bony horses.

When at last the moment came when the "Gee" was spoken and the wagons lurched into motion, Micah, Thomas, and September were in the back of the last wagon, trying to comfort Philip Ramirez. He feared the desecration of his routine above all things. The last few days had been sheer hell for him, and this morning most of all. So it was that Micah's last glimpse of the Fold came while enclosing Philip in a bear hug as he tried to leap out of the back of the moving wagon.

They reached the borders of the frequented lands by early afternoon. It was when Bill announced that they would not stop until nightfall, that they would be traveling straight on through, that Micah's heart dropped with a sudden revelation: the road was blocked with fifty years of fallen trees. It had taken him an entire day to fight through the tangle of it, through to the sideroad. With the wagons it would be impossible, and there was no time or strength left for struggle. He jumped out of his wagon and ran to the front of the ragged column to where Arthur drove in the lead.

"Arthur," he gasped, no longer caring who heard him. "It's no good. I forgot . . . I forgot to tell you. The road's blocked from here through to the 15th Sideroad.

The beavers dammed the stream. It's a lake now . . . we'll never make it through with wagons."

Arthur smiled down at him, his eyes twinkling through the tangle of his eyebrows. "Then isn't it fortunate that this winter has come so early and so fierce? Have some faith, and maybe remember that some of us weren't on honeymoon and had time to prepare. Rufus hasn't been sitting on his ass all summer, though you wouldn't know it to look at him." And he spurred the horses on, chuckling, leaving Micah standing in the frozen mud with his mouth open until his wagon came rumbling up and Donny Rasmussen demanded in shrill tones that he return to his place in the back with the Friendly Men. Among them, wrapped in a sheepskin, Martin was smiling a silent, lopsided grin, his finger pointing south.

And sure enough, the wagons kept rolling without pause, all through the afternoon. They crossed the frozen back of the beaver pond and beyond it their wheels found the old road, resurrected from the bush by the labors of the spring. Rufus, riding outlier on his rail-thin horse, cantered up to Micah. "Look what I've been up to! Not just a pretty face, you know. Faith and mystical visions are great, but proper road maintenance also has its place, I think you'll find." It was true. The road ran hard and smooth and straight through the forest, and in a day they traveled a distance that had taken Micah three.

As they skirted Cardoon and the sideroad left the bush, September left Micah and Thomas and took the seat beside Arthur at the head of the column. These had been her family's lands, and it had been decided that she would act as a guide through to Burrows, where they would spend the hungry night. They smoked their pipes together (much to Joanna's disgust) and shared their stories of the lands they were leaving. In the wagons behind them, the afternoon ration was produced and shared around, to the delight and astonishment of the Brothers and Sisters, who had not been informed of the presence of food in the wagons as a preventative measure.

The greenish glow of the setting winter sun still clung to the western sky when they reached the great house on the overpass. They disembarked from the wagons with much stretching and cracking of joints, and September led them up to the great door. She stopped before it, and for a moment her face was again the hard survivor's mask Micah remembered from the day they had met. He came alongside her and took her right hand. Her left wandered up to the swell of her belly and gripped it tight. The moment passed, and September squeezed and released Micah's hand, took the key from her coat pocket, and turned it in the lock. With a visible effort, she pushed through the door, and Micah and the Friendly Men followed her.

Soon the fireplace and the woodstoves were lit, and the old hall was filled again with the happy racket of the living, and September seemed to ease. She directed the Shepherds to the secret hiding places where they unearthed the last of her family's emergency rations. When these had been divided equally among the travelers, they sat in a great circle around the enormous hearth and sang carols and ate their daily bread.

When the morning came, the hearths were quenched and the doors were closed and locked behind them, and their horses brought them to the crest of the ridge as the sun broke the eastern horizon. Across the concrete plain, the white walls of the City glowed pink like a great shell on the shore of the lake. They stayed on the crest of the hill for a long time, every eye probing the silent geometry for any clue as to the nature of their destination. Rufus, who had the best binoculars, finally broke the silence.

"Nothing's moving down there. There's no smoke, no cars, no people. And the gates are open." They went no further that day, despite their desperate need, but watched the city until darkness fell. No movement was seen, and no lights came on after sunset.

The next morning Martin awoke, agitated and trying to speak. Philip began to keen in sympathy, drawing Micah and Rufus running. They sat down beside his bed as he gestured and attempted to vocalize.

"Here, old man," said Rufus, producing a flask. "Take the rest of this." With assistance, Martin drank it down. His eyes widened and he glared at Rufus, a glare that slowly became a grin.

"Last of the communion wine," muttered Rufus to Micah, apologetically. "Needed something for the journey."

The wine seemed to give Martin strength. He struggled into a sitting position and, by a combination of signs and sounds, indicated that he wished to be taken out to the edge of the overpass. Micah and Alan helped him to the outlook and onto a barrel, where he sat with his back against the rear wall of the house, his face to the sun where it rose across the valley. Martin grabbed Micah's arm, pulled him down to stare into his eyes. Then he lifted his right arm and pointed out towards the city. Micah nodded, and looked into Martin's eyes until Martin was no longer in them.

They carried his body with them when they left Burrows an hour later, in the same place in the wagon, wrapped in the same sheepskin, the same crooked smile on his lips. The Friendly Men, though advised to stay in Burrows until Micah, Rufus, and Alan could investigate, refused to leave Martin's body. Philip Ramirez held Martin's hand all that day and wept as it grew cold and stiff.

No one spoke much that last day, as all morning and through the afternoon the wagon eased its steady way down the great empty highway that bisected the burnt and broken grid. There was neither sight nor sound in that dead land, save for the ceaseless cawing of the crows and the growing complaints of hunger and road-weariness from the princes. The early winter evening was reddening the western sky when they reached the city. "Whoa," Micah said to the horses in a low voice. The wagon slowly rattled to a halt, and an utter silence fell.

The great gate hung open like a broken jaw. Out of the gap in the white wall, a drift of abandoned treasures had been vomited out to either side, the heaped and scattered evidence of a sudden, desperate exodus. Sarah's little white tent was nowhere to be seen, lost in a storm-wrack of armed and ruined bodies.

The way was open before them, but the princes and their shepherds stopped before the City in an undeclared, collective pause. A light snow had begun to fall from the rosy cirrus of the evening sky. For a long silent moment no one seemed able to move. Then, the shape of a man, small but distinct, appeared in the space between the walls. The figure raised its one arm high in the air, and beckoned for them to come in.

Philip Ramirez, as if by prearranged signal, left Martin where he lay. He climbed down out of the wagon and walked alone despite his blindness through the gate into the city, where the man took him by the hand. The others stood and watched him as they walked, unhurried and unafraid, through the orphaned riches all around them. Then Philip stopped, and turned, and seemed to stare at Micah with his unseeing eyes.

"Come," he signed. "Eat."

Epilogue: Final Entry

Date: January 1st
Recording Staff: Micah Gault

"In that day, declares the Lord,
I will assemble the lame
and gather those who have been driven away
and those whom I have afflicted;
and the lame I will make a remnant,
and those who were cast off, a strong nation;
and the Lord will reign over them in Mount Zion
from this time forth and forevermore."
Micah 4:7

The End

About the Author

Mike Bonikowsky lives in Melancthon Township, Ontario, with his wife and kids and chickens and rabbits. He works as a caregiver for men and women with developmental disabilities. In 2022, he published his first book of poems, *Red Stuff*, with Solum Literary Press.

www.ingramcontent.com/pod-product-compliance
Lightning Source LLC
Chambersburg PA
CBHW031102020726
47495CB00007B/2007